SENSUAL SEDUCTION

THE SENSUAL SERIES BOOK 1

AVA M. ROSE

Copyright @ 2019 Ava M. Rose

All rights reserved.

ISBN: 979-8-8478-5528-0

No part of this book may be reproduced, stored in a retrieval system, or transmitted by any means without the written permission of the author.

Print information available on the last page.

All characters and events in this book are fictional. Any names, characters, businesses, or events are fictitious.

TABLE OF CONTENTS

TRIGGER WARNING..5

DEDICATION 6

1 ALEJANDRO..8

2 LEXI 13

3 WATCHER 16

4 ELLIE 17

5 CHEMISTRY...20

6 INTOXICATING 25

7 FIRST DATE 29

8 FREESTYLE..37

9 FIRST KISS...40

10 SOCIAL MEDIA 44

11 CLOSER 48

12 DARK WOLF 50

13 SILENT TEARS 58

14 SERIAL KILLER 65

15 PROFILE 68

16 POETRY..73

17 HAYDEN...77

18 THE GIRLS 86

19 RISE AND FALL 91

20 DARK MUSE 99

21 SONG..108

22 DAD..115

23 PICNIC 119

24 I MISS YOU 124

25 BREAKING 130
26 SHOCK 136
27 TREND 142
28 INEVITABLE 149
29 TOUCH 154
30 SOUL SPARK 163
31 DINNER 169
32 SENSUAL 179
33 LISTENING 186
34 POOL 187
35 JACUZZI 194
36 BEDROOM 199
37 NIGHTMARE 202
38 THE PLAYGROUND 210
39 THE SWING 217
40 MUM AND DAD 224
41 DEMONS 232
42 BELT 234
43 STUDIED 243
44 ISOLATION 248
45 CHRISTMAS EVE 254
46 CHRISTMAS MORNING 258
47 CHRISTMAS DAY 263
48 BOXING DAY 272
49 MAKING LOVE 284
50 NEW YEARS EVE 292
BONUS CONTENT 298
ABOUT THE AUTHOR 299

ACKNOWLEDGEMENTS 299

The Sensual Series..300

Book 1 – Sensual Seduction 300

Book 2 – Sensual Danger 300

Book 3 – Sensual Depth 300

TRIGGER WARNING

This story contains material intended for a mature audience, aged 18+ only. It includes topics that may be sensitive to some readers. Reader discretion is advised.

DEDICATION

To my parents and grandparents, I can't begin to tell you how beautiful it was to bring you all back to life in this book. To spend time with you again, talk to you and remember the good old days when we were together. I was given the chance to wrap my arms around you and say some of the things I've missed saying to you. I was able to talk to you on the phone and have a cup of tea with you again, like I used to. I didn't realise all those little things *are* the important things. Your passing left a huge void in my life, sending me on a tailspin of grief and loss for several years. This book helped me to remember the good times before that. It has been an amazing gift to me. I have immortalised my feelings for you, permanently, in black and white. I love you all dearly, and I always will.

To my children... my beautiful girls. Thank you for the gift you are. I know a lot of this book wasn't written with your eyes in mind, but the creative process we shared while writing the family scenes will stay with me forever. Little things you always wanted - like a puppy, giving you names you liked in the book - they fired you up so much and it was beautiful to watch. Writing about your personalities and some of the things that mesmerise me daily, like your sweet nature and your beautiful eyes, completed the wholeness of my first novel, as a representation of everything and everyone that was important to me. My love for you is vast. You mean the world to me, and I thank you for your patience, as I've been tapping away trying to realise this dream of writing my own novel. I hope I was able to inspire your creative nature and show you, with effort, there's nothing you can't do. Live your dreams and your life, doing what brings you alive. I love you.

To the beautiful community of friends, both in real life and online, who supported me through a time of great change, pain, and growth for me, I can't begin to say how much you helped me. From inspiration to laughter, from a shared daily interaction to a belief in both me and my words. Some days felt so dark. But some of you looked after me and spoke to me, sometimes for hours on end, making sure I wasn't alone and didn't feel isolated. You gave up your own time to spend with me and it touched me in ways I can't express. From the bottom of my heart, thank you for not letting go of my hand and for any contribution you made while I wrote this novel.

To my readers, both who have bought the book and fuelled my desire to write publicly, when I was previously both shy and apprehensive to express my true self, thank you. Every positive comment you've left, review you've given, like of my work throughout the last three years has all led me here, to realising a dream.

To Alejandro, who is both inside me, as a representation of my darker times and as a persona I became post grief. And outside me, as a man I have dreamed of. I fell in love with you throughout the writing of this book. I cannot tell you how satisfying it is to have you as my dark muse. You have been exciting, adventurous, and fun. You've held my mind and body in ways I never imagined I could experience emotionally through this journey with you. You are the man I search for; you are the dream.

To Leila, who is the lighter side of me, a representation of the persona I was pre-grief, thank you for giving me an opportunity to reintegrate myself. I was lost in a void before you. I realised all the beauty I had in my life growing up is still here, inside me, just waiting to be released. We both needed to be released, to become our true uninhibited selves again, in so many ways. You were always beautiful, you just needed Alejandro's darkness to make you feel and appreciate the light again. I now love both the light and dark sides of me and feel more whole through the unity of both. I love the beauty, raw talent, and truth of each side and each character. Writing this novel has created balance again.

To you, the person reading this book right now, I hope you learn to understand all the different sides of yourself throughout your life and find ways to ensure you always have balance. Self-care is so important, especially in modern times. Life is so short. Find whatever makes you happy. Thank you, from the bottom of my heart, for allowing me into your lives and taking the time to read my novel. Time is valuable to all of us, and I humbly appreciate yours. I hope you enjoy it and would welcome your feedback in the form of a review.

If you'd like to know more, please refer to my website https://www.authoravamrose.com

Warm hugs and many blessings to you,
Ava M. Rose. Xxx

1 ALEJANDRO

February. Thursday night. Liverpool. Salsa.

My favourite night of the week, salsa. It was the only place I could let my hair down, feel alive and free. I'd been going for months now, and it was a place of refuge, a place where I could empty my overfull mind. I needed that escape. Salsa was my place to shut it all off, be a woman, led by a man, listen to the rhythm, and just feel, respond, and dance.

February knew how to bite at your cheeks, chest, and hands, and I was desperate to dance to warm up. I waited in the crowd of apprehensive new dancers and confident regulars, looking around, wondering who I might end up dancing with tonight. Right before the session was about to begin, an incredibly handsome man walked through the door.

He had a chiselled jaw, structured cheekbones, and a cut-off black T-shirt displaying muscular biceps and an ample chest. I kept glancing in his direction. He looked a little over six-foot in comparison to my five-foot four-inch frame. He had almost-black hair, cut short at the sides with a couple of inches more height on top, and a gorgeous, olive-tanned complexion.

Greek, Spanish, Italian, or French perhaps. I wondered.

Even at a distance, I could see his bright-blue eyes sparkling behind dark, rectangular glasses. He had the appearance of a deeply intelligent Armani model and radiated confidence. To my surprise, after shaking the hand of the man on the door, and exchanging brief pleasantries, he went straight to the front of the class. He wasn't there to learn; he was the new teacher.

How thrilling.

Curiosity started to form immediately, like a strong magnet pulling me toward him. I don't think I was the only one in the class feeling the attraction, considering the way a few of the other women were eyeing him. I had no chance; he was far too handsome.

I checked his ring finger and to my surprise, found there was no evidence he was already taken.

"Okay, class, gather around. I'm your new instructor, and my name is Alejandro."

He spoke in a soft Spanish accent that seemed to drip into my senses. He smiled at the class as we gathered round and briefly made eye contact with me His eyes were a pure cobalt blue, sparkling against his olive skin. I caught my eyes lingering on his upper torso and arms.

"Line up in rows, and we'll go through some basic salsa steps. I'll teach the men how to lead and the women to follow. The men are in total control of the steps, and the women respond to the leaders' cues.

He took centre front and turned around, so it was easier for us to copy him. His back was solid and V-shaped, his waist tapered into his belt, and his faded blue jeans revealed a firm backside and thick thighs. He was a visual delight. I was already imagining how I would feel in his arms.

"Basic," he demonstrated, showing his left foot going forward, shifting the weight onto his front foot, and then onto his right back foot. His hips had a snake-like quality to them. It felt like he was a snake charmer, and I was being slowly mesmerised by his movements. They looked like poetry to me. We copied the steps, and he repeated the move several times, allowing people to get the hang of it before moving on.

"Now, side to side." He moved his left foot to the side, centre, then right side. His hips had a languid sway, and his whole frame was rhythm personified. It flowed through his back, arms, hips, and legs. He looked so artistic as he moved, and I couldn't help but admire that about him.

After a few goes, Alejandro said, "Good. Now the open back move." He demonstrated the left foot opening out to the back.

"Okay, class, you all look like you've got the basics, so I'm going to put some music on, and we'll go over the basic steps to music first."

As the rhythm of the music kicked in, with only minor corrections to the group, everyone eventually started to synchronise.

"Excellent," he said at the end of the song. "We're going to take it up a notch now."

I'd been going for several months now, so the steps came easily. I no longer thought about the specifics of the move, just the flow of them through my body.

He counted out the beat, as the class tried to turn. One woman stumbled in her heels, and four men whom I'd not seen before ended up laughing at their lack of ability. A few of us giggled sympathetically because we'd all been there.

Alejandro went over to the group. "Is this your first time?" he asked the guys.

One of them replied, "Can't you tell?" We all laughed.

"Okay. Follow me slowly," Alejandro said and repeated the move slowly for them a couple more times. "Have you got it now?"

"As much as we ever will," said the funny one.

Not everyone took dancing seriously. For many, it was just a different type of night out, something to do for a giggle, or to try and hook up. After the lesson it was more of a social event. For the diehards like me, dancing was a lifeline. There were only a handful of us who came every week, but those were the people I enjoyed dancing with most.

I loved dancing with the "Boxer," who started when I did, the "Silver fox," a distinguished gentleman who glided, the "Counter," who counted One-Two-Three, Five-Six-Seven to every move. Then there were my four favourites, the "Romanian" who was a beautifully smooth dancer, the "Heartbreaker," who moved sensually, giving great eye contact, the "Charmer," who was gorgeous to dance with and had a cheeky, vibrant personality, and the "Soul of salsa," who was an incredibly warm person, and a truly phenomenal mover.

I used a memorable nickname in my head for everyone, as I was never very good with names. Every week, I avoided the "Hairy biker" with the dark creepy stare, the "Arm cracker," the "Accidental boob grazer," and the "Hip lunger," for obvious reasons. I identified them in ways that helped me remember if I wanted to dance with them or avoid them.

Alejandro called out to the class. "Okay, followers please go to the left-hand side of the room, leaders please go to the right."

We separated to the two different sides and Alejandro asked if there were any regulars in the room, looking at the ladies' side of the room. Aside from me, two other women raised their hands. He smiled and held out his hand to me,

"Would you do the honour of assisting me?"

I blushed, immediately taking it. His hand was firm, and warm. My fingers looked petite in his. Leading me to the front of the class, I desperately tried to keep my composure. Being this close to Alejandro was making me feel aroused and I was struggling with the sensation. When I stood in front of him, I was awestruck by his eyes. Hypnotic blue with gold flecks radiating out from the centre. I tried to stop myself from blushing. Something about his glasses made me feel timid around him, like he was a teacher, and I was his student, although his eyes were warm and inviting. Alejandro flashed a beautiful smile at me and then said to the class,

"Right, now I'm going to show you the cross-body lead. Leaders, this is your step,"

After he was confident the men had the hang of it, he said.

"Now it's your turn, ladies."

I followed the prompt, while Alejandro broke it down in words.

I got a little nervous with everyone watching me. He had me repeat the move a couple of times, then went over to help a lady who was turning the wrong way. There was a beautiful confidence to him I couldn't help but admire.

What was it about him?

Alejandro returned to me.

"Right, now we're going to put the two moves together."

As I stepped back, he opened his stance, leading me perfectly across his body, placing his hand on my back to guide me, gently pulling me through the open space, then using his left hand to support me as I turned. Being at such proximity to his body was intoxicating, as was his hand upon the curve of my spine and the way he held my hand as he guided me around him.

"You have a beautiful flow to your dance steps," he whispered quietly.

I crumbled a little at the softening of his accent. I wasn't expecting him to be lovely, too.

"Right, now we dance salsa. Partner up. Don't be shy, no one will bite you here."

Several members of the class laughed simultaneously, reflecting they felt that way.

"Remember to be respectful to your partner and be careful of your hand placement."

He whispered to me, "Do you mind if I keep you as a partner?"

"I don't mind at all," I said, smiling warmly, trying to maintain my composure.

"Let's go. Basic," he said, raising his voice and we both instinctively felt the move.

The class copied. I started to let the beat flow through me, as Alejandro's hips and mine synchronised perfectly with the rhythm. I could feel a beautiful ache building in my loins and my breathing started to slow. I was so aroused, dancing close to him, and I had no idea how to feel about that because it had never happened before in class. I also knew I shouldn't feel that way about a total stranger.

Alejandro took us through all the moves we'd learned earlier. By the time we'd done a few of each step, you could feel the confidence growing in the group, as if the basics were starting to click. Alejandro took us back to the beginning again and continued to loop through the sequenced moves until everyone looked confident. That naturally closed the beginners' session, and everyone was on a high. What a beautiful and fulfilling hour, and what an incredible feeling he left me with.

"Great work class," Alejandro said, clapping, everyone joining in, applauding their own achievements.

"Have a 15-minute break and we'll resume with the advanced class, for those who wish to stay."

Alejandro was still standing next to me after we'd finished demonstrating. He turned to me.

"May I ask your name?" he asked, with that sexy sparkle in his eyes.

"Leila" I said, completely aware of my flushing cheeks and coy response.

"That's a beautiful name. Are you staying for the advanced class?"

I paused briefly and wondered if there was any way I could stay and then remembered I had to be at work at 7 a.m.

"I can't tonight, I have an early start tomorrow, but I'll be here next week." I was gutted.

"Well, it was a great pleasure dancing with you tonight, Leila. Will you be my glamorous assistant next week?"

As if I could resist that offer.

"Of course, see you next week." As I walked away, he grabbed my hand and kissed me on both cheeks.

My body flushed at the contact, and I felt he registered it before I turned and said,

"Goodnight, Alejandro."

I took a picture of his face with my mental camera. *Point. Click.* I imagined stroking a single finger down his cheek and felt a strong surge going through me to kiss him.

How am I going to control my thoughts around you?

2 LEXI

February. Friday morning. Liverpool. Office.

It was nearly the end of February and a chilly morning, the week thankfully nearly over. The weekend was ringing the bells of freedom in my mind. My yawning was at its peak. I'd had an early start most days this week trying to hit an editing deadline, and I couldn't wait to sleep in.

Criminal journalism could be draining, constantly chasing local stories, completing interviews and transcripts, researching and gathering materials, photos, graphics, and timeline information. Then there were article drafts, double checking for accuracy, checking with the legal department to ensure there's nothing we could get sued for, trying to meet both writing and editing deadlines. I often worked late. I loved my job, but it tended to be mentally intensive. Sometimes, work deeply affected me. On the worst days, I felt overwhelmed, so I had to learn how to shut off and hold some of me back in reserve.

I had worked my way up over my time at *The Liverpool Express*. In addition to assisting criminal investigations, I now conducted in-depth interviews with local crime victims. Some of the people I visited were in a state of mental trauma and that was tough. Ultimately, if I could help these people find justice in any way, it felt like a truly worthwhile career.

Exhaustion often built up over the week, but alcohol normally perked me up on Friday night and I had a blissful lie-in to look forward to each week. I needed these things to stay balanced. I exercised when I could, going for a run or visiting the gym just around the corner. One great thing about Liverpool and city living was I had everything I could possibly need.

"Do you want to hook up for lunch today?" asked Lexi, hovering by my desk.

I quickly replied, "Yes."

The friendship between Lexi and I kept us going. She was my closest friend in the office, and we'd been working together for several years. We were close, and she was the only one that completely understood the work demands we faced, as she had a similar role on another team, as a community reporter.

I met Lexi by her desk.

"You look lovely today," I said.

Lexi was wearing a cream crossover shirt, which curved around her ample shape, and a beige fitted skirt with nude heels. Her perfume was subtle with a slight hint of flowers, which matched her sweet personality. She picked up her beige handbag and grabbed a taupe, mid-thigh length winter coat from the coat rack.

'I'll be back at 1p.m., Tim," she said, as she walked past him.

"Okay, see you later," Tim grumbled, engrossed in writing an email, not even looking up at her as she left.

It was only a short walk to the café.

The weather was bitter, and we wrapped our coats around us, tightly linking arms. There was a lovely warm blast from the heater above us as we walked through the door and approached the till.

"What are you having?" asked Lexi. "It's my turn to buy."

"Hmm, fresh orange and a tuna salad wrap, please," I said, my stomach rumbling.

"Cappuccino and a chicken and bacon wrap. please."

We found a table by the edge of the room and sat down, hanging our coats over the back.

"Soooooo, I met someone I like," I blurted, beaming like an idiot.

"Oh, do tell!" she implored.

"His name's Alejandro, and I met him at salsa last night. He's the instructor. I think he likes me, too. I'm not really sure, but I think he does."

"So, you may or may not have met a guy, then," she said, giggling.

I loved, and always laughed at her dry humour.

"I felt a pull to him Lexi, like nothing I've ever felt before. I can't wait until next week."

I felt overexcited, like a puppy, just thinking about him.

"What does he look like? Age? Hair colour? I want all the gossip," she said, playfully slapping both hands on the table.

"He's Spanish, his eyes are striking." I retrieved his image from my emotional camera, recalling him in detail. "He's around six feet tall and has an accent to die for." The meals arrived and we started eating, carrying on our lively conversation, conscious of the one-hour time slot.

"So, he's definitely single, the really hot amazingly gorgeous Spanish guy with an accent to die for?" Lexi asked and for the first time, my heart sunk.

What if he already has a partner?
What if he is just a flirtatious guy?

"He wasn't wearing a ring and I assume he is single because he was giving off vibes," I said, feeling a bit worried.

"Well, maybe establish that before you get carried away. This isn't like you at all. I've never seen you fawn over a guy before."

"Honestly Lex, I don't know. There's an attraction to him I can't fathom."

"Just be careful. I don't want you to get hurt."

"I know Lex, I'll try and find out a little more about him next week."

"How's that piece on the homeless in Liverpool coming?" I asked, changing the subject.

"Heart-breaking. Most of the people I've spoken to have had back luck and they're struggling to cope– some have lost jobs or have split up with partners and lost their homes. Some don't have family they can turn to. It's sad; it will be an emotional piece when I wrap it up."

Lexi grimaced. "Is Janice still being a cow about not getting the piece?"

"Of course, I have no idea what on earth her problem is, but she's never liked me from day one."

"She's bitter, hunni. She's got such a chip on her shoulder, like the world owes her something. Leave her to it and ignore her," I added.

"I know, she's not worth the aggravation. I only speak to her when I must now. Anyway, I won't waste another breath on Janice. You're so lucky on your team, you're all normal."

Lexi normally had a no-nonsense way of looking at things and she was down to earth. I loved her for that, but with Janice, who could rile even a saint, she found it hard not to engage.

I glanced at my watch. "We'd best head back. Time always flies so fast with you," I said. We headed back to the office giggling and chatting about office politics. I couldn't help but be distracted, my thoughts constantly drifting back to last night and Alejandro, but now with the sombre addition that perhaps he wasn't available and just had a flirty personality. I must stop letting my thoughts get ahead of me with him.

Facts.
Get facts, Leila.
Think with your head.

3 WATCHER

8:37 a.m. You caught my eye, the shape of you, your eyes, your hair, your skin, your smile, the way you made small talk with the stranger next to you and the way you bought a coffee and sandwich for the homeless man sitting outside the shop. You were kind, so sweet and innocent. I wanted you from the first moment I laid eyes on you; to touch you, to hold you, to consume you. I could be anything you wanted me to be.

That was the first day, the first moment I realised you were the one. The next one. That was the first time I started following you. It's been four months now. You're so oblivious to your surroundings, never looking behind you. You feel safe in your world, the route you walk to and from work, the places you visit every week, the way you don't always lock your door when you go into your house. So beautifully unaware of the eyes that follow you, and the desire that builds every time I get just that bit closer to you. I touched you last week, your soft immaculate skin. You didn't even realise. I touched you last week. I will touch you again.

4 ELLIE

February. Saturday. Liverpool. Home.

Finally, the weekend. I had such a long lie-in. When I went downstairs, Ellie was already up, eating cereal.

"Morning sunshine," I blurted, feeling revitalised.

"Morning trouble," she smiled, as I popped the bread in the toaster.

"Do you want a cuppa?"

"Please."

"So, what time do you want to leave to go shopping?" I asked.

"Straight after a shower. So, what's your news then? You sounded all excited to talk to me today."

"Well, I've met someone, and I'm really attracted to him, but I don't actually know if he's single, so I'm trying hard not to be excited."

"Oh Leila, you are funny. What's his name?"

"Alejandro. He's the new salsa instructor. He's Spanish, tall, dark, and handsome." The kettle clicked off after it boiled, and I made the tea while I chatted.

"Hot, Spanish, sexy, and he can dance. This has disaster written all over it, babe."

"I know, right?"

"Take it easy. You'll be fine."

"I know, I don't know what it is about him, it's like an instant connection. Maybe I'm reading all the signs wrong. I'll try to contain myself until I at least know if he's single."

"That's exactly what you should do."

"At least you have a potential prospect. I haven't seen a decent guy for so long, I'm starting to give up on their existence."

"You'll find one, most likely when you stop looking. There could be a hot guy who's an absolute gentleman waiting for you somewhere this week, you don't know."

"And we both know I'd not even see him and head for the bad boy clad in leather behind him."

She had made shockingly bad choices in the past.

"Absolutely no comment," I shrugged mockingly.

"So, what are we shopping for today?"

"Shopping darling, just shopping. We always need dresses; we always need shoes and we will always need retail therapy."

"Are we hitting Liverpool One?"

"Yes, we can have an early tea at that new Italian restaurant, Il Mercato. The food was so good when I was there with Amelia."

"How did that go?" Ellie asked.

"It was such a good night. She's turned into my go to for cultural nights out."

"Oh, I see, it's like that is it?" mocking jealousy with her hand on her hip. "So, what am I good for?"

"You're great at being you," I said, blowing her a kiss.

We had a long afternoon of shopping, hitting at least 10 shops and changing rooms before finishing up with delicious Italian meals.

I was extremely close to Ellie. We'd been living together since we were 19. During the first year we found each other at a university run salsa club, sharing the same passion for dance at the time, although Ellie hadn't kept it up like I had. We shared an instant chemistry, found we shared a similar sense of humour, and started to hang around each other's apartments, also meeting up for nights out on the town. The student accommodation was guaranteed in the first year. By the end of it, we decided we would live together in the second year and found another two housemates to keep the costs down. We'd been living together ever since, our accommodations becoming nicer as our careers advanced. Our current house was a lovely three bedroom. It was very modest and quaint with a beautiful energy to it. We were so open with each other. There was nothing we couldn't say to each other, and no judgments passed between us. She was the best friend I'd always wanted, someone I could laugh with, hang around with, shop with, party with, go to meals with. We had a special friendship and supported each other unconditionally.

I woke up incredibly content and happy, reasonably early for a Sunday. I went downstairs and started grilling sausages, mushrooms, bacon, and tomatoes, which was our standard post-drinking breakfast, and called up the stairs.

I'd heard pottering around before I came down, and I put an egg for each of us into the frying pan. "Your grill up is ready, Ellie."

As I served the eggs, we were both starving and devoured our breakfast, in as ladylike a manner as we both could when ravenous. We were both a little hungover; we'd talked so much the night before.

"Thank you, Leila, that was gorgeous," she said, as she finished the breakfast. "I'm going now."

"No problem, lovely, have a great time at your parents."

"Right, it's about time I chilled out a little bit and wrote some poetry," I muttered to myself.

I responded to my notifications, interacting with comments on my work, and opened a blank post. I closed my eyes briefly, allowing any thoughts to just float through, as if they were being carried away on a breeze, clearing my mind. As an idea formed in my mind, I let it sit there as I played a little to find an angle I agreed with and felt in that moment. I had to mould and shape the idea or thought. My mind, of course, returned to Alejandro and his beautiful face and how I wanted to kiss him. Everything I wrote involved escapism to some degree. So, I allowed myself, even if only briefly, to imagine what it would be like to kiss Alejandro. It was his eyes I remembered most. The pupils were so dilated and dark at one point I could see myself in them. So, I played with that thought and then wrote:

"Looking deep
into your hypnotic eyes
like they're portals in time,
showing me somewhere
I want to travel to,
exploring the
light+dark I see
in the duality of you,
like a true
reflection of me.
I want to know
what it feels like
to free fall into you;
through your kiss+touch..."

Then a simpler one to vary styles:

"Kiss me slowly,
start with my mind..."

And, while thinking about what he looked like in his glasses, I continued.

"The most perfect kiss
is an intellectual mind..."

Is anyone in modern society still interested in poetry, writing, or words though?

5 CHEMISTRY

March. Tuesday. Liverpool. Home.

It felt like an extraordinarily long week. My anticipation for Thursday was overwhelming, and I couldn't wait to be in Alejandro's arms. I'd been thinking about him throughout the week and was nervous about seeing him again. I feared these unknown feelings. I was afraid of losing control of my emotions.

By the time Thursday came around, my heart was racing as I got ready. I was particularly careful picking out an outfit. As I trawled through the rails in my wardrobe, I picked out a bright red top with a sweetheart neckline. I wore red lingerie, hoping the upper curves of my breasts would tantalise him a little. A few well-placed sprays of perfume upon my wrists, neck, and upper breasts, and I was good to go.

As I walked in, I saw Alejandro standing in the corner by the bar, pouring a glass of water. I felt my skin starting to flush.

Tonight, I was on a fact-finding mission. I needed to know if he was single. I couldn't afford to take my mind down a road I couldn't travel.

When he turned around, I was already looking at him, much to my embarrassment. He flashed a beautiful smile at me. I returned a coy one to him. He briefly looked me up and down, not in a leering manner, but enough to make my legs go a little weak.

"Okay, class, let's get started," he instructed.

His confidence was so appealing. We went through the same routine for the beginner's class each week, so I always knew what was coming during that section of the night. The advanced lesson always threw in some interesting surprises. I needed capable hands for the advanced class, to make the most of the session.

Alejandro repeated the same basic steps just as he had the week before. We caught eyes several times throughout the class. When it came to the cross-body lead, he turned to me.

"Leila, would you be my glamorous assistant?"

Without hesitation, I said "of course," and joined him in the centre of the room. I may have looked calm on the outside, but inside I was full of butterflies.

He took hold of me, and I felt him, like thunder racing through my body. The muscular shape of his shoulder under my left hand instantly weakened me. His hand found the soft arch of my back. They felt strong and so incredibly good on my body.

"You look beautiful tonight," he whispered.

"Thank you." I was aware he had glanced briefly at my top.

Great choice, Leila.

Within his subtly strong hold, he demonstrated moves to the rest of the class, much in the same way he had the week before, and then told everyone to "partner up." When the room settled, he started the music and we started to move our feet, his hand on the small of my back the entire time. The music had a deep bass line, feeding our need to move, rhythm instinctively flowing through our bodies. Our dancing felt smooth and the chemistry between us was palpable.

"Basic," "side-step," "open back," "left-hand turn," Alejandro instructed to the class individually after a few turns at each move.

"Right hand turn," he called out next.

After several of the left-hand turns, my vertigo kicked in a little and I lost balance and tumbled toward him, my head spinning slightly. He caught me, and for the briefest of moments I was held, tightly pressed against his thick, solid chest.

"Sorry," I offered, embarrassed, my cheeks flushing.

"It's okay, I've got you," he smiled, trying to pull me upright, his phrase echoing through my mind.

"I've got you."

When I centred, I realised we were looking directly into each other's eyes. They were twinkling like fireworks at midnight, and I felt every single one of them burst inside me.

The space between us kept inadvertently closing; he didn't flinch. I felt myself fighting against the strength of that certain feeling again.

"Okay, class. Have a 15-minute break and we'll continue with the advanced class. Feel free to join in. Help yourself to drinks at the bar. There are jugs of water out, too, if you'd like some. After the second class wraps up, you can enjoy the rest of your night at our salsa party."

Tonight, I was staying and didn't care if I was tired the next day. He turned to me.

"You're a great dancer Leila, you have so much potential," he said with genuine depth in his voice.

"I'm as good as the leader I'm with," I rebuffed. We naturally flirted with each other, without any effort at all. I never flirted, but with him, it felt completely natural.

"Then, hopefully you will let me lead you to become the dancer I know you are capable of becoming."

He excited me, the way he spoke, the way he moved.

"I'd like that," I offered shyly.

"Good, because I have a couple moves in the second half, I think you'll love."

My interest piqued.

I walked off to refresh my perfume in the ladies and check if I was blushing as much as I thought. I wanted to look perfect for him.

When I re-joined the room, the class had started to gather in the centre, and I noticed some of the regular advanced dancers had arrived.

"Okay, this is the advanced class. If you are struggling with any of the moves, feel free to ask me, or if you don't feel ready, you're welcome to watch and maybe try again next week. I'm going to teach a choreographed set of moves that will interlink with each other."

I was already excited at the prospect of learning more complex moves.

"Leila," he said, his hand beckoning mine. He sounded quite authoritative, and I rapidly responded to him.

"The first move is a double hand spin," Alejandro informed the class. He held both of my hands above my head, creating an arch like two swan necks between us.

"Leaders, don't hold her hands tight, keep them in a loose hold so when you turn her clockwise, like this," he demonstrated, turning me around "you can complete the move without hurting her."

The class copied; that move was quite easy for most to adapt to.

"Now extend the same move, so you end side to side, with your left arm around her shoulder".

He repeated the double hand spin but manoeuvred both my arms, extending them so his left arm was around my shoulder and my right was extended up and around his V-shaped back. We were symmetrical in stance. Being this close to him with my arm around him made my heart flutter and the heat in my face doubled. I noticed one of the other women smiling at me; she knew the exact reason why. He was catching the attention of a lot of the women in the class. We repeated both moves and then the class tried, some more successfully than others. Each move with Alejandro felt more sensual than the previous one. The accidental hip touches as we aligned, the definition I felt through his T-shirt; my body was pulsing, and I felt every part of me responding to him.

"Now undo her arms using the reverse of what you've just done and go into a cross body lead."

"This time leaders, when you hold both of her hands, just use your left hand," he demonstrated to the men. "You are going to find the loop to step inside, between her two arms."

He found the space between and put his head through my arms. My arms slowly slid down the back of his hair, over his neck and onto his broad shoulders.

"Like this," he said to the class, as my body ached.

That feels so sensuous.

"Okay, now practice all of those moves up until that point," Alejandro said.

As we all repeated the moves a few more times and the class became more independent, the intimacy shooting between our eyes intensified. I think I felt my soul stall at one point.

"Right, the next two moves are particularly nice. The first is a corkscrew."

He demonstrated the move, which ended with a beautiful rotation and his left hand holding my knee.

"Leaders, make sure you are supporting her back, so she doesn't overbalance."

Is he doing this on purpose?

It felt sexual and I felt like a goddess in his arms. Alejandro spotted a couple of people who were having difficulty with the move and went to help. My breath was quiet, but jagged, revelling in the heady sensation of him.

"Okay, the last move is one of my favourites. After this, we'll practise the whole set a few times. Think of yourself as a matador, leaders. The move is dramatic and over the top, so act it out as you do the move. Shape your hands into a fist and perform a large arc, so she knows the move you are about to do. This is her cue. Dramatically complete a circular move, splitting her hands apart using the top part of your forearms, raising her arms up into a flamenco like stance, like this," he explained. "Followers, allow him to raise your arms and then leave them up."

When he demonstrated the move, it felt domineering and powerful, his strong arms lifting mine like they were feathers. It had echoes of bullfighting and I liked being the bull to his matador.

"Now leaders, watch closely. You're going to drop your arms, leaving hers up, grab onto her left hip with your right hand, push it back and then spin her full circle anti-clockwise. But be ready to steady her when she comes back around."

As he demonstrated, I felt his hand grip my hip firmly. All I wanted to do was kiss him. When he spun me, I overbalanced a little with inexperience of the move, and he caught me, firmly. The dramatic arm raise, the hand on my hip and then the push pull spin, were making my head spin, too.

"Right now, we're going to put all of the moves together and practise them a few times."

After six times of him running through the whole sequence and going over every delicious nuance of the moves, we perfected them and had the whole piece nailed. It felt fluent and sexy, instinctive, and beautiful. The primal rhythm and choreography felt so stunning as a set piece. I'd never felt so aroused dancing before. I never even thought it was possible.

"Okay, class dismissed. Go have some fun. The salsa music will play for the next three hours, courtesy of DJ Wayne Groves. "Practise makes perfect," he added.

Alejandro moved me to the side of the class. "You don't just dance the steps, you feel them too, don't you?"

"I dance from the soul, Alejandro. It makes me feel alive. I just let my body respond to the flow of the beat and the hand of your leadership."

He smiled at me, sexier and deeper. Something had changed in his eyes that I felt instantly. Something darkened, other than his pupils.

"You're a great follower, not many women truly know how to let a man lead," he said.

I smiled because I'd seen other women trying to push the man, like dancing was a battle. Dance chemistry was incredibly rare, and damn, did I feel it with Alejandro.

"A woman is as creative as the man who leads her," I smiled, realising how utterly satisfying it felt being flirtatious with him.

I adore the way you lead me.

6 INTOXICATING

March. Thursday. Liverpool. Salsa.

As the class was dismissed, Alejandro turned to me and said, "Can I buy you a drink, Leila?"

"I'd love that."

This was finally my opportunity to find out if he was single and whether I was imagining our chemistry. He was polite with everyone, helpful and charming, but his special smiles and attention felt like they were being directed toward me. He didn't come across as a player and that reassured me, but I had to know.

"What would you like?" he asked, while pulling out a thin, tan leather wallet.

"A white wine, please."

He asked the barman for two glasses of white wine.

"Sauvignon or pinot?" the barman asked.

"I'd guess Sauvignon for you, Leila, am I right?" he smiled, with a hint of cheekiness.

I liked him trying to read me for some reason.

"You're correct."

"So, before I try and guess anything else about you, I want to know one thing," he said. "Are you in a relationship?"

"No, I'm not in a relationship right now. Are you?" I braced myself for a potential rejection.

"No, I'm not and now I don't have to concern myself with any guilt if I flirt shamelessly with you." We both smiled at the same time. There was a difference now though; I knew all that chemistry could potentially lead somewhere. I'd say it was also inevitable. Everything changed in that split second. It was like lightning shooting through the core of me, and I flushed at the real possibility of him.

"Cheers mate," Alejandro said to the barman, as he handed over our drinks. We moved over to the corner. I was against the wall and Alejandro was facing me. It felt like there was only us there.

"I enjoy dancing with you, Leila. You are the first woman I've felt an instinctive connection with. That's rare," he said.

"That's because I feel the moves, instead of thinking about them," I offered truthfully.

"Do you feel everything so deeply, Leila?" he asked, holding my gaze steadily. I felt a little like I was being interrogated with his questions, but in a way that made me ache. His questions were deeper and more searching than other men had asked, like he really wanted to get to know me. I liked that.

"It's both a blessing and a curse. I feel energy from others. I feel drained around the wrong people, or people with malintent. Other than work, I control who I'm around to try and minimise negativity."

"Isn't it exhausting for you trying to control that?" he asked.

"It is, I've been like that for most of my life. I have a small group of close friends that know me well and I trust them completely. I have lots of acquaintances outside of that, but I don't let people inside my circle easily. I haven't for that exact reason," I added honestly, as that was the only way I knew how to be.

"How did your friends make their way inside your circle of trust?" he probed, with a focused attention on me that was laser-like. It made me feel like I needed the wall just to hold me up.

"Through always being consistent and being there for me, as I am for them. I'd drop anything for any one of them if they needed me, and I know they'd do the same for me. I'm drawn to open-minded intelligent people that both listen and contribute. I struggle with people who talk *at* me, with no intention of listening *to* me. I find that draining. All my friends in my close circle talk *to* me," searching for answers as I was speaking.

"I'm sure they're lucky to have you."

He looked for a few seconds too long into my eyes, rendering me useless for a moment. He came across as intellectual and thoughtful, as well as curious and playful.

You fascinate me.

"Do you trust people easily, Alejandro?" I asked.

"No. My circle is so small I literally have my father and one close friend in it. They both have partners. Other than that, I keep myself to myself. They're the only ones I trust now. I haven't been in a close relationship with anyone for about five years, and rarely share anything about my personal life with either associates or strangers," he added, looking a little flat as he shared. I had the distinct feeling there was far more to his story than a gorgeous face and body. Far more.

"I don't understand how you could be single for so long when you're like that…" I blurted. Another bad habit of mine.

"Like what, Leila?" he leaned a little closer into my space. I imagined him leaning forward and kissing me, pressing my back against the wall, and seducing my body, the same way he was seducing my mind.

"Attractive, sexy, intriguing..."

Just saying those words aroused me deeply. He had this way of extracting information out of me, like nobody ever had with me before.

You are intoxicating. I can feel your power over me.

"I think you're one of the most beautiful women I've ever seen."

He lacked any form of inhibition, and it threw me off completely.

"Your features look Spanish. Beautifully long dark curly hair. Chocolate eyes I can't help but want to look into. Full lips. Stunning figure, and beautifully gentle hands."

He reeled them off and I realised he was studying me like I studied him.

"No Spanish relatives to my knowledge. I never think of, or see myself, like that," I answered.

"And you're also humble. You've just become even more beautiful to me."

"Are you always this intense?"

"Never."

It made me shiver and gave me goose bumps. His magnetism felt like I was floating, and he was trying to reel me in. I didn't know whether to run or pull him closer.

"So, is that a good thing?"

"There's something about you. I'd like to get to know you better and yes, that's definitely a good thing. Will you have dinner with me on Saturday night?"

Yes!

I didn't have to think twice.

"I'd love to," I said, my voice trembling a little, reflecting what was happening inside me.

"Smart or casual wear?" I asked.

"Smart. Wear something pretty," he said, smiling.

What have you got planned, Alejandro?

"Have you got a paper and pen to write your address? I'll pick you up at 7:30 p.m."

"Yes," I said, pulling out a piece of paper.

"If you have a mobile number, can you write that down, too? In case I need to contact you about Saturday," he added cheekily, while winking at me.

I wouldn't normally give out my details so soon, but there was something about him I couldn't and didn't want to resist.

We carried on dancing a little before I left; another early start was looming at the office.

As I danced, I kept thinking the same thing, over and over.

I want you.

Why so much, though?

7 FIRST DATE

March. Saturday. Liverpool. Home.

I'd spent longer than I normally would getting ready than on most other Saturday nights. Ellie was out with her parents. We had a good chat the night before. I'd caught her up on the events of Thursday night. I gave my mum a cut down version on the phone too, leaving out the chemistry references, of course. My mum was a devout Catholic and, although she was more modern than the previous generation of Catholics, she was still a traditionalist.

After an aromatherapy bath, my legs felt smooth as silk. My skin was lightly scented with lavender and jasmine sensual oil. As Alejandro's arrival time started to approach, I realised how nervous I was, which surprised me. I didn't expect to feel so fluttery.

Alejandro rang the doorbell to pick me up at exactly 7:25 p.m. He's punctual. I like that. Everyone, at some point, has had to wait for someone, wondering whether they were going to be stood up. His promptness instantly reassured me. It was a perfect start to our date. As I opened the door, I tried so hard not to leave my mouth agape. He looked so handsome in a deep navy tailored suit, with a crisp white shirt and silver tie. Such a contrast to the T-shirt and jeans he wore when we were dancing and yet, somehow, he looked sexy as hell in both. This look was like dynamite to the rhythm of my heart. I started to feel aroused before either of us spoke. The intensity hung in the air between us.

I can't control it.

"You look beautiful Leila, truly stunning," he said, looking at my three-quarter length fitted dress and black strappy heels. He greeted me with a tender kiss on both cheeks. "You suit teal."

As he leaned into me, I could smell his aftershave. It was a modern fragrance, punchy and slightly sweet, but with a provocative masculine depth to it. I instantly wanted to bury myself between his neck and shoulder. That dark, magical mysterious pull he had on me was both delicious and nerve-wracking.

"I love your aftershave," I said honestly.

He smiled.

We were already struggling not to drop everything and kiss each other right then and there.

Patience.

"Where are you taking me, anyway?"

"By the docks, so make sure you wear a heavy coat, the early March air still has a cold bite to it."

I grabbed a stylish black coat that had a thick belt I wrapped around my waist. I picked up my keys and locked the front door. We walked down the pathway with large stepping-stones. Alejandro took my hand, which felt more intimate than being offered an arm.

As I looked up, I realised there was an incredibly beautiful, brand-new silver Audi R8 parked outside my rather modest three bedroomed house. I loved Audis. They were always out of my price range. My dad owned nice cars and took pride in them, and I developed an appreciation of them as a result.

"Is that R8 yours?" I asked, the surprise clearly showing in my tone.

"Yes, do you like cars?"

"I've always loved cars. My dad had sports cars. I'd help him clean and polish them when I was little."

I smiled, recollecting all the wonderful things my dad taught me over the years.

"That's good to know, Leila. Maybe I'll let you drive it sometime if tonight goes well," he added.

He had a dark sense of humour that matched my own, having grown up with Scouse humour, my dad being born and bred in Liverpool. I liked the instant feeling of trust that resided in that statement, even more so knowing how hard he found it to trust people.

Why is it so hard for you to trust people that you need to isolate yourself?

Alejandro pressed the key fob to unlock the doors and opened the passenger door for me, like a true gentleman. The interior was beautiful; red leather seats and interior side door panels, contrasting against the black dash trim. The dashboard lit up like a cockpit when he settled in the driver's side and put the key in the ignition. It was so pretty. It was only a short journey to the docks.

"Do you live alone, Leila? I didn't think to ask you."

"No, I live with my housemate Ellie. We've lived together since I was 19 and we're thick as thieves. Do you?" I asked.

"I've never lived with anyone else as an adult. I'm quite a recluse, truth be told."

What else do you do besides salsa to afford such a beautiful car?

At the docks, we parked in an underground car park, walking along the front, past three iconic buildings on the waterfront called "the three graces," and passed in front of the ferry crossing. Alejandro was right, the wind had a bitter bite to it, coming in from the Mersey River. There was something about early March; the British winter seemed to hold you in a death grip. We always seem to have a bitter spell, just before it turns to spring, like it was trying, and failing, to let go of winter. I wondered which restaurant Alejandro was taking me to, as we had already gone past Liverpool One, which contained most of the trendy restaurants. As we got closer, I realised where we were going. My pulse raced a little arriving at The View, a swanky, high-rise building. I knew I was in for a treat. The restaurant was exclusive. It offered an incredible view of the docks and river. I'd never been inside.

"Let's get you in before you freeze."

We went in, taking the elevator up through the modern glass building. A young woman came over. Alejandro smiled and said,

"Table for two, booked under the name Fernandez."

I loved the way that rolled off his tongue. *Fernandez.* After a quick reference to the restaurant bookings, she said,

"Very good, sir, please follow me."

She escorted us to a table for two by one of the large glass windows. The view was every bit as breath-taking as I had imagined, with what felt like a million lights sparkling just as brightly as my eyes, which were now reflecting them.

As I looked at Alejandro, everyone else in the restaurant seemed to disappear. He was my entire focus. There was a large lit candle inside a glass, tulip-shaped vase on the table, giving his eyes a sensually soft flickering glow. The waitress came back with menus, handing to each of us in turn, asking,

"What would you like to drink?"

"Would you like a glass of white wine?" Alejandro asked, quickly scouring the menu. "Yes please," I replied, before he ordered two glasses of one of the most expensive choices on the wine list, clearly unphased by the price.

There's more to you than meets the eye.

"I'll have one with you and then switch to water," he said.

"So, what do you for a living, Leila?"

That was the question I wanted to ask him.

"I'm an investigative journalist. I work for a local paper, about a 15-minute walk from where I live – *The Liverpool Express.*"

The waitress returned with the wine and filled our glasses. We both took a sip, quickly scanning the menus for our selections. So many beautiful choices to pick from. I spotted the one I wanted.

"What made you choose journalism?" Alejandro asked.

"Being a reporter challenges my left brain and I like being part of the justice system. I do more research than writing most days, but it's always rewarding when I finish a piece, often heart-breaking, too, if I'm being honest. There are a lot of villains and heroes in the area, not that you'd even suspect. They never look quite how you imagine."

"What do you cover?"

"All crime. Burglary, rape, abuse. You're trusted with bigger cases as your career progresses, and you prove yourself. My boss has been saying for a while I am ready for a bigger challenge."

"So, what do you do for a living, Alejandro, other than teach salsa in Liverpool? I have a sneaky suspicion you wouldn't be able to afford an Audi R8 from that alone."

I wanted to know everything about him, but I knew letting the journalist in me out would be overbearing, so I restricted my questions. He smiled.

"I'm a songwriter, but I'm private about it. Hardly anyone knows and I'd like it to stay that way."

"Of course. Wow, what a beautiful thing to do for a living. How did you get into that?"

"My mother taught me how to play guitar when I lived in Spain; I've been playing since I was eight years old. I wrote my first song at 10. It's a natural fit for me, song writing. My guitar is one of my greatest companions," he said, with an air of confidence. There was something else etched upon his face. Something I could sense but couldn't quite put my finger on.

Who are you, Alejandro?

"When did you move to England then?"

"I moved over when I was 14, after my mother died. I briefly stayed with an aunt in Spain, but ultimately returned to England to live with my father, who lives here in Liverpool. I moved to Chester a few years ago, but I visit Liverpool regularly to see both he and my best friend."

There was a darkness I felt, a sadness trapped behind his eyes, an energetic shift in emotion when he spoke about his mother.

"I'm so sorry to hear about your mother, especially at such a young age and having to relocate. That must have been traumatic as a teenager. What did she die of if you don't mind me asking?"

"Breast cancer. She was diagnosed when I was 12. It was painful to watch her suffer. It took her slowly, first her body, then her spirit. It was difficult. My mother encouraged me to write songs throughout that period to express myself. I sang many of my songs to her. It comforted her."

"What a beautiful thing to do for her."

"She was an extremely independent woman and she always showed strength, right up to the end. I expressed the pain I felt she hid. She was always trying to protect me, but I knew. The last song I wrote for her evoked the only tears I'd ever seen her cry. I think she knew in her heart it wouldn't be long. She died two weeks later."

"You must have been a great blessing to her, Alejandro. She must have loved you a great deal. Did you have any help from anyone while she was ill?"

I was very aware he sounded like he was on his own.

"An aunt, Gabriela, came to stay with us and looked after us both. I learned to cook early on, so she didn't have the sole burden, and there were times when it was just my mother and I, so I had to be able to take care of her. Nursing staff from a charitable organisation, organised by the local hospital, visited as her health declined. We were quite isolated other than that, just a small family with a few local friends that called in occasionally."

The waitress came over, asking if we were ready to order. We looked briefly at the menus and Alejandro offered up his hand as if to say, 'ladies first.'

"I'll have the Cornish coast halibut, with a side of roasted carrots, tarragon, and honey, please."

"Thank you," the waitress said, smiling.

"And for you, sir?"

"I'll have the pork loin with curried pear, and a side of mange tout, horseradish, and walnut, please."

He ordered with the kind of assured masculinity I already adored.

"Excellent choices," the waitress smiled as she collected our menus.

"Could I order another glass of wine for the lady and a glass of water for me too please?" he asked.

"Certainly, sir," she said, walking off.

"So, how does it work with your song writing?"

"I have a recording studio in my home, with some high-tech computer equipment and software. I write the lyrics, then come up with an arrangement I like, normally that way, but occasionally the melody hits me before the lyrics. I'll then meet up with my manager and the guys at the record label to discuss the track. They make suggestions and fine tune my initial arrangement, and then we record the final version at their studio. My manager handles where it goes from there. I've never had to worry about anything other than writing and the creative side. I often meditate before I write to get into the right frame of mind. It's a job I love."

"Do you have any creative pursuits, Leila?" I loved the way he referenced my name as he spoke.

"I paint and I write poetry. It's often referred to as poetry, anyway. I started out writing rhyming words but tend to write free-form prose now. I understand what you mean about finding that creative space. It's like quieting your active mind and all your thoughts, so that you can listen to what your soul and your inner voice has to say."

"I've never met a poetess before, how beautiful. Also, we both write, in our own unique way. That both intrigues and excites me. I'd love to see some of your poetry, will you show me?"

"Of course, it thrills me you are interested. I'll write down the handle for you."

I got a pen and small notepad from my bag, always prepared to write as an idea comes to me, and I wrote down my Scribe @ for him.

I handed it over. "Do you use social media for your work?"

"Yes, it's a vital to marketing these days. The record label takes care of all the promotions, and I'm anonymous personally. I use branding to sell my lyrics, not my real name. Here..." he said, handing me his business card.

I read it briefly. It said "Soul Lyrics" at the top. Underneath, it said "Creative Records," with all of his Social Media details.

"I stay anonymous and let my manager take care of everything, posting links to the artists who have recorded my songs, but I occasionally make time to interact with people on some of the posts, too. I value constructive feedback. Not everyone is constructive, sadly. I keep it professional and don't give away any personal information, but I like to pass on my appreciation to people who support my work. I see you are using a pen name too – MoonlitRose, that's a very pretty name," he said.

"Yes, I write using a pen name so I can write freely," I added.

"So, what exactly does the record label do then, other than to provide the facilities to record the final versions of the songs?"

"They cover the full range of management of artists: management, production, promoting, booking gigs for those that want to perform, vocal coaching, music/promo videos, photo shoots, and live gigs and tour opportunities. Since I don't perform, to remain anonymous, I only use the recording and promoting aspects of their services. Their goal is to evolve original artists and promote them, but they're looking for a niche type of artist. They're very selective who they take on. Creative Records have direct contact with the artists to make connections for those interested in recording and releasing my songs. So, they're the middleman, so to speak. This allows me to stay anonymous. That's something I requested from the start. Even when I work directly with the artists, it has to be discreet."

You fascinate me.

"So, will you accept me as a friend if I request it?" I giggled.

"I'd like to add you as more than that."

I liked him teasing me.

"Any contact will have to remain anonymous. I don't want anyone to find out who I am," he said, a little more solemnly.

"That's fine by me, there are Direct Messages and text to discuss anything privately," I said.

The meals, and a second round of drinks, arrived, just as I was taking my last sip. The aroma was delicious, filling my senses. The food tasted particularly nice when followed with a sip of the wine.

"Mmm, delicious. How is yours?"

"So good."

"So how did you get into poetry?"

"Boredom," I replied laughing, to which he laughed too.

"I have an active imagination and wanted to do something as a creative outlet, so I set up a social media account and started to write. I wanted to express and challenge myself."

"Now I'm curious. I'll enjoy reading through your account the next chance I get. I'll create an anonymous account, so I can interact with you without anyone else knowing. Look out for anything to do with a wolf in my handle; that's my spirit animal."

"Interesting choice, I'll do just that. So, who normally wants to record your songs?"

"I write bespoke work for artists my manager makes deals with, for new albums or ventures. You build-up a relationship with these artists, getting to know what they want and what type of sound they're looking for. I get royalties from the music they sell based on my lyrics."

"How fascinating. So, what excites you? What else are you passionate about?"

"Working out, reading... you."

Great answer.

"How about you, Leila?"

"Anything that makes my soul feel alive. That's why I dance, why I write, why I paint, and how I breathe."

His gaze on me became more focused and intent when I mentioned what brought my soul to life. There was a smouldering glint

I couldn't take my eyes off. His eyes met mine with such intensity, I felt like I stopped breathing for a second.

How do you do that?

I felt like I was being drawn in by some mystical power, one I couldn't resist and didn't want to unhook from.

"Would you like dessert?" he offered, but I already felt full.

"That's just right for me, thank you, but feel free if you would like to."

"No, I generally prefer savoury food, with the exception of fruit, perhaps."

"I'll get the bill. Would you like to go dancing? There's a Brazilian venue a few streets up if you fancy seeing how crazy we can get freestyling?"

That sounded like music to my ears.

"I'd love to dance with you tonight," I replied, smiling at the thought of us freestyling.

"Can we have the bill please?" he said to the waitress, when she came to collect the plates.

"Certainly, sir, are you paying by card?"

"Yes," he said.

"Let me give you half toward the bill," I said.

I always liked to pay my way.

"No, I'd rather treat you, in as many ways as I can, my beautiful."

He smirked slightly as he said it. I tingled at the thought of spending time with him.

My beautiful. My. His.

The waitress brought the card reader over and Alejandro settled the bill, leaving a generous tip on the table.

She brought our coats over and we both said, "thank you" on our way out.

"Thank you," she said.

I mentally photographed the image of the city, docks, lights, and candles before I left. Such a gorgeous memory for a first date.

Thank you, Alejandro, for making this so special.

8 FREESTYLE

March. Saturday. Liverpool. Town.

As we stepped into the elevator, Alejandro pressed the ground floor button. The sexual tension between us was palpable. As the doors shut, he closed the space between us, making my heart race. He put his left hand on my jaw, cupping the right side of my face, stroking my hair behind my left ear with his other hand.

"I think you're extraordinary, Leila. I want to kiss you right now. But I don't want to rush something as important as a first kiss. It's taking everything I have in me to control myself."

He leaned a little closer, his tone soft. I could feel his building need to kiss me and his desire to stand close, touching me.

"I wanted to kiss you from the first moment I saw you," I confessed. "I know that was wrong, but I felt drawn to you."

He cupped my face with both hands.

"There is *nothing* wrong with this, with what we have between us... *nothing*," he said, emphasising his point. "Why would you think that?" he asked.

"I've never felt so instantly attracted to anyone before. I'm not supposed to feel that way."

"Don't fight against it, embrace it. This type of chemistry doesn't come around very often."

"I'm trying. I've never felt anything this strong before," I said, as we passed the first floor.

"I haven't either," he said, before kissing my forehead and releasing me.

The elevator doors opened.

Even the way you kiss my forehead is sexy.
Kiss me, baby.

I tied my belt as we walked outside, bracing myself for the bite, which was worse now. The walk wasn't long, but it was bitter. Alejandro put his arm around me, offering me some of his warmth. I was grateful for the heat. It didn't take long to walk to Cabana, a

Brazilian restaurant with an upstairs floor doubled as both a club and dance hall, depending on the night. The music was pumping. Everyone was laughing, dancing, having fun. It was just the type of place we loved, and the blend of music was perfect for us. Cuban, Latin, Brazilian... all catering to salsa, bachata, and kizomba. My hips and shoulders were finding the beat as we stood waiting at the bar.

Alejandro stood in front of me, offering his hand to me.

"May I have this dance?"

He made me feel so special with small gestures. I'm not sure if he was even aware of them. I was, though.

"You may, my handsome date."

Alejandro didn't have to say anything to me once we started dancing. His cues were enough. They were subtle, beautifully crafted with his body movements. With a soft raise of his left or right hand, I knew he wanted me to turn. With his hand in the small of my back, guiding me with a semi-firm pull or push, I knew which direction he was leading me, whether for a cross body lead, or any other move. The combination of the voltaic beats and the powerful rhythm between was exciting. It was instinctual. I didn't even have to think. What a beautiful sensation, clearing my mind, my body simply responding. I felt the beat and I felt him. I wasn't thinking about steps at all. He could place me exactly where he wanted me, with any combination of moves.

I was responding without a moment's thought. I already knew a lot of the steps, but he showed me some new ones too. I loved him teaching me. I felt delirious in his arms. It felt so romantic. The space between us had closed. Every time he brushed my arm, every prolonged glance, carried a raw ache I could feel in the air.

He wrapped me in his arms and paused for a second, breathing close to my neck, before spinning me back out, double hand spins flowing into various moves, small, choreographed steps he repeated until they felt fluent, with subtle leg raises and twists. There were moments when our hips gravitated toward each other, his hands naturally finding the curve of my hips, my hands sliding down his arms, pulling him closer to me. Our hips, arms, extensions, spins, and fluency between the moves intoxicated me. It was sensual, sexual, and everything in between.

We weren't speaking, but the conversation we were having between our bodies was unforgettable. The intimacy becoming more tangible with every move, the heat running through me was pure, unadulterated, passion. There was a trust and understanding that grew with him leading and me following; a synchronised partnership that fulfilled me. I knew I wouldn't be able to surpass the ecstasy imbued in the chemistry we shared. That night, my soul danced for the very first time.

"I'm feeling a bit tipsy now," I said, after a noticeable whirl had started forming in my head after so many spins.

"It's getting quite late. Shall I take you home?" he offered.

"That might be a sensible idea, yes,"

We went downstairs, gathering our coats and heading toward the exit, before walking to the car. The alcohol was warming me. The cold didn't seem as harsh on the short walk back, which I knew was only an illusion.

Are you going to kiss me tonight?

9 FIRST KISS

March. Saturday. Liverpool. Car.

We listened to sensual jazz on the way home. I felt incredibly relaxed. Even more so as he kept putting his hand on my thigh in between gear changes. Such a comforting thing to do. As we pulled up to my house, he came around to open the passenger door, offering me a steady hand to help me out. I felt nervous walking up the path with him, wondering what was going to happen next. I wanted to fall into bed with him, but I also wanted to get to know him first, to find out who he really was. So, I made myself a vow to not risk ruining anything by sleeping together too soon. I would wait.

I searched my bag for the house keys, fumbling a little with the alcohol and cold. Only the landing light was on in the house and all the downstairs lights were off, so I knew Ellie had already gone to bed. The house was lovely and warm when we entered. The atmosphere was thick between us and growing by the second. The lingering desire was palpable.

We entered the living room, shutting the door quietly behind us. I turned on the electric fire and went to stand by it. As I turned around, I knew we couldn't contain it any longer. I was ready to implode. Alejandro stepped toward me. No smiles this time, no grinning. The only thing in his eyes was raw passion, like the glare of a gracefully hungry wolf.

It was a moment mellifluous in every nuance. My hand was on the back of his neck, tracing his strong, defined jawline with a single finger. I paused, reading him, looking into his eyes, feeling his racing heartbeat against my chest as his grip around my waist tightened, drawing our bodies together. His mouth closed in on mine, sensually and slowly, stalling before my lips to breathe me in one last time. I felt both disarmed and enchanted by him. I could have stayed in that moment forever, in anticipation of our first kiss.

Alejandro held my face, looking deeply into my eyes.

"I've been wanting to do this since I first danced with you."

My breath hitched. One of his hands was holding my face. The other was on my lower back. He leaned in close, not taking his eyes off me. My mouth parted slightly as his lips found mine. He had soft, full, warm, beautiful lips. His tongue gently touched my lips, tracing them slowly, outlining both the top and the bottom, before opening his mouth and delicately gliding his tongue into mine. My heart changed rhythm, passion surging through my entire body. I melted into him.

I whimpered softly into his mouth, our tongues dancing our most perfect dance yet. He pulled me toward him by my back, his kiss probing softer and deeper. Our hips naturally pressed together. I felt an electrical charge pulsing through me, the core of my body heating on contact. My desire for him was consuming, every cell of my body felt overwhelmed by a deep rush, stoked by pure emotion.

The kiss became deeper. It felt like ocean waves were crashing against my body, the ebb and flow of our passion, our need to kiss and touch. Neck, shoulders, upper chest, arms, hands, backs, hips. Yet he was a gentleman, not once grabbing me. He seemed totally in control.

I'm the one who isn't.

He was turning me on, with beautifully orchestrated, small, sensual touches, leaving my body aroused amidst epic rushes of tingling sensations. Such small movements, yet I couldn't begin to explain the impact of them. The way he stopped to look at me, one finger tenderly stroking my hairline, tucking my hair behind one ear as he kissed me again, his hand moving down the centre of my back. He had a soft yet delicate grip of my long curly locks as he kissed my lips with wild tenderness. The way he was holding my neck with gentle strength. The way he was pulling me closer to him, stroking softly up and down my neck with the tips of his fingers. His hand descending slowly from my waist to the upper curve of my bum cheeks, while going no further.

You have perfect restraint.
I bet you're an amazing lover.

That one thought was repeated with every sensual caress, and my body wanted to be touched. Badly.

We kissed for what seemed like an hour, exploring, teasing, moulding our lips to each other, perfecting the way our mouths slid together amid the crescendo of each kiss. Every single one started slowly, building passion. I was never one to rush beautiful things. I wanted to linger in the moment, feeling every single second dancing through my senses. I knew we could never replay this night and I wanted to fall into him, slowly and exquisitely, savouring every taste along the way. There was a sensation of intrigue building inside me. I wanted to know everything about him. Even more now. I'd had a taste.

The agony of sweet torture in the build-up, the torment of a torrid desire, was ironic bliss to my mind, body, and soul. My body was aching with dark need, as he consumed every single thought I had. He made me feel like a leaf drifting in spirals, twirling within the eye of a storm in slow motion.

I can't get enough of you. I don't think I ever want to.

"You are so exquisitely delicious, Leila. I could kiss you all night long."

He meant it. I could feel it. He had more restraint than I'd ever seen from a man.

"I would love that, Alejandro; I can think of nothing I'd enjoy more."

I was swooning at the mere thought.

"I know," he said. "But, with you, I want to move slowly."

"I do, too. Let's savour every second."

"I should probably go, then. I'm having a difficult time holding back already."

"Really? You look like you're in perfect control."

"I don't want to leave, you know that. But I have to. I know I should," he said, gently caressing my hair, trailing its length over an open palm. "I want to take my time getting to know you, Leila. I want you to feel safe with me. I want you to trust me. Completely."

I melted into his words.

"Nothing would give me more pleasure."

I wanted to languidly draw out every exquisite moment, feeling the full depth of every single one.

"When will I see you next?"

"My agent has called a meeting with me Tuesday, but we could meet for a coffee after work. I know you'll have to be up early, so I won't keep you too late, I promise," he said, smiling.

"That sounds perfect, where do you want to meet? Shall I come to your house in Chester?"

"No, let's meet at Café Rouge on Baker Street. 7 p.m. Sharp."

Why don't you want me to go to your place?

We went into the hall, facing each other. His last kiss was the most tender of them all. He held my chin with both hands, gently pressing the fullness of his lips onto mine with a delicate and velvet softness, gently squeezing my face.

"See you Tuesday."

He collected his coat from the coat stand.

"Thank you. For a truly amazing first date. I loved every second of tonight, Alejandro," I said, squeezing his hand before he left.

"Likewise, I loved it, too."

He smiled as he opened the door and left.

I stood there waving him off, every second of the cold air worth it as I exhaled him one last time.

There's a good chance I'm going to lose my mind with you.
I'm scared I might never get it back.

10 SOCIAL MEDIA

March. Sunday. Liverpool. Home.

Waking up, I felt particularly blissful. Stretching out like a cat, I was relaxed, content. Thoughts of last night's kissing left a smile on my face that was growing by the second. My body gently ached. I turned to the alarm clock. 9:30 a.m. Still early. It wasn't that he *had* kissed me. It was the *way* he kissed me. I couldn't get it out of my mind. The gentle touches, the sensuality of everything. He left me wanting him in a way I couldn't describe, setting fire to the deepest part of me. My fingers slipped between the sheets and under the hemline of my short silk nightie, needing to satisfy this ache and craving he'd left in me. The taste of him on my lips lingered, and I was deeply aroused by thoughts of his hands on me.

I jumped in the shower. I heard Ellie boiling the kettle downstairs when I stepped out. I lightly towelled my hair. I hadn't seen much of her this week, and I was keen to chat with her. I quickly threw on a pair of jeans and a casual sports top, practically skipping downstairs, smiling to myself like an idiot.

"Someone's in a good mood," Ellie said, drawing out the words as I walked into the kitchen.

"Good morning," I said, smiling at her.

"I was out as soon as my head hit the pillow, as per usual. Did somebody get laid last night?"

We both giggled.

"No, but Alejandro did kiss me for a solid hour, and it was nothing short of breath-taking," I sighed.

"Lucky sod!" she rebuffed.

"So, tell me more about him. So far, you've only said what he looks like and how hot he is."

"That is an indisputable fact. You'll understand when you see him. Well… he's a songwriter, but he doesn't want anyone to know. He's also a dancer, highly creative, very sensual, and an incredibly attractive man who randomly has a very nice car."

"Why the use of the word randomly?" she probed.

"I don't know, it doesn't really add up. How does a dancer and songwriter afford such a nice car?"

The journalist in me was suspicious.

"Have you looked him up on the internet?"

"I forgot he gave me his card with all his social media details on. I'll go fetch it."

I retrieved it from the hall. I had nowhere to be. Now was a great time to investigate him.

"You fire up the iPad and get comfy in the lounge. I'll make you a drink."

I went into the lounge, turned on my iPad on and opened Scribe. Ellie made tea, placing it in front of me on the coffee table, sliding in beside me.

I typed his name into Scribe and as soon as I opened his page, I had to double check to see if I typed in the right address. Ellie was looking at the screen too.

"Friggin' hell, Leila, why has your boyfriend got over one *million* followers on Scribe?" she asked, looking shocked.

"Hmm, I don't know. Okay, so he might be a little more popular than I'd thought. I don't understand."

"Didn't he give you any clues to go on when you spoke to him?"

"Not a lot. He said he writes songs for artists. His manager at Creative Records deals with all customers and new work, so he can just concentrate on song writing. He said it was imperative he stay anonymous, so you can't tell anyone, and you must promise that. It's important to him."

"You know I can keep a secret, Leila," Ellie reassured me.

We started looking at his page for more details.

His bio read "Songwriter/Musician" with no additional details as we scrolled down. Trawling down his timeline, we found some promotional posts stating the most recent song he'd written was "Searching."

"Oh my God, that's sung by "Elizabeth Bell," Ellie said. Bell was a ballad queen in the UK. "I've heard this on the radio. She's an absolute powerhouse. You know the one. It goes '*I'm searching for a moment to be lost inside your arms.*'"

Ellie sung it pitch perfect. I recognised it immediately.

"Yes, I know the one. Wow. That's his song, he wrote that?"

I was shocked he was associated with a song I knew. Not only that, but a massive hit.

"No wonder he's got a nice car! That song went straight to the top of the charts about two months ago," Ellie added.

"Not just that one, though," Ellie said, as she carried on scrolling.

"Letitia Moon, Mark Johnson, Jason Rhine. Leila, these are really, big names. Like wow. Isn't it weird how you don't hear of the songwriters so much, you just recognise the songs?"

It rang true with me.

"I think songwriters in general like to be out of the spotlight. Alejandro definitely does."

"I wouldn't have a clue who wrote what. I always assumed the artist wrote it for themselves. I guess I've never really thought about it before."

"I'm guessing these one million people do have a clue. And love his work. Must be hard to stay anonymous though," she pondered.

"Hmm, I wonder if that's why he is a self-confessed recluse. Maybe he hates the idea of anyone finding out about him, or becoming famous, because he prefers the peace to write songs. I think he just likes the creative side. Plus, he couldn't teach salsa if everyone knew who he was and that's his other great passion in life."

"Sooo, it's kinda hot his identity is a secret, a bit like dating Batman."

"Mmm, I could live with that. Wonder if he has a bat cave?" I said, both of us roaring with laughter.

I had so many questions I wanted to ask Alejandro. I knew I had to be careful not to scare him away.

"Does it bother you dating someone with a secret life?" Ellie asked.

"I don't know. I can't quite get my head around it all to be honest. He was just a salsa instructor to me last week. Today I've discovered he's written a handful of famous songs. I'm not sure what it all means."

I felt a little uncomfortable with the idea as it felt surreal to me, so I shifted the conversation.

"How was your mum's surprise party? Was it at the Legion?" I asked, taking a few sips of tea.

"It went well. And it was, yes. It was in the smaller room, not the large one they use for functions. Quite a few people showed up, some I hadn't seen in a while, some I hadn't wanted to see in a while," she said, rolling her eyes. "The main family members and their partners all came. That nutter Jeremy was there."

"Is that your cousin's boyfriend? The guy who keeps secretly creeping you out and being inappropriate?"

"Yes, the odd accidental touch here and there, you know the sort, a bit like Eddie, the ginger lad who grinds on you when you dance."

We knew each other's secrets.

"I can't tell you how many accidental boob grazes and hip touches I've had now. I try to avoid him. He makes such a play for me. I can't always get away from him. I grimace the second he gets close to me. Between him and Matthew, the guy at the coffee shop, who keeps perving at me if we're working out in Peak Fitness. I'm sure he doesn't realise I can see him in the mirror. If he lifted his eyes away from my bum, he might notice the shock registering on my face at his blatancy."

"The pitfalls of being a woman," I said, rolling my eyes.

We tried to make light of it, but it was a serious issue; one that many women often face alone.

"Did you still want to go shopping this afternoon?"

"Yes, I don't need much, but I am nearly out of perfume."

"I could do with a new one, too, now you've mentioned it. Go get ready. Let's leave in about 20 minutes"

"Perfect," Ellie answered.

We left for the shops. Alejandro was always at the back of my mind; having been there since the first time I spoke to him. His reclusive lifestyle and today's discoveries were playing on my mind now.

I want to know more about you, about the secret side of you, the side you don't share with anyone.

11 CLOSER

11:56 a.m.
　I've always loved following you. I needed to see you today. I missed you yesterday. I knew you were about to leave, and I waited for you. I've been so patient with you, more than I was with the others. You intrigue me more. I watched the sashay of your hips as you walked ahead of me. You and your housemate are both a pleasure to watch. But you... there's something about you I crave. Your jeans were hugging your thighs and bum, giving me a much better idea of the shape of you, revealed by your short furry coat, tapered sexily at the waist. You looked so pretty. You were smiling when you came out of the house. Your happy personality and sweet side have been a blessing to watch. Your bag was over your arm, slightly open. The devil is in the details.
　The last time you were wearing higher heels, on your way to work, you headed into the Green Café, before flashing a warm smile to the woman behind the counter as you said, "Have a great day." I like your positivity. I'm so dark inside. I'm constantly fighting my own demons, but your warmth is effortless and adorable. I wanted to feel it. Feel you. Closer. I didn't have the courage that day. Today I did. You were oblivious to me following. You're in your own world so much you barely register your surroundings. I've become a master of disguise. I need to get close to you.
　Halfway into your shopping trip, I followed you both into Cafe Bean. You were in line directly in front of me. La Lune, the perfume you bought, suited you perfectly. Light and sexy, not too much. You were talking intently to your housemate. You didn't register anyone around you. Nor did she. You didn't even make eye contact with most people you walked by today. To be so close to you, after watching you all this time, was incredible. I stood behind you as you placed your order with the young man, requesting a mocha and latte to go. You put your bags on the floor, as they were starting to hurt your fingers. You had a new handbag in a box, and it was bulky to hold.

I couldn't help but notice you left your bag open on the floor. So trustworthy, so innocent. Your small red diary was popping out slightly and proved far too tempting for me to resist. You will question how you lost it, but you won't suspect me. I'm not on your radar. You were unaware of how easy it was to lean down, pretending to pick something up I hadn't dropped. A quick sleight of hand and it was mine. An easy steal.

You've never met anyone like me. I've trained myself to be invisible. I'm drawn to people who are trustworthy and naïve; people who won't question my lies because they assume, I'm telling the truth. I'm adept at deception, thinking on my feet. Now, I have access to where you will be, for the next few weeks at least. Show me your plans, beautiful. Where else can I follow you? My hunger to get closer is increasing.

12 DARK WOLF

March. Monday. Liverpool. Office.

I couldn't help thinking about Alejandro and the way we had kissed and danced. My mind wandered to all the ways I wanted to kiss him, touch him, hold him, be held. There it was, that falling sensation again, like I was losing control. I always hated being out of control. I fought against it. I was too trusting and open. The problem was I felt something from him I'd never felt from anyone. He had power over me. It scared and excited me. It was a conflict with the potential to ruin me.

When noon came, I went to the kitchen. I wanted a little peace and quiet, maybe write a quick poem. My boss called me in for a meeting late that afternoon. I wasn't sure what it was about, but he'd saved an hour-long slot, which was longer than most of our meetings.

Sipping on water, I opened my phone. More than 20 notifications, which probably meant at least 40. Scrolling through them, a handful caught my eye.

'DarkWolf followed you.'

Alejandro?

He said to look out for a wolf. It was compounded by the fact he'd "liked" 70 posts. Seventy?! Nobody had ever done a deep dive on my timeline quite like that before. He was reading me. No, he was learning me.

He'd gone through the last three months of my writing, leaving comments on six poems. I opened them to see which ones he was drawn to and what he had written. Interestingly, he almost instinctively picked up on the ones written about him in the last month.

This I wrote after the first night I met him:

"He knows,
from the way I move,
the sway of my hips,
the way I feel the rhythm
starting to pump
through my body+

in every response
to the beat,
accentuated with
shoulders, hands+feet.
He knows
when the rhythm has got me,
how it takes me,
fills me,
makes me thrive+
feel alive…"

    DarkWolf replied: "The beat of the music flowing through your body makes you feel alive, doesn't it?"

    He was openly flirting with me on an anonymous account. How intriguing. I followed him.

    MoonlitRose: "I feel music through every part of me."

    He picked up on another dancing related prose too, from a couple of months earlier:

    "Sometimes it's just
the sway that I crave,
the wind blowing
through the trees,
a slight rock
within your embrace,
or the intimacy
of a sensual dance
where you hold me tight,
press my hand to your chest+
tell me that every beat
is an echo of poetry
that whispers my name…"

    DarkWolf: "This sounds so beautiful. Just a gentle dance in a close hold."

    The thought made me swoon, that I might be able to do this, with him.

    To this, relating to connection:

    "You feel the difference,
when words touch you
somewhere deeper inside,
like a gentle caress to your
exposed aching soul,
one that you don't understand,
you just fucking feel it+
it burns+heals you

within the same breath;
that's the power
of a true connection
between sapio minds..."

    DarkWolf: "This sounds intoxicating, something that should be explored. Sapio minds are some of the most intriguing minds in the world."

    My heart raced at the prospect of him wanting to explore my mind, and that he might be a sapio, too.

    MoonlitRose: "It would be incredibly intoxicating."

    The next one was escapist, and magical:

    "She was an enchantress,
a spell maker,
binding you to her mind,
seducing you
with the hips of a siren+
the mouth of a goddess,
creating wave after wave
of thunder+lightning
within your body,
as she tumbles
through your thoughts+
leaves your shore aching
for another taste of her..."

    DarkWolf: "An enchantress like that, capable of such seduction, will require a strong man with a versatile imagination to channel her desire and cater to her needs."

    His eloquence.

    MoonlitRose: "Not many men are capable of such a challenge."

    "Be my refuge,
my fire, then my calm+
I will show you a kingdom
worth more than
a million pieces of gold;
I will show you a mind
that adores you+
a body that will worship you.
It all starts with trust+
ends with your hands
all over me..."

    DarkWolf: "I would love to feel that."

The things he was responding to were the things he related to, things he wanted. The most beautiful part of it all was, I think he wanted to feel them with me.

After our first date:
"Our souls only
had to touch once
to understand
that it felt different..."

DarkWolf: "An absolute truth," which made my heart pound.

I wanted to know what type of anonymous account he'd set up to converse with me through. His photo avatar was a black wolf, with piercing blue eyes and flecks of silver in his fur. I must admit there was something about the wolf I found quite hypnotic, maybe the connective associations of hunting and protecting, and the duality of the two. They fascinated me, the imagery of them howling against the moonlight was very strong and a metaphor often used in poetry.

I opened his page, at the top in his bio he just had the words "The call of the wild."

It intrigued me. He'd used symbology wild and feral in nature yet came across so calm.

Is there a secret side to you I don't know yet?

Maybe that mysterious side I felt in awe of was hiding far more than I knew. I turned his notifications on, so I knew when he posted. There were 10 posts on his page. I'm not sure if he was going to play a character on his wolf account or be himself.

His posts were short and to the point, masculine and strong. I instantly fell in love with the way he wrote. This wasn't about song writing, just expression. Interestingly, his posts were in short format. I would have expected long, like his lyrics. He had my full attention regardless. His posts read:

DarkWolf: "They are more than just words. They are pieces of your heart and soul."

DarkWolf: "Your beautiful mouth and all the poetry I feel when I look at it."

DarkWolf: "Dancing with you is the sexiest form of connection I've ever felt."

I got goose bumps. This one *must* be about me. Does that mean I am a muse to him? How exciting, how erotic.

DarkWolf: "I need a slow dance and sensual kisses. I need you in my arms for both."

DarkWolf: "I can only imagine the curve of your hip against the moonlight and all the ways I would howl on the inside."

MoonlitRose: "Beautiful, DarkWolf," I responded. The thought of him musing about me naked against the moonlight made me feel instantly carnal.
DarkWolf: "You don't know it yet, but I have dark corners waiting for you in my mind. These will excite you the most."

MoonlitRose: "Now I'm curious."
The sense of mystery around him grew.
DarkWolf: "I don't ever want to feel lonely again."
That was incredibly open, honest, and expressive. He caught my eye because of things like this, things I couldn't interpret yet. The journalist in me wanted to ask questions.
DarkWolf: "Trust is the single most beautiful thing I could give you."
MoonlitRose: "This is the key to every door."
DarkWolf: "My dark wants to play with your light."
I found this incredibly provocative. Maybe it was the balance between light and dark and the inference of playing together between the two, but this one turned me on, and I felt that pull, even to his words.
Do you see yourself as dark and me light?
What an erotic thought, one that made me desire him instantly. I felt myself pulse and tingle, in response to the thought of his darker side. Intelligence was an incredible turn on for me. So were words. He could clearly use both. Just the thought of that trifecta, when combined with his looks, was intoxicating.
DarkWolf: "It's your mind I want to explore the most."
MoonlitRose: "I love this."
This demonstrated patience and a desire to get to know me. To explore someone's mind took effort. Effort was the sexiest and most powerful gift you could give another person; you are gifting time from your life.
There was so much I could interpret if I dare assume, they were about me. I sent a quick Direct Message to him.
"Hi, I assume this is you, A? Are these beautiful words about me? I don't want to make any assumptions."
I had to admit, if he was going to write about me, that was one hell of a way to woo me.
Alejandro had inspired me. All I wanted to do was write back, so after I finished my lunch, I centred myself for a minute, composing my mind, letting thoughts drift away, to see what I felt and what I wanted

to say. I allowed the way his words made me feel sit still in my mind. Each post felt like a personal message. I'd never had a muse I felt connected to. I'd always just imagined words without a face behind them. I always thought it would be beautiful though, to spark off a muse and write for each other, for it to be mutual.

That felt incredibly romantic to me.

I wrote:

"I feel you;
in the emotion
that you write from
underneath the words,
in the spaces+what
you don't say..."

Sometimes I really feel it when I write. Other times, not so much. I can tell where each piece of writing comes from. Verses with no muse often come from my head. When something has touched my emotions, it comes from the heart. When something touches every part of me and moves me, that's my soul voice speaking. I'm convinced people reading it can feel the difference.

Just before I went to pack up lunch, I received notifications.

In response to his post about trust, he'd written:
DarkWolf: "One I would love to open with you."

In response to my "now I'm curious," comment about his dark corners, he replied,

DarkWolf: "They are safe spaces, to free you."

What do you mean by that?

Reluctantly, I returned to work.

I carried on with shorter pieces of writing until my 3 p.m. meeting. I went into see my boss, Mike, and sat down.

"Right, Leila, this is a big day for you," he said, getting straight to the point. "There's a fourth victim just been found in a murder case. I want you to cover it. I think you're ready for a big story. How do you feel about that?" he asked, his bushy white eyebrows raised for the question.

"I'm overwhelmed you think I'm ready for such a big case."

"Joshua has left a gap, but I think you're the perfect replacement to cover. Your work has been excellent, you've excelled in your last few pieces."

"Thank you for the vote of confidence, Mike. I would be honoured. What is known currently?"

"There is a report here for you with the facts so far. The victim was from Childwall. Crystal Wilkinson, 26. Long, curly, blonde hair and blue eyes. Cause of death according to the forensic report is choking asphyxia. Her body was buried in the Childwall forest, in a shallow grave, the earth had been washed away by several storms and the recent torrential rain had revealed partial skeletal remains. A dog walker reported it to the police. Crystal was wearing a floral dress and a choker necklace when she was buried. You can arrange an interview with the family. The details are all in here. If you need any advice, Timothy was working closely with Joshua and did a lot of research for him on the last few murder cases. Police are referring to The Choker because of the necklace he adorns his victims with and the strangulation. The other case files are in this box," Mike said, handing over a small, brown box.

"Thank you, Mike. It sounds like an interesting, albeit harrowing case if it's linked to those other murders. From memory, they were also young women, 20 to 30. I'll read through all the case files and start fact finding,"

I felt a little daunted by the idea of reporting such a significant case.

"The police are doing everything they can, but we are here to support and help them find a lead that may help solve the crime. All local exposure increases their chance of catching the killer. We can reach out to a wide audience for potential witnesses, or vital information from the public. This is a big case, Leila, you're ready. I have faith in your work."

"I'm very fortunate I've been given this opportunity. I'll arrange a meeting with Timothy when I get back to my desk. Is there anything else?"

"No, that's all. Thank you, Leila."

I went back to my desk, scanning my calendar to see when Timothy was free. He wasn't in tomorrow, so I set up a meeting for Wednesday at 11 a.m., forwarding the request. Done. I started to prepare a checklist of everything I needed to do in preparation for the case. I was exhausted just thinking about it. There was so much I needed to do. It would be an early night for me.

My dad called to see how I was, so I filled him in on what had happened. He didn't know whether to congratulate me or commiserate with me. He knew it was a big deal and showed an advance in my career, which he was incredibly proud of, but he was also concerned about being exposed to the details of such a case. Dad was always trying to protect me. He knew how sensitive I could be. I love how much he cared about me, how much I always felt that, through his actions more than his words.

I love you, Dad.

13 SILENT TEARS

March. Tuesday. Liverpool. Home.

It was a difficult day at work, reading through case notes, arranging interviews with key people and transcribing anything that could form part of my report. There was a lot of fact finding. These types of investigative reports built up over many months. Every fact was recorded clearly so it could be quoted, with the source included.

I'd agreed to meet Alejandro at Café Rouge, a quiet little diner only a five-minute walk from where I lived. Seven p.m. gave me enough time to freshen up after work, throw on a casual outfit, have a quick drink, and speak to my mum briefly before I left.

Alejandro was waiting for me at the door, early as ever. He didn't beam the way he had previously when he greeted me. He kissed my cheek. He looked nervous. I felt a shift in the atmosphere. We sat at a table by the window. Everything felt heavy suddenly, not at all what it felt like the last time we were together. The tension emanating from him was dark, ominous, loaded. It felt like anxiety bleeding through into the air. It was intensified 100-fold, and just hung there, in the space between us. His hands went to reach for mine. He struggled to look me in the eye after he sat down. I didn't know what he was about to tell me, but I already knew I wouldn't like it.

"Are you okay? Has something happened?"

"You know the second something is wrong, don't you?"

"I sense it."

"That beautiful empath in you. It makes me want to kiss you, hold you, protect you, look after you. I'm devastated I won't be able to." he said, lowering his eyes.

No, baby.

Don't break up with me.

At the least opportune moment, right as my heart was sinking like an anchor in a vast sea, the waitress came over.

"Would you like any drinks. Are you eating tonight, sir and madam?" noticing we didn't even have our menus open.

"I'm not feeling hungry. Leila, are you?" Alejandro asked.

"Not now, no."

I'd lost my appetite.

"Can I have a latte, please?"

"Certainly madam. And what would you like?"

"Cappuccino."

"Thank you," the waitress said as she walked off, provocatively sashaying her hips. He didn't pay her the blindest bit of attention.

"What's wrong?"

"I had a meeting today, Leila. The outcome will change my life for a while, so I won't be able to see you."

Just my luck, after I meet a perfect man.

"Are you ending our relationship, Alejandro?"

I hadn't even realised how quickly I'd gotten attached until that moment. He looked to see my eyes filling with emotion.

"That's up to you, beautiful," he gently stroked my cheek.

The fact he didn't reassure me straight away made my eyes fill up more.

Why is it up to me?

I don't understand.

"It depends if you want to wait for me or not."

"Where are you going?" a single tear caressed my cheek.

He wiped it away, down the wet line on my cheek.

"Canada," he said.

"How long?"

"Six months," he said.

The disappointment was clear on his face.

"Six months, that will mean you're not back until… September," I exclaimed in shock.

"I know, but this is a once in a lifetime opportunity for me. It won't come around again."

Find out what it is before you react.

"What is the opportunity?"

It wasn't a permanent change unless I wanted it to be. I didn't have to lose him. I just had to be prepared to wait for him. What a relief. I was so scared of being separated from him.

Why so much fear?

The waitress brought over our hot drinks, laying out the cream and sugar lumps on the table.

"Thank you," we both offered in unison.

"Have you heard of Brandon Trent?" Alejandro asked.

"Upcoming country star in Canada and across America? Yes, of course."

"It's a deal with him. Brandon wants me to tour with him, writing songs while we're on the road, while he gets material together for his next album. He's on the rise. It's a great time to associate with such a potentially huge star."

"Wow. Do you know why he picked you?"

"My agent has been chatting with his manager, and Brandon likes my work. My style of writing fits his genre. He said my lyrics spoke to him on a deeper level. He also suffered a bereavement a year ago and is looking to convey depth in his songs. He knows my background. That's part of the reason he wanted me, because he felt my words so strongly and connected to the song I wrote after my mother died."

"That's a massive compliment. Your talent is being acknowledged by a prestigious artist. It's a sad thing to connect with. But tragedy can often unite people who are meant to be together."

"Brandon is looking for a storyteller. He's a country artist. Country is all storytelling. I can't let an opportunity like this slide."

This is the part where it starts to hurt.

"I know you can't. I know," I said, my eyes filling up again. "I'll just miss you. I've only just found you."

There was a wet glint in his eye too. He tried to cover it.

"Will you wait for me?" he asked impulsively. "Will you stay devoted to me while I'm away? I think we have something incredibly special and rare. I've never felt a connection like I have with you. Will you wait for me?" he repeated.

"That's a lot to ask. Six months is a long time. I know this is a great opportunity for you, and I understand you've got to go, but we've only just begun. We've literally just started our journey together. The thought of being separated from you makes me emotional."

"I understand that. I give you my word. I'll be faithful to you. I know you're worth waiting for. I know you're special."

"But how can you know that? You know nothing about me."

"I feel it. It's a sixth sense, a gut feeling. I trust it when I feel it."

"I have absolutely no guarantees about anything you're telling me right now. I don't know the real you well enough yet."

I was so aware of this; it was ludicrous by most people's standards.

"You have my word," he said, strongly.

"Nobody else believes in anything like that anymore."

"I'm not like anyone else, Leila."

"You could be. You could easily be spinning me a line. I wouldn't have a clue. I could literally be waiting for you like an idiot while you're off out hooking up with some of Brent's groupies."

"I would never do that. You don't know me."

"Isn't that the point? I don't know you well enough to make that kind of promise to you."

"What would it take for you to believe me?"

"Knowing you thought of me every day. Not letting us slip into an abyss of silence."

"I will phone you, every single day I have a signal. Seven p.m., every night. Brandon and I will be writing during the day, but my evenings are free while he performs. I'll watch some, but I'll be free most nights. I want to be in your life, to be there with you in spirit, even if I can't in body. I know I'm reliable. I can and will prove that to you."

"I've never had anyone prove anything like that to me."

"I will prove it to you, Leila. I know it's early on to be banding around big words, but you can trust me. I promise."

"Honestly, Alejandro, I don't know if I can believe that. I've been betrayed before. I've never met anyone I'd trust with that type of decision, especially so early on. It's not normal to ask something like that."

"I know. It's ridiculous. It's a romantic notion no normal couple at the beginning of a relationship would go for. But we're not normal, Leila. You're a poet. I'm a songwriter. We are romantics. I'm asking for a chance to prove I'm nothing like every man you've dated. Or your friends have. Or you've heard about. Or been reporting on every single day for years now. I'm asking you to believe in your gut instinct. I know you feel it, too. I know you feel our connection. I can see it in your eyes, I sense it in your touch, in the way you kiss me. What we have is special and you know it."

"Even if what we had was amazing, and you did want to return to it, you will have access to hundreds of female fans. Most would find you attractive. I'm pretty sure temptation will be all around you, as well as opportunity, and all you have to do would be casually chat. You're bound to have chemistry with someone. Then where does that leave me? Clueless, waiting at home for you, while you're off with a beautiful woman having a nice time and I'm none the wiser. You wouldn't have to tell me. I'd never know. I think it's easier if we leave it and forget about us. Being faithful to someone I barely know sounds like a worry I don't need. Just wait until you're back, and then we can talk. Isn't that easier?"

Where the hell are all these feelings coming from?

"Yes, it is. But that's not what I want. Deep down, I don't think that's what you want, either. Speak from your heart, Leila. Not your head. Your feelings are strong for me, aren't they?"

"Yes."

"You're scared I will lie to you because everybody else in your life did?"

"Yes."

"But you love the idea of taking a risk for love, of the poetry and romance in that. I could be telling the truth, and we could have something breath-taking here, something that would be worth the risk."

"Maybe."

"I'm willing to take that risk. I'm willing to gamble on us and believe we can build a strong connection while I'm away. I know because I'm willing to put in the effort. I will prove to you I'm everything I say I am. I won't put myself into situations where my loyalty to you might be tested. My focus is on you, just you. I don't care who else is out there. Something temporary will never interest me in place of what we have, real chemistry. I'd never make you question me."

"That's a bold statement, Alejandro. Don't say things you might regret."

"Has someone lied to you so much in the past you struggle to believe I'm telling the truth at all?"

"More than you can imagine. It confuses me. I want to believe you more than anything, but I'm a realist. I know how attractive you are, how kind, how thoughtful and considerate you can be. Other women will see that, too, and honestly, there aren't many men can turn down attention from a beautiful woman. I know you'll be flitting from one place to the next and won't be around the same women week to week, but I am struggling with the idea of how easy it would be for you to hook up and I'd never know."

"Please, let me restore your faith in men. I promise I'm not going to seek the company of other women. I won't do anything to encourage anyone. You are the only one I want to be with. I'm not going to lose sight of that. I'm not an idiot."

"Why is this so hard?"

"You just don't know me well enough. I don't encourage women. I don't want to give out signals that could potentially end up hurting anyone. Women can get attached, fast. I've seen it too many times. I'm not like that. I don't flirt with anyone. I won't encourage anyone unless I'm in a relationship or want to be in a relationship with them. The second I put doubt in your mind, I know I can never undo it. You deserve the type of laser focus I've always craved. Give me a chance to prove it?"

My eyes were overflowing now. There was so much passion in his speech. So much determination. Conviction. He was worth the risk.

"Okay. I will stay open to all possibilities with you. But I can't eliminate my concerns overnight."

"You won't have to. I'll prove it to you. I have faith in us. You will too over time. I promise."

I craved his strength and conviction. He was adamant about our declaration to each other.

"You are so fucking beautiful to me. I don't want to lose you. When I was looking through your poetry the other day, I couldn't stop reading you, wanting to understand how your mind works. I was lost in the fantasies you create with words, the way you feel things. I was captivated by your imagination. It made me feel alive, creative. I wrote a song within the hour. I love you being my muse. I found it so much easier to write thinking of you. I'd like to keep us in that bubble, to both be muses for each other, if you would let me?"

"You are officially my stalker now."

"Maybe."

"I'm flattered you couldn't stop reading me."

"I want you. Does that frighten you? I'm aware I'm being intense. That's a part of me. I just know what I want."

"It does frighten me. I can't deny that. Thinking I was losing you, these tears hitting me, out of nowhere, they're all trying to tell me something."

"Give us a shot. I promise I'll make it up to you when I come back."

I paused for a minute to consider everything he had said.

"Okay. I will do my very best to stay open to you, so we remain focused on just each other."

"That's a relief to hear you say that."

"When is it you're leaving?" I asked, hoping it would be a few weeks yet and we could have a few nights together.

"This Saturday. It's an 11:15 a.m. flight from Manchester."

"Oh."

There was no time for intimacy at all.

"I assume you'll have to do some shopping and pack for the rest of the week then?" I asked.

"Yes, sadly, so I won't be able to see you after tonight. I'm so sorry, Leila. I can only promise, with all of me, I won't change how I feel."

He pulled both my hands to his face, kissing them. I felt the passion in his voice, his kisses, the conviction in every word.

I believed him, for now, anyway.

The realist in me also knows things change.

"Okay, Alejandro. I hope I don't live to regret this but, I promise I will wait for you" I said, my eyes filling up again.

A tear fell from my left eye, always my left eye. That tear was filled with so much emotion.

"Thank you, Leila."

"I'll settle the bill and drive you home."

What a strong and protective gent he was. I'll miss that. I knew there was so much more I hadn't discovered about him yet. Alejandro was deep - his pull, the magnetic force of him drew me in, like the moon pulls the tide.

After a short drive, when we got to my house, I asked "Would you like to come in?"

He looked deep into my eyes.

"If I come in, I won't want to leave. I can't possibly do justice to the way I feel for you in a couple of hours. I need all night to even begin to show you."

He was right. I knew he was. This tormenting ache for him would only grow while he was away.

He got out and came around to open the passenger door.

The atmosphere, that shifting heaviness of change, fell upon us.

After he shut the door, he pressed me against the car door. In a passionate way, in a way that stole my breath. His mouth sought mine as he pressed the fullest part of our lips together before they parted, and our tongues and soft moans expressed themselves as they wished. We both desperately needed one last kiss. Pausing for breath, eyes searching each other momentarily, we didn't want to stop. A beautiful, swan-like movement of his tongue left me in a state of total demise.

I looked up momentarily. The stars had lined up to form the most beautiful backdrop for our kiss. How stunning this moment was, laced with emotion. How temporary this moment felt; such a clear and known impermanence.

As we parted, he simply said "I will keep in touch. I'll still be there for you. Just us, okay? Just you and me."

Gentle tears streamed silently and slowly down my face as I closed the door.

What if six months of separation breaks us?

14 SERIAL KILLER

March. Wednesday. Liverpool. Home.

I woke up and logged in to Scribe. With a heavy heart, I wrote:
"The falling of
a single silent tear,
perpetually replenishing
from the soul;
the deepest river on earth..."
"She was flesh, blood,
heart, soul+tear stained
parchment. She bore
every facet of herself
for the passion
of her art..."

I was devastated after Alejandro's announcement. I had a choice to make. I could wallow in self-pity and let myself slip slowly into depression. Or throw myself into work. As the latter involved potentially saving another woman's life and making the local area safer, that's what I chose. I shook off thoughts of Alejandro for now. I knew he was coming back in a few months and there was nothing I could do about it. He promised he'd keep in touch, so I had to wait and see.

When I got to work, I immediately started thinking about the case and the checklist I'd outlined. Ahead of my meeting with Timothy, I decided to look over the case files and analyse the psychological profile of a serial killer.

Case Files
They were tough to read, particularly details of the torture The Choker subjected his victims to right before he killed them. This was part of the job I least enjoyed, learning about how evil some individuals could be. Knowing so much about criminals made it hard for me to trust people. I had to rely solely on instinct.

Rape was something I dealt with a lot, but in my previous reports, the victim always survived. I hadn't covered a murder case. In each of these murders, he raped them while they were tied up. Forensics indicated they'd been like that for several hours before he strangled them. There were so many things about the crime scenes that disturbed me.

The killer had taken items to each of the scenes, as if he were wooing his victim. He chose things very personal to them. He took the time to get to know them first. It was macabre. The first three victims had been killed in their homes, where he managed to both enter and exit completely undetected. No prints, no DNA.

In the first three cases, the killer had taken a single white rose and laid it on the victim's chest, almost as a last romantic gesture. I wondered why he chose his victims. I couldn't see an obvious link between them geographically, through family relations, high school, common interests, or anything else, really.

I need to research more about serial killers, sociopaths, psychopaths.

Statements from friends and family stated the victims had all been stalked beforehand. The victims all reported they were being followed, increasing in frequency and intensity with each victim. The killer was sending them gifts. They were aware they had a secret admirer but couldn't understand the personalised nature of the gifts. Some were gifts they wanted, things they mentioned in private to someone, items they'd searched for; things he couldn't possibly have known. They felt like someone was reading their minds. Certain things couldn't be explained. There was far more to this case than bodies.

What is your motive?

I couldn't wait to get home and hop in the bath. Between Alejandro leaving and this case, my head was full of rubbish. Questions, facts, thoughts, analysis, overthinking, anxiety, worries. It was all rolling around in my mind, with nothing to stop the overflow. I wanted to stop the world for a bit.

The only thing that helped was water. A bath, shower, swimming, a still lake, waterfall, the ocean. It calmed me. Alejandro had sent me a text, asking me to give him a quick call that evening. I told him I was going to have a bath, a glass of wine, and try to still my mind.

I hadn't had a chance to discuss the murder case with him. I decided to tell him.

Would they ever catch The Choker?
Would I play any part in his capture?

15 PROFILE

March. Thursday. Liverpool. Office.

The time between one victim and the next wasn't that long. I began researching psychopathic behaviour of serial killers. I wanted to understand more about possible motives. Or how and where to start looking for links or angles.

Several things in the articles stood out.

"The psychopathic behaviour associated with serial killers includes a lack of remorse or guilt, impulsivity, the need for control, and predatory behaviour. Psychopaths can often seem quite normal and charming."

How can someone so evil come across as charming?

This perplexed me. I was baffled this kind of duality existed within the same person. Psychology had been analysing such duality for years.

In terms of underlying cause, references were made to early childhood trauma. Sexual, emotional, or psychological abuse by family members was reported. Feeling bullied or isolated as children. This often set up a pattern of deviant behaviour. Emotional neglect has a huge bearing.

This is how they end up hating people.

Most serial killers have a tendency toward crime from an early age. Some possess low IQ, although appear to lead normal lives and hold down careers.

So, basically anyone. Not helpful.

Parents with drug or alcohol dependency tend to leave their children feeling neglected, placing them in a situation where they might fantasise about a world they control. Development often happens in the fantasy world, not the real one; therefore, they don't learn the concepts of right, wrong, and empathy.

Of course.

They have no real role models. Nobody teaches them right from wrong. Their fantasy worlds are often complicated, with interactions they've imagined, from an unrealistic perspective, in a world they've created to escape into.

Boundaries aren't defined, often leading to fantasies of control, dominance, sexual conquest, violence, and ultimately murder. A dissociative state allows the killer to detach from their victims.

I knew disassociation was a method used by people to remove themselves from a painful situation.

I didn't realise murderers used this, allowing them to kill with no remorse.

Organised killers plan meticulously, often possessing a solid knowledge of forensic science to cover their tracks. Disorganised killers are impulsive, often using weapons at hand.

He's an organised killer.

Everything is pre-planned. He leaves no traceable evidence at the scenes.

They often fool those around them into thinking they are kind, unlikely to hurt anyone.

How can people not sense them?

How is a killer so clever at disguising their true nature?

They tend to be loners, unemployed, frequently out of work.

But I knew from earlier research, they could also be intelligent and able to hold down a career.

Serial killers often have a need to form a relationship with their victims.

True in this case.

Why is that?

There are four categories of motives for their murders.

A visionary killer breaks with reality, starting to believe they're someone else.

The mission killer believes they're ridding the world of certain types of less desirable people. Their victims are often prostitutes, or the homeless.

A hedonistic killer simply seeks pleasure from killing. They fall in lust with their victims, with the thrill of inducing terror, but also sometimes for material gain.

Then there's the killer who loves power, loves the control they exert over their terrified victims.

Some are motivated by fame.

So, who's our guy?

Power and control – must be.

He enjoys their fear, knowing he's out there, watching them.

There were so many factors that could have shaped him and maybe we'd never know what they were, but I'd love to think we'd find him before he hurt anyone else. At least with additional publicity, women would know not to ignore stalking incidents and unusual gifts being delivered.

At 11 a.m., knocked on Timothy's office door.

"Come in, Leila. Take a seat."

"Hi, Timothy. I'm happy to have someone to talk to. My head is already spinning, so thank you for agreeing to help me. I brought my iPad to make notes."

"That's great. It's a pleasure to help. I worked on many cases with Joshua and can point you in the right direction. I have some contacts too."

Timothy was pleasant, gentle, and kind, with a helpful demeanour. He was in his late forties, with light brown hair, thick salt and pepper stubble, and rectangular thick glasses with green eyes.

"I jotted down some questions going through the files. The thing I don't understand is how they come across as such nice people. I should try and understand what type of man he is first."

"It's part of their con. Everything is manipulation. They practise conning people for the sake of it, fine tuning their devious skills, preparing for their next victim. They provoke, and look for, reactions, to see who is gullible. There are certain indicators they look for to see what level of control they can hold over them. Stealing their virtue. Tormenting and corrupting. These victims represent something the killers can never be. It's a level of innocence they secretly crave."

"I read the data on The Choker. I think there may be a pattern here. The white rose gives it away. He also decorates his victims with a choker necklace. He wants to make them look pretty, but is it also like a collar, that he owns them? Beauty and purity, that appears to be what he seeks."

"The rose would have been buried with the fourth victim, so you won't know for sure if he did it with Crystal, too. Serial killers have absolutely no empathy. You need to understand this to understand them. The characteristics they look for involve a suggestible personality, someone with low self-esteem. Maybe they apologize a lot or show a lack of confidence. Someone who cares about how other people feel and most of all, someone they can control. They sense it in their victims, people who are receptive to the fear they create. Often believe they're intelligent, one step ahead. Some are and can get away with it for several years. You'll need to analyse all evidence. But the police are focusing on, and are asking for our help with, the following things. What are the common factors?"

I started making notes as he spoke.

"What links the victims? What are his possible motives? Does he go for a specific type of victim? Looks or personality?"

"So far, there aren't any links in terms of appearance, Tim," I said. "Different hair colour, body type, eye colour. I can't find any link between schools they attend. None of them have a similar social circle."

"Okay, so maybe you're looking at personality type, then."

"Are there any eyewitnesses? Who was close to the victim?"

"I've arranged interviews with key family members and friends to establish a relationship with them."

"Good, it's important they trust you. There are things they will be able to tell you that will hopefully help your research."

"Had the victims said anything unusual to them? Dig deeper. When did they first start feeling like they were being followed? When did they know for sure? To what extent was he stalking them? What exactly was he doing?"

"I'll take all of these questions with me, and fact find as much as I can from friends and family," I said.

"You often get more from the friends closest to the victims. People often protect their families from worry," Timothy added.

"That's a good tip, thank you."

"You need to establish commonalities between how the victims were approached, and what was different."

"Was it the same in every case, or has it changed with each victim? Was there anything unusual on the coroners' reports? Did they sense anything different on the build-up to their death? Were there any precursors to their death, any signs he was going to attack just before he killed them, that can be identified? Patterns to indicate their death was imminent."

"The police will focus heavily on forensic evidence and the scene of the crime. That's not the area you need to focus on. People and information are your focus. Look for links and go with any hunches you have. Gut instinct is important when acting on leads. We need to help the police connect dots in any way we can. That's our job. Start looking for all the things we've discussed. As you're sifting through, make a note of anything you'd like to question with any of the witnesses. You can't keep going back to them all the time. It's hard enough for them to deal with everything as it is, so try and consolidate meetings and questions."

"This has helped me so much. Thank you. I'll leave you to it and go look for more links," I added, as I folded the cover of my Bluetooth keyboard over my iPad.

"Any time."
Where do I start?
I dialled the local police station. "Detective Grayson, please."
"Connecting."
"Good afternoon, Detective Grayson speaking."
"Hey, it's Leila. How are you?"
"I'm good thank you, busy but can't complain as it's part of the job. How is your year shaping up?"
"Challenging. I'm now covering The Choker case."
"That's one hell of a promotion, congratulations."
"Thank you. I'm hoping I can rely on you for extra tips relating to the case."
"Of course, what would you like to know?"
"I'm curious about the necklaces. Can you send me some detailed pictures? I haven't seen any close ups."
"You mean they weren't supplied in the reporters' pack?"
"No," I giggled.
"I'll see what I can do kid."
"Thanks, I'll catch you later."
"Sure. I'll email you."
There's something niggling me about the choker necklaces. Attention to details. I have to try and think like him.

16 POETRY

April. Saturday. Liverpool. Home.

I was glad to see the weather settling down after a windy and very wet winter. I woke up gently, stretching my way into the weekend and feeling rested. Alejandro was in the airport, getting ready to board the plane shortly for his long flight to Canada. Six months. How was I going to cope with not seeing him for six whole months, when it felt like a lightning rod had connected and bound us together? I promised to stay faithful to him, and I meant it. He was the only one I wanted to sleep with. I was struggling to breathe thinking about it. My head was full. I needed to still my mind.

Poetry. I needed poetry.

Great idea, Leila.

Poetry was my retreat, my way of outing the contents of my mind. It fulfilled something beautiful and creative inside me, from somewhere deeper, and I found it hard to name. Calling it my soul voice was the closest I came to be able to describe it. The words from there were more powerful. I felt them. I experienced them. They weren't simply narrated. The trick was stilling my mind long enough to hear whatever my soul wanted to say. I had to let go of all the useless clutter built up in my mind from the day.

I had such beautiful visions when I did this. They surprised me, thrilled me, consumed me, led me, touched me, evoked emotion. They were from my core. If I wrote without getting into my soul-space first, they were just words, containing no emotion or real meaning. That wasn't what I was about. I wanted the reader to feel what I'd written. For that, I needed to feel it first.

I was deeply drawn to sensual words and imagery. To sit inside a moment mentally, exploring it with romance. Projecting into it was beautiful. The image often portrayed couples being intimate or loving, which appealed to the fantasist in me, either touching me with emotion from the connectivity I perceived between them or arousing me, stirring me from inside the daydream.

Words had the same power over me, often spinning my mind into thoughts of kissing and touching, moments of tenderness and intimacy. I never really had a muse before, not one I had a connection with. I fantasised about a dark muse in my poetry. These words came from the deepest part of me. This hidden place fascinated me most. I fantasised about connecting with a man so dark and powerful I could lose all sense of myself with him. I often wondered if part of me wanted to surrender to him because I'd always been in control and had to be strong and independent. Maybe someone taking care of me was appealing because I was too scared to let go, too frightened of what would happen if I gave someone else control of the reigns. Of me.

The internal fight was real. I never felt safe enough to hand control over to anyone. I had a lethal dose of Catholic guilt getting in my way, too. I was raised in a devout family, and we went to church every Sunday growing up. The priest, and all discussions of intimacy as I grew up, were clear about provocative thoughts being sinful. The type of thoughts running through my mind sometimes were supposedly the devil's work. The thing is, I kept thinking them. My fascination with the darker side of my mind was increasing all the time, as was my suppressed desire. My fantasies of Alejandro and the dark muse were starting to synch, making it dangerous. It could become more than simply a fantasy with him. The yearning I felt, in the arms of my dark muse, was identical to the yearning I felt for Alejandro.

The safer I felt, the more I would naturally open to him.

I sat at the kitchen table to write. I focused on my breathing, going into a meditative state of observation.

I let my thoughts drift by. As they cleared and my mind became still, I swam deeper, starting to tread water, turning inward to reflect on what my soul voice wanted to say today. Then I waited, for a feeling, for a sensation, for an idea to form. If I was using a poetry prompt, I would have thought of the word first and then started to focus on it as my mind cleared, to see what came forward.

As it happened, not surprisingly, all I could think about, all that rose to the surface, was Alejandro.

Just a simple thought of him had me aroused, my heartbeat deepening, my chest rising and falling as I became more turned on. I allowed myself to completely immerse within the sensation, exploring it, recalling it, adding to it, deepening the deliciousness of that one moment, until it expanded in my mind and words started to form.

"That soft sensual slide,
eyes closed,
lost inside the depth of a kiss,
lips moulding in perfect harmony,

tender skin that erupts
like fireworks under skilled lips+
an ache that can detonate
my mind, body+soul.
Set me on fire ..."

    I thought about our date, the first time Alejandro and I danced together, how I felt. I focused on the dark pull that we had, that magnetic force I couldn't resist.

"Feel the energy
interchange,
that instant lock of eyes+
our bodies raise hell
as you put your hands on me+
feel the rhythm
flow through our bodies
as the beat drops.
The passion you feel
as we synchronise,
is just a preview
of a fire that can
endlessly burn
within our dark chemistry..."

    I thought about Alejandro. How creative he was, how artistic. I started to think of him as an artist, metaphorically. I wonder if he could make beautiful art of me, if he had that ability as DarkWolf. It was an enticing thought.

'Paint me
in the colours
of your craving,
with the acrylic
vibrancy of passion+
the soul+depth of oil,
while you taste the emotion
in my watercolours.
Trace me in pastels+
feel me respond
in a blaze of colours.
My body
is your canvas,
under the paintbrush
of your mind..."

    I wanted the reader to put themselves inside my words and continue it in their own minds, with their own interpretations.

Once the thoughts left my mind, they no longer belonged to me.

17 HAYDEN

April. Saturday. Liverpool. Home.

Ellie and I were in the house getting ready for our big night out.

It was exactly what I needed to stop me pining over Alejandro. I was becoming obsessive, constantly thinking about him. Him leaving left me depressed. Despite having planned this night about a month ago, it couldn't have been timed better.

"Which one?" I said, walking to Ellie in my silk underwear, holding up two dresses. "There's the tight, black, short one. A classic. Or the more flamboyant, knee-length cherry red with flare at the bottom."

"Hmmm," she said, looking the dresses and I over. "I'd go with the red one. It has a cheerfulness about it that suits where we're going. Besides, we both want to dance and have fun, don't we?" Ellie added, with a wink.

"I'm not hooking up. I promised Alejandro I'd be faithful, and I meant it. I don't want to sleep with anyone else. You, my dear, can do whatever you want," I said, winking back. "What are you wearing?"

"That little aqua blue, floaty silk dress we picked up at Tequila Sunrise."

Ellie was much more organised when it came to fashion and cared far more about it. I just wanted to look pretty. She was more impulsive than I was, which made her extremely good fun, showing me there were other ways to be that didn't involve being a control freak. She always made me laugh, too. I loved that about her.

"So, you're on the prowl tonight, huh?" I teased her, with a wind-up smile.

"Aren't I always?"

She finished applying her mascara in the mirror above her dressing table. Somehow, she even looked elegant in a silk nightgown perched on her tiptoes. Ellie was one of those drop-dead gorgeous girls most men couldn't take their eyes off. She was tall, five feet, ten inches, with long, flowing blonde, curly hair, beautiful big blue eyes, a pert little nose, and heart shaped face. She was slim, with a medium sized bust, gently sloping shoulders, with a prominent back arch curving into a high shapely bottom.

She looked innocent. She wasn't.

"Let me rephrase that, are you going to go for someone nice this time?"

"Oi you, it's not my fault I'm a magnet for tall, attractive assholes, dressed up in nice clothes, pretending to be nice people," adding, "I really need to start going for personality instead, don't I?!"

"Yup. It's not like you'd go for short guys at your height, is it?"

"Barry wasn't so bad."

Barry was the most recent bad choice.

"You mean the guy who ignored you most of the time because he'd rather play golf with the posh boys?"

"Yes, that one. At least he was faithful, unlike Tim. What a disaster he was."

"Girl, he ripped your heart out like the savage he was. He was too good looking and everyone else wanted him, too. Just a pity he couldn't keep it in his pants. At least it was only a year with him. It could have been a lot worse."

At least she didn't end up marrying him.

"He was such a bloody player, but damn if I wasn't a fool for him at the start," Ellie said.

"Who was worse, Tim or Owen?"

"Owen, without a shadow of a doubt. He wasn't a player like Tim, but mentally hurt me a lot more. I believed in him, in his mind, in his intelligence. I never had anyone wine or dine me or talk to me like he did. He was so attentive, so thorough in his pursuit of me, so erotic in every way. He wooed me and made me feel special before he turned on me and started trying to control everything I did. Everything became a competition, like he didn't want me to be happy. He was horrible sometimes, nasty to me. I had no idea what a normal relationship was after we split up. It's hardly surprising I went from one idiot to the next. Next time I want a normal guy, just normal. I was always rooting for you and Grant. I was sad for you when it didn't work out."

"I was too. We were well matched intellectually. He was so much older than me though and I was young and naive. Few years ago, but, for obvious reasons, it's still hard sometimes."

"I really thought he was the one for you and for the life of me, I can't understand why he had an affair. You guys were so good together and I thought he genuinely loved you," she puzzled.

"I know and even after it ended, he still said he loved me. I think it hit him what he'd done. He expressed a lot of regret and guilt. I was just too young for him at the time. Cassandra seduced him as a mature woman and got pregnant, I think deliberately to be honest. Her body clock was ticking, and she was ready to settle down. She knew he was a decent guy and would want to stick by her, especially with his job. What a scandal that would have caused him. I had no chance because she set out to reel him in as soon as she started working with him. He was always a catch. Handsome, great prospects, caring. Nobody knew what went down with him and I. Our relationship had always been in secret because he didn't want to be judged for the age difference and I loved him at the time. I wouldn't have jeopardised his career."

"You haven't got a vindictive bone in your body, Leila. You did the right thing, he didn't sadly. I still remember trying to help you pick up the pieces afterward."

"It took a while, didn't it? I think I missed the way he looked after me the most. I've never let anyone get close since. Once you've had your heart torn out, the appeal goes away. If I couldn't trust him, who could I trust?"

"I know, right? Your time may have come now though. At least you've found your dream guy now, missy."

I beamed uncontrollably at the thought of Alejandro.

"I can't wait until he's back," I said, making a puppy pining sound.

"You have got it bad, Leila. To be fair, I would, too. Dark looks, bright blue eyes, intelligence, creativity, caring protective nature, that sexy accent, is there anything Alejandro hasn't got?"

"Not so far. There's something about him I can't put my finger on. He's like a mystery I want to solve. He pulls me in without trying. Our chemistry is off the charts. I know it's early days, but I've never been around someone I want to kiss, hug, talk to, and make out with at the same time. And it's every second I'm with him. Even without. He's been phoning me every night since he left virtually, and he reassures me daily."

"How does he manage to talk to you every night?" she asked.

"He's on a big touring coach with Brandon. There's a place he sleeps at the back of the bus. He lies down to call me if they're travelling, and he is free whenever they have a show. The guys laugh at him, but he doesn't care. They stop so many times at truck stops for food, petrol, showers, and to stretch their legs. He often sends a quick post or two, or goes through mine, leaving comments and showing support. It's nice."

"What on earth do you guys talk about all the time?"

"Everything and nothing. He always wants to know how my day went, what I'm working on, who I've spoken to. He's concerned about me working on this case, how it affects me mentally, so he chats it out with me every night, to clear anything I struggle with. I talk to Mum a lot about him and vice versa. It's like he's trying to find out everything he can about me and my life. It's refreshing. I've never had anyone taking this kind of interest in me before. There's something about the way he speaks to me and wants to protect and care for me. It's more than that, though. We have deep talks, too, like you and me. He's got such depth and an open mind that leads our conversations into random and unusual places. He excites me."

"That's so nice he does. I completely understand why it's reassuring. Sounds to me like you're smitten, hunni."

"I really am, aren't I?"

"Yes, and you totally deserve someone to sweep you off your feet. You're sweet, sexy, talented, smart, beautiful, nurturing, intuitive, loyal, kind, and caring; you deserve the same in return."

"You humble me. Is that how you see me?"

"Truly. I think you're amazing and you deserve to be with someone amazing."

"Thank you, beautiful. I feel so blessed to have you as a friend."

"We are both blessed we found each other. Now, go get ready."

Divert myself with the night out, that's the plan.

When the taxi came, I was excited for a night out. We had cocktails at several smaller pubs first, knowing we wanted to end up at Vibe by the end of the night. It was a trendy club that had been open a year or so in the heart of the city centre.

By 11 p.m., we were already tipsy, so we headed for the club, knowing we would either dance it off or get worse. We had a 50-50 chance, anyway.

Vibe was buzzing, as it often was by 11 p.m., everyone wanting in on a Saturday night. Tonight, it was busy, but not so you couldn't move. There was breathing space in the club and a great atmosphere, full of people having a good time. We waited for a long time at the bar to get a drink and, true to form, Ellie had already made eye contact, smiling at a hot guy by the bar.

He didn't make his way straight over like a lot of the other guys that pursued her. He was happy exchanging smiles. We were there for a solid 10 minutes without getting served our mojitos and he didn't come over, but she could do a coy look like no one.

"He's hot," she said, nodding in his direction as she collected the drinks from the bar and turned to me.

We headed straight to the dance floor. We both knew how to work a floor after a few drinks if we liked the music. We spent a lot of time goofing around, dancing back-to-back wiggling our asses together, or doing Tina Turner-style hand rolling; generally having a good laugh. A lot of guys were looking over while we were dancing. We exuded a fun vibe guys seemed to sense, but the guy by the bar before was intensely watching Ellie now.

"Do you like him?" I shouted into her ear.

"Yes, he's gorgeous, who wouldn't? I'll go and get a drink close to him at the bar and see if he's going to make a move, or if he just wants to watch me all night. Do you want the same again?"

"Please" I said to Ellie, as she grabbed my hand and led me toward the bar. Sure enough, the hot guy intercepted her this time, probably driven to distraction by her hips as she danced.

"Can I get you a drink?"

He had all the charm of a guy from an old movie.

"I'd love one, please," Ellie stated.

"What can I get you and your friend?" he asked confidently.

"Two mojitos, please"

Ellie changed around him instantly, turning into a girly mess. Maybe he and the alcohol together were a fatal concoction, I giggled to myself. The music was too loud, and I couldn't hear exactly what he was saying beyond the interaction to pass me the drink, which I thanked him for. I could read their body language perfectly. Arm touches, bodies' leaning into each other, mirroring, long gazes into each other's eyes. Within a few minutes of them fawning over each other and me standing there like a lemon, I started to feel decidedly conscious. I made a beeline to talk to one of the four male friends he was out with who were standing close by, opting for the least threatening looking. I had my promise to Alejandro in mind.

As his friend and I chatted superficially, I was mesmerised at the change in Ellie. She was visibly shuddering when he touched her arm, or he held her back.

"I think your friend is a hit, what's his name?" I asked.

"The guy chatting up your friend is Hayden. I'm Terence," he said, extending his hand.

"I'm Leila, my friend is Ellie," I said, looking over at them.

Hayden was incredibly handsome – blonde hair, cut short all over, which he wore like a model. Ice-like pale blue eyes, thickset eyebrows, and a chiselled nose and chin, with prominent cheekbones. Tall, maybe six foot two inches, muscular in appearance and smartly dressed in a dark grey suit with crisp white shirt and navy tie. They looked striking together.

"So, are you all celebrating something together?" I asked Terence.

"No, it's just an ice breaker. We are all in IT security, specialising in complex safety systems. Hayden is a contractor who recently joined us. The rest of us have been there for a few years now," he said.

That would explain the expensive designer suits then. It must be a lucrative career. Terence didn't appear to know much about him other than that, though. He was interesting enough to talk to, spoke about the firm a bit, and I was grateful for the company as Ellie had given me the thumbs up, as if to say, "I've pulled" and "I'm going to be here a while."

I nodded and smiled, which she knew was my way of giving approval.

Over the next couple of hours, Terence and I spoke about many things. We virtually set the economy and the universe to rights with polite chit chat. I intermittently glanced over at Ellie and Hayden. They were chatting together quite happily, intermingled with flirtatious touches, like they couldn't keep their hands off each other.

At the end of the night, Ellie and Hayden came over. Ellie asked if Hayden could share a taxi back with us.

"Of course!" I said, knowing I needed to make myself scarce in the house afterward.

We went outside after saying goodbye to the rest of the group and walked a couple of minutes through the town centre before arriving at a taxi rank. Ellie was, by this stage, swooning all over Hayden. He was charming, tall, and good looking – Ellie's trifecta. He might also have the bonus of being intelligent, too.

We quickly found a cab, who niftily took us through some back roads to get to our house faster.

"So, you're in IT security then, Hayden?" I asked.

"Yes, it's a great job but just on a six-month contract for now. Sometimes they extend the contract before you leave," he said, holding Ellie's hand.

"Where do you live?" I inquired.

"I live about 15 minutes from here. I was born on the Wirral but moved to Liverpool about seven years ago as there's more work on this side of the water. Where do you work?" Hayden asked me, in a polite return.

"I'm a criminal reporter at *The Liverpool Express*.," I replied, enthusiastically as always.

"Oh, that sounds interesting. I love CSI documentaries. On Scotty Road?" he quickly rebuffed.

"Yes, that's the one. I love my job, even though it can be demanding emotionally and stressful at times."

"It must be dealing with crime all the time," he added thoughtfully.

He was charming. I could see how Ellie was doting on his company already.

"I try and find the positives as much as I can. I'm trying to get the public involved. I want justice to prevail," I said, as the taxi pulled up outside our house.

"A very noble line of work in that case then," Hayden added, and I could see Ellie smiling approvingly as he spoke.

Hayden kindly paid the taxi driver and wouldn't hear of taking a penny from us.

When we got inside the house, I asked if either of them would like a hot drink, a glass of wine or a nightcap. "I'm in the mood for a hot chocolate to warm up again," I added.

"No thanks, but I'll take a bottle of wine up with me, Leila. See you in the morning," Ellie said with a smile on her face and brief wink at me, opening the fridge and pulling one out, while grabbing two glasses from the cupboard.

"Goodnight, Leila," Hayden smiled at me, a slight smirk forming on his mouth, probably in anticipation of what the next few hours would have in store for him.

"Goodnight, guys."

I went to turn on the electric fire. I finished making the hot chocolate, placing it on the coffee table mat in front of the fire, before grabbing a comfy throw from the storage box. I sat on the couch, reaching for the remote. I put on the music channel so I could zone out for a bit. Also, so the noise provided a bit of discretion for Ellie and Hayden. I reached for my phone.

There was a text from Alejandro.

"Have a nice night, beautiful. Don't get into any trouble. Got another song down today, I think this one will be a hit. I miss you, baby."

I smiled instantly, wishing he'd been with us.

I missed dancing with him, holding him, kissing him, touching him. I was still going to salsa every Thursday, but it didn't feel as magical without him. My passion for the dance was still strong and my growing friendship circle gave me something fun to look forward to each week. I got on particularly well with Valerie, Charlie and Kerry and loved spending time with them. I just missed him. I texted back.

"Wish you could have been there. Ellie has met a new guy tonight. Hope he's not just another one-night stand. Well done on your song, I hope it flies for you. Missing you so much."

My eyes were blurry with keys, as alcohol messed with my vision. I finished the hot chocolate.

I heard the bed squeaking intermittently upstairs, laying my head on the large, soft cushion on the couch. My head was spinning a little and I felt so cosy. I drifted off to sleep in no time.

When I woke up, I checked my phone. Five a.m. I turned everything off and made my way upstairs. No work, which meant a lie-in. I loved Sunday mornings. Everything was quiet in Ellie's room down the hall. I went into my room, changed into pyjamas and wrapped myself in the duvet.

Late morning, I heard the clanging of cups and pans, catching a waft of bacon from downstairs. As soon as Ellie heard me moving around upstairs, she shouted up "Would you like a cooked breakfast, Leila?"

"No thanks, Ellie, I'm still hungover, I'm going back to bed," I shouted down, thinking I'd give them as much privacy as possible. I had to be at work in the morning and Sunday mornings were the only times I got to cuddle my duvet.

A couple of hours later, I woke up, got dressed and went downstairs. Ellie was there alone, beaming from ear to ear.

"Good night, hunni?" I smiled at her.

"The very best."

"So glad to hear it. Well?"

We never discussed intimate details, but we gave just enough discreet info we could at least gauge whether there might be a follow-up date.

"So, Hayden is a God in bed and the best kisser, ever. He's an attentive lover and I can't wait to see him again."

"Have you already setup a second date?"

"We're going out again mid-week. He does shift work that varies week to week. He's working late the next two nights. Then he's off for three days. He's going to take me to the Thai restaurant in Liverpool One you really like."

"I'm so incredibly pleased for you, Ellie. You made an attractive couple and it's nice to see you with someone you instantly like so much."

We spent the rest of the day chilling out, mulling over our connections. We were both happy. Well, apart from Alejandro not actually being with me that was. With all the phone calls, texts, and interactions between our poetry accounts, which we did daily, both of us writing and romancing each other in some way, I somehow felt like we were together. He always left his essence with me, keeping me safe, watching over me. Our relationship was growing and our connection

strengthening, week by week, as we opened to one another. He was actively breaking down my defences and getting me to let him in, slowly but surely. Alejandro's last post simply read,
"You're worth it all."
You're worth it too, baby.

18 THE GIRLS

April. Saturday. Liverpool. Home.

The seven-seater taxi arrived at 7 p.m. with Amelia, Farrah, Jacqueline, Nia, and Lexi already inside.
Amelia knocked at the door, just as I was calling.
"The taxi is here, Ellie."
I opened the door and Amelia said,
"Hello, you," kissing me on the cheek, looking chirpy, as always. She was a brilliant organiser and had been planning outings for us for about two years. Amelia had been single for many years, through choice. I admired her resilience. She had to be tough mentally to work as a Doctor. It was a demanding job, involving many hours of work. She deserved to let her hair down.
"Waiting for you know who to hurry up," I said, giggling.
"Shocker," Amelia said.
"Here she is, finally."
Ellie came down the stairs, looking flustered, as always.
"Have you got everything – handbag, money, perfume, lippy, your phone?" I said, teasing.
"Alright, alright. I'm good, I think," she flustered.
Ellie and I had a very playful relationship.
"Hey, Amelia," Ellie said, air kissing so no one smudged any lipstick.
We grabbed our coats, locked up, and made our way to the taxi.
"Hi girls," we both said, almost simultaneously, while climbing into the taxi.
A staggered,
"Hiiii," echoed through the taxi from Farrah, Lexi, Nia, and Jacqueline.
"Where to, ladies?" the taxi driver said, not quite knowing which one of us he was asking.
"Savannah, please," Amelia offered.

About 10 minutes and a few giggles later, we all arrived at the Savannah, a funky Spanish restaurant relatively new in Liverpool One, which hosted most of the exclusive restaurants within Liverpool, after an extensive renovation of the area.

"Here we are," Farrah said.

I always felt so small next to her. She wore ridiculously high heels she always ended up carrying by the end of the night. Farrah had long auburn hair she could wear curly or straight. Tonight, she'd opted with straight. Farrah was pale with freckles; they multiplied every time she sat in the sun. She was such a lovely girl, quite shy, and introverted before alcohol but uninhibited after it.

We arrived at the restaurant, and I had a brief look around. The restaurant was predominantly wood. There were grape vines trailing along some of the upper wooden beams, which made it seem as if you were in an enchanted garden, white fairy lights suspended above us and wrapped around the many olive trees in the room. The tiles were rust coloured, a deep burnt orange, with a green leaf pattern. We were greeted by a handsome boy. His name card said Miguel.

"Do you have a reservation, ladies?" His lilting accent reminded me of Alejandro.

"Sutton," Amelia volunteered.

"Follow me," he said, ushering us to a secluded bay window area. The table was circular, with deep tan colour seats in a three-quarter circle.

"May I take your coats, ladies?"

"Thanks."

We handed them over, shuffling around the table. The waiter returned a couple of minutes later.

"What can I get you to drink?"

"A bottle of chardonnay, please," Amelia responded.

"Certainly, madam," he said, before leaving us to look at the menus.

"Let's figure out our order before we start chatting. Once we start, we won't stop," Lexi said, picking up her menu. "Are we all going for tapas or main meals?" she directed to all of us.

"Let's go tapas. We can all share, try a bit of everything," Amelia said.

We began to look through menus, pinpointing our selections. The waiter came over carrying a bottle. He poured us each a glass, except for Lexi, who normally stuck to water.

"Are you ready to order?" We ordered, choosing two small tapas selections each. Lexi then added a few general tapas selections, in addition to a few sides.

"Excellent, thank you," Miguel added, before collecting the menus.

"So, guess who booked a trip to Tokyo today?" Lexi piped up.

"You maybe? So, when's that then?" I asked.

Lexi was always traveling to such interesting destinations. She came back with the most fantastic stories.

"August. Matt wants to run the Tokyo marathon. He's participated in so many marathons in the western part of the world, he wanted to run in an eastern country this time," she explained.

"Is he already training?" Nia asked.

She was the only one of us that could do long distance running. She regularly ran half marathons and had completed a full marathon three times.

"Yes, he's on a steady build-up now, increasing the number of kilometres he runs each week. He's so fit I can't keep up with the food shopping. He's like an animal when he's in training, with the appetite of a savage," Lexi said, widening her eyes.

We all laughed. Some of her facial expressions were hilarious.

"You're going to need to train your legs too, you know," Jackie said, a smirk forming on her face.

Jackie had backpacked through India, Asia, and Japan, exploring the world for two years, settling in Thailand most of that time. She was a free spirit, a gypsy at heart, and she loved to travel. I felt she was trying to find the truth in her spirituality. Jackie was a Buddhist, and eastern values allow for a much stronger connection with Buddhism.

"Why?" Lexi asked.

"Have you seen the toilets that are nothing more than a hole in the floor?" Jackie asked, snort laughing.

"Yes, I have and no, I'm not looking forward to them. No wonder Japanese women have such beautiful, strong legs," Lexi giggled.

"You'll need to start practising hovering now and build-up," Ellie added.

We let the laughter simmer until it faded.

"So, what's the latest with you, Ellie?" Amelia inquired, as Miguel brought over the tapas selections and filled up the space on the table. There was barely enough room for all the plates. We'd finished the bottle of chardonnay.

"May we order another bottle, please?"

"Certainly, madam."

"Well," Ellie started, "as Leila knows but you won't yet, I met someone a few weeks ago and he's gorgeous. Hayden. We literally can't keep our hands off each other. It's hot and fiery," she added, beaming.

"I'm so jealous right now, details please," Nia added, motioning with her hands and fingers. Nia and Amelia had been single forever. Amelia's reason, not that anyone needed one, was a very distinct choice, mainly because she liked her independence and genuinely had no need for a man in her life.

Nia was different. Nia was the strongest woman I'd ever met, yet she had a gentleness about her that was striking. She was a barrister. A brilliant one at that. She wouldn't suffer fools gladly. Intelligent, beautiful, kind, fierce, athletic, motivated, inspiring, confident. Her reason for being single had more to do with a predisposition to being attracted to men who were stronger than she was. That reduced her options to virtually none.

"IT security contractor. Tall with short, blonde hair. Well built. His body is to die for, and I cannot get enough of that chiselled face," Ellie added.

"Eye colour?" Amelia enquired.

"Light blue, like ice," Ellie confirmed.

"Compatibility?" Nia asked.

"He's charming and intelligent. Always has something interesting to say and holds my attention easily. I'm not used to that. Plus, he's on fire in bed, too," Ellie sighed.

"Sounds ideal for you," Nia added.

Amelia chipped in with "It's been so many years since I dated properly, I can't even remember what that feels like."

"It's better to be alone than with the wrong person," Nia said wisely.

"So, Hayden is a hot tamale and you may have a future with him?" Farrah asked.

"Yes, and I'm permanently flushed. I've booked us a sexy weekend next week in a spa hotel, I can't wait," Ellie grinned.

"Enjoy it girl, enjoy." Jackie added and then turned to me. "So, Leila, what's happening with you? I haven't caught up with you for over three months now," she added.

"I know. We must grab a coffee soon. I met the man of my dreams. Alejandro. Felt sparks that even the gods of thunder would be proud of, but he's had to leave for six months. I'm devastated."

"She is pining like an idiot," Ellie added.

"He's everything I ever wanted. We have amazing chemistry. There's a powerful and magnetic connection between us. We chat every night on the phone. He keeps in close contact and there hasn't been any wavering at all, from either side. I told him I'd wait for him, emotionally, and not sleep with anyone else. I really do mean it," I added, a little embarrassed now I'd vocalised it.

"You have absolutely no guarantee he's going to be faithful to you, why would you do that?" Jackie asked.

"Because he promised he wouldn't and asked me to," I added.

"Do you trust him that much in such a short space of time?" Jackie asked.

"I didn't at first, but he has proven he is consistent, reliable, and trustworthy. He does what he says, and I trust him from a deeper part of me. I'm not sure I can even explain. We have a type of raw chemistry where we are open with each other. Alejandro asks me detailed questions, opens me up. He's always trying to get to know me, inside and out, beyond anything I'm used to."

"That sounds powerful, Leila. I hope everything works out for you both. The whole being faithful to someone you've only just met thing though, that's a strong statement," Jackie added.

"Unless he's lying, of course, but fingers crossed he's not," Farrah added, a little unhelpfully. Her view of men was often they were rats. This was, however, based on genuine experiences with men who were indeed rats. I offered to stay faithful for half a year to a man I don't know and haven't even been intimate with yet. It sounded stupid. On every level.

It feels right to me though.

The rest of the night was such a good laugh. We had so much food and wine, there was no room left for dessert. The company was just what I needed to take my mind off Alejandro. Damn those niggling worries that weave into your mind. As a woman who was in control of how I felt normally, I hated when my overactive mind latched onto doubt and let it linger in my mind, nagging at me repeatedly.

What if he's lying.

19 RISE AND FALL

May. Saturday. Liverpool. Home.

I was loving the early summer heat shining through the windows. The following weekend arrived, and Ellie and Hayden were away at their spa weekend. I had the whole weekend to myself now. I must admit peace and solitude were things I often craved. Time for relaxing and poetry.
Bliss.
What is it about Alejandro that drives me so wild for him, I asked my muse?
"It's your dark side
that makes me
weak at the knees;
the taste of mystery+desire
that I crave upon my lips..."
He was a mystery. We talked every day, for weeks now, yet parts of him were still locked away. I could feel it. He was open in so many ways, but he kept parts of himself buried.
I want to know why.
I focused on his gentleness. How I crave that part of him, too. How I want to touch his body, have his hands on mine. How our hearts beating would be the only rhythm I would need.
"I desire something soft,
something sensual,
for you to take my words+
let them touch you,
as they weave into your soul+
become part of the history
that I write upon your body;
my hand as the pen,
my voice as the music+
your heartbeat as the rhythm
that we lock within our pages..."

I crave physical contact with him, closeness. That's all I want. It didn't even need to be sexual; it was intimacy I needed from him.

I just wanted him back.

"The press of your
chest against mine,
a hand that pulls me
closer to your warmth+
a desire to wrap my body
within the security of your arms..."

My mind was full of contradictions. I loved the way Alejandro felt in my mind, but the frustration in my body was growing.

I'm finding it so hard to contain my desire.

"I've never felt such intimacy
toward a man I've never
been naked with before.
The way you pull me close,
using just your mind
is an intoxication
my soul has never felt.
I miss you baby.
You leave me craving
the taste of you+
I need to know all the ways
we can fit together..."

I put the phone down for a while. As I was in the kitchen making a drink, I heard it ping several times.

I picked it back up, my heart immediately racing. Alejandro's alter ego was liking my work and replying to my poems.

In response to the poem called "I desire something soft," DarkWolf wrote, "I crave the artistry of your pen."

The innuendo made me ache.

To "The press of your chest against mine," he wrote, "His arms will always be safe."

He was reassuring me, even from a distance. It meant so much to me, given the thoughts nagging my mind last night.

MoonlitRose: "Nothing reassures her more than knowing that."

To "I've never felt such intimacy":

DarkWolf: "Your body craves the intimacy of reality, but your mind needs the stimulation of fantasy. What does your heart crave?"

This response threw me. He hadn't ever asked about my heart.

MoonlitRose: "My heart craves the peace of a union within a connection, somewhere between fantasy and reality."

DarkWolf: "That, would be verging on perfection."

I didn't reply, my thoughts swirling with ideas of how we could blend fantasy and reality. It felt powerful, stirring my mind.

I finished the afternoon off with grocery shopping for the next two weeks, and necessary household chores.

As evening approached, I felt excitement building about my regular call from Alejandro.

Alejandro was by my side emotionally on days I was happy, sad, excited, frustrated, tired, or stressed out. Not once did he ever show anything but patience and calm. He was more consistent than anyone I knew. The amount of time he was willing to spend with me was something I deeply appreciated.

One day, I will make it up to him.

When my mobile rang, my heart skipped a beat seeing "Alejandro" displayed on the screen. My heart was fluttering as I answered the phone, distorting my voice immediately. "Hi," I managed.

"Hey, beautiful, how are you?"

"Missing you, so badly."

"I know, me too. Remember, it's short term. With patience, we'll be able to spend so much time together. I need this to show what I'm capable of," he said.

I understood. This was a great opportunity for him. But I couldn't help how I felt.

"I'm finding the distance hard. My feelings grow each week. Is that wrong of me?" I asked.

I felt like I had an overbearing crush.

"No, our feelings for each other aren't wrong. I don't want to leave you on your own again. I want to be there with you, to protect you," he said, picking up on my anxiety.

From everything I experienced, or heard from other people, I feel what we have is different. It feels special, stronger, like it was planned by kismet and the universe. Maybe it is just wishful thinking on my part. I was practical at times, a hopeless romantic at others. This was another clash within me.

"I don't need you to protect me," I said, wondering why I've always been feisty about my independence. In the past, I didn't rely on men for anything. I prided myself on it. I was a New Age, modern, career-oriented woman. My conflict was always how to let go of this independence, with any man. With Alejandro, I felt a strong internal battle, flipping constantly between needing him and wanting to not need him.

"I know you don't, Leila. I sense that about you. I also know no woman should have to be strong all the time. I want to take some of that responsibility off your shoulders if you'll let me?"

Alejandro had a way of saying things like he was taming a wild horse. There was a calmness about him, centring me and drawing my focus. His voice was placid, soothing me easily. It was on par with his kiss.

I craved both.

"That's hard for me, Alejandro. I'm so used to being responsible for everything. And I mean everything."

"I feel your resistance. You have a naturally defiant streak, Leila, but by allowing me in and trusting me, you won't need any resistance."

There was nothing he did to rile or annoy me. He simply calmed me. Trusting him was something I craved, instinctively, but it was a big leap for me.

"I don't mean to be defiant. I'm not used to having anyone else look out for me."

"You have strong, high walls, Leila. That's exactly why I want to take them down. I think what lies behind them will stun us both. Have you ever truly let down your guard for anyone before?" he asked.

"Never. My first boyfriend broke my heart. I hated the feeling so much I vowed I would never lose control of my emotions or be in that position again. Ever. I've been hurt more than once. Trust is a huge issue for me, so my resistance is naturally strong, and my walls are high as a result. I know it's wrong, but I can't help it" I added.

I even annoyed myself with the way I kept people out, as it ultimately made me feel lonelier. It's like shooting yourself in your own foot. You have something wonderful and special right in front of you, and yet, for some reason, you don't let them in. It's self-sabotage.

Alejandro replied softly,

"You can if you want to. You're right, putting a wall around you will protect your heart, and minimise your potential for getting hurt. There's not a single person alive likes being hurt, but the control you're trying to exert is boxing you in and keeping people out. You're not letting anyone truly love you," he said, with point blank directness.

"I have a lot of love with my family, though, so I don't feel like I'm missing out" I answered honestly.

My parents are so loving, in every way. They're always there for me, at the drop of a hat. They provide so much emotional security.

"That's different than intimate love, though, Leila. Your love for your family is caring and key to the beautiful person you are today. It's your foundation. You and I both know there is another level, one with a partner who will satisfy your soul, too."

I must admit, whenever he spoke about this deeper level, I couldn't relate. I hadn't experienced depth of that sort with anyone. It was appealing to the romantic in me, though, to the poet, and I love knowing he believed in it, too.

"When you talk about it, I'm curious. I want to understand that feeling," I added.

"I want to show you, Leila. I want to free you."

"I'm not sure I understand what freeing me means."

"You have to trust me, let me into your mind completely. That means the darker parts, the parts you're afraid to open, the parts you may be ashamed or scared to reveal. I know it's incredibly hard, but you have to be willing to let go."

He gently presented his idea in a way that intimidated at first, yet still intrigued me.

"I don't know if that's possible," I admitted.

The control freak in me was battling an internal war. Part of me wanted to try; the other part wanted to run.

So much conflict.

"It is," he told me. "You will find a level of peace you've never even imagined; a peace you've only dreamt about. I promise it will free you. There's only so much we can do at a distance, but intimacy is about opening yourself up like a flower, petal by petal, layer by layer. This comes from your mind first, body second."

"You also need to trust I'm not going to hurt you," he added.

"If it's important to you, I promise I will try," I said. "I can't say much more than that right now. I simply don't know exactly what you mean, yet."

My head was spinning, confused at the notion.

"Our physical chemistry is already sexy. You're an amazing kisser, Alejandro. I could spend hours kissing you. What excites me most, though, is our mental connection. My heart starts to race, and my blood starts to pump when we have conversations like these," I said honestly.

"I can't wait to spend hours kissing you, Leila. I know as soon as we start, we won't be able to stop."

I loved it. There was nothing ambiguous in what he was saying. He wants me. He's made it completely clear, in every way, and I was flattered. Once the conversation shifted, I felt arousal stirring my body, more aware of my chest suddenly, like everything was slowing down and deepening inside me. It only happened with him.

"When you talk to me about anything intimate, my chest starts to rise and fall. Is that something you feel, too?"

"Yes. That's part of our pull to each other, the strength of our connection. It's like an overwhelming form of arousal. It will deepen, growing more severe over time. That's how I know you're the one I want to invest my time getting to know. I trust the feeling."

"I've never felt it before,"

"This rarely happens. Do you believe in soulmates, Leila?"

Alejandro had a way with words. It felt as if he was searching for the raw truth of who I was, underneath the external, social layer I showed the world. He thrived on the intensity of a tortile penetration of my mind. I was starting to, as well.

"I do believe in fate. Although I believe we're compatible with many people to some degree, I think there's one person out there who can touch us in an entirely different kind of way. Someone with whom sparks fly, like a thunderstorm between you, the intensity perpetually building and releasing, before building again" he explained.

"I believe that person, for me, is you."

My heart was beating fast, pounding in my chest.

How do you do that?

I fell silent for a short while, processing what he said. He thinks I'm the one. *His soulmate.* This beautiful, sexy, intelligent, creative, thoughtful, caring, protective man, thinks I'm his soulmate. I wanted to kiss him.

"Soul sparks, yes. I'm feeling it right now. I don't have to understand it conceptually, my body is explaining it as we speak," I said, my breath jagged.

"Do you feel a little lightheaded? Is your breath deepening and your chest rising and falling at just the thought of me kissing you?" he asked.

"Yes," I replied. I felt shy, as if it was affecting my ability to think and speak.

"What if I said I want to twist your hair up, away from your elegant neck, and kiss it? That I want my tongue to trace down the full length of it, then butterfly kiss on the way back up, with gentle nibbles and teasing sucks? How would you feel then?" he asked, deliberately teasing me.

I felt this huge shift in our energy, in a way I couldn't begin to describe.

I felt weak, drugged. My responses changed as I focused on the thought of him on my neck, tormenting me with beautiful attention to detail.

"It makes me feel delirious," I said, my voice quickening.

"What if I pulled your body in close, losing myself in the crevice of your neck? My fingers tracing down the centre of your spine, then back up your arms, until I cup my hand around the back of your head, underneath the hairline. How would you feel then?" he asked.

I liked the way he was probing me for a reaction, knowing full well he was turning me on.

"My chest is pounding heavily, my mind is trembling, shivers are running through my body," I added, feeling exactly the way I said.

He was kryptonite. I was weakening the more he spoke. I think he was thriving off the impact.

"What if I were to lift your chin up and make you look into my eyes, while I told you I needed to kiss you deeply? What if I stalled before I kissed you, what if I made you wait in that pause, anticipating me? How would you feel then?" he prodded.

"Sensually charged, my body starting to pulse in anticipation of your tongue in my mouth." I couldn't be sure, but I thought I heard him softly moan. "When our mouths part and I tilt the angle of my head to find yours, we meld together. My tongue sliding into your mouth, dancing together, swan-like movements, graceful, elegant, gentle, how would you feel then?" he continued.

He was surprising me. I hadn't realised how deeply sensual a telephone conversation could be, or how vast a man's potential effect on me could be. I was virtually rendered speechless at this point, waves of erotic sensation sweeping through my body.

"I wouldn't be able to talk."

"Your voice has changed. It is quiet and wispy, sensual and soft. You're deeply aroused, aren't you?" he asked.

I felt like I was being slowly hypnotised by his voice.

"Yes."

I was unable to say anything else, feeling lost in the sensations I was experiencing.

"Follow my lead and trust me now. Okay?" he asked.

"Yes," I muttered.

"If you want to travel deeper with me, your first instruction is to go to bed early tonight. And I want you to imagine me doing all those things to you. Allow your hands to wander. Pretend they're mine. Will you do that for me?"

Damn.

I knew exactly what he was asking of me. I also knew I had to free this wretched heart rhythm. I felt so sexually charged; I needed the release. To do it because he'd instructed me to, that was hot. It felt deliciously naughty.

"I will," I replied, my voice quaking.

"I won't make you speak anymore. Close your eyes and lose yourself. There are only four months until I bring it all to life for you. Take care of you, okay?" he insisted.

"I can't wait. I will. Goodnight," I answered, my breath ragged.

"Goodnight, beautiful," he closed with.

I put the phone down, filled a glass of water, and went upstairs, removing my clothes and climbing in bed naked. I had no idea what happened, but I knew I needed to touch myself; the ache inside my body left me feeling overwhelmed. I knew it wouldn't go away on its own.

Something incredibly powerful was sparking between us. I could feel my wetness. I couldn't breathe normally. My back was arching naturally as I thought of him, letting my fingers roam underneath the duvet. Touching. Thinking of him kissing my neck. Longing. Yearning. Craving his touch. It roared through me like a fire, building and building, until the final sigh, the last gasp, the beautiful release. It was all because of him; his voice, his instruction, his thoughts, his mind, our connection.

You are sexy as fuck, Alejandro.

20 DARK MUSE

June. Saturday. Liverpool. Home.

What a beautiful day. I was sunbathing in the garden for most of it, relaxing after a late-night dancing salsa, bachata and kizomba with my dance friends. Ellie was at Hayden's for the weekend again. I hadn't seen her much recently and was getting used to spending more time alone.

Ellie and Hayden were obsessed with each other. They kept to themselves over at his place. He popped in for an occasional coffee, but not often. With all her other boyfriends, she kept in close contact with me. But she was slipping away with Hayden. Maybe it was because it was early days in their relationship. They were in the honeymoon phase right now, after all.

I was thinking about everything I'd achieved this week. The Choker case was much more involved at this point. I'd spent time making connections with the family and friends of each of the victims, building up a network of people.

Alejandro and Timothy were great with me, discussing the case regularly and coming up with new angles, things that might not have crossed my mind. Alejandro was more than a sounding board; he was an intellectual who helped me think outside of the box. Plus, he encouraged me to vent and release, so I didn't become too stressed.

Timothy was full of knowledge from working with Justin, and regularly gave me tips on next steps, things I may have missed, or new angles to work. He also helped with the presentation of facts when writing my articles. We made some key contacts from public feedback and had a host of people offering information about the victims. I felt as if I was overlooking something, though. Doubts about why the last victim was different lingered in my mind. All other victims were found at the crime scenes where they were murdered.

This last murder was different. Crystal had been buried.
Why?
What was different about her?

I'd mull that over in depth during the week and reread the case history. The appearances of the victims didn't follow a pattern. The only pattern I could find at all was their personality type. Every single one of the victims was adored by everyone. None had enemies. They were literally sweethearts who wouldn't hurt a fly.

Why would you be so evil to such lovely women?
What's the relevance of trying to romance them first?

My phone bleeped at 7 p.m. A text from Alejandro.

"Just checking if you're free for a phone call. I want you comfortable for this one," it read.

My heart immediately reacted, pulse quickening. I missed him so much the thought of just his voice excited me, let alone thoughts of what he might speak of.

"Give me half an hour if that's okay. I was just going to jump into the shower. I've been in the garden all day sunbathing and was so hungry, I made tea early."

"Half an hour? Now you are teasing me," came the response.

Exactly half an hour later, he called. I was sitting on the bed with a towel around me, hair freshly brushed and wet in ringlets after gently towel drying it. I placed a dry towel on the pillow for my wet hair, ready to speak to Alejandro.

"Hi," I answered.

"Hey, beautiful," he said, with that gorgeous Spanish lilt to his voice.

"How long have you got left out there?" I pined.

"It's been over three months, we're more than halfway there."

In a way, I was grateful I had a case to work on. It gave me something to completely throw myself into, an important focus.

"Thank goodness for that. Every week feels like a month. My concept of time is all screwed up."

Eleven weeks, I can do this.

"Eleven weeks," I chanted, like a mantra.

Alejandro laughed on the other end.

"Are you missing me that much?" he teased.

"I've been on fire since I met you, and it's starting to burn a little now, if I'm being honest. This ache isn't going anywhere. Nothing gets rid of it. Sometimes it twists inside and hurts a little," I said, feeling that stirring deep inside my core.

"I might be able to help you with that, Leila, if you'll let me?" his voice softening and deepening.

My chest started to pound in slow motion again, as it did as soon as we connected intimately.

"My chest is losing control again, Alejandro."

"Mmm. You become aroused so easily at the thought of me, like I do with you," he said, his voice deepening. "My body is doing the same thing. Your heart beats deeper and faster because of the sheer strength and power of your soul's voice calling out for its soulmate."

I liked that explanation a lot. He had a way of seeing everything a little deeper than anyone I'd ever spoken to before. I found it mesmerising.

My mum could talk deeply to me, and I spoke at great length with her most weeks, but never with a partner. No man ever understood me like Alejandro, not even a fraction as much.

"You're interested in everything I say, everything I think, everything I feel. I can feel you raging like wildfire through my poetry and thoughts. The effect you have on me, the way you make me feel, is almost overwhelming at times."

I felt emotional.

"I can feel you when you write. You're this beautiful living book and I get to journey with you, even when we're apart, by reading what you write, seeing what you like, what you connect to, on any given day. It's like having an insight into your heart, and everything you're thinking and feeling. You literally wear your heart on your sleeve."

"It means a lot you like what I write." I added gratefully.

"You are too modest. I'm clearly not the only one who reads you" he added, trying to boost confidence in my talent.

I suspected he liked that about me, too, though. There's a line with confidence; it's not attractive when someone crosses over into cockiness. I'd rather be on the humble side of confident any day.

"Okay, well, you're the only one I truly care about who reads me."

"I love the way you do that, the way you make me feel so important in your life. You make me feel wanted, Leila. I adore that," Alejandro said, and my heart tugged as I felt a smile in his voice.

I miss you.

"It's unfair I can't touch you. I can barely contain my passion. You leave me aching, all the time," I said.

"It will be worth the wait. Let me explore your mind while we're apart. It will be far more powerful when I touch your body, I promise."

I melted at the thought.

"That sounds sexy. Why is it you want to explore my mind so much?" musing over why it felt so powerful.

"Because I know you have a beautiful soul. I can't think of a single reason why I *wouldn't* want to explore it. Your intelligence is an aphrodisiac. I'd like to see the full range of what you hold in that pretty mind of yours, to journey it to full depth. Even the darkest parts, baby."

My jagged intake of breath said it all.

"I know you've already started by the hundreds of questions you've asked me so far, getting to know all about my past, my youth, my aspirations for the future, my hopes, my dreams. How would you explore me further beyond that?"

"By pushing you past your limits."

There was a hint of darkness I hadn't heard in his voice before.

"How do you know what my limits are?"

My chest started to pound at nearly full force, tension shifting between us.

"That's what I'd like to find out."

"In what way?"

"I want to discuss that in person. Don't worry about that for now. I just want to get to know you a little better, week by week," he said.

"I'd like to know three things tonight" he said confidently, piquing my interest.

"First, I want to know where you would most like to travel on a short European trip?" he asked, in that beautiful Spanish voice.

"Paris. Or Italy. Maybe Venice or Florence."

My heart fluttered.

"Perfectly romantic," he said.

"Where would you like to go?" I asked out of curiosity.

"Italy would be my first choice."

"What was the second?"

I was enjoying his little quiz.

"Do you prefer gold, silver, or bronze?"

What an unusual question, I thought, but knew the answer straight away.

"A shiny polished silver with a slight sparkle, not matte. I like things that sparkle. I think I was a magpie in a former life. I quite like rose gold and gold, too, but I'd say silver out of all of them."

Why on earth was he asking me such bizarre questions?

"Are you ready for the third?" he teased.

"Yes."

"I want to know what you sound like when you come for me."

His directness truly and utterly shocked me. Damn, if my body didn't respond to him saying it, though. The heat through my cheeks felt like a furnace.

"Now you're just being naughty, mister."

"No. I want you to be with me, here and now. I want to hear you and sense you."

He said it so sensually, his voice deepening as he became aroused.

"I've never done that before."

The thought secretly turned me on.

"I know it probably feels naughty to you because you explained your background, but you know how much I miss you. I need to connect with you. We are both healthy, single adults. There is absolutely nothing to be ashamed of. I'll tell you what, I'll just talk to you and let you decide. Okay?" he asked.

"Okay," I said, nervously, aware the energy had shifted between us.

"I want you to close your eyes, focusing on my voice. Imagine I'm there with you right now. I lean into your face and brush my lips softly against your cheek, sweeping your hair back behind your ear, kissing softly along your jaw."

His voice was sultry and sexy.

"Mmm, that sounds nice."

"I tilt your head gently, exposing your soft neck. As I lean over you, I can sense you starting to quiver as you feel my warm breath against you."

My body was tingling at the erotic way he was talking. Nobody had ever spoken to me erotically before, not like this. It feels wrong to me, yet I couldn't help but enjoy the sensation of giving in to the feelings.

"I place kisses gently down one side of your exposed neck, my lips soft and warm, before parting them, my tongue softly tracing wet lines from underneath your ear, down to the crook of your neck."

I gasped softly, imagining exactly how it would feel if he were with me. My imagination was so powerful I could physically feel everything he described.

"I like that noise," he said. "I don't want you to say anything, I just want you to listen," he added.

That helped. It took away any pressure associated with staying silent in a conversation, which I normally would feel obliged to fill. He took away my need to do so.

"My hands are caressing gentle lines over your shoulders, down your arms, as I reach in to kiss your collarbone and the rounds of your shoulders, before moving back up to find your mouth, yours parting instinctively," he said, teasing me with a directness I hadn't known before.

My breathing changed audibly, chest heaving. Arousal was steadily building inside me. I was wet; such a warm feeling I knew to be an instinctive response to the things he was saying to me.

Nothing felt uncomfortable with him. Nothing. I felt shy, but it was so natural for him to talk openly with me, erotically.

This is naughty.

"I can hear your breath changing, Leila, as I begin to lean in and softly lick over the shape of your lips, partially penetrating your mouth. You're so beautiful."

Alejandro was responding to the sound of my breath as a cue. He knew when I started to lose control of my senses. Only he could do this to me. Only he had this kind of power over me. I never wanted to lose control of myself before now. Yet the sensations felt so sexy in this aroused state, listening to the way words fell effortlessly and sensually from his lips. My mouth parted on the phone, as I imagined his mouth next to mine.

"Our kiss is long and slow, starting off shallow, becoming deeper as we taste each other. Our tongues are sliding over each other. I can feel your moans softly landing in my mouth as you begin to lose control of your responses. These are the sounds I adore, the natural ones, the instinctive responses your body makes," he said seductively.

I moaned involuntarily, directly into the mouthpiece. As it hit him, he responded with a similar sound. It didn't matter what we did, everything felt sensual, erotic, sexy, beautiful. He was becoming like a drug to me, his voice an aphrodisiac, and he was making me high.

"I trace my fingers down to slowly peel off your towel, revealing your warm, soft flesh."

A gasp escaped my lips as I undid my towel.

"I'm naked for you," I said, truthfully, a little afraid of the vulnerability.

"That's such a beautiful thought, Leila. Lie back, baby, I want to tell you what I want to do to you."

I readjusted myself on the pillow, allowing the towel to fall away from my body.

"I'm right next to you, standing up, looking over you, at the beautiful shape of your breasts and body. You're so sexy, Leila. I ache at the thought of you. Caress your breasts for me. Use my hands in your mind. I'm touching you," he commanded softly.

To my surprise, I found myself doing what he asked.

"I'm caressing my breasts, imagining they're your hands. Are you touching your body, too, Alejandro?" I asked, curious if this was mutual.

"No, beautiful. I only want to please you tonight. I want you at my mercy."

The word *mercy* made me whimper.

Whether he intended to or not, my body was responding. I was so wet. I felt the warmth within me. The way he commanded me was something so different.

I enjoy being at his mercy.

Why?

I stroked my nails gently over my breasts in circles, squeezing each gently with one hand when I got to the fullest part, before tracing in circles again.

"I'm gently cupping your breasts, thumbing your nipples, before leaning down to take one in my mouth. I tease it, flicking softly with the tip of my tongue, before sucking on you, gently at first, then firmer," he said, sexily.

There was something about the way he said it that had me inhaling deeply, my back arching at the thought.

"Touch yourself," he gently demanded.

His voice was masculine, but soft and sultry. My fingers automatically followed his commands.

"Okay," I whispered, suddenly losing the ability to speak.

My hands started to wander as he continued to arouse me, and I followed his words, re-enacting everything he said.

"My hands trace you in a line, tickling over the side of your breasts. I'm sucking softly on your nipples, licking them firmly."

I loudly gasped.

"My fingers are tracing you at the same time, down the centre of your body, over your belly. Until I reach that moist line, so beautifully wet, and then dip my finger into your warmth."

He carried on as I moaned into the receiver, my fingers traced wherever he told me to go.

"I follow the line over your clit," he said, pausing, knowing even saying that would arouse me. He was freezing the moment for me. I flinched as my fingers rubbed over my clit, gasping on the first pass.

"Does that feel good?" he softly asked.

I felt myself arching, pressing my fingers harder.

"I want you to rub it softly for me now, in diagonal small lines. Rub, not flick," he said.

The feeling of doing this with him, and for him, overwhelmed me with desire.

"Now press a little firmer, move a little faster," he said. "I'm rubbing your clit and suckling your nipples. The firmer I suck, the more your body aches."

He was right, the thought of it drove me crazy. I started to rub firmly over my clit, the moisture flowing freely now, making the slide over the firm swollen area so sensual.

"I'm switching to all four fingers now. I'm going to press only lightly in a hovering motion, like a rapid but very light rub."

I did the same.

"That feels so beautiful."

My voice cracked with arousal.

"Mmm, good. Now I want to steal your breath."

I moaned responsively.

"I want you to speed up, pressing harder. I want to hear the hitch in your breath, the increasing demand in your moans. Harder."

This feels so wrong.

"The way I'm touching you now is like a rapid vibration, almost tantric. When your desire turns into a very real need, I want you to come."

I didn't need much motion to make myself come. I touched myself with all four fingers, moving rapidly, using the same technique he instructed. Then I was grinding, moaning, pushing against my fingers. I applied full pressure, the four fingers gliding across my wet surface, as I caught my clit on every pass.

"I've found your sweet spot, beautiful. I'm not moving off that clit until you give yourself to me completely."

Fuck.

I felt it. I felt exactly what he described, starting to rub vigorously. My breath caught down the phone on every hard pass, as I lost myself in the sensation.

"Mmm, that sounds nice. Harder."

I increased the pressure, rubbing furiously over myself.

"Now, baby. Lose yourself. Let go completely," he instructed.

I let go.

"Mmmmhmm," I moaned, the sensation building through my core, detonating in what felt like a million nerve endings underneath my fingertips. As I rubbed, hard, the waves rushed over me and I was overwhelmed, in every way. My breath was broken and panting, moaning, and whimpering, all at once.

"Mmm, that's so beautiful," he said, and I knew it was turning him on to hear me. I continued rubbing myself, moaning through the sensation as it spun through me, then slowly started to de-escalate. It took so long for my body to still completely, to feel sated. Eventually, a sense of peace came over me.

"That was everything I imagined. You sound divine giving yourself to me. That was so sensual. You are everything I desire, and so much more. I can't wait until I can touch you for real, when I can make you come, then hold you tight in my arms. I want to hold you and talk to you afterwards, too."

I whimpered again at the thought of his aftercare.

"I can't talk, Alejandro," I replied jaggedly.

I was too overcome and overpowered with emotions to be able to speak properly. I couldn't form a complete sentence in my mind, let alone with my mouth.

"Then do the following for me," he added. "Pull the duvet over yourself and get cosy. Lean onto your side. I want you to imagine I'm in your bed with you, facing you, my hands tenderly stroking down your arms and back up again. I want you to feel safe, as I kiss along your shoulders and collarbone, stroking your hair," he said.

I felt the combination of his voice and my body, as I pulsed and twitched through the last sensations of my orgasm. There was something incredibly hypnotic and soothing about the feeling, almost like I was in a trance.

My dark muse.

21 SONG

June. Thursday. Liverpool. Home.

It was one of the warmest summers I could remember. We rarely had long periods of unbroken summer weather. My mobile rang, as usual, at 7 p.m. Alejandro didn't keep me waiting. I was never left guessing. He hadn't let me down once. I smiled as I realised how attractive his absolute consistency was.

We chatted several times since our "first" erotic call and couldn't help ourselves anymore. I was starting to feel a dark form of need for him, like I couldn't get enough. He'd done this to me from day one. Something clicked the first time we touched, and I don't think I could imagine life without him now. How can that happen when we haven't even slept together? How could I form an emotional dependence on someone without a physical relationship? He made me feel the contrast of all these thoughts.

"Hey, beautiful," Alejandro smouldered, with his sexy accent.

"Hey, handsome."

I was barely able to hide my excitement speaking to him. He knew. He could hear it in my voice. He felt it from me; he knew me that well.

"How was your day?"

"A day. How was yours?" I asked.

"Productive and exciting. I wrote a song for Brandon. He absolutely loves it; wants it to be the first release on his new album."

"That's great. I love hearing you're happy."

"We've already got six songs for the album, but the one I played to him today was his favourite."

He sounded so full of energy, and I wanted to kiss him.

"So, I'm not allowed to tell anyone about the contents of the song, but if you give me your word not to tell anyone, which I trust, I want to show you. This one is special to me," he said.

"I'd love to, as long as it doesn't get you in trouble."

"I'm sending the lyrics now. It's called *All that's left of me*," he said, and a Gmail message popped up on my open laptop. I clicked on it and started to read.

Verse 1:
You touch me without hands,
I feel you through words you use.
A song in my mind like poetry,
You've become everything, my muse...
I feel our souls fusing together,
That fire, locked deep in our kiss.
You draw me to you like a magnet,
The close ache of your beauty, I miss...
Bridge:
I feel you building inside me,
Like a storm within a glass jar.
You fill me with thunder and rain,
Bottled with patience, from afar...
Chorus:
You can take the best of me,
As you deserve the rest of me.
Take my tender and aching heart,
real love is all that's left of me...
Verse 2:
All my resistance now shed,
You echo through corridors of my mind.
Reaching depths I've never known,
With each breath, we inevitably bind...
Take off every inhibition,
I want to show you who you really are.
Dive into my ocean eyes,
I want to feel the longing in your heart...
Bridge:
I felt you building inside me,
Like a storm within a glass jar.
You fill me with thunder and rain,
Bottled with patience, from afar...
Chorus:
You can take the best of me,
As you deserve the rest of me.
Take my tender and aching heart,
real love is all that's left of me...

Chorus to fade:
You can take the best of me,
As you deserve the rest of me.
Take my tender and aching heart,
real love is all that's left of me...

I realised the significance.
"It's all about me, isn't it?"
"Yes."
I paused for breath as I realised, he'd used the words *real love*. I wondered if he could possibly love me when we hadn't even touched.
It's just a line in a song, it's just for sales.
Surely you can't love a stranger without touching. As I said it to myself, I realised I was wrong. I'd been falling for him since day one. My emotions were so intrinsically tied to him, that they surged reading he might love me.
Why am I starting to lose control of my emotions like this?
I decided not to ask him. Even if he did mean it, I wanted us to be face-to-face for the first time one of us said it. I wanted to be kissed and held the first time he said it. Surely, he couldn't be in love with me, not without sex.
The thing is, I realised in that second, *I did love him.*
I'd fallen in love with him.
I'm in love with Alejandro.
"I really wanted to show you. Brandon has big plans for the song as the title track. You'll love the tune, too. It sounds so beautiful when the harmonies are thrown in. I can't play it until it's ready."
"I can't wait to hear it on the radio."
I wondered if this was as close as anyone could get to being serenaded.
"I'm in awe you wrote it thinking of me. Thank you so much for sharing it" I said, aware of how much emotion I was carrying.
My eyes filled up again, a single tear falling softly down my cheek, laying a gentle, wet glistening line of pure feeling on my skin.
"Since I'm in the flow and it's such a great day, I'm going to write another song. My creative juices flow just talking to you. I couldn't adore you more for that. If I were there, I'd kiss your forehead, pulling you into me, caring for you."
I melted at the thought.
"Okay, lovely. Go for it. I'll speak to you tomorrow," I added.
"Goodnight," he said.
As I got off the phone, I posted.

"When you get
to know their mind
before you've ever touched,
the intimacy is so much deeper.
You know what they like+
how they want to be touched.
When you know how
intelligent they are,
you are simply at the mercy
of each other's creativity.
What a beautiful way to breathe..."
"He kisses me in places
I've never been kissed before;
my eyelids, forehead+soul..."
"Perfecting the art
of kissing with words+
touch without hands.
How the surface
of my skin
tingles+surges
at the mere
thought of your
verse wrapped
firmly around mine+
how your eyes
would pierce my soul..."

DarkWolf liked them immediately, replying "Beautiful" with both a rose and kiss emoji.

I wrote one more, thinking about our connection.

"Someone
you want to
kiss, hug, talk to,
laugh, make out with,
get lost, be found+
discover who
you are with.
That..."

DarkWolf: "That makes beautiful inspiration"

MoonlitRose: "We are both inspired then."

I sat there, wondering what Alejandro was going to write next, what his other songs were like on the album. How beautiful it was to inspire him. A creative, mutual muse pairing.

I jumped a little when the house telephone rang, momentarily lost in thought.

Picking it up after having a look at the caller display, I said "Hi, Mum."

"Hi, Leila, how was your day?"

Mum was always sweet and was a natural conversationalist, always leading with compassion and intelligence toward those she spoke to.

"It was busy today. I'm trying to hit a deadline for next week's editing schedule."

"Are you on target?" she asked.

"Fortunately, yes, so I won't be working until 4 a.m. like last time, which is a relief. To be fair, it wasn't my fault, but that's not the point. How was your day, Mum?" I asked, wondering what the jewellery trade had been like.

"Had four engagements come in, so it was a big sales day. You know how I love selling engagement rings."

I could sense her smiling.

"Yes, something to do with people being ecstatically happy. And huge diamonds appealing to your inner magpie, perhaps."

Mum loved working with jewellery. It had always fascinated her.

"How is Dad?"

I was always a proper daddy's girl when I was little. I still was, I suppose.

"He finished an hour late today. Payroll run. They had a few issues with the system. His team were trying to fix it, with tech support over the phone." she added.

"Ah okay, send him my love and an extra big squeeze when you see him."

Dad was lovable in every way. I didn't know anyone who didn't get on with him. He was warm, kind, generous to a fault, always giving his time and helping people wherever he could, in any way possible. They were both affectionate. Mum was far more demonstrative than Dad. I was lucky, I felt incredibly loved growing up. For that, I was truly grateful.

"Have you spoken to Alejandro tonight?" she asked, always curious to hear what he'd said.

Mum and I spoke a couple of times a week, at least. Caitlyn often met me there with her children. It was so nice to see Grace and Lilybeth, my beautiful nieces.

We were a close-knit family. I regularly went out with them on weekends for a meal. Often Caitlyn was there, too. We got on well as sisters, despite being like chalk and cheese. I was emotional, she wasn't. I was open, she was closed. I was affectionate, she was cool. I'm not even sure how we ended up so different, but that didn't stop us from loving each other, or being there to support each other when needed. She was my best friend. I loved having a sister I was close with.

"Yes, we just spoke. A big night."

"Oh really, why?" she asked.

"I think I've fallen for him, Mum."

I wondered if she would be shocked, happy, or disappointed.

"You are talking about the guy you've hardly ever seen and barely spent any physical time with whatsoever, that Alejandro?" she asked.

I giggled at her sarcasm because I knew it sounded crazy.

"Yes, exactly that Alejandro," I laughed.

"So how does that happen when he's thousands of miles away? I know we've spoken about him a fair bit but love?"

Mum always liked to question everything. She worried, all the time, about small things, about big things, about life, and people in general. She didn't buy into fantasies, so she was often sceptical. Whereas I was both a fantasist and romanticist.

"I'll try to explain, but I'm not entirely sure I can because it's something I feel from my heart, not something that makes sense in my head. That's where a sense of conflict comes in. It's something I feel. It's instinctual," I replied.

"That makes no sense and already sounds like love then."

"He's been here for me, every single night since he's been away. Not once has he left my side mentally. He's always interested in everything I have to say. He doesn't talk *at* me. He talks *to* me. Our chemistry is unlike anything I've ever felt before. I've never had anyone question me the way he does, other than you, that is."

"He wants to get to know me. How I think, what I like doing now, what I'd like to do in the future, what dreams I have, what secrets I've kept inside my mind. It keeps getting deeper and deeper, week by week. It's getting closer to when we see each other again, and I know it's going to be so special when we do. I realised when I was talking to him tonight, my feelings for him have expanded rapidly."

"Sounds like your dad and I when we were younger. He was so smart and handsome and different from all the boys my age. You are a woman now; you know exactly who you are. You've had some bad experiences. It's like you've always been searching for something, and you've never found it before. The mental stimulation and connection you're talking about is so incredibly rare."

Mum was knowledgeable on many levels, as well as clever academically. She was an incredibly intelligent woman who was a strong female role model to grow up with. Dad was quietly clever, a lot more streetwise than my mum. He was quieter, too. Again, he was a great role model as he taught both Caitlyn and I about having a strong work ethic early on in life. Everything in his career he built from scratch and pure graft.

He loved Mum so very much and was incredibly dedicated to all of us. Dad was a strong head of the family, making us all feel loved.

Soulmates, could there be anything more poetic?

"I'm so happy for you, Leila. It sounds like this is your time now. He's handsome, creative, intellectual, loves words, he's stimulating you, and he dances. I can't wait to meet him. Neither can your dad."

"Your sister is coming up for a day out Saturday with the girls, if you fancy it?"

"That sounds lovely, I adore my little munchkins. I'll pop around in the morning."

"I'm going to run a bath now. I want a long soak. Hope you can settle down after all the excitement. I'm truly happy for you. Goodnight, sweetheart," she added warmly at the end.

"Sleep tight and I'll see you Saturday."

I needed anything to distract me until Alejandro came back, when I could kiss him in the flesh and feel safe within his strong arms again. From tonight's incredulous discovery, I realised I was also looking forward to all the hours I wanted to spend loving him.

I'm in love with him.

22 DAD

July. Friday. Liverpool. Home.

"Hey, curly," Dad said, arms open. I threw my arms around him.
"I missed you so much."
He gave me a gentle, but incredibly reassuring squeeze right at the end, before releasing his hold.
"I missed you too, sweetheart," he said, in a voice I would always find endearing, simply because it was his.
"Would you like a cuppa?"
"Is the Pope a Catholic?" he retorted.
The corner of his mouth curled up slightly.
"You really need some new jokes, Dad!"
"Why, when the old ones work so well?" he smiled.
He had a cheeky grin and a lip twitch and purse he did when he was being cheeky.
"Come on, we'll get comfy in the lounge."
I placed the mugs on the low coffee table, sitting on the white leather couch. My dad sat, as always, on the floor next to me, leaning his arm on my knee. Such a simple thing, but one I treasured. It was his way of keeping connected to me.
"So, how's it going at work, kiddo?"
He sipped his tea.
"Coming up on a deadline for that case about The Choker. The more I investigate, the more it gets to me. I haven't spoken to you much about it, Mum more so."
"What's happening?"
"It's horrendous, the things he's done to those poor women. There are four victims so far, the sad part is they all had a long ordeal before they were murdered. He follows them with the same MO each time. He torments them, plays with them, breaks them down psychologically first. He stalks them, making them paranoid. He's horrible, Dad" I explained.
"I despise men like that. Is there any commonality?"

"They're all local women, within a 15-mile radius. I interviewed friends and family of the victims in detail. They just want him caught and put away. He became braver with each victim, the duration of each stalking escalating lasting longer each time. His first victim felt like she was being watched for four months, the second was eight months, the third was 10 and the last was 12."

"Did he ever speak to any of them? Or just watch them before he killed them?"

"We'll never know. Not that they were aware of. The more information we can give the public, the better. We need to work together as a community to catch this guy. He didn't just kill his victims, he tormented them psychologically, playing horrendous mind games with them first," I added. "They all had big hearts and didn't deserve to die. Not that anybody does, but it's so sad in these cases. They were all popular, well-liked, and gentle."

"How has he managed to get away with four local murders right under everyone's nose?"

"He's clever, incredibly intelligent. There's no evidence at any of the crime scenes. The victims all wore a choker necklace. That's his trademark. He's meticulous about not leaving a single trace for forensics to study. No hairs, semen, prints, nothing. He enters their homes at a time when he, assumedly, knows they'll be alone, so he must know their exact routine. He ties them up and 'does things' with them, more than once. Each ordeal lasted longer, like he knew when the finale was planned and he tries to draw it out, after a culmination of several months watching and studying them. He enjoys playing with them, toying with them, like a cat with a mouse."

I was disturbed, recounting this information.

"I can't understand the psychology behind anyone who would want to hurt people that way. It makes me want to know what the hell happened to him to make him so twisted, so horrendously evil. How did he kill them in the end?" Dad asked.

His face contorted as he asked. He was so gentle. I was the mirror of him in many ways.

"Asphyxiation, with his hands around their throat. There are some weird twists in the story, which I can't get my head around," I said, before finishing my tea.

"In what way?"

"He's deranged enough to romance them before he kills them. That's the part that doesn't make sense. Each victim had meaningful, untraceable gestures which you would assume were affectionate, that was how they knew they were being watched. Flowers, their favourite chocolates, gifts personalised to them, books they liked to read, jewellery they preferred, things that took intimate knowledge. Nobody understands how he found out. Each victim told someone they knew their stalker bought things only ever mentioned in conversation or referenced online."

"He was stalking everything about their lives. It sounds like he was learning them."

"Yes, it's sinister. He wanted to give them gifts that meant something, that nobody else would have been attentive enough to find, but then he took their life away. It doesn't make sense. It's like he wanted to be everything to them, but then killed them, anyway. In each crime scene, he left a white rose upon their chest, almost like a symbol of pure love and affection toward them, like a final parting gift, which creeps me out."

Dad could see goose bumps forming on my arms and gave me a gentle rub, warming me up. The chill in the room was from The Choker, from the inside though. Trying to understand him made me feel such negative and confused emotions.

"I get the creeps every time I think about him. Anyway, that's enough about me and my crazy deadlines. How have you been?" I asked, trying to divert the subject.

"Before I answer that, tell me one thing. Have you got a personal alarm for walking around Liverpool?" he asked, squeezing my knee.

"No, I haven't. I've never felt unsafe in Liverpool," I added.

"I know, but knowing this guy operates close in proximity is enough that you should be cautious. I'm going to buy you and Ellie a personal alarm, okay?" he said.

"You don't have to do that, Dad."

"I know but it would make *me* feel better knowing you had at least some form of protection. Please, for me, do as you're told, and always keep it with you. Do you promise?"

"If it would make you happier, of course I will."

"Good," he said. "Getting back to your question, we're good. "I'm looking forward to seeing your sister and my beautiful grandkids on Sunday. I was going to suggest a picnic by the river. Fancy it?" he asked.

Every time he spoke about Caitlyn, Grace, and Lilybeth, he couldn't help but smile. He adored all kids, but his own and his grandchildren were the best things ever to happen in his life.

"I'd love that. I love your impulsive days out. I'll text Caitlyn and see if she's up for it," I said, pulling out my phone.

I could see Scribe notifications from DarkWolf.

Hey you.

I closed it down and sent her a text.

My phone bleeped. Message from Caitlyn.

"Yes, they are extremely excited about a picnic. The girls are jumping up and down, apparently. Jay is out with his friends playing golf Sunday, so it will just be us and the girls," I relayed.

"Excellent. I'll bring that hamper you all love. The weather is supposed to be gorgeous this weekend. Let's meet at our place at 11 a.m."

"I'll tell Caitlyn."

"I'm going to head off and catch the shops before they close. I want to buy a few things on the way home," he said, standing up.

"Give me a big hug."

He opened his arms to me, wrapping me up in them.

"Really excited about Sunday now, Dad. Thank you for always wanting to take us places and share experiences. It means a lot to all of us, and the kids will grow up knowing how important family time is, too. I love you."

23 PICNIC

July. Saturday. Liverpool. Home.

My day consisted of flirty poetry between Alejandro and I and a very long and comforting chat with him that night. The band was performing, and he went to the hotel they were sleeping in. This time we talked for eight hours continuously, with no breaks. We didn't even touch on anything erotic.
We spent the whole time getting to know each other to greater depth. The conversation was fluent between us. We were great conversationalists. There were never any gaps, even during all those hours. He asked me about my week, and I told him about the family picnic. He was happy I was excited. He told me to have fun, not to be careful, like past boyfriends had. I fell asleep fast after our long conversation,
I awoke at 9 a.m. on Sunday, which was much later than normal. I drove to mum and dad's house by 11 a.m. Caitlyn and the kids were already there, and I gave everyone a hug when I walked in. Mum was first to the door. She held me so tight. I squeezed her back.
I leaned over to give her a kiss on the cheek, spotting Grace in the kitchen.
"Where are my favourite nieces in the whole wide world then?"
Grace and Lilybeth came running. Lilybeth jumped into my arms, and I lifted her into the air, cuddling her into me as she wrapped her arms and legs around me, squeezing tightly. I never had enough words to describe how beautiful it felt, and how completely adorable she was to me. Scrumptious, delicious, wonderful moments of affection. I clicked my emotional camera.
Lilybeth beamed whenever she saw me. She trusted me completely. She wasn't comfortable in the company of strangers. She had a natural wariness about new people, particularly tall men. The only people she let in were those she saw regularly. You had to earn the trust of those dark chocolate eyes, through reliability and patience. You had to win her over, and I loved that.

Grace ran toward me from around the corner, putting her arm around my waist.

"Hi, Aunty Leila," she said in her sweet, angelic voice.

Grace and Lilybeth were complete opposites in their approach to others. Grace had a big, beautiful heart which beamed for miles around. She could melt anyone at 50 paces with her naturally long, dark lashes and hazel eyes. She was funny and warm, hugging and loving everyone.

"Hey, beautiful," I said, shifting Lilybeth's weight to one hip and putting my arm around Grace, stroking her hair.

My sister was leaning by the kitchen door.

"Hey, Leila. I see you have your arms full already, their favourite aunt," she said, smiling.

"They've only got one," I said playfully.

"Are you ready to have some fun, kids?" my dad said as he walked through the room, giving me a kiss on the cheek before carrying the picnic hamper out to the car.

"We're going on a picnic," the girls said in unison, Grace jumping up and down on the spot. Lilybeth was squeezing me so tight with excitement I could barely breathe.

Dad threw my mum the keys, so he could finish up the last few bits,

"Can you lock up, Marie?"

"Of course, let's go people," she said, and I realised how beautiful my family was.

What a beautiful family I have.

The picnic site was in North Wales, but, as these beautiful rivers often are, it was down some tiny little twisted country lane my mum and dad somehow remembered. The sun was bursting through. There wasn't a cloud in sight.

Grace shouted first, "Look, the river, the river."

Dad targeted the gentle area of the stream, so the kids could play safely. The air was fresh. Just what I needed after all this focus on murder.

"Okay, kids, what do you want to do first, play or eat?" Mum asked.

"Play, play," Lilybeth said, looking excited just to be there. She was humble. Whenever we went anywhere, it was the best thing to ever happen to her. Lilybeth and Grace were an absolute pleasure to be around. I hoped I'd have children like them one day.

They had a little keepsake jar to put shells into back home. Each was a reminder of a different place visited, so it was a collection of experiences, not things.

"Frank, shall we set up the picnic while the girls play in the stream?" Mum said.

"Okay, love," Dad replied. "Go have some fun kids," he said, beaming, as we all started taking our shoes off.

It was a little cool stepping in, and Caitlyn and I had hold of one child each to make sure they didn't fall over, as we had to step over some rocks before we got to the soft sand bed. We had buckets and net scoops in the other.

Caitlyn and I started to catch up while the girls began to play.

"So, how's your week been lovely?" I asked Caitlyn.

"A bit hectic, tests and lots of revision this week. Typical me volunteering for more work."

"You aim high, hunni. You should, you're an intelligent woman with a lot of potential. Take it as far as you can."

"I'll get there. It's that extra bit of confidence I need. I know I can do it. Having the likes of Nia to chat with can be quite inspiring. I enjoyed it when you and I went out for a meal with her. She's such a strong, incredible powerhouse of a woman," Caitlyn added.

"Nia's phenomenal. She's mentally strong, but fair and kind. She's the best person I could think of to be putting away criminals," I said.

"I'd love to be as powerful as her mentally. I'm not sure I'm one for getting up in front of everyone, though, to be honest," Caitlyn added.

"Being a barrister wouldn't be a career choice for everyone, it takes a certain type of person."

"I know, she had so many years of dedicated study to get to where she is. It's nice to have someone to talk to who's ahead of me in a similar profession. How's it going with Alejandro?"

"I admire her, too," I answered, pausing. "I'm in love with him, Caitlyn."

"In love? Have you even kissed him?"

Caitlyn wasn't a romantic like me. If anything, we were like chalk and cheese. She was logical, fully left-brained, rarely using or feeling intuition. Everything had to be proved factually for her, which was similar to how she operated as a lawyer. There was no room for movement at all. She was a self-confessed cynic, and I was pretty used to her by now. I giggled at her inability to embrace any romance whatsoever.

"Yes, I've kissed him. We've hugged, too," I said, jokingly.

"Oh well, that's all right then."

The girls were having a blast in the background playing with the fishing nets. Mum and dad were nearly finished setting up the picnic.

"Seriously, how on earth do you think you're in love with him?"

"I just feel it. Alejandro and I have gotten closer while he's been away. We've spoken almost every night. The other night we chatted for eight hours straight. He's reliable, consistent, supportive, caring, thoughtful, kind, takes an interest in what I say, how I feel and some of the crazy thoughts that go through my mind. He wants to know the real me, inside. It feels wonderful to be seen, felt, and heard," I said, feeling like I was trying to convince her.

"Nah, still think it's weird."

"Cynic."

"Unrealistic romantic," she retorted.

There was an element of truth in this. I could romance a notion or idea of someone. Her subtle reminders were her way of saying *be careful, don't lose your head and don't go all in until you know*.

The problem was, I was already all in.

"It will be fine. I just can't wait until he's back."

"That will be when you find out for sure how compatible you are. When does he get back?" she asked.

"Third week in September. It's killing me."

I was yearning for him like an idiot by this point.

"That's not that long, lovely. We're nearly August anyway, so you've only got six or seven weeks to wait. Last hurdle. Just focus on your work and dancing and it will go fast. You'll see."

"Salsa helps a lot. I'm so glad I carried on going every week. Our original teacher returned in Alejandro's place. His teaching style suits me. Not as much as Alejandro's, of course."

I mocked a downturned mouth.

"Last few weeks and it's all over, and you can be together then."

"So true. Shall we see if we can find some fish and go grab some of that picnic? I'm so hungry now."

"Yes. Kids let's see if we can spot some fish. Dad, can you pass me a piece of bread?" Caitlyn shouted over, as she went to the edge to collect it from him.

As soon as she crumbled it into the water, a few fish came over, swimming by us. Clever girl. Lilybeth had a lot of fun trying to catch them with the net. Grace managed to catch one on her own. We put any we caught in a bucket. The joy on their faces was a delight to observe.

Grace wanted to release them. After the girls had both studied and fed them, she lowered the bucket and let them slip away. Lilybeth jumped with excitement as they swam out.

Such beautiful innocence.

It was a perfect day. We stayed there for a few hours, taking in the scenery, catching up on chit chat to see what everyone was doing.

On the way home, the kids fell asleep in the car.

When we got to Caitlyn's house, Dad handed Caitlyn an envelope quickly.

"It has a personal attack alarm in it. I got one each for Leila and Ellie, too. Please carry it with you to keep your old dad happy," he said, giving her another hug.

"Okay, just for you Dad," Caitlyn added.

"I love you and I worship those kids of yours. It was a perfect day," Mum said, giving Caitlyn a heartfelt hug. Her eyes filled up as she walked away. Only I saw it. I gave her a huge hug before we got back in the car. She felt things so very deeply. She loved to the core.

"Right, let's get you home," Dad ruffled the top of my hair playfully.

It was only a few minutes' drive.

I hugged each of them, long and tight.

"Goodnight, curly," Dad said, winking.

"Au revoir, ma fille," Mum called out.

"Au revoir, ma mere," I replied.

I waited by the open door, as I always did, for one last wave goodbye and to ensure safety getting in.

I love you both. More than you'll ever know.

24 I MISS YOU

August. Wednesday. Liverpool. Home.

Alejandro and I will see each other next month. I can finally say *next month*. It's been a prolonged and agonising form of torture, all this waiting. The closer we got to the date, the more it pained me to carry this desire for him. It was the ache of an unexpressed love twisting a knot inside me that doesn't go away, only burns with a slow heat. Never fully igniting, but never dying out.

Since it was Wednesday, it was my turn to cook. I'd gone to the gym on the way home, doing a few light weights and floor exercises. I bumped into my workout buddy, Ray, who was there most nights. I'd picked up the food on the way home the day before. Tonight, I was preparing chicken marsala sauce.

"Thank you. That looks and smells delicious," Ellie said, sitting down at the table as I placed the meal in front of her.

"So how was your day, Leila?"

We were a great source of support for the other and had natural chemistry. There was nothing we wouldn't share. We had big hearts, but were wary to let others in. It was difficult for us to trust people.

Ellie was a former wild child, having been instinctively drawn to every bad boy she could find between the ages of 13 and 20. She was so pretty; it was always the alpha men that went for her. She was a sucker for a muscular body, playing the field a lot as a teenage rebel and then throughout university. Ellie settled down for some longer relationships between 21 and 29, but none that stuck for a long time. Mainly because they were idiots. She had an absolute heart of gold; despite being hurt by many of said idiots. She still wore it on her sleeve and was warm to everyone she met. She couldn't help it.

"My day was hectic, coming up to an end of month deadline. I was burning the midnight oil last night trying to finish composure on it, so my editor has time to make changes for deadline before it goes to graphics."

"How is it going?" Ellie asked, looking interested, as we ate and talked. "This is so tasty."

"The police have made no significant steps in the case so far. The killer is clearly leading them all on a merry dance. Anyway, I won't dwell on it as I'm up to here with him this week," I said, motioning a horizontal line at the top of my forehead.

"How's your job going, Ellie? Is Maureen still doing your head in?" I asked.

"Honestly, after what you're working on, my workday seems particularly boring," Ellie added.

"There's nothing wrong with being a business analyst, hunni. I think it's kind of sweet how you ended up back at the university you got your degree in," I said, knowing it was a good environment she was working in, despite yet another reorganisation being mentioned, which meant more job cuts on the way.

"I know, there's not a lot going on. The start of the reorg isn't for another couple of months at least. The most interesting thing that happens in my daily working life is whether Maureen has a massive diva strop."

We both burst out laughing.

"What is the problem with that woman?"

"I have no idea, but she's so full of herself and her own self-importance that the rest of us cringe at her antics. She thinks she's better than everyone else and tries to belittle people. The thing is, it backfires on her, because everyone hates people trying to one up others. By trying to make someone else look stupid, you end up doing that to yourself. I genuinely think she's unaware of it," Ellie said, topping our glasses off with wine.

"Muppet."

Maureen's antics had become the butt of many of our giggles, because if Ellie didn't laugh about it, she'd end up crying.

"Had a bit of a weird coincidence at lunch today. I bumped into Owen. Or he bumped into me I should say, when I was in the market area. I was civil, but it was awkward as hell. He started asking me if I was with anyone, if I was still working in the same place, if I wanted to go for a coffee and meet for a proper chat," Ellie continued.

"After everything he put you through? As if," I said, with a look of pure disgust on my face.

"I know, right?"

"That's a distinct swerve. I hope you told him to get lost."

"I said no, I didn't think it was a good idea."

"You're way too polite and easy-going. I would have told him to shove it where the sun didn't shine. Bet it was satisfying to knock him back?"

"Very," she said.

The night had drawn in fast, becoming pitch black outside before we knew it, velvet darkness descending rapidly.

Our garden was hidden in the back; nothing overlooked it. There were also 20-foot conifers at the rear growing larger every day, sheltering us even more. We had a large, rear dining window and a full-length patio door in the kitchen, leading to the back garden. We never closed the curtains, enjoying the view when it was daylight. There was a low fence on either side of a long, nice sized garden.

The neighbourhood was quiet. Our house was semi-detached. We were on the right side. The neighbours to our left were an elderly couple in their early 80's. Other than the tele being occasionally loud because they were hard of hearing, we rarely heard them, exchanging pleasantries when we saw them or their visiting family. It was windy. I heard rustling through the trees and could hear the building sway. There was something utterly hypnotic about the sound to me. Whenever the wind howled, the house banged, creaking with the gusts. Every now and then, the patio doors vibrated in such a way that it felt as if the wind had reached inside our house.

Ellie and I were sitting opposite each other, continuing our conversation. I was facing outside; she was facing me.

"So how is your Dad, Ellie?" I asked, knowing he'd had some tests run recently.

"Blood test results came back inconclusive," she added. "They want him to go for a scan now, so I'm quite anxious about it. When he went initially, it was just a routine appointment, but they called him back with abnormal test results."

Concerned for him, and for Ellie, too. "Is he experiencing any unusual symptoms?"

I loved her parents to bits. They'd always been good to me. I'd spent many a barbeque at theirs over the years.

"A little bleeding, but no pain as such, no. I'm a little confused about what they want to test him for. It's probably nothing, but they have this way of instilling worry in you," she reflected, looking down, lowering her head, and resting it on her arms.

Suddenly, out of nowhere, I froze. My eyes were fixed firmly outside in the space where her head had been, like a rabbit in the headlights.

Fear.

Instant fear.

Ellie's head stayed down, and I couldn't even speak up, my eyes staring outside at the shadow I saw. A figure I could barely make out the shape of was moving, in OUR garden. A tall figure was about all I could determine, which made me suspect it was a man. That compounded my fear even further. Two women alone in a house and a STRANGER in OUR back garden. There was something about the absolute invasion of it, that made it feel so much worse. He was stationary as I looked at him, which struck fear through my core. He was watching us. He was out there, looking at us in the kitchen, watching us. I couldn't speak.

Why on earth would anyone be watching us?
How long was he out there?

Once he realised, I'd clocked him, he moved swiftly to the right as I looked out, jumping over the fence, down the alleyway, to the side of the house. I couldn't react. Fear had not only taken my voice, I froze and couldn't move, either. Ellie raised her head, immediately seeing the fear in my eyes.

"What's wrong?" she asked.

When I didn't respond immediately, she asked again, "what is it?"

I composed myself, snapping out of it, knowing I'd seen him leap over the fence. He wasn't there anymore.

Are we safe?

"I just saw a man, Ellie, in our back garden. Standing over to the right, by the shed," I said with a shaky voice.

"Oh my God, you're trembling. Is he gone?" she asked, turning to look outside while holding my hand to steady me.

"Yes, I saw him jump over the fence," I tried to reassure both of us simultaneously.

"What if he comes back?" Ellie questioned. "I'll call the police," she added.

I was moving slowly; Ellie was reacting much quicker. Going into the other room, she grabbed the phone and came back in.

As she was dialling, I looked at the garden, briefly reassuring myself I couldn't see anything.

"What was he wearing?" she asked quickly.

"A navy hoodie, with a double red stripe on his left arm, highlighted by the streetlight, and dark jeans. His face was obscured by the hood."

"Yes, police, please," I heard, before Ellie was redirected.

She was answering questions before starting to report what we'd seen.

"There was a man in the back garden," I heard her say, zoning out slightly as she continued to describe the brief details I had relayed. I wondered why the hell anyone would want to watch us. Even weirder, we were just eating. Ellie recounted our address to the police. They said they would look briefly around the area and call in to check on us.

"They've advised we double check all of the windows and locks for now," she said.

When the call ended, we went around and checked everything. I must admit I felt hesitant going anywhere near the patio door suddenly. I didn't know whether to pull the curtains across or not. I didn't know if it was better to see and know, or not to see. About 20 minutes later, there was a knock on the door. Two police officers were showing their badges, detailing their names to us for verification. Officer Scott Riley and Officer Brian Dudley.

"We had a drive around the vicinity and can't see anyone matching your description, ladies. The roads are quiet tonight. There's hardly anyone out in the neighbourhood on foot."

"Is there anything else you can tell me about the man you saw? Height, weight, distinguishing features, anything about his face?" Officer Riley asked.

"He was tall, over six feet, athletic build. I couldn't tell you anything about his face. It was dark, and his hood was obscuring it. The hoodie had a double red stripe running the full length down his left arm, which I saw clearly," I added, trying to recall as much detail as I could.

"We've taken down your details and will be in touch if we find out anything," he added, standing up. He wrote down a reference number for us, handing it to us on his business card, along with an information sheet.

"Thank you, Officer Riley," I said, leading both officers to the door.

"Well, that's freaked us both out," I said, after the door closed.

"Yes, it's creeped me out. There's no chance I'm going to sleep tonight now. I might go and phone Hayden," Ellie added.

"I'm so glad you have someone you feel safe to chat to, hunni. Maybe this is the one for you," I added, trying to distract her.

"I hope so, I really like him," she added.

"I'm going to shower and then message Alejandro to see if he's free, so I can tell him what happened. He's so reassuring and calming, hopefully I'll stop thinking about it after we've spoken. Goodnight, hunni," I said, giving Ellie a big hug with a strong squeeze in.

We both needed it.

I was in the shower for ages. It relaxed me most when it was nearly piping hot, and I stepped out with steam coming off my skin.

I heard Ellie chatting away to Hayden on the house phone. He had her giggling so that was a very positive sign. He seemed so right for her.

I sent a long text message to Alejandro. As soon as he read it, he rang my mobile. We were on the phone for an hour. He was worried, but he downplayed it, choosing to take a protective, soothing role, instead, which completely calmed me. He had a way of settling my chaos that felt like he was nurturing me. I adored it. He spoke softly, reassuring me. He was there for me.

"I'm so glad you told me. Always do. Please. Always be open with me, especially about anything that upsets you. I can't bear the thought of not being there when you need me," he said.

"I'd feel so lost without you," I said, realising for the first time I genuinely meant it.

"I've never left you, not once, and I don't intend to now. Please try and get some sleep while you're relaxed."

He didn't speak of any of the drama, steering me away from it beautifully, redirecting me to a calm place. It was one of the most intelligent things he could have done with me then. I got comfy in bed, my wet hair freshly brushed and laid out on the towel to dry as I slept. Wrapping the duvet around me, listening to the wind and Alejandro's voice, I relaxed more.

After I said goodnight, I turned my mobile off so it could charge next to my bed. I realised he'd grown to mean so very much to me. Every time, just like tonight, when he was there for me, when I felt alone and lost, when I didn't know how to breathe, my feelings went a notch further and a bit deeper. That had stacked up to a hell of a lot of feelings over time.

I feel fragile tonight and I'm falling for you so hard.

It still feels like such a long time until I see you again, and I can't handle it right now, not today.

I miss you.

I need your arms wrapped around me, right now, here, in my bed.

I fucking need you.

25 BREAKING

August. Friday. Liverpool. Home.

The stalker was playing through my mind on a loop, like a movie I couldn't turn off, and I felt more vulnerable than usual. Thoughts of him were freaking me out, and I was struggling badly. My eyes kept filling up, a single tear finding its way down my cheek. I had been hiding it all day at work, slumped down behind my monitor so nobody could see me wiping tears from my eyes. Emotionally, I felt totally lost. I realised, somewhere during the drama, the thing I needed most was Alejandro.

It was only one month until he was back, and I couldn't wait. Life was agonising without him, knowing how much I felt for him, but not being able to get anywhere near him. I desperately craved his arms. I felt a constant pull toward him. If he wasn't arousing me physically, he was supporting me emotionally. It was as if there was no distance between us. Yet the ache to touch him physically was killing me, to feel like this and not be able to touch him.

Alejandro was the only man who could calm me or fire me up equally, the only man who seemed to understand me, or want to. In all the hours we clocked up talking to each other, every single one of them developed and deepened our relationship, and the strength of our communication. We knew so much about each other, because we would pose questions about how we felt about different things. Some of them were light. Others were soul searching and deep. Our adventure hadn't even started.

I had no idea it was possible to develop such an intimate relationship with anyone remotely. I'd always thought this type of thing was make believe. All I wanted was to look him in the eye and be with him. I knew that was all I needed. My resolve to be strong would crumble in his arms. The physical ache I had to talk to him or read his words, knowing how I felt, was almost unbearable. I constantly spun between feeling deeply aroused, sensually tormented, and peacefully calm. His voice was soothing for me, as were the simple reassurances he constantly gave me. I'd never met anyone so attentive and caring. He's more than I could ask for.

The stalker left me feeling lonely and isolated, anxious, and worried. I suspected Ellie felt the same. It was like a dark shadow had been cast onto our lives, one which neither of us understood or felt comfortable with. It was made worse because it didn't feel like someone just peering into the window. We knew he had stood there, specifically watching us.

How long was he there? Why?

When I was alone in the house now, I was always creeped out. Goose bumps formed on my arms, a deep anxiety took hold whenever I looked out the window, wondering if anyone was there. My thoughts were irrational. I knew this, but it depended on the reason why we were being watched, as to the likelihood of whether he would come back. I was panicking about it. That's all anxiety needs, the possibility of something negative to happen.

Why would he pick us?

There was nothing about us anyone would want to stalk. We were normal women, attractive, granted, but just normal women at the end of the day. Then a chill went through me, a horrendous deep chill, making the hairs on my arms stand up immediately as I remembered what case I was working on for *The Liverpool Express*.

What if there is a link to The Choker?

What if he's specifically targeted me, because of my job and relationship to the case?

My name is on the article.

No. No. No.

Fuck.

I was instantly physically sick, heartbeat fluttering vigorously, my breathing erratic. My chest was tight. The thought it could be the serial killer, despite however irrational it might seem, had triggered my first full panic attack.

Fuck, how do I stop this?

I didn't know what to do. I couldn't calm myself down. The first person I thought of was Alejandro, so I texted him.

"I'm in the middle of a massive panic attack and I don't know what to do."

I started to cry, feeling helpless, out of control. My heartbeats were completely erratic now, fluttering, jumping, racing, and thudding in a flurry. It was like my heart was trying to escape and jump out of my body. Then my heart stopped completely for a few seconds, before a flooding rush hit me, like a scramble of heartbeats hitting me in rapid succession all at once. It felt like a heart attack.

What on earth is happening?

My mobile rang. Alejandro. Thank God.

"Okay, don't say anything, make a noise when you can and only talk if you're ready. My mum had these sometimes and the most important thing is to stay calm, so I'm going to keep talking to you until that happens, until your breathing is normal again. Focus on me. Alright?" he asked.

"Uhuh," I mumbled, in between tears and interlocking heartbeats that wouldn't let me catch my breath.

"Whatever the thought was that triggered your panic attack, I want you to completely forget about it. We can deal with that after. For now, I just want you to do some breathing exercises for me. I'll talk to you while you breathe. So, I want you to do what I tell you for a while. Start by breathing in through your nose for a count of eight, then blowing out through your mouth for eight. Okay, deep breath in," he said, starting to count. "One, two, three, four, five, six, seven, eight. Now out for eight. Slowly."

My heart raced as I followed his instructions.

"In for eight. Out for eight. " Somehow, with him counting and me only focusing on the numbers and the sound of his voice, I was becoming calmer, more focused.

"In for eight. Out for eight."

He had so much patience with me, repeating the pattern over and over, constantly, until my breathing started to sound less erratic, and tears stopped falling.

Once I was nearly calm, he said, "Okay, now I want you to carry on doing just that. Count in your head, while I take you somewhere pretty that you can imagine for the rest of today. Okay?"

"Yes."

"There's my baby."

There was something about his tone. It was care, that was all I ever felt from him. He could say anything, and it wouldn't matter *what* he said. It was the *way* he said it, which calmed me completely.

"Okay, you keep breathing. I'll know if you stop because I won't be able to hear you," he said, trying to lighten me a little.

"I'm going to take you somewhere special now. Since I started writing for DarkWolf, I discovered something incredible that's there, only for us. It's a portal. I can take you anywhere in this world, or anywhere within the universe. There's no limit, the only limit exists within our imagination. Everywhere I take you is completely safe. We can use it to paint poetic images in our minds, of places where you can be free to be yourself. No worries, no hassles, no stress, just beauty, intrigue, or adventure. Whatever you wish for," he detailed.

"That sounds perfect," I added, the tightening in my chest releasing its hold on me. I continued breathing, counting in my head, loving the relaxing sound of Alejandro's voice.

"Okay, the place I imagined for the portal to take us has been programmed in. Please hold my hand and we'll be there in a second," he said, his creativity overtaking his narrative.

"As the portal rests us down within our programmed destination and the door opens, we step out holding hands."

I imagined the bliss of that one simple thing, holding his hand.

"You see the ocean, this beautiful azure blue, calm, relaxing ocean on a paradise beach with pure white sands. There are many palm trees ahead and a gentle swing I've put in for you, standing inside the water's edge, in the very shallow part, so your feet are in the water. The ocean's waves are tumbling gently onto the beach. Focus on your breathing and the sound of the ocean. Are you with me? Can you see it?" he asked.

"I can see it perfectly, it's beautiful," I answered calmly, my heart returning to just the odd mis-timed racing heartbeat now.

"I'm holding your hand a little tighter now, walking you over. I'm imagining you in a short, white summer dress, with a peach bikini underneath. Peach would suit your dark features. I'm wearing swim shorts, navy on top, white on bottom. There's a large, comfy lounging bed to the right, where we can relax in the sun. I put three books I think you'll like to the left of the lounger. I've got drinks, fruit, and a selection of food for lunch in the cooler bag, along with wipes, as we all know what eating melon can be like," he paused.

You are perfect.

"I want us to go on the swing first. Would you like that?" His voice was so soft with me right now.

"I would love to," I said gently. This was just what I needed, to go somewhere and feel safe with him. To feel him next to me.

"There's a step on the side frame for you to get onto the swing. Or alternatively, I can lift you up."

"Lift me, please," I asked, just wanting to be in his arms.

"I hold you and kiss you tenderly before placing you on the swing and climbing up to join you. I push off in the water and we start to swing very gently. The rhythm is soothing and calming. The only sounds are the whoosh of gentle air, sea birds flying above us, and the ocean tumbling and lapping at the shore. I want you to relax, enjoy the sensation for a while. Whoosh, whoosh, that's all you need to focus on," he added.

His mental imagery and storytelling were second to none.

I can't stop falling for you.

I imagined being there, everything he described, and I felt at peace. Despite how chaotic my mind was earlier, I felt completely calm now.

What a gift you have, Alejandro.

How lucky I am you chose me, when I didn't even know what you were capable of.

"How are you feeling?"

"Thank you. I feel much more relaxed. I don't know what I would have done without you."

I was genuinely humbled at his heart and mind.

"I'm glad I could help. My mum used to have attacks like this near the end, overwhelmed by what she knew was going to happen, facing her own mortality, fearing what might happen to me. The only thing that would soothe her were my songs. That's why I started writing stories inside them. I imagined places she needed to go or things she might need to hear," he said.

"You have a talent. Such an amazing unique gift. I'm overwhelmed you want to share it with me. Your mum sounds like such a special person. You loved her so very much. I'd love to hear some of the songs you wrote for her, if you would play them for me," I asked.

"Thank you. I've never played some of them for anyone else. Only her. I would play them for you, though. When the time is right," he added.

I was in awe of him again, that he wanted to open for me after having been so closed off for so much of his life.

"I'm tired now. It's getting late and my eyes are batting."

I was emotionally and mentally exhausted. Yet he had soothed me somehow, until I was calm enough to be able to sleep. If my heart were still racing, there's not a chance in hell I'd be able to sleep, with that internal rhythm pounding.

"Take me up to bed with you and get changed. I'll wait on the phone and make sure you get to sleep," he requested.

"Okay. I'll just grab some water to take up," I said, going into the kitchen to grab a drink to take up, sipping on the way.

"I'll put you down for one second," I said, going into the bathroom to get ready for bed. When I came back out, I picked up the phone.

"Okay, I'm cosy now. My eyes feel so heavy."

"I want you to close them, think about everything we just did. You're in a relaxed state on the beach lounger, listening to the waves. Your skin is protected and heating up under the sun. You can go to sleep enjoying this thought now," he added.

"What a beautiful reverie. What a very special man you are, Alejandro. Thank you, for everything you did tonight. You are selfless. You dropped everything to look after me. Thank you for being there for me," I said.

A single tear fell down my cheek. This time, they were tears of happiness.

"Goodnight, angel. If you wake up, or that happens again, you call me, any time of the day or night. I will drop whatever I'm doing for you, okay? Now you sleep well. Imagine I'm right next to you, with my hand in yours. I've got you," he said, reassuring me in a way I'd never imagined.

"Okay I will. Thank you. Goodnight," I said, hanging up the phone.

I love you.

26 SHOCK

August. Saturday. Liverpool. Home.

I was ready for a long lie-in, the anxiety of the week catching up with me, that niggling question still in the back of my head.

What if the stalker in our garden was related to The Choker?

The fact nothing had happened since Wednesday was good news. I needed, for my own sanity, to conclude it was a one-off incident. I couldn't allow anxiety to ruin my life over something which was probably nothing.

Ellie was already in the kitchen, preparing to make an elaborate grilled breakfast. I hadn't had much chance to see her since it happened. She stayed over at Hayden's Thursday night, taking the day off yesterday to be with him, and returning first thing this morning. She must feel safe with him. I felt even lonelier without her there.

I went over to her, giving her a heart-warming hug.

"How are you feeling, hunni?"

"A little shook if I'm being honest, Leila. I can't stop thinking about it and I didn't want to be anywhere near the house. Shock probably. All I wanted was to be with Hayden."

I knew exactly what she meant.

"What did he say about all of it?"

I wondered if Hayden was a protective man, like Alejandro.

"When I told him on the phone what had happened and that I felt nervous being in the house, he told me to pack an overnight bag and see if I could take Friday off, so we could spend some time together. It was gorgeous yesterday, so we spent the day wandering around town and visited Sefton Park. It's pretty and peaceful there. Just what I needed. We spent most of the night making out. It was such an emotionally fragile and erotic night. I'm shattered, mentally and physically. As soon as we've caught up and had breakfast, I'm going straight to bed. All I want to do is sleep," she added.

"I'm glad Hayden looked after you, Ellie. I wish Alejandro was here, too. God, I miss him so much. I had a panic attack last night and he talked me through it, calmed me down."

My eyes filled up before I finished the thought.

"Oh no, I'm so sorry. I completely understand because it left me feeling a similar way. Come here, sweetheart," she said, arms outstretched to me, having instantly registered my blurry eyes.

Ellie held me tight and didn't let go for a long time. I think she sensed my fear.

"Would you like a full hit grill-up?" she asked, having already prepped mushrooms, tomatoes, and onions. The sausages and bacon had been taken out of the fridge and the egg box carried over too.

"One of your infamous grill-ups? You're damn right I would!"

Ellie was clearly trying to distract me.

About 20 minutes later, when everything was cooked, and after some catch-up news about family, we ate.

"This is delicious, Ellie. Nobody cooks grilled mushrooms and tomatoes like you do."

The sweet, watery flavours of the tomato exploded in my mouth.

"Doesn't taste the same unless they are perfectly ripe," she added.

The doorbell rang halfway through.

"I'll get it," Ellie said. After a brief exchange with the delivery man, she came back with the most beautiful flower arrangement in a pretty basket, tied with a large, red silk bow. White roses and deep pink lilies, complemented with green fern, leaves, and those pretty, tiny white flowers, baby's breath, I think.

"Oh wow, they're beautiful, Ellie. Who are they from?" I asked.

"There's no card anywhere, so I'm not sure, but they're for one of us. I'm guessing it's Alejandro or Hayden," she added.

"It's unlikely it's Alejandro all the way from Canada."

"It could be, Leila. He's rich, missing you, and knows you've had a rough week."

I realised that was entirely true. Plus, I knew how romantic he could be.

"Could be from Hayden, too, to show his thanks for a vigorous night," I said, winking at her.

Ellie filled a large vase with cold water, arranging the flowers before carrying them over.

"They brighten up the table so much."

After we ate, and I watched Ellie yawn about 10 times, I said, "I'll clean up, you go to bed."

"Sounds like a brilliant idea, thanks, Leila."

After she went up the stairs, my thoughts turned to Alejandro again. How I missed him. The thought the flowers might be from him cheered me up slightly. What a sweet, kind gesture. He was so thoughtful.

Less than a month to go.

What a wretched curse this waiting was. All these feelings with nowhere to go. It was all very well expressing yourself, poetically and over the phone, but the reality was it hurt not to have an outlet to express our emotions physically. It felt like a waste of our present affection, which I found overwhelming at times. Today was one of the days where the ache hurt. I needed to write out some raw emotions. Time for some poetry, I thought, pulling out my phone.

"There's
as much pain
in love with no touch,
as there is in touch,
with no love…"

I wanted to get close to him to see if I could trust him in person, the same way my gut instinct told me I could. That was all I needed to know, so I could let go and fall for him.

"All she needed,
to give you everything,
to open up+find strength+awe
in how you wanted
to cradle the vulnerability
of her gentle heart,
was your strong hands+
the safety of trust.
She felt that
the first moment you held her,
as she lost herself,
deep in your ocean eyes…"

All I could think about was how special our connection was.

"It's so much more
than the anticipation of you;
it's the way you wrap me
in your light+dark.
Conversation+connection
has become our
perpetual foreplay.
There's never a point
in time where we aren't
yearning to touch

or that I can't
feel you with me..."
 Keeping on the same theme:
"Intimacy
should be a
fully immersive
experience; mental
foreplay, sensual music,
candles, gentle caresses+
deep connection-soul
sex to die for..."
 "Someone
that touches your heart,
who finds
depth in your mind,
that carries something
about their personality
that reaches you,
that makes you feel more.
A connection
of mind, body+souls;
the type of muse
you can't get enough of+
can never get enough of you..."
 All I craved right now was touch.
 "I can't think of
anything more erotic
than a connection where
every part of us is touching;
both inside+out. I want
to feel your soul..."
 "Sometimes
all it takes is just
one person to see
your mind as beautiful,
to become part of your
world+change your life in
a way that you could never
have understood beforehand-
the power of intense connection..."
 Ellie had a good three hours of sleep, as I wrote poetry and went about several house chores, catching up for the week. A little washing

and ironing, some cleaning, bleaching, mail sorting - the usual weekend chores too boring to mention.

No "good morning beautiful," text from Alejandro this morning, and no response to my text, so I felt a little bit meh about today, given what happened last night. Not every day could be a good day. I still couldn't eliminate the feeling of unease from Wednesday, either.

When Ellie came down, she looked refreshed.

"Sooo, I was thinking, as we've both been so flat, I think we should go out tonight. And I mean out-out. Get your prettiest, sexiest outfit. We'll go to Chester to the gorgeous new cocktail bar, Trend. I was told the vibe in that place is exquisite. I've been dying to see what it's like. Plus, it saves you from moping around the house on a Saturday night, too. Come on, let's be impulsive," she pleaded, with puppy dog eyes and a fake whimper.

"Okay, let's do it," I said, thinking why the hell not. "What are you going to wear?" I asked, wondering if I had anything flash enough for the venue. It sounded so posh.

"The pretty, yellow, flowy dress we picked out last time we went shopping. You have the beautiful, fitted, black and red strappy dress with the zip-up back. It goes perfectly with your dark features. I remember you bought it as a set, with matching underwear."

"Perfect! This is exactly the reason we both like shopping, so we can be impulsive whenever we want and we're still prepared," I said, beaming. "Yes, I'd love to wear it. Do you know what? I haven't had a leisurely get ready for a girly night out for ages, I might even start in a bit and have a nice long bath, with some fancy oils, and put on some pretty smelling cream, and do my hair all soft and curly."

I realised I hadn't done that since the last time I went out with Alejandro.

I miss you.

"Sounds perfect. I can't wait. I'll book a taxi for seven p.m. You go run your bath and take your time," she organised.

"Okay, hunni."

This lifted me. She was right. I needed to get out, change scenery for a while. I looked in the cupboard, finding the strappy black and red dress. I pulled it out, along with a pair of red under sided black heels. Such a beautiful outfit. I went over to the set of drawers to retrieve the stunning red satin and black lace underwear set I'd bought to go with it. Perfect.

I heard Ellie jumping in the shower as I began to apply makeup, paying extra attention to my eyes and lips. By the time I was finished, Ellie's hair dryer was going, and I was excited about the night out. I put on my pretty underwear and dress, carrying my shoes, and handbag, and went downstairs, shouting "I'm ready Ellie. I'll pour us a drink."

I went in the kitchen, reaching for two wine glasses and taking a bottle of white wine out of the fridge. I looked outside briefly, that flutter coming back. No sign of anyone, relax. Nobody is out there.

It must have been a one-off.

It's all okay.

"How are we doing for time?" Ellie asked.

"Taxi should be here in 10 minutes."

It arrived just after we finished our last glass.

We took our jackets in case it got cool later. I locked up and we excitedly hopped in.

"Where to, ladies?" asked the taxi drive, looking in his mirror.

"Trend in Chester, please."

"Oooh, posh," he said, jokingly.

"I know, not sure a couple of Scousers are going to fit in, to be honest."

As I said it, all three of us burst out laughing.

"Well, you both look the part anyway. That's what counts to get into Trend," he said.

"Thank you," Ellie said. "We scrub up okay, I suppose."

She had a smirk that always gave away her dry sense of humour. We had aligned ours together perfectly over our years living together. It was about a 35-minute taxi drive to Chester, and we chatted nonstop on the way there. The journey seemed quite short overall.

I can't wait to let my hair down tonight.

Will I be able to get through the night without feeling any anxiety?

27 TREND

August. Saturday. Chester. Town.

When we pulled up outside Trend, there was already a long queue. We had anticipated that, though; we'd heard it was exclusive and were prepared to wait. Even as we were getting out of the taxi, a group of lads were getting turned away for their attire. There was a strict dress code to be adhered to. Ellie had already spoken to a colleague who had been here before to get the lowdown. We waited patiently, glad of the warm night so we weren't cold standing in line. When we got to the front of the queue, two huge, burly, well dressed bouncers said, "good evening, ladies" as we walked in.

First impressions: wow, what an amazing place. It was stunning. It had the vibe of a refurbished, modern, funky warehouse. There was a wide-open space for the dance floor to the right, a bar to the immediate left, a high seated table area further to the left, and a small upper section overlooking the dance floor. It looked like a VIP area. There was a winding staircase leading up to it, with a red rope cordoning it off, and a less intimidating bouncer standing by. There were a lot of large windows on the upper half of the building, which was unusual, and there was a neon blue light fading in and out, giving the whole place a cool, funky vibe.

Everyone was dressed to the nines. The DJ was to the right. We had arrived at a good time. Ellie said it didn't get rammed until about 11 p.m., and there were still tables left. Pleasantly, the music wasn't blasting at an unbearable decibel level. Some places deafen you, but this was more of a medium volume. Loud, but not overpowering.

What a cool place.

"Let's go get some drinks," I said. "Would you like an apple martini, pink gin, or a mojito?" I asked Ellie.

"I'm gonna go with a mojito tonight," she said, briefly pulling out her phone to send a text.

The drinks arrived in pretty, round glasses, with a centre bluestem, decorated with mint and lime garnishing. Neon blue was the predominant colour in the room. Everything was coordinated to match the lighting.

We chatted away and danced on the spot, as girls often do, for about 20 minutes.

Our drinks were starting to get low when a man came walking over toward us, looking directly at me. He was wearing a smart tailored suit with a dicky bow and silver tray, carrying two more mojitos on it. As he got closer, I realised I wasn't imagining it, he was walking straight toward me.

When he arrived at the table, he said, "These are compliments of the gentleman standing in the VIP area, he'd like you both to join him."

Just as I was about to send the man on an about turn with a *Thanks but no thanks* message, I looked up to the VIP area and my legs immediately started to tremble, goose bumps forming all over my arms. I pressed my hand to my heart.

I'd know that shape anywhere.

Alejandro.

My eyes filled up as I saw him standing with one arm on the ledge, beaming at me with a big, gorgeous smile.

What? When? Why?

How long are you here?

Just to make my legs buckle completely, he was there in a tailored black suit, with a crisp white shirt, and black tie. Handsome, tanned face, chiselled shape, white teeth, gorgeous hair, and eyebrows. What an absolute vision. It wasn't just physical now, the feelings I had for him were overwhelming me completely. He raised his glass to me, nodding his head to the side, as if to say, *come here, baby.*

I'd been waiting so long for this moment.

I looked over at Ellie. She was beaming like an idiot watching me.

"How?" was the only question I could get out.

"He contacted me on Scribe. He wanted to fly back early and surprise you, so I've been trying to act normal all day, because he literally dropped everything after your panic attack, spoke to Brandon, and sorted it all out so he could be here tonight. I've been dying to tell you, but he made me promise. Come on, gorgeous, it's your time now, let's go and get your man," she said warmly, embracing me, squeezing tightly.

He was watching me as I walked over. His eyes didn't flinch. The waiter was guiding the way with our drinks on a tray held at shoulder height. My eyes didn't break from Alejandro's until I got to the stairs.

I'm trembling.

A sophisticated bouncer un-roped the entrance so we could walk up. As we approached the top of the stairs, Alejandro stood there facing us. I was walking ahead of Ellie and couldn't take my eyes off him. My heart was fluttering; it was racing. He was looking me up and down in such an affectionate way. He had a soft smile on his face, his head was cocked very slightly to the right, as he did. He was taking in everything about me, all at once.

As I got closer, we were both beaming. I swear it was like lightning flashing inside the building and sweet soft rain starting to fall upon my skin. My body was glowing with affection for him and as I got closer, I couldn't say a word. I was too choked up. I wrapped my arms around his neck and felt everything folding into him all at once, my body, my mind, my heart, and my soul. It was as if I was fusing into him, our souls were locking together, binding us tightly. Every word we'd ever spoken hung in the air between us and inside us. It was so powerful, so potent. I felt it. I knew he could, too.

His body felt so strong and firm against my soft breasts. I'd forgotten how overwhelmed I became when my body pressed against his.

"Hey, beautiful," he whispered in my ear.

Emotionally, I was somewhere between smiling and crying. It was one of the most incredibly joyous moments of my life. I'd never been so happy to see someone before.

"Hey, handsome."

Alejandro pulled me into him, pressing me firmly into a squeeze, before releasing slightly to bend down and kiss me on each cheek. I was conscious I'd momentarily abandoned Ellie behind me and she would probably feel a little awkward. I also knew she was ecstatically happy for me, though.

The waiter had discreetly placed the drinks on the table and Alejandro took hold of my hand, so as not to break contact with me and leaned over to Ellie.

"Hi, Ellie, nice to meet you. I've heard so many wonderful things about you from Leila," he said, kissing her on both cheeks.

"Likewise, Alejandro. I've heard some amazing things. And the way you wanted to meet her tonight and surprise her in here was simply perfect," Ellie replied.

"Shall we all sit?" he smiled, gesturing to the seats. I could only nod; I couldn't stop staring at him.

"It's so good to see you. Tell me how and why you're back early? You're nearly one month ahead of schedule. Are you back just for the weekend? Do you have to go back for the last month next week?" I questioned. I had to know.

"After what happened to you at the house, then with your panic attack, I went straight to Brandon and explained the situation, saying I wanted to be with my girlfriend to make sure she was safe."

Alejandro's girlfriend.

"Brandon completely understood and said he would want to do the same if it was his girlfriend, so we discussed the last two songs to write for the album, and he said we could do it remotely. We were already ahead of schedule, and we've laid down all the other tracks. There's just these last two left now to complete his album. I can work on those in the studio at my house, send them to him digitally, and then he can record them with his guys, tweaking the arrangement to suit him. I'm back for good," he explained.

I felt myself choking up emotionally. Ellie sensed it, taking over with the conversation.

"That's great news," she said.

I squeezed Alejandro's hand to acknowledge him, as Ellie continued to ask,

"Have you enjoyed writing for Brandon?"

She was genuinely interested, I could tell. He was charming as hell. I could feel myself swooning in such proximity. The pull was stronger than ever.

"I have, Ellie. He has such a massive future ahead of him. He's brilliant. He knows exactly what he wants, and he's focused and dedicated. The way he delivers a song is so powerful; he sings lyrics with great depth and emotion. His voice is mesmerising. Personally, I think he's on the verge of breaking through. I wish him every success, he's a top bloke," he said, clearly impressed by Brandon.

"I'm so glad you worked together so well, and I'm really glad to see you. I literally couldn't be happier to have you back in my arms," I gushed.

"I hated being away from you, Leila," he said, looking into my eyes for a few seconds too long, and I knew exactly how much he wanted to be with me then. From that one look.

"So, I hear the big news is you've met someone?" Alejandro said, directing the question to Ellie, trying to make sure she was included.

We intermittently sipped our drinks. Alejandro hadn't let go of my hand, squeezing it regularly. It was taking all my strength not to kiss him then and there.

"Yes, Hayden and I are like rocket fuel together. We've spent a lot of time together recently, so I've probably not been around as much as I should have with Leila," she said, looking a little guilty.

"Hey, don't worry about me. I told you that. You're in a relationship with Hayden. I would expect you to be with him most of the time and we still have tea together most weeks," I said without thinking, realising I'd seen her a lot less on those days recently, too.

"Hayden's so different from anyone I've ever dated. He's full on. We're still in the stage of the relationship where we want to spend all our time in bed," she smiled.

"Ellie!" I said, looking shocked.

"Whaaat?" she replied, smirking.

Alejandro responded by saying,

"I'm looking forward to that stage, too," while looking me right in the eyes.

Boom, instant melt. I was so glad to see him; I hadn't even got that far in my mind. But yes, I knew exactly what we would be spending a lot of our time doing shortly.

Ellie called the waiter over to ask for another round of drinks and when she was talking, I whispered coyly to Alejandro.

"So, when exactly is that likely to start?"

He looked straight into my eyes, putting his hand on my cheek.

"Tonight, baby. I need you tonight."

Fuck me.

Goosebumps instantly formed on my arms and my breathing started to become erratic. My mind surged in waves of passion, instantly overwhelming my body. Alejandro spotted my chest rising and falling, knowing exactly what to look for.

"Breathe, baby, breathe…" he said, and then I realised, we were going to make love this very night, for the first time ever.

The arousal was unlike anything I'd ever felt before.

Ellie said, after ordering our next round,

"We should get together, all four of us. I'll arrange something in the next couple of weeks if you'd like?"

"That would be great, Ellie. I'd love to meet Hayden," Alejandro replied.

We carried on drinking and chatting and had a few dances. How I missed dancing with him. It wasn't salsa, but it was fun regardless, and great for the three of us to let our hair down. Alejandro could move to anything. He had the most beautiful and natural sense of rhythm, and his timing and coordination were phenomenal.

It was strange, because I felt like I knew him inside and out, yet I didn't know him face to face. I didn't know him in person. What a bizarre feeling. We had to get to know each other all over again, but in a very different way this time. We couldn't read each other's words anymore. We had to learn how to read eyes and body language instead. How intoxicating.

Ellie said, "I think I should be heading back now, I'm sure you two have a lot of catching up to do. I'll order a taxi."

"No need. I've a driver standing by. Let me text him and he will come and pick the three of us up, take Leila and myself back to my house, then safely drop you off at your house, or Hayden's, wherever you wish," Alejandro insisted.

I was genuinely impressed at his thoughtfulness.

"I'll text Hayden and see if he minds me coming back to his," Ellie said, pulling out her phone and tapping away.

Alejandro leaned over to me, whispering,

"You're nearly *all mine.*"

I shuddered, replying,

"I have been since the day you walked into my life."

He was stroking my arm softly, tracing a single finger down the centre of my arm and I could feel such beautiful sensuality pouring out of him.

You're as hungry for me as I am for you.

"Hayden said that's fine, so I'd like to go back to his, instead of being in the house on my own, if that's alright?"

She was happy to end up spending the night in Hayden's arms.

"Yes, that's fine, Ellie. My driver is trustworthy, and you can feel safe with him," he added reassuringly.

We collected our coats, stepping outside. Alejandro had his arm linked with mine, pulling me tight to him. I could feel his strength. The driver pulled up in a newer, shiny, black, car with tinted windows.

"Good evening, Mr. Fernandez," he said respectfully.

"Good evening, George."

After we got in Alejandro added,

"Please drop myself and Leila off at my house, then make sure Ellie gets back safely to her boyfriend's house? She'll give you directions on the way."

"I certainly will, Mr. Fernandez."

As George drove, I realised I would see Alejandro's house for the first time. To end the evening with Alejandro, in his arms, made this night, one of the most memorable and special of my life.

I was losing the ability to speak, to utter a word. I was becoming increasingly aroused. Alejandro knew this and covered for me, making light conversation with Ellie on the way back. After a while, we started to slow down, and I realised this must be his road. We were nearly there. My stomach filled with butterflies.

Alejandro pulled a gadget out of his pocket, pressing the button, aiming at a very large house in the darkness. I couldn't see it clearly, but then the gate opened, and a bright light came on as we drove through. We pulled up outside an exquisite house. I was awestruck.

It was a mixture of cream and beige brick, with grey windows and roof trimmings, including an arched door entrance with two elegant plant pots either side, a set of three windows above the door, and a strong triangle shaped apex to the roof. There were small, round windows projecting out from the roof, and a large, beautiful turret style section to the house with large windows.

To the left, there was a plush and well-maintained grass area and an outhouse garage, in the same cream and beige brick, with three garage doors. To the right, there were beautiful tall trees and a tiered fountain feature in the centre of a pond area with a bench next to it. It looked like the equivalent of a small mansion. It was situated in a very wealthy area, judging from the approach as we drove in. Finally, I was going to enter his house, knowing we were about to make love for the first time.

As we drew to a stop, Ellie leaned over to kiss me on the cheek and said, "Enjoy the rest of your evening, guys."

"Thank you for helping organise such a wonderful surprise for me," I said, briefly squeezing her hand affectionately, to show her I was both nervous and excited.

She understood and smiled back, winking at me out of Alejandro's line of vision.

"You too, Ellie. Have a good night. Thanks again for everything," Alejandro replied.

"No problem at all. I was glad to help. Have fun guys," she said, while Alejandro stepped out of the car, turning to offer me his hand, guiding me smoothly out.

Such a gentleman.

For now, at least.

My cheeks were flushed, my heart was racing with nerves.

I need you.

I need you inside me.

28 INEVITABLE

August. Saturday. Chester. Alejandro's.

    The atmosphere between us was loaded. It was inevitable. We both knew we were headed for an intimate liaison. We needed it for our bodies to breathe and souls to exhale. Finally. As he unlocked the front door, the car turned around in the drive and I waved goodbye to Ellie, knowing she would be safe with Hayden tonight.
    Alejandro opened the door, flicking a switch just inside, the lights suddenly coming on. What a stunning hallway. It was classy and modern, with beech wood floors. It was large, with cathedral ceilings. A winding staircase to the right, significantly wider than standard. The stairs were wooden and dark brown, with white trim and a dark brown handrail beautifully winding their length. The floorboards and tall ceilings, including an intricately detailed coving, were white.
    I was curious how many doors came off the hallway. By going down a small set of steps, I could see two more at the rear of the hallway. It looked like the house continued out the back beyond the door, too, like a modern extension had been added. The house was exquisite. Alejandro locked the door behind us, coming up behind me.
    "May I take your jacket beautiful?" as he put his hand by my shoulders.
    I shuddered at the contact. It had been so long. I was aching for him to touch me. Badly.
    "Yes, please. You have such a beautiful home, Alejandro."
    "You haven't seen a fraction of it yet," he said, winking at me.
    Interesting comment.
    "I've been thinking about this night, imagining how you would react, knowing I was back for good."
    "Do you mean that, Alejandro? What if another contract came up again next month?"
    He hung my coat on the coat stand.
    "I already told my label I don't want to spend months away again. I can do the odd week when it's necessary for bigger contracts, but I

predominantly want to write remotely. My agent knew I could have my initial meetings in person, and then come back here and lay down some tracks, based on the ideas we've brainstormed together. Others do this already. Then we can set up meetings and I can visit to collaborate at key milestones. It means I would never have to be away from you for long periods of time," he said.

My eyes started to fill up.

I've become so attached to you.

Alejandro walked over to the door on his right, turning around to beckon me in. It was his lounge. A beautiful, open space, with a modern, low corner couch in white that looked comfy. There was a light and airy feel to the room. Most of it was in white or light beige, with only green accessories and silver frames with artwork carrying any significant colour in the room.

"I'll go get drinks, please sit down and make yourself comfortable."

In front of the couch, there was a modern floating fire, embedded in the wall and encased in glass a few feet above the carpet. He turned it on before he left the room. It looked real, the flames moving in a mesmerising way. I couldn't take my eyes off their seductive dance, hypnotised by each flame, enticing me with moves like a belly dancer.

Alejandro came back into the room, carrying a metal wine chiller full of ice, a bottle of white, and two stemmed wine glasses. He placed them on the coffee table by the couch, smiling at me as he lit four chunky candles placed in focal points around the room. A strong, sweet vanilla scent drifted slowly toward me as it spread, the air filling with warmth. He walked over to a small table with an unusual wooden folding latticework divide which stood tall on the tabletop.

"I love this effect," he said.

I looked curiously at what he was doing. I realised after he placed a large candle on a decorative plate in front of the lattice that the light had started to filter through the shapes and gaps. The lattice was projecting flickers of candlelight onto the walls, creating beautiful shapes of dancing light and shade. The visual atmosphere it created was soft and pretty, as if the movement of the flicker was creating an ambient light show for us. Light patterns stretched, filling the wall and ceiling.

The candlelight flickered in his eyes as he turned to me.

His suit and crisp, white shirt looked alluring on him in the cocktail bar, but here, by the flicker of candlelight, his eyes were blowing me away. Such beautiful, cobalt blue, oceanic eyes.

You're so fucking sexy.

Butterflies filled my body as he poured a glass of wine for each of us. You could cut the sexual tension with a knife when his eyes locked on mine as he handed me my glass.

Fuck me.

I took a sip.

"That's such a lovely, rich flavour."

The piquancy of the liquid swirled around my palette, dancing on my taste buds.

"Sauvignon Val del Loire," he said. "I thought you might like it. I have three people who work for me, helping to maintain the house or drive. I let Janet know I was returning and what to purchase. She was maintaining the house while I was gone."

Alejandro went over to the portable speaker. There was an automated message when it connected to his phone. He scrolled, selecting from a playlist he'd made. The first track that came on had a wickedly sensual vibe to it, the sound of saxophone filling the room. A male vocalist who performed effortlessly captured my attention with his dulcet velvet tones. The volume wasn't too loud.

"Are you hungry?"

"A little, not much."

"I'll be back in a minute."

He came back through the door with a small cheese board, complete with finely cut mild cheese, small crackers, and biscuits, accompanied by black grapes and strawberries.

Perfect.

Not enough to fill me and just enough so the sweet taste of the fruit would linger ahead of our inevitable kissing.

With a sexy teasing glance, he placed the tray on the coffee table, sitting down on a white rug next to the fire and motioning for me to join him.

I smiled sweetly at him, joining him on the rug. We were facing each other, in opposite directions in front of the fire, the rug soft underneath us. Our eyes were dancing with the reflective flicker of the flames. He picked up one of the cube cuts of cheese with a cocktail stick, holding it out to me, looking at me while he did. He didn't just want to make out, he wanted to seduce me. Every detail he'd paid attention to was doing exactly that. The atmosphere, the fire, the heat, the music, vanilla scent, the dancing ambient flicker around the room, the look in his eyes, the offering to my taste buds. He was seducing every single one of my senses, simultaneously.

Fuck.

I had the feeling he had been from the very first word he ever spoke to me, which left me overwhelmed, in the sexiest of ways.

Alejandro then picked up a dark grape, popping it into my mouth. The contrast of the drier cheese against the juicy sweetness of the grapes was delicious. He watched my mouth closely as it closed around the small morsel, while he was hand feeding me. My lips caught on his fingers momentarily and a surge went through my body at the contact, at his finger inside my mouth. I offered no resistance as he fed me another sweet grape to flavour my mouth. It was succulent and sexy, the way he was feeding me without even saying anything, like words were superfluous at this point.

I picked up a grape in the same way, offering it to him slowly. Our eye contact was intense, the atmosphere between us thick and heavy. It had turned sexual so quickly without so much as a word, beautifully crafted by this intimacy he'd engineered.

After a couple more grapes each, he picked up a strawberry and deliberately offered me one that was too large to fit in my mouth. I had to bite and suck it a little at the same time, to stop the juice running over my lower lip. It was sweet and grainy, falling onto my tongue as I shifted it and swallowed softly. He placed the remainder in my mouth and his thumb lingered, caressing my top lip as he looked deeply into my eyes. I felt overwhelmed as he leaned toward me, his fingers wrapping around the back of my neck through my hair. I swallowed softly, watching him move closer.

Alejandro kissed me tenderly, pressing softly against my lips with his. They parted for him naturally. He paused, hovering close to my mouth before gently moving in toward me, letting his tongue slide slowly, but deeply, inside my mouth. The sweet aftertaste of the strawberries, mixed with the delicious heat of his tongue, formed a hypnotic concoction. Every part of me started to ache wildly. I placed my arms around his neck and lost myself within his kiss.

You're such a beautiful kisser.

With his right hand he moved the board to the side and pulled me closer into him, wrapping around me, dangerously close, my breasts now pressed against his chest. My heart started to race as he brushed my hair over my left shoulder and down my back, tickling me through the lace of my dress. His tongue traced a wet line down my neck, sucking slightly at the skin before reaching the crevice of my neck and enclosing his lips around me, like a bite with no teeth. His tongue started to work this particularly sensitive area of my neck with a circular motion, licks, and gentle sucks. I felt my body starting to pulse, deep inside, with the combination of physical contact and the rhythmic swell and retreat of his tongue on my neck.

Please don't stop.

My heart was starting to feel like thunder as he generated a palpable electricity between us, a building static. There were surges racing through my body as he held my face, raising my chin with one finger to meet his mouth again. He changed his position to sweep my hair over the other side, drawing out its length and my curls over the back of his hand. He paid equal attention to the other side, his tongue expertly flicking down my neck before enclosing his lips around me, ravishing me with a precision which both heated my skin and gave me goose bumps simultaneously. He'd paid such attention to the details of our conversations. I felt like he knew me inside and out before he ever touched me. How incredible it was, to feel that level of emotion through a kiss.

I want to do the same for you. I want to make you feel special.

29 TOUCH

August. Saturday. Chester. Alejandro's.

As I looked into Alejandro's eyes, I knew without a shadow of a doubt, I was already in love with him. Excitement rushed through my whole body. My core felt like it had been set alight with fireworks. His six-foot muscular frame was pressing against my chest, and even from this position, it made my heart beat wildly. My mind was already his. It had been from the first moment I laid eyes on him. My body longed to follow.

Our eyes locked together in this intimate space. There was a softening depth in his cobalt eyes that captivated me, deep blue flecks mesmerising me as I looked into them. He had an air of mystery. Despite having spoken a hundred times. There was still so much to discover.

What makes you go weak at the knees?
What makes you feel alive?
What makes you thrive?
I want to know everything.

I couldn't, for the life of me, understand the hold Alejandro had over me. He had already penetrated my mind and my body was flushed. I didn't just *want* more of him, I *needed* more of him. He laid soft kisses upon my mouth, tender and sensual, whilst arousing every nerve ending in my body simultaneously. He knelt up slowly, holding my hand, bidding me to do the same, pulling me tight against his body.

An involuntary moan escaped, reverberating into his open mouth, as his tongue found mine inside a kiss, I felt soul deep. I felt him harden against me.

"Does that feel good?"
"I've never been kissed like this, not with passion like yours."
My voice was timid, lost in arousal.
"Then you've never been truly kissed."

His air of surety was sexy as hell, like he already knew what he could do to me. I felt his overwhelming power, drawing me in.

Surges of emotion tingled over my skin.

Everything Alejandro did was in crescendos, the passion building between us. I was enchanted. He was like an erotic form of a dark sensual art, igniting me in waves as my hips arched forward. Magnetically, I gravitated toward the delectable heat pulsing inside his jeans. The most beautiful part, though, was every touch was laced with feelings. We had been building toward this moment from the very first moment our eyes connected. I needed to express it physically now.

I need your body on mine. I need you inside me.

Tracing a nail softly over his shoulders, through his crisp white shirt and down the centre of his back, I felt the shape of him, ripped muscles underneath his skin. He shuddered under my nails. It was as if that tipped him over the edge, and he pulled back, offering me his hand so I could stand up.

He turned me around by the hips, without a single word. He untied the necktie that was keeping the upper part of the dress in place and then reached for my zipper, slowly unzipping my dress.

Alejandro teased the undone necktie slowly over my arm, tickling my skin, as his fingers grazed me gently. I inhaled sharply. He teased the other side off, in the same provocative manner. I shuddered visibly as he tugged briefly at it, with just enough force to reveal my bra, and he turned me around by my hips again. He leaned back a little just to look at me. I found it deeply arousing, watching his eyes look intensely at the upper curves of my breasts and my pretty red and black lace bra.

"God, you're beautiful," he said, without the slightest hesitation, biting his lower lip, in a masculine, sexy way.

The heat of his stare melted me. He was studying me intently. He slowly traced a finger across my clavicle, over my shoulder, down the side of my arm, then back up and over. It was very deliberate and painfully slow, his finger softly tracing the upper curves of my breasts, dipping gently at the top of my cleavage, following it down and back up on the other side. He pulled me toward him, kissing my stomach. He left his mouth close enough I could feel his warm breath on me as he swiftly yanked off my unzipped dress.

Sexy as fuck.

Alejandro held me for balance as I stepped out of my dress and moved it carefully to one side. Then he gently pulled my thighs, covered in black lace thigh high stockings and suspenders, toward him, cradling the back of my thigh with one hand. He traced the outline of my pretty bra. He did this, and everything else, slowly, every move deliberately prolonged. My groin pulsed deeply. I could feel how wet I was. I hungered for his hands touching me all over in the same way.

I'm already lost.

There was something about me standing there in my underwear and him in his full tuxedo, looking like a handsome James Bond, that was incredibly seductive and powerful. The imbalance aroused me far more than I anticipated.

I put my hand out and he stood up. He knew I wanted his clothes off. He could see my hunger.

"Your eyes have darkened. They're misty and sexy," his voice deepened.

"Arousal looks like that on me," my voice sounded sultry, crumbling as I spoke.

"I'm particularly turned on by that look in your eye."

That spurred me on more.

Undoing his tie, peeling it away slowly as I unbuttoned his shirt, looking him in the eyes, my mind was somewhere between not wanting to undress him because he looked so sexy and wanting to rip everything off.

Patience, Leila.

As his shirt opened, the sight of his chest and stomach nearly floored me. He was ripped in a way I'd never seen up close. As I pulled his crisp white shirt over his back and down his arms slowly, the contrast of his dark skin against it was a stunning sight. The definition of his chest and abdominal muscles against the contours of his hips as they popped through the top of his dress trousers was sexy as hell.

"I've never seen a body like yours before, you're so perfect," I said, blushing.

With that, Alejandro wrapped his arms around me, pulling me into him, reaching up toward the clasp of my bra and unhooking it with precision. My bra clung naturally to my shape even after the clasp was released. He peeled it away slowly, erotically. It was so sexy. Being exposed in front of him felt powerful. I was trembling inside. As my bra tumbled to the floor, he looked at my breasts, grunting softly, animalistic, as he pulled me in tight against his chest, my breasts pressing against him. We were skin to skin for the first time.

Fucking hell.

I was tantalised by the strength of his firm, padded chest against my soft, feminine curves, my flushed nipples grazing his. When he kissed me next, I felt it soul deep. The passion of our tongues and the sensual way our bodies came together was delicious. It was nirvana, the greatest rush I'd ever felt.

Your passion blows me away.

The music was playing in the background, changing to the next track in his playlist automatically. I suspect he may have engineered this playlist with our imminent rendezvous in mind. This song was soulful, with a hard, sexy beat. I wanted to grind against him. He came around my back, standing behind me, his hands on my hips, gently pushing side to side, making us sway to the beat together.

"This is so sensual," I said, nearly whispering.

Alejandro had sexy hip movements, tantalising me, kissing my neck from behind with an attentive, eager mouth, while our hips swayed naturally to the beat. His hands reached through my arms, cupping my full breasts, kneading them gently, taking in their shape and working my nipples between his thumbs and forefingers. I moaned softly as he pinched a little. He growled lightly into my neck, and I could feel the hard press of his arousal against me now.

Fucking hell.

My knees are going weak.

I was standing in a red silk thong with black lace trim, stockings, suspenders, and heels. He pulled me closer, his left hand working my breast, his right trailing a finger in caressing circles over my right breast and down my stomach. He worked his way gently toward my panty line. As he traced one finger along the top ridge, my heart started pounding, lost in the sensation of his kisses on my neck, his fingers gently squeezing my nipple, his other finger teasing me.

"Do you like that?" he whispered seductively into my ear.

"Very much so," I whimpered, unable to offer much else as my responses were slow. His fingers were traveling, slowly making their way into my pants, searching to see what he had done to me, sliding softly into my wetness, gliding effortlessly to find my clit.

"Uhhh," he moaned. "You're so wet for me."

"Mmm," I murmured, my bum leaning back against him for balance.

I could feel his hard ridge sitting perfectly between my cheeks. I went to move my hand to touch him, and he said,

"No," sternly, surprising me.

Alejandro didn't want me to touch him at all. He had phenomenal, almost unnatural, control over himself. He moved slowly with medium pressure, his fingers crossing over my clit several times, making my head delirious with such precise attention. He found the underside of my clit, working it slowly, finding the small dip just to the side of it, letting his finger sit inside the pocket, rubbing slowly while always maintaining contact with the side of my clit. That slow rub was divine, like he was learning my body, tuning into me.

"I want you so much," he whispered into my ear.

My knees started to buckle under the intense physical sensation and his words. I was overwhelmed being dominated in such a sexy way. Everything strong about me as a woman felt so perversely weak. It was both immobilising and sexy at the same time. It was such a contrasting sensation, but it was one I didn't think I could ever get enough of.

Why do you affect me so much?

I arched my back, my head pushing against his strong shoulders. He had me pinned, supporting me. He kissed my neck deeper, starting to work against the warmth of my raw, wet ache, alternating between circular movements, light flicks, long double finger strokes, and a harder rubbing motion.

As I became more and more aroused, my chest pounded like a set of bass drums. My breath was erratic. He enjoyed every second of rendering me into this state. I could sense it. Alejandro loved having this control over me. My core was aching and pulsing with every sensation, every throb. As my legs started to tense, he knew I was getting close to the edge. He pushed harder and firmer against my clit, rubbing with a pace my body had no choice but to respond to. He pinned me hard against him. The feel of his erection pressing against me aroused me further.

"Let go. You need this. Right now. There will be more, I promise."

Telling me he wanted me to let go completely tipped me over the edge. I came in surges, in waves travelling through my body with such a force my entire body tensed, as I started to rock and buck against him. That just made him pin me harder, so he could feel every single writhing movement of mine against him. He rubbed much harder as I spun out of control.

My breath was jagged and needy. I moaned heavily in waves, my whole body pulsing repeatedly. His strong arms supported me as I caved into the pleasure. I shattered in his arms. I let myself be lost in a moment of complete abandonment. He felt it with me, experienced how it felt, through my body, my breath, and the way my legs buckled. He was learning my responses. The build-up was delicious, making the orgasm much stronger. For every wave and moan, he pinned me against him tighter, enjoying the sensation of me trembling against him. That was the most intoxicating part, the way he wanted to feel it with me. He held me there as my body twitched, until he felt all of me relaxing slowly against him, allowing the chaos to finally leave me.

For now.

Alejandro turned me around, sucking softly on his fingers, before kissing me wildly, more passionately than I ever remember being kissed.

"Fuck. You taste beautiful. I need to be inside you now," he said, with an urgency that made me tremble more.

I undid the button on his suit trousers, peeling them open, tugging them down over his wide and well-formed thighs before pulling them off completely. It was the first time I'd seen the shape of him. Through his boxer briefs, I saw he was well endowed. I squeezed him playfully through his boxers and he throbbed inside my hand. I felt his girth immediately, the thickness of his manhood.

Damn, that's sexy.

I rubbed my thumb over the length of him, circling the tip slowly, while still gripping the width of him with my other fingers. My groin started to ache. A deep ache born of raw carnality.

"I need you inside me."

We had discussed I was on the pill in one of our conversations and knew we were medically safe, which was one less worry now.

"Come inside me. I trust you."

Alejandro lay me down on the rug, stripping my silk pants off slowly, eyeing my naked body before him.

"I love your curves."

He stood up briefly, tugging off his boxers. The sheer size of him, in height, stature, and girth, which was now fully erect above me, weakened me at first sight. His muscles were defined, abs ripped, firm chest, wide biceps, thick thighs, shapely calves. I licked my lips without even realising. I was so turned on, I couldn't speak.

Alejandro knelt before me, parting my legs gently before positioning himself over me. Looking at my face and body, he lowered himself further, hooking himself underneath my shoulders, resting on his forearms. He positioned himself with the tip of his erection just touching the moisture around my clit.

He kissed me. As the kissing intensified, he slowly rubbed up and down my silky sex in a smooth motion, making me ache for him to be inside me. His hands were gripping me a little firmer on the shoulders and his tender kisses became deeper.

As his tongue slid further into my mouth, he started to enter me, his wide tip pushing slowly inside me, deliriously slowly.

Fuck me.

He had such perfect control, to kiss like that, yet enter me slowly at the same time. As I enclosed him with my warmth, he slowly started to fill me with his girth, pushing into me. My muscles were still contracting, the tail end of my orgasm still pulsing in small waves around him. I let out a deep moan as he reached full depth inside me, a slight gnaw to the ache. He groaned a little as I did.

"Fucking beautiful," he whispered in my ear.

His kisses were deepening as he eased himself nearly all the way out, then slowly thrust inside me again, rubbing against my inner walls as they contracted, filling me up.

We lost ourselves in the moment. My back arched naturally, slowly, and he filled me deeper. I felt him getting harder and thicker inside me, throbbing as I arched. He knew how hungry I was for the sensation of his warmth, for his width and the way he made me gasp involuntarily on each thrust. I had absolutely no control over my responses now. I was turned on. He filled me in such a way, I had no choice but to gasp or moan on virtually every stroke inside me. A twisted ache was building up inside again for him. We both needed to feel sated and release months of build-up, right now. We had all the time in the world to explore each other to great depths. For now, I just wanted him to come inside me, to complete me, to unite us.

I wanted him to become part of me tonight.

"More," I whispered, pleading with my eyes for him to ravage me.

He thrust sharply and I whimpered, unable to control my responses. Pulling out more harshly, he thrust into me again and I gripped onto the back of his shoulders, pulling him into me deeper still. My hands started to rummage through his hair, and I tugged on it as he finished each stroke inside me, his rhythm picking up speed. He started pumping in and out of me, my head swirling in the mix of all the combined feelings - body, mind, heart, and soul. He was touching all of them simultaneously.

Alejandro was edging me toward another orgasm. I felt it build inside me. A few more thrusts and the sheer depth and motion of the penetration brought another wave of pleasure inside me, as I contracted around him again. This orgasm was so different to the one earlier, like a raging need inside me. I bucked against him, trying to rock, fucking the feeling out of my system. The orgasm was explosive and intense. The feel of him thrusting in and out of me while I was coming drove him faster and harder. While I was moaning, deep in the throes of orgasm, his pumping ramped up suddenly and I felt the tension in his body, and the second he started to lose himself inside me. I bucked around him as he came. He let out a guttural moan when he released into me.

The ache slowly replaced itself with a feeling of warmth inside me. He looked into my eyes, and I saw a few seconds of complete vulnerability within him before he started dropping the pace off slowly. He eased in and out of me, until both of our orgasms faded, our bodies fully relaxed.

He was breathless, with a faint smile on his face.

"That felt so incredible, Leila."

I couldn't help but feel a little emotional, like a part of me I'd been missing had just been completed, even if I never knew I was missing it. He stroked the hair off my face, laying kisses repeatedly on both cheeks, my nose, and forehead. He was so tender, so gentle.

"You have no idea how much I needed to feel you. After all that time, I needed to connect with you so much."

It was intimate and special.

"I needed to connect as much as you did. I struggled to retain any form of control, knowing how I felt about you and with you being all those miles away. I needed you so much."

"I love you, baby."

I felt the softness in his words and the fullness of his emotion.

"I love you, too, Alejandro."

A moment of true perfection, in a world where I see so little. I took out my emotional camera. Point. Click. I wanted to store this feeling forever, relive it over and over.

I was grateful we were both patient people waiting for this. It felt so special.

We stayed by the fire for several minutes. He leaned up on his elbow, stroking my hair with one hand, looking deep into my eyes. It was like we were talking, without even saying anything. All those times we said *I miss you*, all those long conversations, we could feel them all drifting past us in our minds, even within our silence. Our connection was all we had ever needed.

How incredibly beautiful.

It was getting quite late at this point.

"Would you like to go upstairs to the bedroom or cuddle up on the couch?" Alejandro asked.

The ambience in the room was perfect.

"I'm happy to sleep on the couch, it's plenty wide enough for both of us."

"Okay beautiful, I'll go clean up and grab a throw and some pillows for us. There's a pack of new toothbrushes in the bathroom downstairs you can use – that's the opposite door in the hall."

He slowly eased out of me and went upstairs while I went to the bathroom downstairs. When he came back, he was carrying a flat sheet, two comfy looking pillows and a beige/cream comfy looking throw, along with a t-shirt of his for me to sleep in.

How thoughtful.

Alejandro prepared the couch and blew out the candles. He lay there, propped up on an elbow, just looking into my eyes as the firelight flickered in them. I felt relaxed, almost in a meditative state, with nothing but a blissful peace in my heart.

We're in love with each other.

Alejandro kissed me again, particularly softly and tenderly this time, eventually lifting his arm up so I could place my head on his shoulder. As I got cosy, he wrapped his thick upper arm around me.

I've wanted this moment for such a long time.

He kissed my forehead, pressing it firmly and with feeling. My eyes eventually glazed over as I watched the flames dancing in his eyes. I realised, as I started to drift and my eyes started batting, I didn't know how to handle this, or what to do with this kind of love or happiness. I'd never felt like this before. I had no idea what to expect or what happened next.

What a beautiful mystery you are to me.

30 SOUL SPARK

August. Sunday. Chester. Alejandro's.

After such a beautiful night, I didn't want to leave, but Alejandro needed to touch base with his dad and best friend, Jason, now he was back, and I knew we would be seeing a lot of each other over the coming months.

"I'd like you to meet my dad and Jason sometime, Leila. I think it's important the people I care about meet. They're all I have in the world."

"I'd love to. Tell me more about them."

"Dad has a new partner, Elizabeth. She's sweet and bubbly, a very open person with a lot of warmth, which my dad needs because he's quite emotionally closed as a person. He always has been. He struggles to emotionally open up, rarely talking about my mother, which saddens me. Occasionally, when he's drunk, he will take a trip down memory lane with me, but not often."

"I've been friends with Jason since I started high school here. He got me through a really hard time. I was lost and depressed after Mum died. Jason had lost his grandmother, who he was close to and missed. It was a difficult time for us both, so we bonded, hanging out all the time. He's a fireman, into weights. He's a huge guy. Ginger with pale face and freckles; the opposite of me."

I like it when you open and let me in.

"Jason has always been a heroic guy, going way back. Together, we saved the underdog wherever we went. We both reached full height at the age of 15. Jason, six feet, four inches, so you can imagine how we carried a lot of clout on the school playground. Whenever we saw anyone being picked on, we intervened. People knew to back off as soon as we walked over. They would scurry away. It wasn't always easy, though. We took some things to the streets. I won't go into that. If they wouldn't stop bullying, they deserved what happened next. We didn't allow it, especially if a girl was being picked on. We had a reputation for being fearless. Got pasted a couple of times, but we always got back up and were given respect for it. Jason has a tough chin. Other than that, we kept to ourselves. Nobody really knew anything about us. That's the way we liked it. A little mystery seemed to help our street cred. More like brothers than friends, really."

"I love how you see him as a brother. I'm happy you had someone close looking out for you after you lost your mum. It must have been hard, moving to a different country on top of everything you'd been through. You were so isolated in Spain. I think it's great when guys bond and form close friendships. So many just have acquaintances or sports related friends. Does he have a partner?"

I wondered if we would all get along and become close eventually.

"Yes, he's been with the same woman for about four years now, engaged for one. Cara. She's Irish. You'll like her, she's a little shy at first, but sweet and compassionate. She's a teaching assistant for children with special needs. They're a great match, they both care about people. She can't have kids, sadly, but she doesn't let it get her down. She channels her attention to the children she works with. It's a very rewarding job for her. From what Jason's said, the kids adore her."

"It's sad they can't have kids, but lovely she's found a way to have a close link with children regardless. Have they already booked somewhere to get married or are they having a leisurely engagement?"

"They've booked something for next year, but they're being secretive about it. All I know is there's a secret smile and a glint in their eyes whenever they look at each other and mention it. They're not telling anybody anything. It's all classified. They could tell you, but then they'd have to shoot you."

We both laughed.

I like this chatty, fun side to you, Alejandro.
Your personality has such versatility.

"Should be interesting. I look forward to meeting them. Does he know you have a steady girlfriend now?" I asked, blushing.

This was the first time I referred to myself as his girlfriend. I was pretty sure a declaration of love secured that.

"Mmm, my girlfriend, now that does have a beautiful ring to it. Thinking of you being *mine* is so sexy."

I smiled, knowing there's nothing I'd rather be, or anyone else I'd rather be with.

My phone beeped twice from inside my bag. As I pulled it out, the banner said "Ellie." I opened it, reading the text.

"Ooh, Ellie has offered to cook for us tonight if you'd like to come and meet Hayden? Would you have time after you visit your dad and Jason?"

After looking at his watch, he said, "Yes, it's only 9:30. That gives me plenty of time. It will only be a coffee with Jason anyway. We can organise a proper get-together another time and no doubt, now I'm back, he'll start calling round to work out in the gym with me. We do that a lot."

"You have a gym?"

"I do. I also have a pool and jacuzzi. You're welcome to use any of them at any time. Even if I'm not in. I'll contact Janet for you, and she will let you in."

"Wow, your own pool. Now that's cool. That's very thoughtful of you, Alejandro, thank you. I'd rather do both with you, though. I have a real thing for water."

I would love to swim with you so much.

"Then perhaps we can start doing that during the week or on weekends. I'm flexible. I'd love to workout with you, go for a swim, sauna, and a jacuzzi," he added.

"The weekends would probably be better, but Tuesday night after I've seen family I could do, too. Ellie and I normally cook for each other on Mondays and Wednesdays, so I wouldn't want a workout after a meal. Ellie has been spending a lot of time with Hayden recently, though, so sometimes I'm free those nights, too. Thursdays are reserved for salsa, always. Will you be teaching again?"

"Of course. I spoke to Charlie, who organises it. He wants me to take the Thursday night class still. I love teaching. I love developing a person's natural passion for salsa and giving them confidence at it," he said. "I also love dancing with you. You can be my beautiful assistant."

"That sounds like fun to me! Besides, every time I dance with you, I get aroused," I said, playfully biting my lip.

"Then that would make perfect foreplay for a weekend together then, Miss Quinn," he said, grinning. "We can work out in the gym or go for a run outside on a Saturday or Sunday. We'd be going into Monday positively every week then."

"I'd love us to run together, Mr. Fernandez. I can think of nothing lovelier than spending time together as a couple."

"I'd love to get to know Ellie and Hayden, too. She's important to you, in the same way Jason is to me. I think it's nice to include each other in our friendship circles. Besides, I want to spend as much time with you as possible. I've missed you so much."

"I know, me too."

"Ellie is asking what time suits us. What should I say?"

"Seven p.m.?" he suggested. "I don't want to keep you up too late, given you have work first thing in the morning. Plus, I want to crack on with these last two songs this week. I can't wait for him to release the album."

"When will the album be ready for release?" I said, starting to text back.

"In the new year."

"That will be really exciting for you both. Is there anything you don't like or can't eat by the way?"

"No, my stomach is made of cast iron after having been raised on concoctions of all sorts."

I laughed.

"I can imagine. I'll add you're fine with all foods, as that will be her next question. She loves it when I pre-empt her."

"Okay, I'll drop you off at yours, then go see Jason first for a good catch up, then I can go and spend the afternoon with my dad and Elizabeth. I'll have an early night tomorrow night to catch up on sleep. I'm feeling a little jetlagged still."

As he drove me home, I held onto his thigh. I was almost scared to let him go in case he left again. It might take a while to lose that feeling. By the time I was getting out to leave, I felt a little emotional, which was stupid because I was seeing him later. But I couldn't help it.

"Have fun with Jason and your dad," I said, kissing him softly goodbye.

"Will do. Thank you. I loved last night. I'll see you later," he said, blowing a kiss up the drive as I stood at the door to wave.

Not only did I feel connected to Alejandro, now I got to fall in love with him in person, face to face. Words just wanted to spill from me:

"When a person
embraces your soul+
not your body.
It feels different.
The connection
runs much deeper..."

"The more deeply
you connect
with a woman's mind,
the stronger
your ability to
arouse her will be..."

"She loves the way
you want to learn her+
reach into her soul,
to understand her fully..."

"It's in the way
he senses her needs,
the way he
connects with her desire
as it burns+
visibly heaves
inside her chest
when he's near;
he loves the way
he induces her rapture…"
"Still time,
before you kiss me.
Undress me,
now slowly tease me.
Taste my words;
do you really see me?
Blow my mind,
now softly free me.
Tend my soul,
until you heal me.
Now love me,
until you can feel me…"
"The soft sensual slide,
eyes closed,
lost inside
the depth of a kiss,
lips moulding
in perfect harmony,
tender skin that erupts
like fireworks
under skilled hands+
the ache that
detonates my mind,
body+soul.
Set me on fire…"
"A connection
where souls caress+
you feel alive with magic;
where romantic eroticism
sustains a perpetual state
of falling in love…"
I loved last night so much.
And you.

The fact I feel so ecstatically happy is something I want to save and preserve through poetry today, to mark Alejandro coming back.
Poetry is how I hold onto my most beautiful moments, like an emotional diary.

31 DINNER

August. Sunday. Liverpool. Home.

Hayden came to our house a little earlier to help Ellie prepare for dinner. I heard him chatting to her in the kitchen as I was getting ready. I went downstairs at 10 to seven, knowing how punctual Alejandro always was.

"Hi, Leila," Hayden said, as I walked in.

"Hi, Hayden. What have you guys been busy preparing? The kitchen smells delicious."

"Creamy garlic parmesan chicken. You're impressed already, I can tell," Hayden said.

He had a charm about him, beautiful smiley eyes, and a very playful disposition.

At five minutes to seven, the doorbell rang. I rushed to answer, and I could hear the guys muttering and giggling at my enthusiastic sprint.

"Hey, beautiful," he smiled, as I opened the door.

I instantly beamed, throwing my arms around his neck.

"Hi lover."

"Mmm, I like that greeting."

He pulled out a beautiful bouquet of flowers from behind his back, kissing my cheek on both sides.

"Aww, you didn't have to do that."

"Just say thank you when someone pays you a compliment. You deserve beautiful things."

My spirit felt lighter the second he walked in. I felt almost giddy in his company. I wondered how long the feeling would last.

"Thank you," I said, smiling. "Come in. Let me introduce you."

I took his jacket.

"Did you drive?"

"No, George dropped me off."

"Oh great, that means you can have a drink, too. I've got meetings first thing, but it will be nice to have a couple."

As we walked into the kitchen, I introduced the guys.

"Hayden, this is Alejandro. You two can finally meet."

I took the flowers over to the sink, reaching for a vase to fill with water and arrange them in.

Hayden extended his hand first. "Nice to meet you, bro, I've heard a lot about you, and I mean a lot," he laughed.

Clearly Ellie had been keeping him up to date with what was going on.

"Nice to meet you too, bud. I believe you're in tech?" Alejandro asked, opening a line of conversation to break the ice.

"I'm an IT security specialist. I work on safety systems and web-based code technology platforms I'm a contractor. I like to move around," he said, grabbing Ellie's waist as she walked past.

"Would you like some wine?" Ellie asked Alejandro, giggling and moving out of Hayden's hold.

"Yes, please."

"White or red?" Ellie clarified.

"What is the meal?" Alejandro asked.

"Creamy garlic parmesan chicken."

"Sounds gorgeous. In that case, I'll have white, please."

"Hayden, would you do the honours and pour us a drink?" Ellie asked.

"Sure, where are the glasses?"

"Behind you in that overhead cupboard."

As he pulled out glasses, he held them up to the light briefly, going over to get paper towels, wiping each around the top. He grabbed a bottle of chilled white out of the fridge, pouring each of us a glass, handing them out one by one.

"Cheers, bud," Alejandro said, receiving his.

"No problem."

"So, you've been on the road, recording with some Canadian from what I can gather?" Hayden said.

"Yes, but you'll have to keep it to yourself. I'm very selective about who knows, so no further than this room, please. He's called Brandon Trent. Have you heard of him?" Alejandro asked.

I was surprised that Ellie hadn't asked me if it was okay to tell Hayden. I know they're close, but it was a little presumptuous.

"I have. I listen to a lot of music, especially in the gym. I'm not a fan of silence. He's not my thing, if I'm being honest, but I believe it's potentially a big deal for you, and a lot of people love him."

"Yes, it could be huge. He's at the point where he's breaking out," Alejandro replied, perching on one of our high stools. "To be chosen to write exclusively for an artist on an album is one of the greatest honours. It was a privilege to get to know how his mind works, what he wanted me to write about, experiences and emotions he wanted me to capture, etcetera. We had some great collaborative moments. He's an intelligent guy."

"Ellie said you have been successful and have a huge house," Hayden said, while Ellie shot him a slightly embarrassed look.

"I had the right people believe in my work at the right times. All I wanted to do was play and write. I didn't go out of my way to find this career path or life, it pretty much found me," he explained.

"Well, you've certainly landed on your feet, lucky bastard," Hayden said, offering a toast with his wine glass.

"I'm not sure I'd call it luck, the first song that became a hit for me was one I wrote about my mum dying," he replied sarcastically, with just a tiny indication Hayden's comment had grated at him.

"Can someone set the table for me please? Dinner will be ready in less than 10 minutes," Ellie requested, stirring a simmering pot of pasta, and starting to get the plates out for us.

"The cutlery is in that drawer over there," she motioned with her hand.

Alejandro jumped up, "I'll set it."

"Yes, please," Ellie added. "And while you're there, can you put the flowers on the table for me too, please?" I said, pointing at the vase. They looked so vibrant.

"Spoiling me with another beautiful bunch," I said, smiling appreciatively.

"This is the first arrangement I've bought you," he said as he picked up the vase, a puzzled expression on his face.

"You bought me that beautiful bunch the other day, with lilies in," I said, bemused.

"Nope, I'd remember if I had. Didn't they come with a card?"

"No, there was no card. We assumed it was from one of you guys," I said, looking at both Hayden and Alejandro in turn.

"They weren't from me, I'm not the slightest bit romantic," Hayden said, shrugging his shoulders.

"Well, who the hell were they from then?" Ellie said, looking at me, puzzled.

"I have no idea," I replied, feeling a little creeped out suddenly.

"Maybe they were from your dad," Alejandro added.

"I'll check with him next time I speak to him, but honestly, that's not the type of thing he would normally do through the post. I've been trying to get him to be more romantic with mum for years, to no avail."

Something didn't feel right. Alejandro picked up on it, too, or was left with the same nagging doubt, because he briefly kissed me on the cheek as he carried the cutlery and flowers to the table.

The timer went off on the stove and Ellie turned it off.

"Can you grab a colander for the pasta please, Hayden? It's in that large cupboard below the sink."

As he opened the cupboard, he pulled out the silver colander, placing it in the sink, ready for Ellie to pour the pasta into.

"Hey, look at you two, you're quite the duo in the kitchen, aren't you?"

"Oh, I'm no chef, Ellie is much better. I just make an excellent assistant," Hayden volunteered.

It raised a laugh from all of us.

"We haven't even had a chance to cook together yet, have we?" Alejandro said, directing his question to me.

"We've hardly had a chance to do anything together yet, Alejandro," I said.

I remembered last night in an instant however, looking down, a partial smile forming involuntarily on my mouth. It was only brief, but when I looked up, he was smiling at me. He knew, of course. Sexy mind reader.

How do you do that?

"You will," Ellie jumped in. "You'll have loads of time together to do whatever you want now. Thank you, Alejandro, for coming back early, maybe now she will stop moping around and pining for you like a lost puppy."

She gave me a wicked grin, sticking her tongue out at me playfully.

"Oh, thanks a lot missy," I retorted playfully, slightly embarrassed she'd outed my sappiness.

"I was exactly the same," Alejandro said back to Ellie, winking at me.

I really liked the playful side of Alejandro. He had such contrasts within his nature. He could go from such great depths to having a complete laugh and being silly with me. I loved both ends of the spectrum. I loved him in his entirety.

I touched my lower lip, dragging my thumb along it slowly for the briefest of seconds, thinking of him kissing me. He clocked that, too. I'm not sure if he is highly observant, or if it's because he was struggling to keep his eyes off me.

"So, she's already under your skin then, Alejandro?" Ellie responded.

"Well and truly. It feels a lot like love," he volunteered.

Did he just declare in front of them both he was in love with me?
I blushed immediately, going bright red.

"Oh wow, I knew you guys were close, but I didn't realise you were that close. I'm so delighted for you," she said warmly, shooting me one of those looks as if to say, *oh dear Lord, that's adorable.*

Alejandro was incredibly proud of me, and I'd never felt that so strongly from anyone before. Someone who wanted to show me off and be vocal about how he felt for me, even in front of other people. I'd been used to people who were closed off emotionally in public. I had no idea what to say.

Hayden didn't know how to respond either, saying nothing, choosing to finish dishing up pasta onto each of the four plates, before moving out of Ellie's way, touching her hip as he did.

"Okay, guys," Ellie said, as she carried two plates over to the table. Alejandro and I sat next to each other on one side of the six-seater table, and Ellie brought over the final two meals to us and then sat opposite. The guys were sitting opposite each other.

"This looks delicious Ellie, Hayden. Thank you so much for your hospitality," Alejandro said, as he raised his glass and said, "Cheers."

"Cheers," Ellie said, tipping her glass to clink back as Hayden and I joined in also.

Finally, she could sit down, relax, and join us now. It was often stressful prepping for everyone.

"Beautiful," Alejandro said simply after a taste. "So, have you always been local Hayden? Have you got family here?"

"I've always lived in Liverpool, yes. My father walked out on my mother when I was a teenager. He wasn't a nice man. I have no good memories of him at all. No siblings," Hayden added.

"Have you seen your dad since he left?" I asked.

"No. It is what it is. Him leaving affected us both, in different ways. He was a sergeant in the army and a very strict man. It was his way or the highway and there was a lot of hurt there. Mum gets very frustrated over the way her life has panned out." he detailed.

"Did she marry again?"

"She tried other relationships, but none of them were healthy. I think she's given up now, to be honest. She became bitter over the years, started to despise all men. I understand, though, she's had a hard time with them," Hayden explained.

"Do you think she'll ever move on and be happy again?"

"I don't think she will. She attracts the wrong sorts of men. They weren't nice to her, at all. She's had it rough. And honestly, I think she always wanted a daughter who would be her best friend, so I'm a disappointment to her."

"Has she ever said that to you?"

"Yes. It's fine, I'm used to it now. She struggles, because I look a lot like my dad and it's hard for her to separate us in her mind sometimes."

I wasn't getting a good impression of either of his parents from him. I was sympathetic.

"That's sad," I said. "All children are a gift."

There was an awkward pause in conversation.

"So, tell me about your work, Ellie," said Alejandro.

He felt the dip in conversation, jumping in at the right time.

"Being a business analyst doesn't bear much in the way of excitement; it's the people I like. The university is an interesting place to work. It's a positive place and environment. All about students and investing in youth. I love it. It's nowhere near as exciting as song writing or what Leila does, though," Ellie added. "How is the freak case going, Leila?"

"I'm sufficiently freaked out, to say the least, which I assume is normal for my first murder case. This man is twisted as hell. Reading case files, trying to understand his psyche, it's just horrible. It's made me more determined, made me realise what I do is important. I open a channel to the public and community, which helps the police do their work."

"Are you allowed to discuss the details?" Hayden asked.

"Some of the case information is confidential, but I can share facts that have been shared with the public. I have an editing deadline I need to hit, with a big article being released the week after next which contains the story so far. I need to make sure it gets submitted on time. It might be a tough week," I said, quickly shovelling in a mouthful.

My plate was very nearly empty, as was everybody else's. Alejandro had already finished. Being the healthy workout guy and wolf that he is, his appetite is voracious.

"So, is it one murder you're reporting on?" Hayden asked.

"No, he's classed as a serial killer now, his last victim made it number four. By definition, a serial killer is someone who commits three or more murders. He's known as The Choker because he leaves a choker necklace around his victims' neck. Also, because all the girls were killed by asphyxiation. He leaves a white rose on their chest, too. It's like a twisted and sick form of romance to him," I said.

Looking over at the first bunch of flowers, I was unsettled suddenly. I realized they were pink lilies and white roses. Alejandro noticed the change in my demeanour, frowning. He must have had the same thought.

"From everything I've read and discussed, he stalks them first, romances them, sends them gifts. They're often very specific gifts, but what is perplexing is nobody understands how he knows what they like, because they're often bespoke, tailored gifts just for the woman he's obsessed with. He focuses very specifically on one victim at a time, analysing everything about them before eventually murdering them," I said, chills forming up and down my body as I spoke.

"The whole thing gives me the creeps," Ellie replied. "He makes my skin crawl."

"There must be some evidence he leaves behind, surely?" Hayden stated, looking puzzled.

"No evidence whatsoever. No hair. No semen. No fingerprints. Everything wiped down and completely clear. The police have no leads whatsoever. Why the romance, though? Why make them think they're special before he kills them? How twisted is that?" I added.

"That's the disturbing part, isn't it? It's bound to affect you, working on a case like this," Alejandro said, looking concerned.

"The details get to me, especially the rapes and strangulation. He tortures them for hours at the end, like his final climax, getting longer with each victim as he gets braver with what he does to them. I find it hard to switch off after I've discussed or read information like that. This week might be tough because I have to climb into his mind to write a really good article," I fretted.

"I'll be here whenever you need this week, every night if you want, okay?" Alejandro added thoughtfully.

"Thanks, babe," I said, smiling.

"Is there any more news from the police on your random garden watcher that night?" Hayden asked Ellie.

"No, the police searched briefly through local CCTV, but couldn't find anything that could lead to a possible arrest. They said to stay vigilant," Ellic stated.

"You can stay at mine whenever you want," Hayden added.

"Thank you. Leila and I are happy if we know you boys are on dial to protect us anytime we need your help. That gives us a lot of security," Ellie smiled at Hayden.

He smiled back at her, putting his arm around her.

"I've got your back," he said.

I loved them together. He was so caring with her, in the same way Alejandro was with me. Protective and strong.

"We're lucky girls, Ellie."

"We are," she retorted.

"That was absolutely delicious, Ellie and Hayden. Thank you for cooking tonight."

I stood up to clear the plates away.

Ellie smiled. "You're very welcome, I couldn't wait for everyone to meet."

"Shall we go into the lounge to have an aperitif?" Ellie asked.

"I'm going to switch to tea. Monday morning is looming, and I can't have a big head for this week. I've got far too much to do," I said.

"I'm going to do the same, Leila," said Ellie, going over to turn the kettle on.

"It's so much harder to think with a hangover. You guys go through to the lounge, and we'll follow you in."

"Looks like it's just you and me drinking then, bud," Alejandro said.

"There are spirits in the central drinks' cabinet. Tumblers too. If you need ice, let me know."

"Okay, thanks," Hayden said.

The boys walked into the next room as we got coffee ready in the kitchen.

"They seem to be getting on well. I'm so glad. I've been hoping we could do the odd double date together," I said, grabbing the mugs out of the cupboard.

"That would be lovely. It's always nice when we get out of the house and go somewhere, we can get dressed up, too," Ellie added.

"Alejandro is amazing. He's so gorgeous, not just in looks but personality, too, and he's clearly gaga over you and not afraid of anyone knowing it. I'm absolutely thrilled for you."

"You and Hayden make quite the team, too, Ellie."

"For the first time ever, we're both happy with someone."

"I know, it's amazing."

I couldn't get my head around it.

We carried our tea and coffee into the lounge and found the boys chatting away, both sitting with a tumbler in their hands and a neat whiskey.

"What are you boys chatting about?" Ellie asked.

"Where we've travelled abroad and some of the places we've visited," Alejandro said.

"Alejandro is a lot more well-travelled than I am," Hayden added.

"Oh yeah, where was your favourite destination?" Ellie asked.

"Seychelles, without a doubt. I've never seen anywhere more beautiful in my life. The beaches were beyond description, even for a poet," he said, winking at me.

"Is that a challenge, Alejandro?" I asked.

"Would you like the chance to try sometime?"

I couldn't tell if he was joking or not.

"Yeah, right."

"I never say anything I don't mean, Leila. We can go. I'll take you and show you why it blew me away."

My jaw nearly dropped to the floor.

"I'd love to travel with you, Alejandro, anywhere actually, but there, wow, I'd love that so much,"

I felt a little overwhelmed.

"So, would you like to go to some European destinations on smaller weekend trips, too?" he asked me.

"Hell yes. There are so many places I've never been. I've explored minimally in France. I've never been to Italy, and I've only been to a couple of places in Spain. I've never been to Sweden or Holland. Come to think of it, I've hardly travelled at all, really. There's a whole world out there I don't know about," I added reflectively, wondering what the hell I'd been doing with my life.

"Then I'd love to show you."

We carried on chatting for ages about the adventures each of us had been on, but Hayden was right, Alejandro was far better travelled than any of us. Other than some venturing with his best friend Jason, he'd sadly done a lot of it alone. He seemed happy about it, though, perfectly independent, and quite a solitary man in his existence. I knew he was happy in his own space, but I still thought he deserved someone who wanted to be with him to do all these things.

Let that person be me.

I started yawning at about 11:10 p.m. At 11:30 I said, "I think it's time I hit the sack."

"I concur," Ellie said.

"We'll leave you guys to drink and chat. Help yourselves to water before you come upstairs, and you know where the bathroom is. There is a new pack of toothbrushes there, so help yourselves to them, too. Thank you for a lovely evening," I said, as I walked over to kiss Alejandro's forehead and say goodnight.

"I'll try not to disturb you when I come up," he said softly to me.

"Okay, thanks babe," I replied.

"Goodnight, Leila," Hayden said.

Ellie kissed Hayden, saying "goodnight" to the room at large as she left.

"Goodnight, Ellie," Alejandro called out.

As we went up the stairs Ellie said, "I wonder how long they'll take?"

"As long as it takes for boys to bond with a short in their hands," I replied, smiling at her.

"Goodnight, sweetie," she said at the top of the stairs.

"Goodnight, babe," I replied.
Who the hell were those flowers from?

32 SENSUAL

September. Saturday. Liverpool. Home.

The weather was wet through August, and September looked like it would follow the same pattern. Burnt orange, reds, and yellows were all around and everywhere I drove looked like a painting.

After a hard week trying to make my editing deadline, Friday night necessitated a random pass out, where I just crashed on Alejandro's lap at my house at 10 p.m., while he was stroking my hair.

What a party animal.

I awoke to the sound of a clinking tray, then saw Alejandro carrying one into the room.

On it were croissants and two glasses of fresh orange juice, with a small pot of butter and jam, and two cups, along with a pot of tea, sugar bowl, and a small porcelain jug of milk.

"Morning, baby," he ushered with a smile, as I stretched and then sat up in bed.

"Morning. How lovely of you to wake me with such a beautiful surprise," I muttered, yawning.

"It's been a hard week for you with late nights, I wanted to treat you."

"Thank you. It was sweet of you to stroke my hair until I fell asleep. I don't think anyone has ever done that for me before," softly caressing his arm and hand with my palm.

"If you're still hungry, we can go out for lunch later."

"As much as I'd love to, I need to go out today. I'd completely forgotten until he texted last night, but I promised my Portuguese friend, Carlos, I'd visit a local gallery. He has some artwork in a display at the docks. I want to show up to support him."

"Oh. I hoped we'd be spending the day and night together."

"You're welcome to come, too," I said quickly. "I like to be reliable for my friends and follow through on my promises, that's all."

"I know, reliability is one of your greatest assets and something I admire deeply about you. I'd love to come. If we can spend the whole night together, too. I need to get close to you," a look of urgency on his face.

"You know I don't just want to spend the night with you, I need to. We've barely started our journey together. I need more of you."

I tugged softly at the hair on the back of his head, my body pulsing at the thought.

"That's exactly what I wanted to hear. So, how do you know Carlos?"

"We know each other through earlier classes of salsa, but he hasn't been for a while, he's too busy sketching and painting all the time now. Carlos is a fantastic artist. I love his work. He's lucky. He makes a good living from his artwork, not many do."

"Do I need to worry about him being another handsome international man who might sweep you off your feet?"

I wasn't sure if he was joking or not.

"No. He's a wonderful friend, but if I'm with you, Alejandro, I'm with you. You have my full focus. Do you understand?" I added quickly to reassure him.

"That's good to know. I'm dedicated and very loyal. You have my full attention. I would never even flirt with another woman, because I wouldn't want anyone else to think I was interested in them. I don't think it's right to give out false impressions, as I think it detracts from you. I would want them to know unequivocally you were the only one I was interested in."

"That's like music to my ears. You couldn't have said anything more perfect."

"I wasn't questioning you. I'm trying to keep you safe. It's important I know you're mine and only mine, and you know I'm yours and only yours. I'm scared of losing you, Leila. I'm falling so deeply in love with you."

My heart melted instantly, somewhere between the fragility he was showing and those as last words echoing through my mind.

I'm falling so deeply in love with you.

"Then you should know I'm falling deeper, too. Please don't worry about my commitment to you. You have nothing to feel insecure about. You're the one that I want, just you and no one else. Do you understand?"

"I needed to hear it; I think. We've never said it before, not clearly like that. It's important to know, as I want you to share all of yourself with me, and you need to feel safe enough to do that." He said, embracing me, kissing my forehead.

"You have a darker side to the way you say things sometimes, in your words, the things you say. I hope one day you will let me in fully and show me the parts of you that you hide. I want to know and understand *all* of you. I don't want you to hide anything."

"There are things in my past that hurt me, changed me, shaped me, as a young man, as an adolescent and adult. I will open up about them when I'm ready," he said.

I sensed pain.

"There are dark things in my past, but there are also things in my present, secret fantasies, and desires I've never explored. I'd like to share them with you, but I'm worried about how you would react, and I'm scared of losing you."

"Alejandro, there is nothing you could tell me about you that would put me off, and there's nothing I wouldn't do for you. I've always been all or nothing. I want all of you," I tried to reassure him. I didn't take love lightly and I meant it with full sincerity. "Please, tell me."

"Okay, but please keep an open mind. There is no obligation, just a fascination I can't seem to let go. My fantasies are deep and dark and would involve you giving me complete control of your mind. You have a submissive nature, but you don't understand yet because you're in deep conflict about relinquishing control. I see it in you because of the dominant side to me."

This wasn't anything I expected him to say.

"What do you mean by submissive and dominant, I don't understand?" I asked, curious and slightly nervous where we were headed with the conversation. I wasn't sure if this was something that would strengthen or destroy our relationship.

"I would class myself as a 'sensual dominant.' Pleasure oriented. As a couple, we would be two opposing sides of a powerful relationship, based entirely on trust. It's a very special type of relationship that goes much deeper. It allows us to become a lot closer in our partnership, by freeing us both of desires we have buried," he explained.

"I'm not aware of burying any secret desires, though," I said, confused.

"I know you're not, but because of who I am, I see them, or the potential within you. The way you look at things, the way you feel things. I have a sense of what you will enjoy. But you would have to let me in first. Our communication needs to be completely open for this type of relationship to work. You need to trust me, fully, and let me train you, so I can free your mind completely. I promise you that your mind will feel vacant of all the noise and chaos you currently carry around."

Part of me felt shocked, and another part of me felt deeply curious about what he was saying.

Is it possible to still a mind as chaotic as mine?

What would that mean for our relationship?
I can't jeopardise what we have.

"Have you trained anyone before, Alejandro?" I asked nervously, imagining him having special trust relationships with other partners and feeling jealousy creep in at the thought.

"Never. I was waiting for someone I love. That was so important to me as part of my fantasy. It's a very special and intimate level of relationship I wanted to wait for. It's not something I could do with someone I didn't love. This connection we have, it's so special. You can feel the pull between us, can't you?"

Yes, it's powerful and strong.

"The pull I feel toward you is as intense as thunder, and I feel it deeply and constantly, sometimes on a low rumble and sometimes with a deep echo and ache that rumbles with power inside me. I haven't been able to stop thinking about you since I met you. You are playing on constant loop in my mind. I feel like I can't breathe sometimes, like I'm aroused just at the thought of being near you. My mind is constantly chaotic. Thoughts whir around my head for hours on end and it never seems to settle. Sometimes it feels so loud."

"The feelings you describe, the obsession you have for me is the same I have for you. You and I are two halves of the same puzzle. The chaos you mention in your mind. I know how to make that stop, baby. You won't know and understand your true self until I show you, free you, and take you into what is often referred to as subspace," he offered gently.

"What is that?"

My curiosity was piqued at the notion there was a way to still my thoughts.

"It's a way of giving you everything your mind and body needs until your mind is still and completely vacant, through my own, very unique version of BDSM."

He looked a little apprehensive as he said it.

"I thought BDSM was a kink about people being tortured and humiliated? Why would you want to hurt me?"

I felt upset at the thought.

"It's nothing like that, not for me, anyway. That's not what I want for us. It must be what you are comfortable with, what you *want* to do. There's no forcing or pushing further than you yourself volunteer to go, but over time, I suspect you will want your boundaries taken a little further. I love you and want to protect you, so let me make it clear so you have no apprehension about it. It's about sharing a deeper intimacy and connection than a normal relationship, about a bond which connects and expresses our love through acts of complete trust.

There are different levels to BDSM. I'm only interested in the sensual side of it, the side of it that's about pleasure and connecting us to a deeper level. Which is why I refer to my adapted version RSD – Restraint and Sensual Domination. It's like an invisible tether, a sensual dominant and submissive relationship is like a special commitment to each other," he said.

I fully believed him and was relaxing more at how he described it, in a gently reassuring way.

"How do you know so much about it?"

I wanted to understand how he had never experienced it before yet wanted it so badly.

"I've known for a few years who I was. I felt myself darken as I went further into myself in my teens, for obvious reasons. When I heard about the d/s dynamic as a late teen, I had a natural curiosity toward it. I researched it to try and understand what I was experiencing. BDSM goes way too far for me, though. Some dominants want none of the connection, only wanting to express sexual kinks. I felt for the men and women, but particularly the women, who craved the dark abusive side of BDSM. I could never be alright with anything abusive. The people I related to and aligned with were the couples who had the strongest connections, those who were deeply in love. It enhanced their relationship, deepening their connection and emotions for each other. I need that, with all of me. That's why I relate more to being a 'Sensual Dominant' and realised RSD fits how I want to pleasure you far more accurately. I've known what I wanted for years, but you're the first person I've felt that pull with," he explained.

"You are the woman I love. I want to own all of you, to love and protect you, with all of me." He spoke with such conviction. "It's a consensual relationship. A lifestyle choice. I want the freedom to explore it with you. I need you to understand my reasons fully, and not feel threatened by this, to understand it is a shared journey. Your consent is the most vital part."

My senses were relaxing. Alejandro made it sound beautiful. Yet as he was talking, I could feel the dark wolf in him, too, with words like *own*. I found it sexy and arousing, while it simultaneously messed with my need to be independent and stay in control, which I was still fighting against mentally. Pretty sure it was my Catholic upbringing struggling with what he was suggesting. There was an underlying association that sexual thoughts are wrong. It was hard to dismiss it all, though I knew the rest of the Bible preached love. That was exactly what we hoped to express for one another. I think that countered the sin part, but I was having trouble convincing my mind.

Alejandro's intelligent explanation gave me a clearer picture of what he wanted without making me feel threatened in any way. I felt him and what his needs were. I understood it wasn't coming from a negative place, only a place of love. So how could that be wrong? How could that be a sin? Who invented all these judgments in the first place? And why do I have to adhere to them? I realised I didn't have to think or believe anything that created a negative association for me. Maybe it was time I challenged some of the thought processes and beliefs that no longer worked for me.

Alejandro wanted to feel loved, to strengthen our bond together, to get closer. He also wanted the security of me giving myself to him entirely; to know I was the surest thing in his life, and he could count on loving me and me loving him.

I got it. My feelings were building, hearing him talk about wanting to love me this way. I still didn't understand the practicalities of what he specifically wanted me to do, however.

"What would it involve? What do you mean by you wanting me to give up control?"

"You'd allow me to explore your mind, to give me complete trust, to explore our deepest darkest fantasies, setting them free, one by one, until you no longer yearn for anything. Because you are complete. Freeing your mind, soul, and body is my ultimate aphrodisiac in this dynamic."

I still didn't understand.

"But what would you want me to do?"

"Trust me with your sensuality, with the expression of your sexuality with me. Allow me to guide you into new experiences where you allow me to pleasure you in particular ways, where you have no control," he explained.

"No control whatsoever?" I panicked.

"Control is an illusion, but it is also a gift. I'd want you to let it go, so I can explore your mind and find what arouses you most. I want you to trust me deeper than anyone before. The key to subspace is this: I give you the freedom of not having any choices to make, no worries or concerns, or a need to think even. I want you to feel. I want you to let me love you in a way that will steal your every breath, so you can breathe freely finally, within your full potential. I will be thorough, enduring, diligent, attentive, and deeply loyal. I don't want you to focus on the how, I want you to focus on the why of it all. The answer is freedom, the answer is love."

My heart could have burst, passion surging through me for the way he wanted to commit to, explore, and love me.

"How long do I have to decide?"

"Take as long as you want and just tell me you're ready should you wish to take this journey with me," he said.

If I want! There's no pressure to do it, which was good. I needed some time to consider it.

Alejandro had a way of making me want him, but this... the way he described it, how he wanted to complete and fulfil me to such depths of love that my breath would be stolen, was tantric. Energy surged through my body at thoughts of connecting deeper. I was also nervous, wondering what he would do to me. Such deep conflict between the two.

"Hold me?" I asked, feeling vulnerable in my confusion.

He saw and felt it, pulling me close to his chest, wrapping his arms around me tightly. My heart was overactive. I was often soothed by his presence but being in his arms tonight was particularly beautiful.

"Shall we go?"

"That'd be great. Bring some extra clothes to my house later for the weekends we spend together. You'll need workout gear and swimwear, as well as casual clothes and nightwear," he suggested.

"I'll bring some over then," my mind spiralled as it drifted into what felt like a deepening abyss.

Will I get lost in it, though?

We had a lovely, cultural afternoon at my friend's exhibition, and both agreed the talent on display was awesome. Carlos and Alejandro got on well. There was no jealousy at all. Once we'd communicated clearly where we stood with each other, and he saw me with Carlos, he realised he didn't have anything to fear. I wasn't like that.

If I'm yours, I'm all yours.
All of me.

33 LISTENING

10:29 a.m.
Did you like the flowers, my angel? You both know about the white roses. Have you pieced it together? Do you know a serial killer is watching you? It's being close to you without you knowing that thrills me, the deception of it all.

As I build it up, I experience the journey with you. It's our very special passage together and you are my current everything. I will give you all of me. I promise. It's like I'm marrying you. I'll be faithful to just you, the whole time, until death do you part. You will have all my time, every single second.

Obsession is required. I need to know everything inside that beautiful mind of yours. What makes you tick. What you love. What you've done in your life. What scares you. All your dirty little secrets and fantasies.

It must be subtle, until it's not. It's the build-up I adore. It's the duality of smiling at you and you not knowing I'm going to kill you.

You've never met anyone like me. And you'll never have the chance again. But... I will adore loving you first. You should feel special. In the end, it's all about my last day with you. But I refuse to rush either phase.

So, lay back and enjoy the ride.
I'm taking you on the scenic route, my angel.
What shall I send you next?
Tell me what you like.

34 POOL

October. Saturday. Liverpool. Home.

When we returned, I packed a few clothes, swimwear, and workout gear, along with toiletries, I could take to Alejandro's. Our relationship felt more like a normal couple now, after yearning for him for months.

I was ready tonight, to connect with him again. The fire that had grown inside me was constantly ready to burst with the slightest brush; a permanent wretched ache only he could cure.

He had such a beautifully intelligent, deep, and intriguing mind. I'd not been bored for a second since I met him, in any of our conversations. He brought me to life. He was stimulating, interesting, exciting, and unique. He asked so many questions, wanting to know all of me, even the parts nobody had asked about, or wanted to get to know, before.

There was an undercurrent in all our conversations, dark passion sitting between us. Our connection was strong now, having been fortified by experiences we shared. He'd held me through deep trauma, been my strength when I had none, could stoke my deepest passion, or provide calm to my chaos.

My mind hadn't been touched in this way before. He was learning all the ways he could protect and love me.

I never stood a chance with you.
How could I not have fallen madly in love?

Alejandro pressed the button, the gates opening to his beautiful house, and my heart started to race. It was early evening, the light just starting to dim as nightfall whispered in anticipative tingles on my body.

There was a beautiful tinge to the sky, as the setting sun blushed, willing to fall into a deep velvet blue. I realised once again how magical dusk was. Perhaps it was because I was in love, but it felt palpable against my skin; a touch of beauty to breathe in as we got out of the car. I wondered how our time together would make me ache tonight.

Alejandro was wearing dark fitted jeans and a slightly ripped grey designer top, like a tiger had mauled him. Subtle movements he made revealed a tiny portion of his abs and in my mind, my hands were already on his torso. He smirked as he caught me looking. I blushed, making him smirk more. I think sometimes he enjoyed making me feel uneasy too.

He knew what I needed. He could read me. This was part of his dominance, his need to control, his need to understand everything about me.

I'm so nervous.

Alejandro's eyes lowered from my eyes to my chest as he looked for my heart rate, only to see what he expected. My breath was shallow, as we were in the zone where sex was inevitable, and I felt deeply aroused building up to it. My groin tingled being close to him, a gathering torment inside me desperately needing release. I looked at his chest; his breathing was shallow in response to mine.

He shut the door behind us and our eyes locked. We knew we couldn't wait for tonight. He turned me around, starting to softly kiss my neck from behind. Slow, gentle nibbles with slight stubble grazing my face, and an aroused growl as his mouth found my skin.

"I can't stop thinking about you. Your mind, your body. I'm obsessed with you," he whispered darkly into my ear.

A soft moan escaped me, my spine naturally arching back to press against him, my hand coming up to find the back of his neck, ruffling through the scruff of his hair. I knew the arch in my back drove him crazy and so I curved it even more. His mouth opened, his tongue driving deeper rotations on my neck.

Both of his hands moved slowly upwards, from my outer thigh, over the curve of my hips, and dipping in at my waist, before curving up, over my breasts. He moaned softly, tweaking my nipples between his thumb and forefinger until they formed a hard peak through the silk teddy under my soft dress. No bra. He squeezed them harder than he had before, a twinge of slight pain adding to my deepening arousal, as my insides convulsed, and my ache spread. I pushed my bottom back against his jeans, feeling the spreading heat of his manhood thickening against me as he squeezed my nipples harder again. He knew exactly what he was doing to me. I started to bite my lower lip.

"You need me right now, don't you?"

"Yes," I replied softly.

His left hand cupped my breast, hard, pinning me firmly against him so I couldn't move, his right hand working its way over my stomach and against my inner thigh, brushing me slightly. I shuddered with the touch. His mouth was working my neck, rotating sides as he pinned me against him. My mind could do nothing but focus on the way his hand was sliding down, raising the lower hem of my short dress. His hand caressing my thighs, his fingers travelling slowly toward my silk knickers, pressing lightly against the centre as he dragged them over and traced me.

"I love how wet you are for me."

I couldn't utter a single word back to him.

Slipping a second finger inside me, he worked my neck while his fingers simultaneously stimulated me, before dragging the ridge of both fingertips back to my clit.

The heat of his jeans pressing against me was like a furnace now, pushing hard against me, as he gently worked his fingers over my clit, then firmer, making circles and long strokes, as the blood flowed through me, my clit now engorged. He spun me around, pressing me against the door, raising my right arm up and pinning it against the wood, while he rubbed me, my body filling with pure heat. As I got closer to climax, he stopped.

"I need to taste you, come with me," he said.

My legs were trembling. He held my hand, leading me down the hall, down the six steps at the rear, and finally opening the last door on the right and down the corridor.

After he opened the door at the end, he turned the dimmer up and my heart stopped. I walked in to see the most exquisite indoor spa pool. It was completely private and visually stunning. It had a cave-like feel, with ambient lighting and a low ceiling, nestled with spotlights to look like stars. There were large stone beige pillars with a dark, red-toned, tan floor.

In the centre of the room was a rectangular pool, with a raised area on the left where a sunken jacuzzi sat. There was a small landing next to underwater steps descending into a brief shallow area, which then sloped into a deep pool, about 20 metres long. There were coloured underwater lights. Currently they were turquoise, fading into sea green.

To the right was a sauna and steam room. To the left, a door marked "gym," that jutted out into the garden area.

"It's stunning. Brilliant design. I love swimming. I know it's a large house, but I had no idea it was this big, or this beautiful. How many other secret rooms have you got and why haven't you given me a tour?" I giggled nervously.

"I'll introduce you to them one by one," he said, with a sexy smile on his face.

I knew instantly he meant we would make love in each room.

His eyes flared with passion and his smile faded as his arousal returned. He led me over to the left side of the room and a large, cream lounger with soft, waterproof pillows.

He raised my arms, looking into my eyes. His eyes sparkled even more in the low light and reflection of the underlit pool, which was now deep blue. He slowly peeled my peach dress up, pausing, looking at the pastel pink silk and lace teddy I was wearing, pulling me to him and wrapping his arm tightly around my waist.

"I want to worship you. I want to fucking devour you," he said, with such passion in his voice I trembled.

His wolf, his beautiful dark wolf.

There you are my sexy beast.

He lifted my teddy over my head, slipping it onto a neighbouring chair. He looked at me, standing in heels and a thin pair of transparent panties, with silk ties at the sides. He tugged at the ribbons, pulling them from me softly before casting them onto the chair.

"Take your clothes off. I need your skin against mine," I pleaded.

Obliging, he took them off, apart from his underwear, undressing sexily. I was aching badly. He pulled me against him, my full breasts pressing against his chest, and grabbed both of my ass cheeks. He pulled at them slightly, stretching the skin around my clit, leaving me tingling. He kissed me soul deep. He paused for a second, speaking to me softly.

"I love you," he said passionately.

"I love you, too."

You are fucking perfect.

"I've been dying to taste you for months. I've fantasised about this moment a million times. Lie down for me," he instructed, in a firm voice.

I did what I was asked. I liked him bossy. It felt like he needed me, right there, right then. He *had* to taste me. My heart thundered with passion, my body twisting inside with this wretched sexual ache that wouldn't stop gnawing at me.

Show me, baby. I need this.

Alejandro threw a cushion down, kneeling before me. I looked at him, framing the moment with my emotional camera.

You are sexy as hell.

Fuck...

My skin flooded with passion, intense anticipation filling my body. He raised my knees, parting them gently. He kissed and licked slowly and sensually up my calves from my ankles, alternating legs. Then he kissed down my raised thigh, before softly nibbling at the inner part, biting them gently, making me gasp.

He paused, hovering over my sex, his breath soft against my warmth, the ache on his face visible, his eyebrows knitted in passion. He loved teasing me, particularly if I could do nothing about it.

The deliberation of the paused breath, the suspense, my clit throbbing feeling his breath so near… it felt like heaven and torture at the same time. He loved making me wait, making me want him. He put his hands under my knees, holding my hips.

That first lick. That mellifluous moment that turns me into a trembling mess of need and desire and ache.

That first lick. Igniting the flames of a thousand fires deep inside my mind and belly.

That first lick. With a slow, wide tongue and a moist warmth making every part of me surrender to carnality.

That first lick. The heat and sensuality of your smooth tongue on me makes me tremble inside.

That first lick. Lost in desire and sensations of delirious bliss as my mind spun out of control.

That first lick. The sultry feel of your carnal need for me, and your need to please me.

That first lick. The power and heat of your tongue, mixed with your need to express your love for me.

So, fucking beautiful.

"Your scent is intoxicating. I need this, I need you."

He reached his hands and arms under my thighs, taking hold of my hands, pinning them firmly at my sides. I trembled as he secured them, beginning to lick, softly, with just the tip of his tongue. From the bottom to the top, he moved along my soft ridges. As he licked my engorged clit, I flinched, but he pinned me down tighter, not letting me move.

This is so erotic.

"Mmm, you taste absolutely beautiful."

He opened his mouth, covering me, his tongue darting out to lick me, while simultaneously sucking on me. It was such a gorgeous, engulfing feeling that it made me whimper his name faintly as I moaned. He tightened his grip on my hands.

You like me whimpering your name?

My clit was sensitive as he flicked over me like a butterfly, then savagely sucking me, my pulse raging against him. My hips were trying to rock, but he wouldn't let me move at all.

He wants to control it.

He wants to control me.

That's fucking sexy. RSD is probably sexier than anything I have ever heard of but to feel how he uses it, is mind blowing. Restraint and Sensuality when paired are an exquisite sensation.

As I arched against him, struggling with the simple act of staying still, he pinned me down even harder, putting his wide tongue on me, lapping me up.

Fuck.

His chin covered now wet, I felt him sliding, French kissing me like he would my mouth. I loved watching him. He loved doing this for me, with me. I could tell by his expressions, the way he moaned, the feral wolf in his eyes as he devoured me. Ravaged me. At one point, he sucked on me so lovingly and sensually my head tipped back, mouth open, gasping for air. I was lost in the sensation, enjoying letting go.

As I lowered my head again, Alejandro moved my hands onto his, running them through his hair. He wants nails. I tugged at his hair, running them through it on either side, taking it down to the base of his neck, dragging them back up. He reached for my nipples, thumbing over them both, tweaking them, while making a beautiful mess of me with his tongue.

Wide, hard, firm licks made me moan. Hard. I was grinding against his face, and he lost control of himself completely.

I could feel the wolf in him howl as if it were a full moon.

"Mmmm, give it to me, baby" he growled into me, tweaking my nipples harder, a small pain shooting through me. I was grinding harder, faster. I'd never felt this free, to move and make noises I liked, to lose myself entirely in a moment. The more I moaned, the harder he devoured me. Firm licks up and over me nailed me every single time. My soft, wet, swollen lips, my grinding hips, my jagged breath. I felt possessed, like a demon in my chest needed to be set free. Tingles and surges were building. I knew he had me right on the edge. We were both moaning hard as he held his tongue wide on my clit and I moved; up and down, until I lost control completely and he clamped around me.

Ffffuuuuccccckkkk.

My ache detonated inside his mouth, pure passion called out of the raging depths of my soul, as a million sensations rushed to that one tiny spot, as I came: hard, needy, and moaning. I pushed myself onto him, savagely, as he braced and held back against me, strong as an ox. Such intoxicating masculinity against my softness. Wave after wave of intensity hit me. He didn't budge an inch.

Ffffuuuuccccckkkk.

He held me in position through every pulse, until every part of me trembled and collapsed. He released me softly, a feeling of peace spreading inside me. A serenity I craved. I don't know if it was the way he built up passion inside me to the absolute tipping point, or if it was just him, but the feeling of calm was much stronger than anything I could do for myself. I needed a release so badly this week.

Pure dynamite.

"You've made such a beautiful mess of the both of us," I said when I finally stilled, looking down at his beautiful, sexy face and his wet chin.

"I had every intention to," his voice deep, growling, not a trace of a smile on his face. He was lost in the intensity of the wolf and his prey.

He stood up, a menacing look in his eyes, pulling down his boxer briefs until his beautiful erection stood proud before me. I eyed it hungrily.

He dropped to one knee, nudging my thigh as if to say *let me in*. I opened them for him, and he placed one of his thighs inside and one on the outer side of my thigh. As he hovered over me, placing his wrists either side of my head, I couldn't help but fall for him a little more. I loved that sexy, sculpted face and his wet chin after giving me the most beautiful and stupendous orgasm I'd ever had.

"Kiss me."

Alejandro knew exactly what I needed. He leaned down slowly, as if doing a push up in a smooth, controlled movement, and his mouth found mine. The sultry taste of me upon his lips, inside his mouth, over his tongue, and all the ways he could make me come undone. So sexy. As he slid his tongue inside my mouth, I sucked on it, tasting myself, my hunger reignited. I sucked his tongue in and out. But now I was hungry for more than just his kiss.

"I need to taste you," I said, the plea evident in the whispering tone of my voice, as it trembled and crumbled with even the thought.

"I need you inside my mouth."

Please.

35 JACUZZI

October. Saturday. Chester. Alejandro's.

Alejandro kissed me, hard, his tongue finding the depths of my mouth. Our connection was on fire. I felt the hunger and need in him.
I need to taste you.
It wasn't even a want or a desire. It was fucking carnal.
I need you in my mouth.
He stood up, holding both hands out for me, knowing my legs would be weak. Guiding me toward the jacuzzi, he flicked a switch on the side and the jacuzzi lit up from underneath, colours of pink, purple, blue, green, and red lighting up the petal shape. Bubbles started to form from the jet streams. There was a lower seated ledge within four of the six petals in the jacuzzi and a directed power jet stream from an overhanging silver arch tap in the fifth. In the sixth there were two steps. It looked beautiful, as the colours changed. The ambience was romantic and powerful.

Alejandro stepped down first, never letting go of my hand. He turned around, looking me in the eye as he guided me toward him into the water. It was like a warm bath. The bubbles swarmed around me, fizzing against my body, and lapping against my ass and belly. The water was at hip height while standing. He pulled me in at the waist, our naked bodies pressed against each other. He kissed me again, as the fire scorched between us, and we lit each other up. My taste all over him was making me feel sexy, wanting, needy.
I must have you.
I held his hand and led him toward one of the petal shaped scallops, briefly holding onto the side and dipping my head and hair back into the water before sitting down. I grabbed his hips to steady and stop him, looking into his eyes. He stood in front of me, fully erect and pulsing, his eyes looking down at me. Hot, sexy, misty eyes as his pupils dilated and arousal flooded him, looking into my eyes, wet lips, and the shape of my mouth.

"I need to taste you as much as you needed to taste me."

My eyes were lost to the same darkness as passion rose inside and flooded me. He cradled my head, his hand smoothing my wet hair. He cupped the back of my head and the curves of my exposed neck, twisting my hair up behind me and holding it like a ponytail.

Sexy as fuck.

Eyeing his virility so close was intoxicating. The surface of his erection was smooth, the odd raised vein, but not prominent, his foreskin partially covered the tip. His pubic area was heavily trimmed, but not bald, and to me, he looked like a work of art. That firm torso, the contour of his abs leading down to prominent, jagged hips that dipped inward, to reveal his masculine shape before me. His girth made me feel weak. I hadn't dated many men, so I didn't have a vast number of comparisons I could make, but he looked perfect. This intoxication and need to be with him in any way, was new to me.

I needed to express how I felt, right now, using nothing but my tongue, mouth, hands, and eyes. I looked up and locked onto his eyes, feeling an overwhelming rush before I dipped my head.

That first taste. Slowly from the base to the tip, using just the tip of my tongue. A soft moan falling from his mouth, guiding me to continue.

That first taste. Licking slowly down the shaft, feeling every single ridge.

That first taste. Using a wider tongue to lick back up the centre, while cupping his balls with one hand.

That first taste. Sucking and sliding down one side of his erection with kisses, briefly tonguing the base.

That first taste. Enclosing my mouth around him on the other side and sliding back up his length.

That first taste. Pausing at the top, waiting for a sharp intake of breath, before licking across the tip and circling around him. Kissing him. Loving him.

That first taste. Wrapping my fingers around his base, squeezing him slightly as I enclosed my mouth around the head, waiting there.

That first taste. I felt the blood rushing through him, the way he pulsed in my mouth, swelling its moist warmth.

That first taste. My tongue swirled softly around the tip, enclosing him fully, warm water bubbling at my chest, splashing up onto my shoulders and face.

That first taste. I want to please you, show you how I feel.

I love you.

I moaned deeply, angling myself, slowly sliding my mouth down around his hot, thick flesh, applying pressure around the base with my hand. Taking in his width, I drew in some of his length, teasing down further with my mouth before sliding back up again. Each time I repeated the action, I took him in a bit further, my mouth feeling more and more deliciously full of him. His hips moved gently. I adjusted my position, angling so I was able to take more of him in. He tilted down slightly, happy to oblige in my obvious need to be full of him.

I held the base firmly as he moved slowly inside my mouth. He was careful not to make any sudden movements or push into me, going only as far as I was guiding him on each slide. As I relaxed more, I guided him deeper into my mouth. I realised I was close to the base of him and moved my hand away, letting him completely fill my mouth. I took him in as far as I could, holding him there, completely still. Breathing through my nose, I realised how much I adored being full of him. I loved the grunts and growls he made, the pleasure I was bringing him.

It only made me crave him further.

He started to rock ever so gently, in and out of my mouth.

Mmm, fuck my mouth.

His breath stalled with each movement. I could sense him losing himself inside of me, losing himself inside the sensuality of my warm hot mouth and rotating tongue.

Delicious.

More.

I could feel him getting close to climax and I backed off, wanting him to enjoy this for a little longer. I secretly adored the ache-tinged stretch in my throat, the feeling of fullness it would leave me with, even after withdrawal.

"You love doing that, don't you?" he asked me.

He was turned on as he watched me.

"I do. I don't know why, but I do so very much."

"I know why. You like to surrender to a moment, giving yourself fully to it. You like to please."

"I like to please you."

"Two givers. How incredibly powerful."

Fuck me.

I squeezed my fingers firmly around the base of his erection, bringing it to full attention, before enclosing my mouth around the tip and lowering my mouth onto him again, taking in his girth deliciously slowly. I released a soft guttural groan, and it vibrated around him as I took him in to full depth. That delicious ache formed in my mouth, where he was almost too much to take.

Mmm, fuck.

Alejandro scooped my hair up and held it in place, as I started to work with him to the tempo, raising and lowering my mouth, as he rocked his hips, pushing himself slowly in and out of me. His gentle thrusting into my throat was fulfilling every one of my needs and cravings. The deeper he thrust, the more we both lost control, the more powerful our moans became. I felt him lose his breath.

I looked up at him, my eyes misty and full of desire.

"I want you to come inside my mouth. Please. I need to taste you."

He saw and felt the need within my eyes and pleas. It wasn't just a desire. I needed him inside me, as a part of me, to fuse with, to combine, to complete me.

"Does that turn you on?"

"Pleasing you turns me on. Finish inside me. Slow fuck my mouth until you're ready to lose yourself."

"Fuck," he said, while guiding himself back inside my mouth. Gasping, I closed around him.

"Mmmmm," I moaned, as he slid inside me, slowly rocking his hips. As he rocked back and forth, pushing softly in and out, trying to stay in control, his breathing became erratic. His moans were more frequent with each new depth he found. I felt him easing further down my throat.

He couldn't help but get carried away as he got closer. I felt the build-up in him, that tingle straining up the centre of his erection while he was in my mouth. He's right on the edge. As his breath started to form a rapid pant, I knew exactly what was going to happen next and prepared myself.

He lifted himself onto his toes in the water and the angle became softer as he cradled my head, holding it steady as a warm, salty, jet of fluid poured down the back of my throat. I sucked on him, hard and he released a sound that was primal. As his warmth released into me, he leaned over, cupping my head affectionately, bringing his head closer, trying to reach mine.

He rocked softly and slowly, until he was empty, and I was full, until the stillness visibly took over him and all we felt was love. I felt it. In the act of giving to each other, all we felt was pure love.

Nothing could have felt more beautiful to me than knowing I had pleased him. Nowhere could have been more beautiful for the first time than in this stunning setting with the bubbles pouring over me and him pulsing inside the very depths of me.

He slid slowly out from my mouth.

"That was so fucking special."

He kissed my forehead tenderly and softly.

"You have no idea how beautiful you are, no fucking idea at all."

"I need you."

"You complete me."

I was in awe of us.

I wrapped my arms around him, and he pulled me in tight to his stomach, pressing my head into him. It felt like a dark erotic enchantment where our souls had fused together entirely. I couldn't tell where he ended, and I began.

You are inside me now, living and moving inside me.

36 BEDROOM

October. Saturday. Chester. Alejandro's.

Alejandro sat in the jacuzzi spa next to me, the warm jets pumped out all around us, softly pummelling our backs. He leaned over to kiss me. It was ecstasy, the way he still wanted to kiss me, knowing I tasted of him.

We spent time just kissing, deepening our connection and the moment. I felt euphoric. Kissing and water were two incredibly beautiful things to me.

We had both come and were sated and relaxed. This was more about us gelling, being free to use our creativity to explore how we kissed. It was absolute bliss. I was storing so many of these moments. Knowing I loved him allowed me to be so much more mindful of every second.

"Would you like to swim with me?" he asked me.

"My costume is in the hall."

"Naked. It's just you and I."

"Mmm, bliss," I said.

He held my hand, and we moved from the jacuzzi to the pool, stepping down slowly into the shallow end. As I pushed off into the water, I felt the drag of the underpull tugging at my nipples. It felt so freeing, so sexy. The strength of the water was caressing my curves, playing with them, tugging and tweaking, moving between my legs, over my wet clit. As I swam in the water, it was like it was sensually teasing me. I realised I would never be able to get enough of Alejandro, or of spending time with him, especially here. It was so beautiful, and my body was only ever sated for a short time, because my mind started to desire him all over again. It was like a perpetual state of desire, in different stages of escalation.

He dived underneath the water, kissing my bum briefly before surfacing again, then swimming next to me. At one point we stopped, and he carried me in his arms, twirling me around playfully. We giggled and had fun. After maybe half an hour, he pulled me in to hug him and I wrapped my legs around him, kissing him deeply.

I will never get enough of you.

After a warm poolside shower with a hot stream jet, where we took turns washing each other, Alejandro wrapped us both in towelette robes from the pool room and, after turning everything off, we headed into the kitchen. I sat around the central island while he cooked a light and fluffy omelette, that he presented beautifully with a side salad.

Swimming always made me ravenous.

We settled in front of the fire for an hour or so, listening to music. I liked everything he played.

"Maybe we could build a playlist together, of songs we both love?" he asked.

"I love that idea. Yes, let's do that."

We cuddled, enjoying being together, chatting about everything and nothing, being creative and spontaneous, as we fell in love with the harmony we felt in each other's presence. Our conversation ranged from great depths to light banter, teasing each other suggestively at times. Everything was so incredibly easy with him.

He turned the fire and lights off, leading me upstairs for the first time up the magnificent staircase and to the master bedroom.

My jaw dropped a little when he turned the dimmer on, the room filling with soft, ambient light. The bedroom was particularly spacious and modern, like all the other rooms in the house. Such a beautifully converted property. There was a large expanse of carpet in a very light beige, almost cream, which amplified the excessive space. The cream leather bed looked huge and was neatly presented with crisp looking linen.

"Is that a super king size bed?" I asked.

"Of course, do I do anything small?"

We both laughed.

"Apparently not."

He was more flamboyant in his own home. I adored watching him come out of his shell.

Classy. The whole room was elegant and classy. Above the bed was a beautiful piece of artwork, a portrait of a couple that were intimately beholden to each other. The tenderness in the image really stood out to me.

He loaded the player.

"I asked Janet to order some nighties and silk short pyjamas for you last week. They're in the drawer under the bed."

I opened the drawer, pulling out a black silk nightie and put it on. How thoughtful.

We cuddled as the movie played. I couldn't get enough of all the ways he romanced me. We had a wonderful playfulness between us, which was a refreshing contrast to the serious and darkly intimate side of us we could exude in our most passionate moments. I think it was all our contrasting elements, both individually and together, that made us so special as a couple.

Just you and me, baby.
Just you and me.

37 NIGHTMARE

October. Sunday. Chester. Alejandro's.

I awoke sharply in the middle of the night to yelling and sounds of complete torment from Alejandro.

He was thrashing around in his sleep, a mild sweat above his brow. His eyes were fluttering, he was deep in REM sleep. He was dreaming, clearly disturbed, shaking his head from side to side, flailing his arms, clenching his fists, and breathing rapidly. His brows were knitted and frowning. His face was scrunched up as if he was in pain.

A quick glance at the clock — 4 a.m. It's October 4th, too, I realised.

What would I want you to do if I was having a nightmare?

I reached over with my hand, stroking his hair, trying to wake him gently. I applied soft strokes with the palm of my hand over the top of his head. I tried to soothe him and still his mind until he started to come to. His torment softened, as I stroked his head, whispering his name until he opened his beautiful cobalt eyes. I could see them glistening in the dim light.

"Hey," I said softly to him.

His eyes filled up and he wrapped his arms around me, holding onto me tightly. That wasn't just a dream, wherever he was, that was pure and absolute terror I'd just witnessed. His need to be held only reaffirmed that. I'd heard of night terrors in discussions at work. Some of the victims had experienced PTSD. Night terrors were often the result of the brain trying to process a traumatic experience.

Alejandro softly wept, and my eyes filled up to see such a strong man show emotion like this. I found the absolute honesty of his emotions endearing, and my heart strings tugged for him. I'd always struggled with men who felt they couldn't show emotion, so many are raised thinking it's a sign of weakness. To me it was a sign of strength and truth.

I fell more in love with him the second that first tear fell down his cheek. He didn't cry with anything more than a whisper, but it wrapped around my heart as I felt his emotions. It didn't last more than a few seconds, but he held me so tight. I squeezed him harder, wrapping him into me. As he raised his head, I kissed a large tear gathering to fall from the corner of his left eye.

How many times has this happened when nobody has been here to comfort you?

"Tell me what you were dreaming about, Alejandro. Let me in," I implored.

A minute or so passed as he gathered himself to speak.

"I couldn't save her," he said, shaking his head.

A single tear traced down the strong contours of his face.

"Who?"

"My twin."

"You have a twin?" I asked, in shock.

Why had he never mentioned her before?

"I did."

He grimaced.

"What happened to her?"

I wanted to get him talking, as this was clearly incredibly important to him. The counselling course I'd taken for victim support gave me a few techniques I could apply gently in any circumstances. The main thing was enabling him to open and share his story. I was trained to listen for keywords in language and intonation. It's subtle, knowing when to listen and when to ask further questions. The rape victims I'd worked with were often left unable to trust anyone and living in a constant state of anxiety and fear. That kind of terror, to the point where you can visibly see it, needed patience and gentle support. They had to know by your repeated actions you were trustworthy. The slightest form of kindness was invaluable toward a person that held deep pain. Alejandro needed mine now.

"She was taken right in front of me, in front of my mother and father. She was abducted," he said. "My mother was gagged and bound. My father was badly beaten, with blood all over him. His face was swollen and deformed from the beating."

My eyes filled up immediately. I was horrified at what he was saying. I felt his pain as he spoke.

"I'm so sorry, baby. That must have been terrifying, for all of you."

"I was seven," he said, lowering his head. "It was a gang of men, all wearing balaclavas. I woke to the sound of things breaking in the other room, my dad trying to fight back. I panicked. I didn't know what to do, so I started yelling for my mum. A man dressed head to toe in black came into my room and rushed over to hold his hand firmly over my mouth. I bit him and he knocked me hard around the head before resuming his hold over my mouth. He carried me out as I kicked and punched him, but my puny frame delivered not the slightest menace to a full-grown man."

Tears began to roll down my cheek and I held Alejandro's hand. The thought of a young boy going through this really hurt me. The thought of his sister being hurt made me feel sick. No child should have to live through terror.

"As I got to the lounge, I saw my mother crying in the chair. Her mouth was gagged with tape but there were no further signs of her having been hurt physically. The four men in the kitchen were taking it in turns to kick and beat my father. One of them held his arms, while the other men punched and kicked him. He tried to fight them back, but there were too many of them. They beat him until he dropped to the floor, until he looked lifeless. It could have only been a few minutes, but I see it in slow motion when I recall it. I tried to scream, but my cries were muffled into the back of the man's hand. All the kicking, shouting, and screaming in the world wouldn't have made the slightest impact. They were strong and overpowering. The torment in my mother's eyes was something I can never erase. She had been made to watch him being beaten. Her chair was angled deliberately to face him."

His eyes welled up again.

"Unimaginable bastards," I said, devastated for them, imagining I was there.

"I was placed on a kitchen chair next to my mother. They wrapped tape around my mouth and tied my hands and feet. I couldn't move. I couldn't do anything. The helplessness, the worthlessness I felt was immobilising. I was unable to stop them, unable to fight, unable to scream, unable to do anything that could help."

He was fully distressed, his face tensed in pure anger.

"After my father was unable to move on the floor, too beaten to be of any threat, one of the men, with a tattoo of a cobra on his neck, went into my sister's room. There's no way she could have been asleep with the noise. She must have been petrified in shock in her room, unable to speak. The man carried Dulce out with a hand across her mouth, like he'd carried me. When she saw us all, she went into shock. She didn't try to hit him or even scream, she looked terrified, immobilised. She was shaking in pure fear. The anger that built inside me was immense. I was kicking and bucking, trying to escape, but it got me nowhere. My mother had tears streaming down the side of her face. I remember it all in such vivid emotional detail," he recalled.

I sat silently, stroking his head and arm, letting him spill his heart. Mine ached deeply for him.

"The man who was carrying Dulce didn't even flinch. He just carried her out, as if she was the reason they were there, as if she was the target. Dulce looked back at us both, her eyes glazed over. The very last look I saw, as she was carried out of the back door, was pure fear. She was absolutely petrified. I couldn't do anything. My mother's heart was literally breaking next to me as she sobbed uncontrollably. My father lay unconscious on the ground. I thought he was dead. We were both strapped there, stuck in a living hell for several hours, perpetually replaying the torment of those few horrendous minutes."

"I'm so sorry, baby," I whispered, tears falling down my cheek.

The emotion I felt from him was overwhelming. He was still deeply distraught, to this very day. He'd carried it around for all those years. I felt the profundity of his trapped pain as he spoke, staring into space.

"After what felt like an eternity, which was maybe about five hours, my dad started to come to, disoriented and groaning from the pain. The relief he was alive, after the fear of him having died before our eyes, was a light in the middle of our darkest hours and deepest sorrow. He took a while to focus before he realised, he wasn't alone in the room. When he looked over, he just said, 'Dear God' and stumbled across to us, wincing with every movement. He carefully removed the tape from my mother's mouth.

'Dulce, where is Dulce?' he asked frantically, because he could see she wasn't with us.

My mother burst into tears, unable to hold back and sobbing uncontrollably.

'They've taken her, Jack, they've taken her.'

'*Not my baby girl, not my baby girl!*' He yelled, sobbing, immediately clutching his ribs with the pain of movement. It was the only time I ever saw him cry. He removed the tape from my mouth and went to one of the kitchen drawers, picked up a pair of scissors and started cutting the super strength tape we were bound with, so that our hands and feet were free. We all held each other when we were free, until we realised how horrendous Dad's pain was."

I squeezed Alejandro's hand tight, trying to show him support as he poured his heart out.

"'*Did they hurt either of you?*' Dad asked, trying to quickly assess if he was the only one damaged."

"'*They were rough, but they didn't hit me Jack,*' my mother said to reassure him quickly."

"'*What about you son. Are you hurt?*' he redirected at me."

"'No, Dad, one of them hit me across the head but I'm ok. They took Dulce, they took Dulce. She was so scared Dad, she looked so scared.' I started sobbing, my head seeking solace in the arms of my mother while my dad hobbled toward the phone."

"'*I need an ambulance and the police,*' I heard him say, before giving our address. He went into his study with the phone and didn't come back for several minutes. After a while it went quiet. Then he was speaking in a different type of voice, clearly talking to someone else then," Alejandro added.

"My mother was trying to reassure me, telling me the police were going to find Dulce. The wait for the emergency services seemed to take so long, but it was probably only minutes. It was the longest night of my life. I've been having nightmares ever since. It's a recurring dream about the fear in Dulce's eyes, and my inability to move or do anything. The helplessness of it all affects me deeply," he added.

"When the police came, we all knew their chances of finding Dulce had vastly decreased with the amount of time that had passed. But, fair play, they did everything they possibly could. Dad had three fractured ribs, a broken nose, and fractured eye socket. He took weeks to heal physically. None of us ever recovered mentally."

I could sense and feel how clogged he was with emotional debris. No wonder he struggled to trust people.

"What did the police do?" I asked, desperate to hear they'd found her alive and well, that they'd tracked down the gang of men and brought them to justice. Then realising he wouldn't still be having night terrors if they had.

"They conducted a search for many months and went international with their enquiries. All I remember is my dad on the phone a lot, getting riled and anxious and shouting as the frustration built up with each day that passed. We were all losing hope and it broke us all in our own ways. They never found her," he said.

The darkness locked inside those four words was immense. I imagined how heavy never knowing and never having closure must feel.

"A while later, my dad left us, suddenly, with very little warning. He said he was moving back to England and he had quit his job. I think it was all far too much for him. He carried so much anger and resentment, and it ate away at him. So that left me and my mother in Spain, on our own. It was tough, just the two of us. My father always kept in touch and sent money, but he couldn't bear to be around the house anymore."

"That's when you needed him the most, though," I said, wondering how selfish a person must be to abandon their wife and child after that had happened.

"I know. My mother and I were heartbroken for the second time and she carried her pain in a different way to Dad, in the same way I did. It didn't come out as anger, we just both became more silent, more solemn and darker. We both struggled with depression. Some months were incredibly intense during the first two to three years after the abduction. Over time, it reduced, but it was still there, always lurking underneath, waiting for a bad day. It was the not knowing made it worse. Not knowing if Dulce was dead or alive, or what she had endured. That thought plays over and over in my mind."

"I can completely understand why that would be so hard," I added as I carried on stroking him, trying to soothe him as he relives the emotion.

"Mum and I missed them both, Dulce and my dad. I was so close to Dulce, for seven years. We were the very best of friends and were never apart. We were the definition of twins in every way, the alike kind who never fight, the kindred spirits, not the type who butt up against each other searching for our own identity. We were always laughing and singing, playing outside together, exploring different parts of our immediate surroundings like it was a huge adventure. We'd play games together, create imaginary friends, have picnics. Our mother often joined in. Dulce and I got our creativity from her. Dad was often working sporadic and long hours, which meant he often wasn't there for dinner, and sometimes didn't come home at all. Looking back, I don't know if he was having affairs or not. It felt like it was just the three of us a lot of the time as we were growing up, but we had these intense outings every now and again with my dad. He made a real effort to be with us all, like he overcompensated for not being there in the week sometimes."

I listened intently to Alejandro, wanting to understand everything about him. In my mind I just kept thinking how awful this must have been for him to live with.

"What happened with you and your mum, after your dad left?" I asked.

"The family felt incomplete and fragmented. It never felt right after that point, but we did our best. My mother tried so hard to be everything I needed, giving me everything she could. We had these beautiful bursts of happiness some days, where we'd be giggling and laughing, or we'd visit somewhere pretty, go for a picnic, go to the ocean, paint or bake something. She was artistic and creative. We were so close. I miss her. We didn't have many people around, other than my mum's sister, Gabriela, and the odd friend from school on some days. We were like hermits, quite quiet and a little introverted and shy around others. Not getting close was easier than explaining a painful past. It became easier to remain isolated. Plus, we were self-contained at this point."

"A very special team from the sound of it," I added.

"Very much so. My mother had asked a local friend if he would teach me guitar as a distraction, encouraging me to sing and enter song writing competitions as I developed. She believed in me with everything she had and kept pushing me in a positive way. We would sing together. After I discovered I could write lyrics, she encouraged me to plough my emotions into songs, and her eyes often filled up when I started to sing a new song to her. I wrote from a place I could never express in speech. I wrote from my heart. I wrote from my soul. All the pain I couldn't discuss turned into ballads. All the joy I so desperately craved went into wistful songs and I realised I was a romantic deep down. I loved all the stories my mum told me about romance and respect and taking care of a woman of my own one day."

"That's so beautiful. You made her proud and happy, and found a way to express yourself. She gave you that. Music was her special gift to you. You repaid her with every word you wrote from the heart and every dream you helped her escape into, through your lyrics. She would be so proud of you now."

"I know she would. I think sometimes, when I'm writing lyrics to a song or I'm recording in my studio, she's with me. I suspect looking back some of the stories she shared with me were her unfulfilled dreams and wishes. That tinges them with a little sadness, she never got the chance to fulfil them or lead a full life. That's what makes me more determined to live mine fully. She never complained, she never said that to me. She gave me as full and beautiful a life as I could have possibly had, given our low budget household. We went to a lot of the local festivals and there was always an abundance of live music and great food. Spain had so much pretty music and ambience to offer, so that became our life. That was where we channelled our energy. That was where we found our peace from all the darkness we had buried."

"You carried that darkness with you for all those years. You haven't been able to settle because you never knew what happened to Dulce. None of you ever got closure."

"Yes. And it carries a lifelong torture. I don't know if she suffered, what happened after they took her, when she died, or how. It hurts, and it hurts even more I could do nothing to stop them. I loved her so much. I still do, I have nowhere to channel the love I have for my mother or Dulce. We were such a close-knit family. Dulce brought me so much light. We understood each other without having to talk sometimes, like we shared a form of psychic communication and connection. My early childhood was fun and there was a lot of love and happiness between us, then everything changed in a matter of minutes. It's like the light went out of my life when she did. All I felt was this wretched darkness afterwards. The captors destroyed everything I believed about the world that night. They didn't just take away someone I loved, they took away my innocence and belief in humanity."

What a sickening thing for a child to lose. Everything began to make sense about Alejandro now. Why he couldn't trust people, why he was often quiet, why he was so deep, and why he needed me to be the one person who was real and consistent in his life. He only had his dad and best friend.

Trust meant everything to him.

Love meant everything to him.

He was yawning, physically and mentally drained from talking about it.

"Go back to sleep for now, baby. Come lay on my chest. Let me stroke your hair."

It took him about ten minutes of me stroking his hair, back, and shoulders before he fell asleep.

I want to show you so much love that it compensates for every day you were hurting.

38 THE PLAYGROUND

October. Sunday. Chester. Alejandro's.

Alejandro was tense most of the day. Even a workout together didn't shift his mood. Talking about his past in the middle of the night had triggered painful memories for him. I knew he needed a release. I prepared a meal for him in the kitchen after the workout, but he was quiet throughout. The air was thick and heavy with his silence.
"What are you thinking now?"
I tried to keep talking, but he was struggling today. He was lost in thought, fresh recollection of the nightmarish events still clogging him emotionally. He was deeper than most people I knew, but that was always a double-edged sword – both a blessing and a curse. I understood that duality of him.
"There are too many things going through my mind right now. I can't focus on any of them."
I knew exactly how he felt. We were both born with chaotic minds. Finding peace amongst the chaos was a real challenge for us both.
"You've suffered so much, Alejandro. The combination of the grief of losing your mother and the tragic loss of your sister weigh heavily on your mind. You relived the fear you felt as a little boy last night. That's hard, even as an adult," I said, now understanding.
"I don't know how to make it go away. I can't stop it from bearing down on me, like a dark mass looming over me. Both those experiences changed me, and I can never fully escape the pain sometimes. It's buried so deep inside my mind. It's like it's there, always trying to chase me, a constant reminder of everything I have no control over in life."
"Is that why you want to control me, to protect me, to have something in your life you know is certain?" I asked, seeking an honest answer.
"I love and respect you. When you give yourself to me, when you relinquish your control to me, I feel wanted in a way I've never felt

more certain of in my life. It's about how beautiful the gift of trust is. I want to please you, to pleasure you, to make you feel safe, for you to know you are loved and adored. And yes, partly, to know there's a part of life I can control, someone who willingly gives that to me. That's exactly what RSD is about. It's sacred love. I need to feel needed by you."

I opened my mind to the beauty of the depth of relationship he wanted for us, to the beauty of the construct he had created. RSD was an entirely new concept I'd never heard of before Alejandro, because he had defined it based on his unique, singular needs for a much more intimate way we could express our love. It filled my belly and loins with a raging, passionate fire.

Alejandro's dark heart made him different than everybody else I knew. It was a little intimidating. It was the unknown; everyone else seemed more predictable. He wasn't. At all. I never knew what he was going to say or do next. Part of me felt intimidated and apprehensive about all the things that could go wrong. What if he lost control of his darkness?

I didn't know how he wanted to utilise the trust he wanted me to give him, or what exactly he wanted to do to me. It felt like a risk, a gamble. I may not like what he wants to do to me. I realised it was my own fear, of giving over control to him, of all the ways he could hurt me which was creating the problem. So far, he'd done nothing to hurt me. There was no evidence to suggest he ever would. I was finding less and less reason for anything to stop me.

I'd thought about submission a lot since it was first mentioned, researching it during the week at home. There were many things that were not for me at all. I would in no way entertain the idea of degradation or any form of abuse. I had self-respect. I wasn't going to allow anything that felt uncomfortable, mentally, or physically. What I agreed to would only ever be consensual intimate acts. I wanted a safe word, so he knew if something felt uncomfortable. I also wanted to know I wasn't completely out of control and could say no at any time. This wasn't a normal type of submission though. It wasn't a BDSM submission, the only reference I could find online - it was an RSD submission, and I wasn't ever going to find that online if it was a construct within Alejandro's mind.

I wanted to say yes. I knew how much it meant to him now. I understood so much more about the dark spaces he carried inside. They scared me a little if I was being honest. His need to still his mind was the same as my own though. Alejandro wanted me to just feel, not think. I could only imagine how blissful it must be. And in so doing, he also could just feel, not think. I knew how much he needed that right now.

"I want to feel that with you tonight," I said, knowing in my heart what we had was extremely powerful. I also wanted him to escape from the heart-breaking place his mind was currently in. "Will you show me, how you need me, who you want me to be? Show me who you need to be?" I asked.

"Will you give me your trust completely?" His eyes were dilated at the suggestion.

"I will," I said. He had a way of making me feel protected and aroused at the same time.

"Then will you come with me now, so I can show you?" he asked.

"I will."

My heart was fluttering rapidly.

Alejandro took my hand, leading me to the hall. My mind was racing in a thousand ways.

At the rear of the hall, opposite the entrance to the spa and pool room, there was another door. As he opened it, I realised there was another level underneath the house. A basement area.

How many rooms are in this house?

He led me very carefully down dimly lit concrete stairs. There was a slightly musty smell in the stairwell. It was an untampered aged part of the building; all other rooms having been modernised above. The pungent smell of maturing wine was drifting into my senses too. He must have a wine cellar.

"Are you sure you're ready, baby?" he asked one last time, standing on the outside of a dark, thick oak door.

"Yes. I want to know."

He turned a lock in the thick oak door, which was covered with black latches and studs. It creaked as it opened, goose bumps forming on my arm. He turned on a low light.

"This is the playground. Our playground. A very adult version," he explained.

The room had a concrete floor, reminding me of a quite spacious castle dungeon. I looked around, seeing what looked like a torture chamber. All the gadgets and different areas shocked me.

"These are all for *your* pleasure," he reassured me quickly.

"It looks like a torture chamber," I said nervously, unable to hide my shock.

"Restraining devices to be utilised for your pleasure and release, though. Big difference," he reaffirmed.

I looked around the room at the predominantly wooden, brick, and old iron features, which he'd restored like part of an old castle. It was a large rectangular room, with a beautiful, antique four-poster bed. It was both erotic and inviting. It had thick, sturdy iron posts and a headboard made of vertical iron bars. There was a solid, horizontal iron bar across the top, framing the four posts.

There was voile tied to each post, covering the top and sides of the bed. It could be left tied back, or untied, enclosing us completely.

Magical.

To the left of the bed was a large oak unit with many drawers. On top was a medieval looking ornate candle holder, with a chunky candle which hadn't been used. On the wall to either side of the bed were strong shelving units, with large unused candles and many suspended crops, and equpwhips hanging from hooks underneath them.

I gasped as I saw them.

I glanced over to the left side of the room, taking in the details before me. Suddenly, I understood why he called it the playground. In the corner to my left was a large circular wooden board on a slight angle, with a rear support structure. At the front was a step. At the base of the circular wooden board, inside the circle, were two footholds with thick leather securing straps, a thick mid-waist securing strap halfway up, and two thick securing straps at the top meant to hold my wrists.

"The roundabout," he offered, following my eyes, watching my reactions.

I smiled nervously, not sure how to take in everything I saw. My cheeks flushed without warning.

To the right of the roundabout, in the top left corner of the room, was a sturdy X-frame, with securing straps at the top and bottom, suspended from chains in between two sturdy rectangular posts.

"The hanging frame," he responded, looking at my flushed cheeks when he brushed my hair affectionately behind my ears, as if he liked to see them.

I lowered my eyes, briefly embarrassed. Visions of what he wanted to do with me on each piece of equipment started a chain reaction of thoughts in my head. Deeply erotic, sexy thoughts. I flushed even more. I could feel the front of my neck turning red. He smiled at me. He knew.

Turning my attention to the right there was a round, leather-edged, flat, three-quarter body length piece of equipment, about shoulder width, with various securing straps. The cushioned strips of wood halfway up looked like knee supports at the rear, and there were smaller and similar cushioned strips, for elbows probably, at the front, too. My nerves kicked in when I imagined what positions I would be in on that one.

"The hobby horse," he said softly, his voice deepening.

You're aroused just showing me, aren't you, baby?

I turned my body slowly to look behind it and to the rear right of the room. Suspended from a double inverted U-frame metal support, glued at the top, was a suspended swing with leg straps and split leather. There was a large area covering the back of the swing It appeared to be rigged up to electronics of some kind. There was a thick gym mat underneath.

"The swing," he said, following my eyes.

To the right of that was a long, angled, leather bench with securing straps at the top.

"Slide, I assume?"

"Yes."

There was a large, extremely thick rug in the centre of the room, and a log burner to the right, although the temperature was cosy, so there must have been another heat source. Built-in, perhaps.

The right side of the door was clear for opening. He closed the door, leading me by the hand over to the bed, where we sat down.

"How do you feel, seeing all of this?"

"I'm aroused, which surprises me. I didn't expect to feel this way. The room shocks me. I want to know when, how, and why, I guess."

"I've only lived here for three years. The rest of the house was designed inside first. This room was only completed a few months ago. As for the why, it's here because I hoped one day to be able to express myself in the way I need, with someone I love."

"When did you know you were a sensual dominant?"

"Everything finally clicked when I started to investigate. I don't think you realised you were submissive though."

"What were the signs?" I wanted to know.

"The way you were so drawn to me in the dancing, as a follower, and respond so naturally to the way I lead you on the dance floor. The way you trust me. The way you tremble and blush around me. The way you liked me enclosing your space and almost pinning you against the wall when we're speaking. The rise and fall of your chest when I take charge in any way. The way you want me to protect you and turn to me. Your dedication to me when I was away, and now that I'm back. Your lack of interest in other me

n because you know there isn't the same type of chemistry with vanilla partners. You're always fighting to stay in control, when the one thing you need is to let go completely. They were all clues you were submissive. And that you were meant for me."

"Wow, I had no idea I gave off so many signs I had no awareness of at all."

"I knew but I don't think you did."

"I definitely didn't but it makes sense now you've reeled them all off."

"I'm sure this room will bring out so much more of that side of you too."

"Have you ever used this room with anyone else before?"

"Never. I designed this room for someone special. I designed it to open up the woman I love to a much deeper love than she'd ever experienced before. I designed it with you in mind. I just hadn't met you yet."

Great answer.

Alejandro had a way of talking which always reassured me. He never did anything to make me feel jealous, even though I could see that other women were attracted to him. Every time we went out, I caught someone looking over at him. I think he's genuinely unaware of how attractive he is, though. He's always so caught up in his own world that nobody else enters it peripherally. He was always fully focused on me, I thought, flicking back through several memories briefly.

"What, in your fantasies, do you want me to do? This is roleplay, right?" I asked, trying to understand the parameters of what he needed from us, in this space.

"It's more than roleplay, it's about the level of commitment where I get to call you '*mine.*' That means everything to me," he said, gently stroking my hair.

It's the little things he does which drive me crazy, attention to detail. I've never known a man who could do that, seduce me with so many things simultaneously.

"In my fantasies, everything starts with you willingly submitting to me, rendering your control completely to me, allowing me to set you free in any way I choose."

"Will you hurt me?" I asked nervously.

"I will *never* hurt you mentally or emotionally. I will never degrade you in any way. I will never do anything you didn't agree to. There are some boundaries I would like to challenge with you physically, to see what brings you the most pleasure. That is what I wish for the most, to bring you sexual and emotional pleasure until you feel free. There's a line between pleasure and pain that can be quite intoxicating, for both of us, if you're willing to explore it with me."

He was so beautifully direct when we were talking about this. Being able to be his natural self was special to him. He'd never been able to share this side of himself with anyone. It lit him up. This conversation and room were like a spark, setting him on fire. I could see his passion looming under the surface, like a sparkler fizzing into life. He didn't seem sad anymore. There wasn't a tinge of it in this room. How beautiful, that simply being here takes that away for him. That made my mind up even further.

"I'm willing to explore our limits together, as long as I know if I don't like anything, you will stop when I ask."

I felt nervous flutters saying it, but I was also deeply excited.

"Deal," he agreed.

"Tell me. Show me," I beckoned, with soft eyes.
Let me free you of your pain, baby.

39 THE SWING

October. Sunday. Chester. Alejandro's.

Alejandro lit the log burner to provide extra warmth in the room. He also lit the various chunky candles scattered around.

"I want you to kneel naked on the rug in the centre of the room, eyes lowered to the floor, your palms open, facing up. This is symbolic of your openness. Your eyes lowered are symbolic of a state of submission. If at any point you change your mind about something that happens in this room or want something to stop, call out 'break' and I will immediately stop what I'm doing. That is your safe word. This is something both of us must want. Expect me to become more assertive as I explore your limits," he explained.

"I'll go get you a drink from upstairs while you think about it. When I return, I'll know by your position if you wish to proceed."

Looking around the candlelit room, listening to the soft roar of the log burner, I realised there was something deeply sensual in the way he had laid the playground out, in the equipment he had chosen. There were no paddles or anything which could cause any serious pain I noted, reinforcing that RSD was focused on pleasure. I still didn't know what exactly he wanted, or how, I just knew it was highly erotic. I was feeling incredibly sexual here. I'd already made up my mind. I wanted our relationship to go as deep as possible.

I choose you.
I choose us.
I choose this.
I choose connection.
I choose exploration.
I choose your dark romance.
The answer is yes.

I stood by the bed and started to undress, placing my clothes in a neatly folded pile by the pillow. When I stripped off my knickers, I was already wet. Just thinking of the vulnerability of what I was about to do was incredibly intense. I walked, like a trembling bag of nerves, to the centre of the room, and knelt, on the soft white rug, facing inwards toward the bed. I placed my hands palm up as requested, lowering my head to the floor, closing my eyes.

Breathe, Leila.
Stay calm and just breathe.

Alejandro took forever to come back. It must have only been five minutes or so, but it felt like 20. My anxiety kicked in as I heard him coming down the stairs, the stunted thud of his shoes on the floor enough to send a soft chill through my body. The door creaked as it opened, a slight draft creeping over my skin.

He stalled his movements. I knew he was looking at me, studying me. I could feel his eyes looking me up and down. I could sense his relief at my choice, within one deep exhale that tumbled from his mouth. I was merely trying to breathe at this point.

After a few long moments, Alejandro walked past me. I heard a chink as he placed glasses on the side unit. A drawer opened, then closed. He walked slowly toward me and stood there. His eyes were running over me. I could feel his intensity, the shift in the room. He leaned down to my ear, lightly holding the back of my head.

"You're beautiful. *Mine*," he growled softly.

Chills went through me. It was the way he said it, arousal deepening his voice. He kissed my forehead, pressing his lips against me in a comforting and nurturing way.

Suddenly, everything was different. Maybe he was right about the things he'd seen in me early on, maybe this was who I was. I understood, for the very first time, how deeply he wanted me to be his. I could fucking feel it.

"Focus on me. Focus on my voice and my commands. Trust me, I'm not going to hurt you. Okay?"

"Okay."

I felt him slipping something silky over my hair and onto my eyes. A blindfold.

Damn.

Everything went black. The blindfold had soft cushions behind both eye pads and an elasticated back, giving a perfect blackout effect.

"How does that make you feel?"

"Excited, nervous, overwhelmed, aroused."

My voice softened with the heady combination of all four sensations fusing together. Something powerful was taking over my mind. My thoughts raced, bumping into each other.

Alejandro traced a finger down from my ear over my neck, across my clavicle, my shoulder, and down my upper chest, before curving over my breasts with the back of his hand. The hairs on his hand were downy soft. I could feel my skin bristle against them. Turning his hand, he cupped my left breast in his right hand, squeezing and gathering it until the upper curve spilled over his fingers. He tweaked my nipple. I gasped. He rubbed it between his thumb and forefinger, rolling his thumb over me. Not being able to see magnified each touch, making it more intense.

Alejandro leaned down. He breathed close to my ears, softly nibbling at my lobes before kissing slowly down my neck. It was intense, his warm mouth enclosing my neck. He was kissing me deeply, as he tongued down to the crevice of my neck. My weak spot. I went to wrap my arms around his leg.

"You can't touch me until I say so. That's a rule," he said.
"What rules?"
"I'll let you know them one by one."
Mysterious. I'm intrigued.

Alejandro lifted his head from my neck, his tongue tracing my lips, before licking along the central horizontal line of my mouth. He kissed me over and over, until I pined and whimpered.

You like me wanting you.
You know I want to touch you.
You like to see it in my face, hear it in my voice, feel it in my tremble.

He took my hand, helping me to stand up, and led me to the bed. He lay me down with his hand behind my back for support, guiding me into the position he wanted. He was assertive like this. Gently dominant. I heard him taking his clothes off, the thought teased me, not being able to see his beautiful body.

Was it being told I couldn't, that made me want to, so much more?

He climbed over me on all fours, using his knee to gently separate my legs. I craved for him to be inside me. He lowered himself above me, his tongue flicking softly over my nipple. He sucked on it slightly before alternating to my other nipple to do the same. Next came a hard lick and a stronger suck, making me gasp hard and my nipple stiffen. I was pulsing.

I went to touch the back of his head.
"No, baby," he said, lifting my hands above my head.
"You can't move until I say so. Keep your hands there."
It was weird, staying still like that, but I did it because he'd told me to. It felt like it was a small test of my obedience.

Alejandro kissed me. His tongue licked my lips, playfully darting inside my mouth as he switched and changed the angle and style of his kisses. He was unpredictable. I didn't know what to expect next. Yet another facet to the lack of control. It frustrated the hell out of me, yet deeply excited me at the same time.

A shift in the weight of the bed and I felt him moving lower and lower. He kissed me in a soft, winding trail, leading down the centre of my stomach. He laid kisses upon me, sensually and with playful bites, always watching for my reaction. His hand was tracing my calf, over my inner thigh.

A deep, erotic ache was burning inside me, as he ran his thumb over silky wet folds, softly, until he triggered the reaction he wanted - my body convulsing, as he thumbed my clit. My back arched. I moaned softly. My chest rose and fell as it deepened. I wanted to touch him. I had no idea how he could control himself to not allow me to.

What could possibly be satisfactory for him about not letting me touch him?

I could feel him as he hovered over me, his warm breath syncing in rhythm with mine, waiting momentarily, before instructing me.

"Open up, like a flower for me."

His tone sent shivers through me, as did his gentle reference. I parted my legs wider.

Alejandro pushed his finger inside me slowly, still breathing over me and I arched against him, pushing further onto his finger. He went deeper inside me. I contracted around him as he started to ease it out and push it back in again, deliciously slowly. It felt so much more erotic because I couldn't see. As he built a rhythm with the rise and fall of my hips, I felt the most beautiful warmth spreading through me as he licked me slowly, from bottom to top, covering both my clit and the soft petalled area that surrounded it. I arched deeper, losing myself completely in this alluring sensation. His tongue flickered with precision over my now engorged clit and he alternated with soft sucks and licking, both soft and hard, while his fingers found rhythm inside me.

Mmm, that feels sexy.

My gasps and moans became involuntary as the combination of sensations started to overwhelm me. The repetition, the variation, the warmth, the depth and the ache inside me were all bursting to be set free. I needed to come so badly. Alejandro knew I was getting close to the edge, the rise and fall of my chest and my jagged breath gave me away.

"I love licking and adoring you this way."

Fuck. I can tell.

He enjoyed pleasuring me. I could feel how much by the care he took going down on me. He sucked a little harder before pulling away, leaving me tingling. I pined as he moved away from me.

"Let me adore you, too?"

"No baby, I have other plans for today."

Alejandro stood up and then scooped me up into his arms, as if it was nothing, as if I were weightless. I had no idea he was this strong. He nestled me against his shoulder, carrying me and placing me, very carefully, in leather seat strappings. It felt wobbly.

The swing.

Fuck.

My heart was pounding wildly.

My back was supported, with a headrest behind my head. He positioned my feet in the leather stirrups. It was more comfortable than I expected. I didn't know what was coming next.

I heard him shuffling about. I sensed him underneath me on the padded floor mat positioned below the swing. I could guess what the aim was by where I felt the air exposing me.

"Don't be alarmed, I'm going to use the controls on the swing, and you may feel a slight jerking motion as it moves" he warned.

"Okay," I stammered nervously.

I heard the motor of the swing above me kick into life, feeling soft jerking motions as the swing lowered. Through the gap he positioned me above, he was guiding the tip of his penis slowly inside me.

Fucking hell.

I can't describe the sensation. It was as if parts of me were floating dreamily, yet the hardness of him being inside me was delicious. It was surreal, feeling both simultaneously.

He lowered me further onto him, and I felt him filling me completely. Then, with the remote control, he set the swing to rotate. It was a soft, slow, gyrating circular rotation, gently spinning me around while he was deep inside me. It was prurient.

Alejandro thrusted at certain angles, holding the exposed parts of my legs from underneath as a guide, and I felt such a delicious tinge with the distension. He pressed another button. The swing started to vibrate, the mix of sensations arousing me to full amplitude, leaving me in a trance.

"I love being inside you," he groaned, his head clearly spinning, too.

We were both lost inside the deep, sensuous swirling, the vibrating rhythm. I was already close to the edge before he carried me over, but now, it was like I was sitting directly on the edge, precariously balanced in a state of pre-orgasm, not being allowed to tip over. Every slow rotation drove me crazy. All I wanted now was for him to fuck me, hard, and to come. He was right, it was a pleasurable form of sweet torture.

His moans deepened, increasing in frequency, like mine. Every delicious swirl around his thick erection, was sending him closer to the edge, too. His breathing was a hard pant, with an aching groan mixed in.

"How does it feel?" I asked.

"I feel swollen. I'm aching and throbbing, teetering on the edge. How do you feel, Leila?"

"I feel tormented, in the nicest way possible. My head and body are spinning. I can see nothing but feel everything. I'm aching. It's delicious, but excruciatingly hard to not let it go, especially the longer it goes on. I need to come. Baby, when can I come?" I pleaded.

I had a deep, twisted knot inside me built up. I desperately needed to release it. I had nothing to propel or push off from, and was left just floating, almost ethereally in this liminal swirling trance.

Alejandro was thrusting harder now, my pleading fuelling him and clearly turning him on. I made a mental note of all the things that turned him on as I discovered them.

"Tell me how much you need it," he teased.

"I've never needed to come so badly."

Clearly, it was the right answer. He turned up the level of vibration on the swing and began to pump deep inside me, making me bounce while I was floating. It was a weird, but very sexy, sensation.

The vibration was intense. I felt my body contract. I felt the swell, the surge through my body rising, overwhelming me as he pounded me from below.

"Fuck me. Please don't stop," I said, becoming lost in the sense of escalation.

I contracted around Alejandro, my breath jagged, uncontrolled. He pounded into me while holding my thighs, his width almost overbearing combined with the vibration and rotation.

As his breath became jagged, too, our moans deepened, becoming more erratic as we let go, both coming simultaneously, overpowered. He kept pumping into me through the tingling burn of a deep, internal orgasm, for as long as we could both bare before the sensitivity became too intense.

I was left breathless and spent. My legs trembled uncontrollably. I'd shattered around him, deep within the rhythm and vibration, as he filled me with warm fluid. There was something so much more intense about our mutual orgasm, here, via the swing, in this room. It was deep, tantric. He eventually turned off the vibration after the intensity passed, but he stayed inside me, breathless, for a few minutes as we returned to earth.

Alejandro stood up. He leaned over me in the swing, kissing me softly and sensually. My tongue was so hungry for him post orgasm. It was a deep, long kiss. I was still pulsing inside. We kissed with a new, wild, and sexy abandonment.

You are so fucking sexy. You're driving me mad.

He removed my blindfold slowly and took my legs out of the stirrups. He knew instinctively my legs had gone completely, so he scooped me up, carrying me over to the bed, like a heroic warrior.

After Alejandro cleaned us both up with wipes and tissues, he covered me with the large feather duvet. It was so cosy. He wrapped himself close, our lower legs touching, as he perched on one elbow, stroking my arms gently. His aftercare was second to none. I adored him even more for it. I was slightly sore, but in such a beautiful way. I knew I would have a reminder of him, of this, our special night together, for several hours.

"How do you feel?" he asked.

"Calm, and peaceful"

"All of the noise in your head has stopped, hasn't it?"

"Yes, how did you know?"

"Because it has in mine."

I feel complete, loved, and free.

40 MUM AND DAD

November. Saturday. Liverpool. Home.

The weather was cold, the trees were stark. Sometimes on weekends, I would wake up and need one thing. The comfort of my mum and dad. I called to see when I could pop by today. I really missed them sometimes. When we grew up, our family was tight, thick as thieves.

I found it hard when I started at university and ultimately moved out. I was used to seeing them every day. I found a lot of comfort living with them. It was difficult to let go. There were days when I wished, even now, I was still living with them in that protected family bubble.

I drove to their house. They'd moved to the Wirral a few years ago. Caitlyn lived on that side of the water, too, but commuted to Liverpool daily. We were still close and visited regularly. I smiled at their beautiful house as I pulled up, the pang of familiarity as I looked at the rose trellis on the fence.

I rang the doorbell.

"Bonjour, ma fille," Mum said, smiling as she opened the door.

"Bonjour, ma mere."

It was the type of hug I didn't want to let go of today, so I didn't for a while. She sensed me.

"Come in, sweetheart."

"Here she is," Dad said, opening his arms.

"Hey, fluffy."

Dad was great at tight, embracing hugs. I couldn't get enough. Ever. They were full of meaning. No words, just meaning.

Dad wasn't the best at expressing himself or articulating his feelings, but I knew how to read him, to sense what he felt. It was one of the most profound forms of communication to me, to understand beyond words. I also learned not everyone expresses their love in the same way.

Mum was the complete opposite. Articulate, open, compassionate, and expressive. They were a total contrast in every way. That's what attracted them to each other.

"You sit down. I'll put the kettle on," he said, seeing me shiver.

"It's cold out, isn't it?" Mum asked.

"Yes, there's quite a bite to the air now. It's only changed in the last two weeks."

"You're a proper early bird this morning, aren't you?" Mum asked.

"I only slept for three and a half hours, so I thought I might as well get up and do something productive."

"What's wrong?" Mum asked.

"Hmm, where to start. There are a few things going on simultaneously. I've been struggling to get to sleep since Tuesday."

"What happened Tuesday?" Dad asked.

"The case I'm working on. I found a link."

"Between the victims?" Mum asked.

Her mind was as analytical as mine. She enjoyed problem solving.

"Yes. And it's bizarre but has quite serious implications."

"Why?" Dad asked.

"Because it means The Choker has already identified his next victim before he kills his current victim. There is no overlap. It's entirely premeditated. His mind has been set on murder since the very first victim."

My head spun with the calculation of it all. A mind that constantly thinks about murder.

"What's the link?" Mum enquired.

"It's the lockets, inside the chokers. The ones he leaves on the women he kills. I always thought they were odd, as they each had a different stone inside the central locket."

"Stones?"

"Yes. I realised, from the multiple visits to your shop, that they looked familiar. So, I trawled through various images on Google and confirmed my suspicions. They are all birthstones."

"So how does that link with the premeditation? I'm confused," Dad asked.

"The first girl who died, Kirsty Thompson, age 23. He watched her for just over six months. On her body, the choker contained a Citrine," I stated.

"Sagittarius," Mum said, knowing her birthstones from the shop.

"Yes. Second victim, Josie Fairfield, age 26. He watched her for at least eight months. Her birthday was the 30th of November. She was a Sagittarius," I recounted.

"Okay but how is that a pattern?" Dad asked.

"Wait for it. Josie was found with an Onyx birthstone in her necklace," I added.

"Leo," Mum said.

"Yes, and the third victim was Julie Long, age 27. He was watching her for at least 10 months. Her birthday was the fifth of August. She was a Leo,"

"And the birthstone Julie was wearing?" Mum asked.

"Sapphire," I said.

"Taurus. Is that what the last victim was I assume?" Mum asked.

"Fourth victim. Crystal Wilkinson, aged 29. He watched her for a year. Her birthday was the fourth of May. Taurus."

"Do you or the police think any of it could be a coincidence?" Dad asked.

"No. I don't believe anything with him is a coincidence. The more I've become involved in the case, the more I've realised how intelligent this man is. It's almost like he's toying with the police, like he's always a few steps ahead and doesn't think he can be caught," I added.

"He's bound to slip up some time, very few get away with it completely, especially if they're conceited enough to be giving clues. So, the relevant question now is, what gemstone was Crystal Wilkinson wearing and how will that help the police?" Mum surmised.

"Crystal was wearing a Garnet, which means Aquarius. The only problem is that roughly one twelfth of the population is Aquarius. When I spoke to the police, they thanked me for the connection and said it was a distinct possibility that he did plan his next victim before he killed his last. Sadly, it only provides a clue, not a lead they can follow up."

"That's why he's done it then, to wind you up. He is toying with all of you because you can't possibly use that information to identify the current victim, despite there being an obvious link," Dad said, frowning.

"Now I know he's leaving clues right in front of our noses, I've been re-reading case files all week, looking for something I've missed. All the family members have made references to him knowing things or sending things of specific relevance they can't understand. Things he couldn't have known from searching through bins or had access to from other people. They just didn't get how he knew. He's an enigma. He's one giant puzzle that needs solving before anyone else gets killed."

"You can't do this on your own though, curly. Everyone needs to pull together," Dad said.

"I know, but it is becoming an obsession, trying to understand how and why he does what he does. After having been watched from my own back garden, I can empathise even more with the victims. It's intimidating. It must have been horrendous for them near the end as he ramped it up. They constantly had to think where they were going, who they were with, who was around them, what they were saying. Any single one of the people they spoke to could have been the killer and they would have had no idea. Even after they realised, they were being stalked, they had no way of knowing his intent was murder."

"Has anything else happened about that guy in your back garden?" Dad asked.

"Nothing. I'm still carrying the personal attack alarm around with me everywhere and always have it within hands reach in my bag. Ellie carries hers, too. It worries both of us. That reminds me. I've been meaning to ask you, Dad. Have you bought me a bouquet of flowers and had them delivered to the house at any point?"

"The only flowers I've ever bought you, your mum, or Caitlyn were given directly to you on your birthday. I've never ordered them, for any of you. Why?" he asked.

"There was a bouquet delivered and we weren't sure who it was from, that's all. Maybe it's something to do with work, or it might be from Ellie's family. I'll get her to check," I said.

"How is Ellie? You haven't mentioned her in ages," Mum asked.

"There's a good reason for that, I've hardly seen her. It was subtle to start, but it's increased more the past few months. I understand she has been in the honeymoon phase with Hayden, but they're always together at his house. After the stalking incident, she's been clinging to him. When I do see her, he is with her, and they aren't staying for much more than a coffee or to pick things up. I get phone calls from her friends at the house asking where she is, because they haven't seen her either. It's like she's stopped seeing all her friends, to be with him," It puzzled me.

"Not sure that sounds like a very healthy relationship," Mum mused.

"People always need their friends, as separate relationships. Particularly with you, though; you've been best friends for years," Dad added.

"I know, right?! We are thick as thieves. That's why I thought it was a little off."

"Maybe you should have a word with Ellie, just to check and see everything is okay. It's easy to make assumptions she's having fun and ignoring you. Check nothing is wrong because that doesn't sound like her at all. You've seen her with previous boyfriends, and she has never been like that. What is Hayden like?" Mum asked.

"Handsome, fit, intelligent. He deals with security hacks for a living. He's charming, especially with women. Alejandro is not as convinced. They had a boy's chat and there's something doesn't sit right with him about Hayden. He goes by his senses a lot, and he thinks something is off. I can't see anything, personally, but then I haven't spent too much time with him."

"What is he unsure of?" Dad asked.

"Alejandro felt Hayden was a little threatened because he is intelligent, too. He responded negatively to a couple of comments made, showing an inferiority complex. Maybe Hayden made assumptions Alejandro wouldn't be academic. Alejandro was a straight A student. Hayden only found out through conversation with him, though," I said.

"Why would it bother him how intelligent Alejandro was?" Dad asked.

"That's what neither of us know. It's like he wants to be the clever one. Like that's the role he's used to taking with people. Alejandro said he made a couple of petty comments. He said he looked visibly irritated and was acting weird," I added.

"Like what?" Dad asked.

"Repetitive actions, like an anxiety thing," I added.

"Sounds odd. Check and see Ellie is okay," Dad said.

"Hmm, I will. Are you looking forward to Christmas and meeting Alejandro?" I asked.

"Can't wait to meet the man who has swept my baby off her feet. He'd better be good enough for my little girl," Dad replied.

"I'm not so little anymore, though, am I?"

"You'll always be my little girl to me."

"And you will always be the first man I ever fell in love with."

Dad smiled affectionately at me.

"How are your friends?" Mum asked.

"Nia's firm won an award for excellence in diversity and inclusion at the Lawyer Awards in London. She looked stunning in a full-length dress. I'm delighted for her, that her company and talent are being recognised," I said proudly.

"That's so impressive. Nia must be incredibly proud. Wish her all the very best from us and offer our congratulations when you next see her," Mum said.

"I will. She's always humble and grateful for your kind thoughts."

I spent another couple of hours with them, catching up on the rest of the family, hearing news about their extended families, both of which I love dearly. My mum has brothers she worships, and my dad has two brothers and a sister. It was very special to grow up with all that love.

I couldn't help but want to include Alejandro in that now, too, to show him what having a larger family was like. He had been so isolated for so many years.

First though, let me love you, baby.
Let me show you the love you deserve.
You deserve all of me.

I needed to write when I got back, to still me, so I focused on my muse.

"He understood about nuances,
creating intoxicating spaces+loyalty,
the beauty of intelligence+
power of choice,
the importance of trust+
care for emotions+
just how intoxicating
the exploration of a mind+
soul can be.
The intuitive power
of a man with a sixth sense..."

"It's the way
you know me,
studied me,
explored me,
felt the way my words
were interwoven
with an innate sensuality,
the way I craved more;
from life, from love.
It's the way you knew
who I hid underneath,
the secret me,
the dark desires that fill me,
as I touch this deep ache..."

"There is
no word
more erotic,
or as compelling
than the written

word *mine*.
There is no flesh
more bonded than
that through a deep
mental connection,
when two minds
touch+savour
the nuances
found within the
darkest corridors
of each other..."

    I could romance the moments all over again. I liked to keep my words sensual, but with an edge, to leave something for the reader's imagination. It was open to interpretation. All poetry was. Readers wouldn't understand the source, but Alejandro would. Every poem was a secret between us, written in a language only we understood, yet shared with thousands.

    Instant notifications. DarkWolf liked all of them. He then started writing his own version of our events, which I always adored, to see both sides, getting an insight into how he felt, too.

    He posted:
"She looked at me like I was art
and maybe that's all I ever needed"
"Once you taste real chemistry
you will never want to let it go"
"Your kisses have a much deeper effect on her
when you take the time to kiss her mind first"
"I tasted you so deeply,
I swear I tasted your soul"
"The key to your trust
is the most beautiful thing
anyone ever gave me"
"I will give you everything
because you ask for nothing"
"Let me seduce you every day
I can think of nothing more beautiful
than to make you feel wanted,
mentally and physically"

    Alejandro and I flirted shamelessly with each other on our timelines, responding to the other's posts. We were both inspired by words and loved being creative while romancing each other. Some words were sweet, others were erotic. We set each other on fire mentally. That was what felt so special, he was engaged in my life and with me.

I couldn't wait to hear more of his songs as they were released. I had a feeling the lyrics could all be poignant, in the same way his poetry was. The things he said in his last post, about wanting to seduce me, that was what we were doing to each other, every single day. We'd been seducing each other all week since the last time we were intimate. It felt like we couldn't get enough of each other's minds. After we were sated, we started to think about the next time. There was a constant craving for each other. It was a need, a mutual obsession.

What happens if you ever have enough of me?
Will you still love me then?
I sent Alejandro a text,
"What time do you want me around tonight?" I asked.

He responded promptly, "Jason is coming over early afternoon and we're going to have a workout then go for a round of golf. I'll cook for us. I'll be starving by then, so make it seven p.m. Sharp. I feel another basement night coming on if you'd like?"

"I'd love to. Enjoy your afternoon. I'll see you later, xxx."

"I look forward to it, sexy, xx," he replied.

I shuddered at the thought.

What do you have planned for me tonight, handsome?

41 DEMONS

9:52 a.m.
So much noise in my head. The demons are talking so loudly today. Such a commotion. They're shouting at me, telling me to strike early, to finish it. They know I won't because I'm stronger than them. It's taken me years to say that but they're so bloody persistent. Always nagging at me, telling me 'She deserves it now, what are you waiting for?' Some days, they try to force me to kill you. They play images in my head. They show me things I don't want to see, and I yell at them to go away. I can't do mess. They know that.

I already spend an inordinate amount of time cleaning up, wiping everything down, using a UV light and a Micro DNA scanner to make sure I haven't left any evidence. Can't buy those in a corner shop you know. It pays to be a highly valued employee of the 'dark lord of tech.'

Yet the voices still hassle me regardless. Do it tonight they say.

Shut up. I'll do it in my own goddam time. I'm not ready. Just SHUT UP.

Always nagging. Telling me to get onto the next one and finish this one, that the build-up is more enjoyable and to get it out of the way. I constantly push back. They're not in charge here, I am.

The women all come to know how I felt. I've seen a demon too, many times. In the shape of a mere man. It's the fear. The absolute terror, as someone you thought you knew becomes possessed by the devil. It never leaves you. You are forever haunted, from that day forward. Wary of everyone, looking into their eyes to check what lurks behind them.

Eventually I destroyed him though, didn't I? When I was stronger than him. Finally. It took so many years, but it was worth it in the end. He got what he deserved. My hands around his throat, looking at the demon in my eyes instead. How does it feel when the shoe is on the other foot? Disgusting, little evil piece of shit, isn't that what you used to call me? His fear was the one thing I always craved. I fantasised about revenge for years. How I savoured that moment.

Now SHUT THE HELL UP. I want some bloody peace.

42 BELT

December. Saturday. Liverpool. Home.

It was rapidly approaching Christmas. I'd been late night shopping in Liverpool One earlier in the week, picking up presents for family and friends. I had a couple of special presents left to order for Alejandro and a few small bits for the kids. After I finished writing, I opened my iPad, finishing off the rest of my Christmas shopping.

Pressing "order," felt like bliss, knowing I had Christmas wrapped up.

Done. Yes!
Now I must wrap them all when they get here.
Sigh.

My family always held a big get-together, which I'd discussed with Alejandro. He was excited to see what a bigger family felt like, and I knew he would be welcomed with open arms.

I was looking forward to meeting his dad, best friend, and their partners. When you speak to someone every day in a relationship, you soon become embroiled in their lives and all the people they regularly communicate with. You build a picture of them in your mind.

I put the Christmas tree up in the week. It was relatively quick as the tree was already pre-sprayed with glitter. It was tasteful. Elegant. I finished wrapping up the last of the presents, placing them under the tree.

I felt like my life had finally come together. A large part due to Alejandro. He stilled the chaos in my mind. I was in awe of him wanting to get to know me so deeply, the way he saw my potential, and our potential together. He believed in us both as individuals and as a couple. What an enchanting, rare and precious gift he'd given to me. His faith, time, mind, care, and love.

At the same time, there were dark, mysterious feelings which excited me and made me pulse, thrilling me with the adventure of not knowing what he was going to do next. He was completely unpredictable. It still made me nervous. But he left me feeling sated and peaceful and I learned to trust this, and him, deeply. I learned to ignore the anxiety and nerves I had about his unpredictability, simply enjoying the sensation of releasing everything to him. I didn't have to think about anything when we were locked together as submissive and sensual dominant. I'd never experienced that before.

I understood it was all about pleasure. I understood his intentions with me and for me. He'd triggered new desires deep inside me, making me feel safe as he explored them. I wanted to talk to him more about my feelings.

Tonight, I wanted a deeper connection. But this time, I wanted him to push me a little.

I started to get ready, paying attention to small, subtle, and sensual details. Like thunder before the rain, my thoughts had begun to rumble, a precursor to our passion. It started to take over, tingling the surface of my skin. It bubbled under constantly, needing to boil, before it could simmer again.

I'd bought a few lingerie items, tops and trousers, some skirts, and dresses after my last payday. I wanted to feel pretty for Alejandro. Tonight, I was wearing a sexy red lingerie set. The bra was sheer, but with small lace roses on it and a silk red trim. The G-string panties were also sheer, but with a silky under section for the crotch and a red silk bow tied at both hips.

Driving to his house that night, everything was whirring around my mind, making my head spin. None of my thoughts would settle. I couldn't stop thinking about him, the things he'd spoken to me about. The RSD submission, dominance, how he wanted to please me, how he wanted to take ownership of me, the way he whispered *mine* in my ear. He'd gotten so far under my skin and into my mind, he was constantly present.

As I pulled up at the house and buzzed the security lock outside the gate, it swung open slowly. I drove in, parked to the left of the house, and nervously went to the door, butterflies rapidly forming inside my stomach.

Alejandro answered the door, every inch of him looking sexy as hell. He wore a revealing navy top and jeans that hung from his angular hips.

"You look ravishing tonight, Leila. I mean absolutely stunning."

"As do you," I said, blushing.

I leaned in, offering my cheek for his standard greeting kiss on either side.

"Dinner will be ready in 10 minutes. I appreciate your punctuality."

I knew that was one of the things he loved and took my lead from him, as he was always so prompt. He hated people being late.

He took my coat, leading me to the dining room. The table looked beautiful. It was a long, mottled, marble-topped table, and there was a classic feel to the room. The carpet was a very light beige. The décor was stunning. The walls were painted in a deeper beige. There were two oval mirrors hung on the wall, with a large, low, centrally hung light. The cutlery was laid out and there was a wine chiller and bottle already at the table, with large bowl-shaped glasses set at both the head of the table and the seat adjacent to it. He had placed us next to each other.

"Would you like to pour the wine, while I bring in the starters?" he asked, pointing to the uncorked bottle.

He left the room, and I poured out the wine into each glass, pouring it to the top of the widest section, as they do in restaurants.

"Please sit."

He carried two small plates of Parma ham and melon, laying them on the table and sitting at the head.

"This looks lovely."

"How was your day?"

He always checked to see how I was. I loved that about him. He'd done it virtually every day since I met him. Nobody had ever been so attentive. I started to cut the Parma ham.

"Other than the writing and wrapping up the Christmas presents and putting them under the tree, I couldn't stop thinking about you. Everything you said was playing through my mind. I can't stop thinking about the ways you want to please and push me. What have you done to me?"

"Nothing that your subconscious didn't already crave. How do you feel about trusting me now, Leila?"

He watched my lips as I ate with delicate bites.

"I want more. More of you. More of what you want to do to me. More of what you believe I need. My body is aching to know and feel you."

"That's how it starts. A natural curiosity you won't be able to sate, a need to be touched in a certain way, loved in a certain way, or commanded in a certain way. Your needs are growing already. That's good. It's a powerful feeling for me to know I've made you feel like that, to bring out the sub only I could sense."

It didn't take long to eat the starters. The way he was looking at me made me sip the wine faster. He leaned over to kiss me on the forehead. It felt tender and loaded with emotion.

He lifted the starter plates and said, "I'll be back in a couple of minutes."

I heard a timer go off on the oven and some general clatter while he was in the kitchen. I finished the last sip and refilled both of our glasses. I rolled it around my palate. He arrived with two plates, steam rising from both. He looked sexy carrying them in, like some master chef. Another way he looked after me.

I love the things you do.

The anticipation was building inside me. What did he have planned? I thought about some of the things he might do to me as they flashed through my mind, but I loved the fact he always kept it as a surprise. It also made me nervous as hell. I think that was what he enjoyed about it though, so I always anticipated being with him.

As he laid down the meals on our placemats, the smell hit me. I saw a succulent piece of white cod, laid on a bed of mash with baby carrots and asparagus placed in criss-cross formation, with a pungent smelling sauce.

"What's the sauce?"

"Chilli and lime. Taste it."

"This is delicious, Alejandro. "

He had this thing about watching my lips. It disturbed the rhythm of my heart. I licked the juice around my lips knowing it teased him. He shifted in his seat slightly.

"Glad you like it."

He alternated his gaze between my eyes and mouth.

"So, are you going to show me tonight?" I asked, with a slight stammer.

I think my shyness turned him on because he played on it.

"I want you to be ready. I will need to prepare you."

There it was, the dark, slightly sinister side to him I would never be in control of. The man he became when his eyes darkened at the thought of me as a sub. I found my body reacting as soon as he said the words *prepare you*. I felt myself starting to pulse on the inside, and I knew I couldn't control the internal flow of my lust or emotions.

"Mmm, that does things to me, when you say you want to prepare me."

"I want to do more than prepare you, I want to own you tonight. I want you to kneel for me again," he said, looking into my eyes.

My breath hitched. He heard it.

"I want you. Finish your meal, Leila."

There it was, that dark dominance that made me go weak at the knees. The turn in his voice. I sipped more wine and proceeded to eat what was left on my plate. Alejandro finished before me and was watching me, like a vulture eyeing its prey, a slight menace sparkling within his cobalt eyes. The atmosphere in the room changed completely.

When I finished, he poured out another glass each of wine and then said,

"Come with me. Now."

His tone was authoritative and sexy as hell. I think he'd deliberately given us a light meal.

I followed him down the stairs to the basement and this time, there was no fear, just nervous energy. It was warm in the room.

Alejandro looked at me and I knew straight away that my *master* was now in the room with me. I lowered my eyes, and he commanded.

"Take off all your clothes and kneel, with your palms facing up, head lowered. The next time I ask, I will just say '*get ready.*'"

He watched me this time. Last time he was out of the room, but this time, he watched me strip. I found it incredibly nerve-wracking, making myself vulnerable in front of him as he watched, as I felt his eyes pouring over my naked flesh.

I knelt, as commanded, on the rug in the centre of the room.

"Good girl," he came over and whispered in my ear.

There was something about the way he said it that made me shiver. Goosebumps formed immediately on my arms and my arm hairs stood on end. As he went around the other side of me, he whispered in the other ear.

"I'm going to show you exactly who you are now. You need no control in this room and I will set you free. Are you ready?"

I didn't even need to think about the answer.

"Yes, *sir*."

"Mmm, I like that response."

Alejandro moved behind me.

"Widen your legs, while you are kneeling."

He lowered himself behind me.

As I widened them, I felt his hand reach from behind, and he slipped a single finger along the ridge of my silken folds, to find my clit. I bit my lip and gasped as he found it.

"That's beautiful, Leila, you're wet through thought alone. Submission is a powerful aid to turn you on, as I suspected. This is the part where I make you even wetter."

It was almost like a gentle, but sexy, threat, as he pressed firmly against my clit, using a small rotational motion to centre the whole of my ache in that singular spot. Slow hard grinds followed with three fingers. I was delirious. He continued using the motion to build me up, interchanging it between circles, vertical, and diagonal strokes.

My clit was burning now, aching, engorged, needing a release. He worked me right up until the edge, until my breath changed, and my chest started heaving, reading my body, reading me. As soon as I was right on the edge, he pulled his hand away.

"No baby, please don't stop."

"Don't use baby in here. Call me *sir* in this room. Stand for me, Leila," he commanded into my ear, as I pouted.

He helped me up. Leading me to the right of the bed, he stood me in front of the hobby horse, like a bench that gymnasts would use to vault over. There were straps for the arms and lower legs, with restraints. He wrapped his arm around my stomach, folding me, bending me over the bench softly. The position was instantly erotic.

The material was soft and warm against my breasts. There was something incredibly sexual about the way he rendered and exposed me, with my sex revealed and my ass protruding out.

He used the restraining devices to secure me. I knew exactly how wet I was then. I felt it on the inside of my upper thighs. He wrapped the leather cuffs around my wrists and secured my ankles. There wasn't much leeway to move at all. I could hear his breath change as he restrained me.

This turns you the fuck on.

I heard the belt on his trousers being slowly slid out and drew through each loop, painfully slow. I gasped.

Are you going to take me right now?

Alejandro took the rest of his clothes off, discarding them. It was as if everything was in slow motion. I waited, vulnerably naked, bearing my soul to him. He leaned over me, his thick hardness pressed briefly against my fleshy cheeks tantalising me, before he kissed down the centre of my spine. So tender. Then came the unexpected warning.

"The next thing I do to you will sting a little. It won't be too hard, and I want you to know you can shout *Break* at any point and I will stop immediately. Do you understand?"

"Yes, *sir*," I replied, my voice trembling.

I had no idea what he was going to do. The next second, I felt something whipping against the soft, fleshy area of my ass. Not hard, but enough to shock me. It stung, but in a way that made me ache erotically. I liked the sensation it left me with, that tingle. He was right. I moaned immediately, my sex twitched automatically.

I lost myself in the sensation, losing control, as he took it from me. The powerlessness was intoxicating. I was restrained and bent over, just for him. All for this beautiful, sexy, powerful man. He was the only one with whom I'd ever let go of control.

"Again?" he confirmed.

"More, please," I whimpered.

He whipped the belt against me again, in a sharp short burst. I had no idea why it felt so beautiful to me, but it did. He had complete and utter power over me, and I had none. I felt intoxicated by the balance shift.

My skin started to smart, yet again I said,

"More."

He repeated the whipping action across my ass, aiming slightly lower this time. It was close to hitting my sex.

"More," I said again, my breath catching as the bite of the movement kicked in.

Soft crack.

"This is your last one. No more than five."

He aimed lower this time and caught my sex, too. I yelped. It stung slightly yet was erotic at the same time.

He dropped the belt to the floor, coming over to stand right behind me, his erection bouncing around my thigh as he ran his hands gently down the side of my breasts, the curve of my waist and hips, then holding my backside.

He bent down to kiss both cheeks softly. Then I felt him start to slide into me.

"Mmm," I moaned, as he entered me slowly.

"You're so wet, Leila."

His width took my breath away as he pushed all the way in. I couldn't breathe for a second, the angle was so deep in this position. He pulled out so just the tip was inside me and then thrust into me, hard. I was neither ready for the depth or prepared for his thrust and I grunted, sharply, loudly. It was almost unbearable.

I couldn't move at all. So, I decided to free myself. I relaxed completely, letting my whole body go limp instead of tense. He pulled out and thrust into me again. It felt easier, relaxing and letting my whole body go.

"You've reached it, baby, right in that second where you relaxed. You're in subspace now."

I could offer no words. I was aroused beyond anything I ever felt before. I was lost deep in the sensation, and offered myself to him wholly, to take as he pleased. He pulled out and penetrated me again, my wetness making him glide to full depth.

As he quickened up the pace, thrusting in and out of me, harder and faster, I couldn't even warn him vocally and started to come. My body quaked in a way I'd never felt before and my legs quivered.

"I love it when you come for me, it tips me over the edge."

He suddenly went into a frenzy when he felt my walls contract, gripping him internally. He came, hard and fast while I was coming, releasing a guttural moan that made me twitch around him.

Fucking gone.

The deep, internal angst disappeared as the feeling subsided gradually, and he finished his last few strokes inside me. I continued to twitch around him, as any power I had left my body completely.

I feel euphoric and dazed, like I'm in a trance.
I feel it.
Subspace.

He gently rocked inside me to ease me out of the feeling slowly. I'd read about having to ease out of subspace and domspace, else it can disorient both of you. He started kissing my spine, stroking my hair, as I lay, motionless, unable to move or think.

My mind is empty.
I finally understand.
I feel complete.

Eventually, he pulled out slowly, as he went to the drawer on the other side of the bed and pulled out some cream. He looked over at me, as I looked vacantly, but caringly, at him. For a second, he watched me, like he was admiring the beauty of my absolute surrender to him. I saw such affection in his eyes, beyond any kind of love I'd seen in a man's eyes before.

Alejandro put some cream on his hands, walking over. He gently rubbed it in circles over the tender areas of my ass. I still couldn't move, not at all. I was completely gone, and he knew it.

"Aftercare," he said with a soft voice. "You will heal much quicker with this."

After he was finished, he released the restraints and then, as I tried and failed to stand up with my *Bambi* legs, he scooped me up and carried me over to the bed, laying me down gently. He covered me in the thick duvet, climbing in beside me. I still couldn't speak.

He lifted one arm, and I leaned onto his chest. I needed to feel close to him, like I was trying to wrap myself in and around him. He comforted me, as he repeatedly kissed my forehead. He sensed how much I needed him. It was an incredibly powerful moment.

"*Mine.* You've got no idea how fucking proud I am of you."

Yours. I'm all yours.

I can't explain that moment, that freedom.

I had no idea how erotic or beautiful or loving this could have felt. It took so much out of both of us. Perhaps that was why we had nothing left.

Rapture.

*Enchantment.
Transcendence.
It was all three.*

43 STUDIED

November. Sunday. Chester. Alejandro's.

When I woke up the next day, I was alone. I heard Alejandro come down the stairs 20 minutes later. He walked in wearing a navy pair of shorts and a thin athletic top, looking very sporty. He was carrying a tray, smiling at me, with a breakfast that looked like it was exactly what I needed. A curvy glass of pure orange juice, a light omelette with two rashers of bacon, grilled tomato, some mushrooms, and a slice of brown bread, toasted and cut in half.
"Good morning, sexy."
I sat up, wincing slightly as I shifted in the bed, aware of my bum mildly stinging, yet unable to take my eyes off him.
"I'll rub some more of the healing balm on your skin after you've had a shower."
"Mmm, thank you."
He lowered the tray onto my lap.
"I'm going for a workout. I assume you won't want one right now?" he asked.
"You assumed correctly."
"Okay, I'll be about an hour. Then we can have a swim together."
He stroked my hair, tucking it behind my ear and continuing to stroke softly over my jawline.
"Is there anything else you need?"
"No, I'll eat this gorgeous breakfast and write some poetry for a while."
I picked up the knife and fork and started eating.
"I went through everything you wrote, going back three years, while I was away on tour. I was trying to understand you, to find out everything you liked. I felt you in your words, what you said, what you didn't. I felt the hidden ache in your words, the yearning. It jumped off the page to me, so badly. You needed me; you just didn't know it."
There was absolute conviction in his voice.

"I can't believe you read through three years of posts."

"I wanted to understand your mind. You never write poetry about love, just erotica, yet you desperately crave intimacy, I can feel it in your words. Why?" he asked.

"I write what I know and feel. I can elaborate experiences, but I can't completely fabricate them. I wasn't in love with anyone."

"You needed a caring dominant, one who made you feel secure and safe enough to open up to love. It was obvious to me as I read you. I can give you everything you crave."

"How would you know what I need?"

"I can feel it emanating through your poetry, Leila. *I can feel and sense it*. It's beautiful to witness the need, the desire in you, blooming."

I physically shuddered.

"Trust me. Trust, I know what's best for you, that I know what you need," he urged.

"I trust you, Alejandro."

"Beautiful," he said, softly kissing my forehead. "I'll see you in an hour or so."

I gathered myself for a few minutes, trying to still the chatter starting to form in response to what he said.

I picked up my phone. I needed poetry. To centre myself. To gain clarity and focus. I thought about how he made me feel.

"It's the way
you wanted to know me,
studied me,
explored me,
felt the way my words
were interwoven
with an innate sensuality+
the way I craved more;
from life, from love.
It's the way you knew
who I hid underneath,
the secret me,
the dark desires that fill me,
as I touch this deep ache..."

Such an erotic thought.

"He was devious and clandestine,
leading me down
into the stairwell of hidden lusts,
seeking rapture
from the lascivious nature

of my deepest fantasies
and my darkest predilections..."

    Last night, I felt a certain darkness to my sensuality was opened further through RSD. I was beginning to understand the way he wanted to explore my mind. It was incredibly arousing, allowing someone to get so close.

    "The first time
darkness wraps
around your mind+
grips your desires,
is a feeling you
will never forget...
the moment
beyond which
your heart will
never again settle+
the taste you
will forever crave...
let it consume you;
lick it from my lips..."

    "She needs someone
who understands
her darkness won't fit
into one hand.
Someone that can
pin her heart,
arouse the unlit corridors
of her mind+
kiss her thoughts
simultaneously.
Passion like hers
needs to be ravaged like fire,
then loved like water..."

    "He made love
to my soul that night+
then cradled my trembling
shell as I pulsed until I
felt still – his aftercare
silenced every
part of me..."

    It felt like everything had changed.
I want to let go completely.
I want to bloom, just for you.

	I felt the purest love I'd ever felt:
	"I want to
make love
to you,
slowly,
with devotion+
the tenderness of
a million butterflies
conversing through
eyes, hands+mouths..."
	"There are days
when all I want
is for you
to make love to me
with a tenderness
that feels
like a lucid dream.
Sensual whispers
cascading into my mouth,
soft kisses
placed gently
on sensitive lips+
emotion so tender
that even my soul
surrenders to you..."
	"You are my
safe haven,
my retreat,
my sanctum.
Here, I offer you
a parallel reality
where we are
both set free.
A place where
I give you all of me+
the greatest gift
I could ever give you;
my complete
emotional submission.
Here, I am yours,
worshipping
your mind, body+soul..."

I wonder what else Alejandro would conjure up for me over the coming months.

I wonder if it would constantly feel like fire and ice with him. The stoking of flames to arouse my passion, and then the soothing aftercare which followed.

I wonder.

44 ISOLATION

November. Sunday. Liverpool. Home.

I got back earlier than normal. Alejandro had looked after me beautifully, but the situation with Ellie was niggling at me. I wanted to check on her. I was getting concerned. I knew her like the back of my hand, and something wasn't right. I texted her to check if she would be in tonight. It was a good time to try and chat with her.

There was no sign of her downstairs, so I pottered around for a while, making myself a quick pasta dish and a hot drink. It was weird she hadn't come down yet. She must have heard me come in. It felt like she was avoiding me, and I had no idea why. There were two more messages from her friends on the answerphone, too.

"Ellie, are you in? Would you like a cuppa?" I shouted up the stairs.

"Yes, I'll be down in a minute."

She came down 10 minutes later. I'd set her drink down by the couch.

"Hey, you," I said.

"Hey."

"Can we chat?"

"Sure," Ellie said, looking down to avoid eye contact.

"I'm worried about you. Something's not right," I said directly.

She blushed slightly, shifting in her seat as if she wasn't comfortable.

"What makes you say that?"

Her whole demeanour changed. She looked defensive.

"I feel like you're avoiding me, like you don't want to speak to me. Even your body language tells me you're clamming up. You've been evasive for several weeks now. I feel like you're avoiding me more as each week passes. I know you. I know when you're struggling, you go inwards. You try to deal with it all yourself. You're struggling with something, aren't you?" I said, trying to encourage her to talk.

Ellie could sometimes get defensive and had to be coaxed out of her shell without invoking that. She could also be shy. Her mother was opinionated and could be domineering. Ellie was the timid stereotypical quiet girl who ultimately went rogue as soon as she was old enough to rebel. I was always gentle with her and non-judgmental. When I looked over to her, Ellie's eyes had begun to fill up.

"I'm not sure where to start."

"Is it your parents? Is everything okay with your family?"

"It's not family."

"Then what's upsetting you?"

"It's Hayden. He's acting weird and I don't know if it's because of me or him."

Her eyes filled up; the glaze sparkled at the corners as the daylight streamed into the room. She looked beautiful, vulnerable, hurt. I felt a pang for her, as I felt her pain starting to brim.

"I thought you guys were happy together. You've literally lived in each other's pockets since you met each other, obsessively. You've hardly been here."

"The last few months have felt like an obsession. I've never known anyone as passionate. Recently, it's like he's changed. The first few months were like falling in love, down a set of rapids and then over a waterfall! There was nothing slow about it. We've been in bed for months, unable to get enough of each other. It was all going so well."

"That's what I thought. What happened, hunni?"

"Hayden started asking weird questions a few weeks ago, easing them in slowly and now, he is constantly checking up on me. He wants to know exactly where I am, who I am with, and what I'm doing. It's easier to just be with him all the time, so he already knows."

Alarm bells started to go off in my head, but she said it like it was a matter of fact.

"That sounds more than a little obsessive Ellie, it sounds like he's trying to control you."

"It seems to be getting more intense, but everything about us is intense. That's the type of relationship we have. We don't just have sex, it's carnal, it's visceral, it's edgy, it's sexy, and we can't stop touching each other. That part of us is perfect. It's like we want to get inside each other, like we're animals."

"I don't understand what changed," I asked, confused.

"That's the thing. I'm not sure I know. I didn't do anything different. I haven't given him any reason to be suspicious of me. I haven't been with anyone else. Nothing changed I'm aware of. The upside has always been the sex. The downside is his constant checking up on me. He won't let me breathe. It's stifling. We've started fighting about it, too."

"What do you mean fighting?"

"We had a massive fight a couple of weeks ago, where he thought I was checking out another man, but I wasn't even looking at him. He's paranoid. I'm not like that. I don't want other men when I'm with someone I love. We've discussed this in the past and both feel the same about it, if you remember, Leila?"

"Yes, we have very similar beliefs."

"The fight was so intense, though. It escalated quickly, from virtually nothing. I didn't see it coming. He shouted at me so loudly, and honestly, he scared me. I wasn't prepared for how angry he was, or the way he called me names. I've never been spoken to like that before in my life, especially over something so trivial. What was worse was everything he said was because of something he'd made up in his head. None of it was true, but he didn't care."

She was visibly shaking at this point.

"Just breathe, hunni," I said, trying to calm her as she took a couple of deep breaths. "How did the argument end?"

"I don't even know how it happened. We ended up having sex afterwards. He was all riled up, then started kissing me. I wasn't aroused, but I was so grateful the shouting had stopped, and he was being loving again, that I didn't stop it. It was the hottest sex we'd ever had. It left me so confused. It was weird. I didn't like the way I felt afterwards, or the next day. I don't want to be the kind of argue and have make-up sex kind of couple, that's not me at all."

"Have you argued like this more than just once?" I asked, trying tried to establish if this was a one-off event, or a pattern.

"Yes, about four times now. He seems to get angrier each time, and the make-up sex is more intense each time. The sad thing is, I'm getting used to the arguments. I know they'll end, and we'll end up having amazing sex afterwards," she said.

She was aware what she was saying didn't sound right. It was causing her conflict just to say the words.

"That sounds like it's turning into a toxic relationship, hunni, one that isn't healthy at all, with no boundaries."

I was a little nervous of how she might take what I said. It's not an easy thing to hear, from anyone, but she knows I always speak the truth.

"I know, that's why I didn't want to say anything to anyone. I didn't want anyone to tell me things I didn't want to hear. The problem is, I'm madly in love with him, like madly, not just a bit. I don't know what to do with, or about that. The thought of not being with him makes me feel like I can't breathe."

She was being as honest as she could with me. I could see it in the pained look in her eyes.

"It sounds like a co-dependent relationship, Ellie. I've seen a lot of examples of this at work. They make you addicted to them first by being whatever you want, and then the real them starts coming out slowly, and they start treating you badly. The women don't often see the change coming. It presents itself one day, when they either let their guard down, or their partner loses control over something. You have 'trauma bonded' and he knows everything you want and need now and will use it to his advantage whenever possible."

"I don't know, Leila, that sounds a bit harsh," Ellie replied.

I got the distinct impression she didn't want to hear what I was saying.

"What are you going to do about it, Ellie?"

"Nothing right now. I'm just telling you because you asked. I've found a few ways of avoiding arguments and they seem to be helping recently, so I feel a little happier."

"Like what?" I asked, curiously.

"I keep my head down when we go anywhere, so he can't think I'm looking at another guy. I avert my eyes around people when I'm with him, so he doesn't get jealous," she said, as if it was the answer.

"But that's changing who you are. You did it when I came into the room, and he isn't even here."

I was confused as to why this was a good thing.

"Yes, but it's easier. This way he doesn't argue with me as much and the sex is still great, not as intense as after an argument, but still amazing. It's like he rewards me for good behaviour, and he seems pleased with me recently," Ellie said, unaware of how it sounded to me.

I struggled a little with how to react. I couldn't stay silent, but I had to tread very carefully with my response. She was clearly being influenced and manipulated by him. She's gone out of her way to change herself out of fear of him. I could see it now, but I don't think she could. It sounded like emotional abuse to me. Most abuse and rape cases I was privy to often started the same way. Their partner showed a temper and then tried to manipulate and control them. The victim would often find evasive methods to avoid their wrath. Sometimes, abusers don't shout, they just make their partner feel horrible when they do something which displeases them and, in the end, it becomes easier to avoid the trigger points which displease the abuser. One is very passive, and one is very aggressive; regardless, they are both manipulative.

"Are you afraid of him?" I asked, probably pushing her out of her comfort zone with the question.

"When he's very mad, yes. My heart races. His eyes change and get colder. All the warmth disappears from them. I don't like it when he argues with me, at all. It hurts me. Some of the things he says make me feel small and worthless. I stand up for myself. You know I can be feisty at times. He hates that side of me though. When I fight back, it riles him. His face changes. When he looks angry, I feel sick inside, like some part of me shrivels."

"He makes me feel as if I've done something bad, as if it's my fault. When I think about it afterwards, I know it's not, but at the time, he makes me think it's me. I know when his eyes look a certain way, devoid of all warmth and looking like glass, not to do *anything* at all to piss him off. I go to bed early or go get a bath. Nothing can trigger him then," she said.

"What do you mean about feeling small?"

"He's so much bigger than me physically, but it's not that. His alpha attitude perhaps. He makes me feel like I'm tiny, childlike. The stronger he becomes, the smaller I feel," she said.

Again, I was trying to be cautious with my responses and stalled a little, thinking.

"I'm worried for you, Ellie. This doesn't sound at all right to me. I don't know what happened or why he changed, he seemed so charming and kind and caring to you. It sounds, if you don't mind me saying, like he is intimidating you. Do you have any physical reactions to him when he's angry or drunk?" I asked, wondering if this was affecting her physical or mental health.

"I get palpitations, crazy mad palpitations, like my heart is pounding, but in an entirely unpleasant way. My chest tightens," she said.

Suddenly, I was deeply worried for her safety.

"Please, go and see a doctor about that. It sounds like anxiety attacks. I had one after the stalker incident and Alejandro helped calm me down. Your health, both physical and mental, are important. Promise me you'll go?" I said emphatically.

"Okay, I'll go the next opportunity I get after I've been away with my parents. We are leaving tomorrow morning first thing," Ellie reassured me.

I had the feeling someone was going to need to look out for her. It sounded like she was in over her head. I could feel her conflict. She clearly didn't want to or wasn't ready to leave him yet. She was in denial. I'd seen too many examples of this type of relationship get out of hand through my work. It never ended well. The sooner they got out, the better, but they often stayed way past the time most people would, due to trauma bonding Their partners often pulled back and acted overly nice in between abusive episodes, to give them hope they're still nice and do love them. They'd often make more effort, over apologise, or ramp up affectionate gestures to win them back over. That's what manipulative behaviour is like, and the victims are left confused and gaslit, as they don't know which version of their abusers is real.

"Have you discussed any of this with your family, or any other friends?" I asked, wondering if she had any other support.

"No. I don't find it easy to talk about things I can't understand. It even feels weird opening up to you about it, and you know I can talk to you about anything."

This led me to suspect she felt ashamed, embarrassed, or wanted to avoid people telling her what she knew in her heart already - she was in an emotionally abusive relationship. Not all damage is external.

"I know, that's partly because you know, without a shadow of doubt, that I will never judge a word you tell me. I try to help because I love you," I said, trying to reassure her.

"I know you do, Leila. I never take offense to anything you tell me for that reason. You have a huge heart. I know it's always in the right place for the people you care about. I'll go see the doctor as soon as I can, I promise. I want to go get some fresh air for a bit and have a little walk somewhere. I need to clear my head," she said.

It was an evasive move. She didn't want to talk about it anymore.

"You know I'm here whenever you need me. Keep talking to me, okay?" I implored, knowing she bottled emotions and there they stayed, festering.

"Okay, I promise," she said with a smile as she stood up.

I stood up and hugged her. Not a normal type of hug. One with deep understanding that tightens at the end. I knew it touched her. Her eyes were full of tears when I let her go.

"Please be careful, hunni. Safety first," I emphasised.

How on earth was I going to be able to convince her to leave him? Toxic relationships were lethal to the mind. Once it escalated in the way she described, it would only get worse. It was a guaranteed pattern I'd seen over and over with emotional or physical abuse victims. The abusers don't always realise they're sick. The mental and physical damage they leave behind can affect people for years. I was worried about her.

You must see it for yourself, though.
You need to want to leave, too.

45 CHRISTMAS EVE

December. Monday. Liverpool. Home.

Alejandro and I spoke about Ellie. I wanted advice. He said what I expected; that she had to see it herself. All we can do is support and try to guide her, but the decision had to come from her. Alejandro had a sixth sense about Hayden as soon as he met him. He had a feeling in his gut that something didn't add up about him. He was the only one who saw beyond his charm. Hiding aspects of his character seemed to be so easy for Hayden. I didn't see it. There were no warning signs, no red flags, no sense of falsity in him, no instinct telling me he could be argumentative, that he was a controlling man sitting behind the face he presented to everyone.

How did I miss it?

Alejandro suggested I checked on her as much as possible, kept an eye on her over the coming weeks, not allow her to hide. He was deeply concerned about the signs of aggression in Hayden, and that, despite all the red flags, Ellie was still under Hayden's control. I decided I would text and phone her regularly, to see how she was, if I couldn't see her. I relaxed a little knowing she was going away with her parents and set about the plans for Christmas.

I was excited about Christmas Eve. I drove to Alejandro's house first thing in the morning, and we went into Chester to do some last-minute shopping. Chester is so pretty at Christmas. It's a beautiful city regardless, but the lights were up all over the city centre and there were street entertainers throughout. So many gorgeous smells wafting our way and unusual sights to look at. It was full of character.

"I'd like to buy you something special for Christmas, Leila. Will you let me?"

"I've already bought gifts for you, so if you want to buy me a present, as your girlfriend, I'm not going to say no."

"Okay, good, because the shop I want to buy you a gift from is just ahead," he said, with a cheeky grin.

I looked ahead, wondering which shop he wanted to take me to. As we got closer, I realised where he was taking me.

Diamond Cut was a quaint, little corner jeweller's shop with fairy lights around the window display. He wanted to buy me jewellery. How special.

"I want this to be a symbol of our bond. I would never ask you to wear a collar to symbolise our relationship, as I think you are far classier than that, but I would like you to wear a necklace, symbolic of our relationship together. Would you do that for me?"

"Of course, I would."

I'd be proud to.

"Hello, sir," said a gentleman with a furry beard and moustache, in a very smart suit and waistcoat, as we walked through the door.

"Good day to you," Alejandro replied.

"Is there anything I can help you with today, sir?"

His soft brown eyes sparkled as he spoke. I could tell he loved what he did, and it was nice to see his enthusiasm and radiance.

"Yes, I'd like you to spoil this young lady with a beautiful necklace and earring set of her choosing please," Alejandro said, guiding my hand forward.

I smiled at the man.

"Excellent, sir. Are you following any budget in particular?"

"No, I'd like the lady to feel really special," he said, winking at the man.

I didn't like it. Even knowing Alejandro had excessive amounts of money, choosing something outrageous didn't sit well with me. I'd been used to following a budget most of my adult working life and I wasn't materialistic in any way. Life for me, was about experiences. Standing there, in a shop, waiting to have a gift bought for me, at no expense spared, felt wrong somehow. I couldn't help how I felt.

"You're worth it," Alejandro leaned in and whispered, knowing me all too well.

I decided to look for the cheaper items, so I didn't feel guilty.

"Certainly, sir. How may I address you?" he said, looking at me.

"Leila," I replied.

"What a beautiful name. Is there any style you are particularly drawn to?" He said, motioning to the abundance of items under the counter and beneath a glass cover.

"Overbearing isn't really my taste, but other than that, not really. I haven't had a chance to think about what I'd like," I said honestly.

"In that case, I'll bring out a selection for you to choose from. Would you prefer something subtle and elegant? How do you feel about jewels or anything a little unusual?" he asked, trying to assess my taste.

"I definitely like simple and elegant, but I also like unique things, too, maybe with a splash of colour. I like jewels for that reason. I favour silver, more than gold."

"Okay, Leila, I will see what I have and bring out a selection for you."

He returned with a selection of open trays, carrying them two at a time, to reveal the most exquisite looking necklace and earrings sets.

"Please, take your time and feel free to ask me anything you'd like."

I scanned through both trays, which had a wide range and typically didn't have price tags, so I couldn't determine how much they cost.

Great, there goes my plan.

"I want you to pick something you love, Leila. It has to mean something."

Such a beautiful sentiment. I looked closer at the trays and saw it after a quick vertical scan. The one.

"This set," I said, indicating my selection with my index finger.

I was often decisive, and the man looked surprised. Clearly, he was used to people who couldn't make their mind up.

"Leila, that's exquisite," Alejandro said, looking impressed at my selection and the detail in it.

It was a pure silver, heart shaped pendant that had a unique centre to it. Between two very thin pieces of glass, sat a miniature red crystal rose, and a silver infinity symbol, which both appeared to be floating within the pendant. There was a diamond inside the very centre of the crystal rose, sparkling. It was the most unique and stunning pendant I'd ever seen.

To accompany it, there were two crystal rose earrings with a diamond in the centre and a second pair of silver heart earrings with a tiny diamond set into the upper right quadrant of the heart. It was such a pretty set. It would be an absolute honour to wear it for Alejandro as a symbol of our special bond.

"Totally unique, just like you."

"I'll gladly wear this as a token of our love. The gesture carries deep symbolism and sentimentality. That means far more to me."

"We'll take this set, please," Alejandro said, beaming at the salesman.

"Excellent choice, Leila."

"Is this okay?" the man asked, sliding a handwritten figure over to Alejandro for his approval, to which he nodded.

"Would you like it gift wrapped?"

"Yes, please," Alejandro replied.

"Very good, sir."

The man carried the trays of jewellery toward the back of the shop.

A few minutes later, he came back with it gift wrapped. The box bore mint paper with a jade bow, inside a clear bouquet style large clear wrapper, which he had layered with flower petals and small crystal looking droplets. I'd never received a gift like it before.

Alejandro handed over his card, punching in the pin code when offered. When he returned with the receipt, Alejandro put it into his pocket discreetly.

"Thank you for your business, sir," he said to Alejandro, as we started to walk out.

"You're welcome. Have a good day," Alejandro said.

"Thank you very much," I chipped in.

As he was opening the door for me, out of earshot of everyone else, he whispered.

"This is a symbol that you're mine. *Mine*. Do you understand?" he said sexily, with a deep, dominant voice.

"I understand, *sir*" I whispered back, understanding fully this was a symbol of our unique and very special RSD d/s relationship.

"We'll get the other small bits of shopping we need, look around the Christmas Market stalls, then grab a couple of bottles of wine to take tomorrow."

"I can't wait for you to spend some real time with my family and see them all together. I know everyone is going to love you, just like I do. Let's get up early. I have a feeling Father Christmas might bring you something," I said, winking at him.

When we got back, I put his presents under the tree in the lounge.

You're going to love what I've got for you.

46 CHRISTMAS MORNING

December. Tuesday. Chester. Alejandro's.

I woke up first, wrapped up in Alejandro, with my head nestled against his chest. I loved sleeping with him. I was too excited to wait and kissed his forehead and temples, trying to sneakily wake him up.

He opened his eyes and found me hovering right over him, waiting like a child.

"Merry Christmas, handsome."

"Mmm, Merry Christmas, beautiful."

He laughed at my playfulness.

"I have some small surprises wrapped up under the tree for you."

"You are going to let me get dressed first, aren't you?"

"Nope. PJs for pressies because I can't wait, and *then* you can get a shower and get ready after. I promise."

"At least today you will be able to open your necklace and wear it for the first time. I can't wait to see you in it."

"It will of course go perfectly with the themed outfits," I said.

"Of course. Why does your dad insist on everyone wearing something red at Christmas?"

"He loves the colour red. Loves the vibrancy of it. He also likes following family traditions."

"Is he by any chance an LFC football supporter?"

He was aware of the local red and blue rivalry, in both Liverpool and Manchester.

"Yes, he's a red. Fully fledged Scouser" I answered.

"Come on then, come and get your present."

"Okay, okay, I'm up. I'm up," he said, smiling, as he climbed out of bed.

"The room looks so pretty with the decorations up. I love Christmas," I said.

"Nick and Janet did a great job," he added.

Sitting on the floor next to the tree, I realised I was nervous.

What if he doesn't like my presents?

I handed him the envelope, a small box, and a larger present. I hoped he'd like them. I knew they wouldn't come close to the value of his presents for me, but I also knew that didn't bother him. He knew we were in different situations financially and handed me my extravagant gift, along with a couple of other presents, including a big box, too.

"You shouldn't have bought anymore," I said.

"You open a present first."

I opened the one I knew first, which was the necklace, and swooned as I eventually got past the wrapping paper, opened the navy velvet box, and saw it again. It was such a stunning set.

"May I?"

He indicated he wanted to put it on me and moved behind me.

"I'd love nothing more."

I twisted my hair up so he could loop through my arms and put it on. He hooked the clasp at the back, tickling my neck as he did.

"It looks exquisite on you. The rose is like a story of its own, inside the framework of the heart. Such a beautiful choice."

"I absolutely adore it… and you. Thank you," I gushed.

I reached over to hug and kiss him.

"Now open that small one of yours."

I handed him a medium sized box, wrapped in silver paper.

"You'll enjoy this one."

He unwrapped it, opening the lid of the box.

"Oh, I know I will enjoy this one," he said, grinning. "You will too, young lady," he said, pulling out the set of leather handcuffs I'd bought for him.

"There was something about the leather I liked more than any of the others."

"You have good taste. They're exactly what I would have chosen for you."

"I think you'll enjoy wearing this today, too," he said, handing me a small box.

I opened it carefully to find a pretty bottle of perfume labelled Blue Mist, in a bottle the colour of the ocean with fading graduated shades of blue.

"I've not seen this one before," I said.

"That's because I had it made for you."

My eyes filled up. I was amazed at the lengths he would go to make me feel special.

I opened the top and sprayed some on my neck and wrist, bringing it up to my nose.

"You've captured the scent of the ocean perfectly. It's crisp and fresh and invigorating. I absolutely love it. Thank you."

I threw my arms around him again and pulled him tighter.

"I thought you'd like that."

He smiled and kissed my forehead, holding my face with both hands. He kissed the tear about to cascade. We took a minute to enjoy the simplicity of the emotion sitting between us.

"Your turn again."

I offered him a tiny box this time.

"Intriguing."

As he took off the lid, inside there was a key.

"This is a key to my house," I said.

"I want you to feel like you can be with me anytime you want," I said, but added "Just make sure you ring the bell if Ellie's car is there and mine isn't, so you don't scare her."

"This is a lovely symbol of how much you trust me. Thank you. This means so much to me. I love the gesture and think it's only fair I return the favour. I have a spare key for here, too. Hold on."

He stood up and went over to the hall.

When he came back in, he had a key on a small keyring for me.

"You are welcome here anytime, too, whether you want a swim or join me in the middle of the night. I don't mind surprises. Feel free to see it as your space, too."

"I knew I wanted to give you something that symbolises trust."

"I love how you know which things will mean the most to me."

"Okay, last box," he said, smiling widely as he handed it to me.

It was a large box.

"Hmm, now I'm the one who's intrigued."

I unwrapped it, removing the lid and flashed him the biggest smile.

There were at least five lingerie sets. Black lace, red satin, blue, gold, and a sheer teddy.

"They are all so beautiful," I said, lifting each out and pressing it to my cheek.

I love the feeling of satin and lace on my skin.

"I'm sure you'll look beautiful in each of them."

His eyes looked a little misty as he said it. The thought aroused him.

"I'll love wearing them all for you."

I loved lingerie.

"There's one more box inside that box," he said.

As I removed the purple tissue paper, there was a long box. I opened the lid.

"Oh, fuck," I said, realising what it was.

An electronic wand! I pulsed at the mere thought of the vibrations touching me, and how intense it must be.

"Is this for me to use alone, or you to use on me?"

"Both," he said, kissing me softly on my neck.

"I can't wait to use it on you," he said, playfully gripping my neck and biting his lip.

Just the thought of him using it on me was incredibly erotic.

"Well, that's a box of potentially hours of fun in it then, isn't it?"

It would give us experiences. That part I loved.

"Last one," I said, handing Alejandro an envelope, snapping out of it quickly.

It was going to be a long day and we needed to get on the road.

"You're good at intriguing me," he said.

"Long may it last."

As he opened the envelope, he pulled out two tickets from inside, reading them carefully.

"Tickets. To Venice," he said, beaming. "I've never been."

"I know. I wanted to take you somewhere you'd never been before and give you a new experience. I've always wanted to go to Italy. I'd love to explore it with you," I said, softly.

"What a beautiful time we'll have. Thank you. I love you so much," he said, kissing me, framing my face with his hands.

"I love you too, more than you know. Thank you for your incredibly beautiful gifts. I couldn't have asked for anything more perfect."

"I have one more surprise," Alejandro said.

He went out of the room, returning with his guitar.

"The last song I wrote to finish Brandon's album is a song I wrote for you. I'd like to sing it now, as a small preview. I wrote it after our sexy night together the other night. I am the moon, you are the sea, and the tide is the magnetic connection we share. Every star in the sky is a kiss I've left for you."

"It's called *Every Star*."

He began to sing.

"Let me clear your thoughts and worries
Show you somewhere you can be free
I'll wrap my love around you, baby
To discover who you're meant to be
I'll believe in you till the end of time
Release all your fears to me
Give me your faith, I won't let you down
I am your moon, and you are my sea

By the tides of our love, I'll pull you in
Such passion watching your crashing waves
Your siren song kills me nightly
I watch and you're all that I crave
You are the ocean that calls to me
My soul's one true counterpart
I'll clear the clouds from your sky
Calming your thoughts and your heart
I know a place you can be happy
A place so deep in your mind
Just take my hand and we'll go there
To the depths you needed to find
I want you to feel me aching
Shining deep in your ocean bed
I promise to love you forever
Every star, a kiss to your head"

I stayed silent, completely mesmerised by the beautiful tone of his voice.

Alejandro, you dark horse, you're not just a songwriter at all. You're a singer, too!

"I thought the necklace was my favourite gift, but this song, is the most beautiful gift you could have given me. The romantic lyrics, the expression, the gorgeous tone in your voice as you sang. That was perfect. I had no idea you could sing like that. Wow. Thank you so much."

I wrapped my arms around him and held him so tight, tighter than I'd ever hugged anyone. I will never forget today.

The less I expect, the more you give me.
YOU are the most perfect gift this year.

47 CHRISTMAS DAY

December. Tuesday. Chester. Alejandro's.

"Okay, let's go. I'm not going to be late meeting your parents for the first time."

"They're going to love you, Alejandro, I know it," I said, kissing him one more time.

George was dropping us off at 11 a.m. He was being paid handsomely just to be available on Christmas night for the return journey. Alejandro had insisted he take a few days off afterwards. George didn't mind, as he didn't have much family.

It also meant Alejandro and I could have a drink together. We were both dressed as stipulated - in anything bearing the colour red. I was wearing a red silk blouse with a scooped neck to show off my new necklace, and navy denim jeans, with red heels.

"Your figure and those eyes will be the death of me," he said, biting his lip after I'd finished getting ready.

"I think it's the necklace that makes the outfit," I said, touching it and smiling proudly.

Only we would know its significance.

I like having secrets with you.

He was wearing blue jeans with a thin, red, polar neck sweater, and a dark suit jacket. He looked impeccable, as always, not a hair out of place.

We arrived at 10:50 a.m. I was so damn proud to walk in with him.

"Mum, this is Alejandro."

She extended her hand, which he shook gently.

"It's such a pleasure to meet you, Marie," he said, kissing each cheek to greet her.

I had warned her about his European charm. I had a feeling Mum would be smitten with him, too.

"I've heard so much about you. Please come in."

I could hear the chatter of both sides of the family in the lounge, kitchen, and dining room. As Mum moved past, Dad came over.

My dad kissed me on the cheek and shared a brief hug. It wouldn't matter who I was with, he would always greet me first.

"This is my dad, Frank."

I was proud as punch of them both.

"So, you're the guy all the fuss is about," he said, with his tell-tale wink so you knew he was joking.

"Oh, you've been making a fuss about me?" He turned his eyes toward me being playful.

"Me? Noooo," I said sarcastically.

Dad offered a strong handshake and Alejandro matched him. Dad nodded a little as he did, a sign of registering he was a man, not a boy.

"Come in," Dad said. "I'll introduce you to the family."

My dad's voice was soft and kind, with an enthusiasm that could be felt and seen. He liked him. He didn't have to tell me; I already knew he liked him. I'd been reading him all my life. I smiled knowing this. As we walked into the lounge, which was reasonably big and housing a lot of family today, my dad made introductions.

"This is my mum, Violet," my dad said, introducing Alejandro to my nana.

She was in her 80's, and still as spritely and quick witted as anyone I knew. In fact, Nana would put some 30-year-olds to shame with her comebacks.

"I've heard I need to watch out for your humour," he teased.

"My reputation precedes me," she giggled.

"A great pleasure to meet you, Violet."

She was huddled onto part of the corner sofa with the rest of my dad's family.

"This is Darren, my brother, Bethany and Kevin, my sister and baby brother."

My Uncle Kevin looked up at my dad with sarcastic eyes at the "baby" reference.

"Nice to meet you all," Alejandro said as he went along the line, shaking hands or kissing cheeks.

"Just to clarify for you, I'm the funny one," Darren said.

"He's the joker," Bethany piped up.

"I wouldn't trust him at all," Kevin audibly whispered.

I giggled at all of them.

"So that's all of my rabble," Dad said.

"Now, we have the dodgy lot over on this side of the room. The in-laws."

He made a joke X sign with his fingers as if he was trying to protect himself from demons.

"Oi, watch it you," said my beautiful grandma.

"She is the biggest troublemaker of the lot of them," my dad said, blowing a cheeky kiss to her.

"This is Dorothy. When she's not being a troublemaker, she's generally making the garden beautiful for my grandkids, feeding stray animals, or even taking them in sometimes," Dad added. "She's got the kindest of hearts," he offered, with full sincerity.

"And you, my dear, are a breath of fresh air," she retorted.

"It's lovely to meet you, Alejandro."

My grandad stood up to shake his hand.

"This cantankerous old man is Alistair," Dad said.

"What a strapping young man you are," he said.

Straight away Alejandro picked up on the accent.

"Cockney?"

"Close, Portsmouth," Grandad said. "I was in the navy during the war. Many an interesting and devastating story I can share."

"I'm up for that over a brandy sometime," Alejandro responded.

"I'd like that very much, young man," my grandad said, smiling.

So far, he's won over everyone based on first impressions.
It wasn't just me who instantly falls for his charm.

"These are my boys, Joseph and Patrick," Alistair said, introducing my mum's brothers.

Each of them held out a hand to shake Alejandro's. They were firm handshakes; protective *don't even think about messing with my niece* handshakes. They made me laugh because I knew they were secretly serious.

"Great to meet you, mate," they both echoed.

"And you," Alejandro replied.

"This is my wife, Letitia, and our two boys, Anthony and David," Joseph said, the youngest of the two, with big, blue eyes and pale blonde hair, sitting on his knee.

"And how old are you, young man?" Alejandro asked, kneeling in front of him so he wasn't as intimidating in stature, and to put him at the same eye level as David.

"Seven," he said, shyly.

"Seven is a really big boy," he said, smiling and trying to put him at ease. "I think we've got something in our sack for you, if you've been a good boy this year," he said.

David smiled.

"I have," he said, nodding enthusiastically. "What is it?"

"Well, that's a surprise. There's one for you and Anthony," he said, melting my heart a little with how natural he was with kids.

"And how old are you, Anthony?" he asked.

"I'm nine. I like aeroplanes and cars."

"Same. I love going on real aeroplanes and I really like shiny cars," he said, shrinking his similar adult male obsessions to relate to a young boy.

"I was like you when I was younger. I used to like thinking about travelling to so many places."

"I'm going to say hello to everyone first, then I'll bring in the present sack for you guys, okay?"

They both nodded, looking excited.

My dad asked, "I believe you have yet to meet my other daughter, too?"

"Yes, I've been looking forward to meeting Caitlyn and her family for a long time," Alejandro enthused.

"She's setting the dining room table for Christmas dinner. Follow me," he said, clearly in his element as king of his castle.

We both followed him through the connected door at the bottom of the lounge. As we walked through, Jay came over first, extending his hand.

"Hey bud, I'm Jay," he said.

"Hi Jay. Accountant, right?" Alejandro asked.

"Yes, that's right. No accountant jokes though, okay?" he asked, laughing.

"Heaven forbid, no," Alejandro said, laughing.

"And you must be the lovely Caitlyn," he took her extended hand, kissing her on both cheeks.

"I am indeed," she said, smiling. "I have been dying to meet you. I'm so pleased I finally get the opportunity."

"Hey, sis," I said, giving her a warm hug. "Love your red dress. You've gone all out this year and are showing the rest of us up."

"Well, you know redheads are bound by law to wear red better than anyone else," she quipped.

"And you of all people should know more about the law than the rest of us, Caitlyn," Dad chipped in.

"Now where are my favourite nieces hiding?" I asked, knowing full well they were shy around tall men, particularly strangers.

I knew they weren't far away, because I could hear them whispering and giggling with each other.

"Kids, come and see your Aunty Leila and her new boyfriend."

Caitlyn elevated her voice above the festive tunes playing in the background. They'd run into the kitchen to hide when they realised Alejandro and I were coming in.

They both ran over and gave me a warm hug. They looked gorgeous in matched dresses. They were both so adorable and affectionate. I loved them to bits. They both backed off a little when they saw how big Alejandro was behind me. He picked up on it immediately and got down on one knee again.

"And what beautiful princesses do we have here?" he asked, oozing sweetness in a soft Spanish voice they couldn't possibly feel intimidated by. The eldest of the two girls responded, while the youngest just looked up at him with big doe eyes that could make anyone melt. It was her superpower.

"I'm Grace and I'm six years old," she said proudly.

"Grace is a beautiful princess name," he said, oozing charm.

Grace had a pretty, sweetheart face with big, hazel eyes.

"I have a heart on my cheek," she announced sweetly, pointing to a beautiful, heart-shaped birthmark.

It only made her more special to all of us.

"That's the prettiest heart I've ever seen," he said, and she giggled.

My younger niece still looked unsure as to what to make of him and, as per normal, she'd become shy. I warned Alejandro she takes a long time to warm up to men and he just saw that as a challenge, which I thought was incredibly cute.

"And what is your princess name?" he asked, smiling warmly at the shy girl with the big deep brown eyes in front of him.

"Her name is Lilybeth," piped up Grace.

"Let her answer for herself, chatterbox," my sister said, smiling.

"Lilybeth. *Is that your name*?" he said. She nodded.

"And how old are you sweetheart?" he said softly to her.

"Four."

"That's such a pretty name. I wish I was called Lilybeth," he said. She giggled at him.

Yes!

"You can't be called Lilybeth, you're a boy."

He had her talking within three minutes. I was so proud of him.

"Well, Lilybeth and Grace, did you get lots of presents from Father Christmas this morning?"

"Yes, we got toys and a bike each," Grace said.

"And what colour is your bike, Grace?"

"Bright pink," she shouted excitedly.

"And what colour is your bike, Lilybeth?"

"Mint green, with sparkly bits and wheels at the back."

"Mint green with sparkles. That's my *favourite*," he said, in a daft voice.

"No, it isn't," Lilybeth said, giggling.

No wonder I fell for him, I thought, giggling to myself at how easily he can charm anyone.

Hmm, is that a good thing or something I need to worry about long term, though?

"So, who thinks it's a good time for presents then?" Alejandro asked.

"Yay, me, me," they said jumping up and down.

"Who thinks it's a good time for a beer?" my dad chirped in, looking at both Alejandro and Jay.

"Yay, me, me," Alejandro said playfully.

We all laughed.

I'd never seen him around people other than me, Ellie, and Hayden. It was so nice to see him relaxed and in a playful mood.

What a beautiful man you are, Alejandro.

Caitlyn caught me watching him and smiled. Every time Caitlyn and I saw each other, there was no distance in between us. Like all solid relationships, family or friends, time doesn't change how close you are.

My dad brought back a can each for Alejandro and Jay, who sat with each other and my dad, while I went to help Mum prepare the food. They must have been enjoying their conversation. We heard nothing but raucous laughter.

It took 20 minutes or so for the kids to open all their toys and a few extra hands, a pair of scissors, and a small screwdriver to unwrap some they wanted to play with. It was worth it, though. There wasn't an adult on this earth who wouldn't enjoy seeing four tiny faces lit up.

When the kids were all happily playing with each other and Caitlyn and Alejandro were sitting on the floor joining in with them, I went back to the kitchen to see what I could do.

"Alejandro is so lovely, Leila. Not just a bit, I mean he is an amazing person. So gentle and sweet. Such a gentleman. You've struck lucky with this one. Did you see the way Grace and Lilybeth took to him?" Mum said.

"I know, he is like the child whisperer. They literally warmed up to him within a few minutes. I've never seen Lilybeth take to anyone like that before. She's approaching him, interacting, smiling, and laughing at him."

"Because he's so approachable. It's his mannerisms. Gorgeous looking, too."

"I'm so in love with him, Mum."

"I know, Leila, I can tell by the way you look at him, talk, and gush about him. I'm so absolutely delighted for you," she said, and I felt grateful she had given me her blessing.

With the way Dad and he were laughing, I'd say it was a double blessing from both my parents. I smiled to myself, feeling really content.

The bleepers on the oven went off and Mum called out to Dad, "Frank, will you come and sort out the gammon and chicken?"

"Sure," Dad shouted back, giving me a squeeze as he went past to get the electric carving knife.

That was the sound of Christmas to me, hearing that knife. That was the last thing before the meal was served.

Everyone grabbed a plate and went along the line, picking out their meat, salad, jackets, and condiments. For this number of people, it was always easier doing a hot buffet style lunch. We ate and laughed until our bellies were bloated. The conversations were light, about jobs or travel this last year, about the delicious food we were eating, or some old family stories.

As the day drew into night, I finally got around to every member of my family, with Alejandro, for a decent amount of time, to be sociable and see how everyone was. It was so nice to feel like part of a couple, to sit there together talking to family and not feel alone. I'd forgotten what that felt like, to be proud of someone. It was a feeling I'd missed.

Alejandro had fluid conversations with each of them and made everyone feel relaxed and at ease. As they started to leave one by one, and we said our goodbyes, we were eventually left with my immediate family. The kids and Caitlyn and Jay were staying over, so Alejandro asked if he could read them both a story once they were changed in their pyjamas, specifying

"Only if you clean your teeth first."

One of the presents we bought for the girls was a full classic collection of Ladybird tales. I'd been ordering presents online for a couple of months. This set was one of my favourites and one that Lilybeth in particular, was extremely excited about. She loved stories, especially when the characters were animated.

"Wow, you both look like fluffy princesses now, in those cute pyjamas. Were they a Christmas present off Santa?" Alejandro asked the girls.

"Yes, we get Christmas pyjamas every year, so we are cosy while it's winter," Grace said. "Last year we got pink, the year before it was purple, the year before it was red, this year it's blue."

"So young ladies, pick a story," he said, offering the box to see which one they wanted.

Lilybeth pointed to *The Gingerbread Man* as soon as she saw it.

"This is my favourite. I love it when Mum reads it," she said, looking up at him with her big deep brown eyes.

"Does she do voices, too?" he asked her.

"Yes, for the fox she does a really sly voice."

Alejandro looked over at Caitlyn.

"Hmm, the pressure's on then."

She giggled.

"Yup, best of luck cause I am really good," she said, teasing him.

"She really is," Grace piped up.

"Right. Are you sitting comfortably? Shall we begin?" he said, as my mum brought in a warm cup of milk for them both, to settle them down after a big day.

"Once upon a time..." he started, capturing the attention of everyone in the room, not just the kids.

Even my dad was smiling as he turned the pages and did each of the animal's justice, giving them each a unique voice.

The adults started joining in on the "Run, run, as fast as you can." as well as the kids. It was nice. It was fun. We were all laughing, and the kids loved it.

My dad patted his knee twice when Lilybeth looked at him, as she had started to look tired. She raced over for a cuddle and cosied up on his chest while he stroked her hair and kissed her forehead intermittently. I remembered that feeling so well. It was so soothing and was my favourite place in the whole world for a long time.

My mum had come in, sitting down in one of the big armchairs. Grace went over to sit next to her and cuddle up. They were very loved as grandchildren, just as Caitlyn and I had been when we were growing up. Even if we couldn't remember everything exactly, you never forget the feeling of love.

Lilybeth fell asleep on Dad's chest during the second story and when it finished, he carried her up to one of the twin beds in the third room. Grace kissed everyone goodnight and gave them a warm hug before saying "night night" sweetly and walking up to bed behind Grandad. She took the book up to carry on looking at the pictures. It wouldn't take her long to doze off.

We all carried on chatting and drinking until after midnight, when Alejandro sent a text to George to come and pick us up. I hugged Jay and Caitlyn, who had been smiling and laughing so much today. Alejandro said his goodbyes to them both.

"It was such a pleasure to meet you both," he said.

"Likewise, Alejandro."

I could tell it was genuine.

I gave Mum a big hug and held on for a long time, squeezing tightly, before whispering,

"Thank you, for a special day, your hospitality, and just being you."

"I love you, Leila. It was a perfect day. I loved every minute of today."

"I love you, too, Mum. I've really missed you. I know I've been busy with deadlines and I'm hoping it eases up."

"It's a huge and very important case for you, Leila. Do it justice and we'll catch up whenever we can," she said, reassuring me she understood.

"Come here, curly," my dad said to me, and I smiled as I swapped with Alejandro, who had been shaking his hand and offering thanks to my dad.

Dad squeezed me so tight, far tighter than normal and kissed my forehead.

"I'm so proud of you, Leila. You look really happy."

"Thank you, Dad, I am. Love you so much," I said, feeling a little emotional as the car pulled up outside.

Christmas day was always so special.

Mum gave us both of our coats.

"See you soon," I said as we left, waving as the car drove off.

"See you soon, Blue Moon," my mum waved.

I'll love you for the whole of my life.

48 BOXING DAY

December. Wednesday. Chester. Alejandro's.

"Are you nearly ready?" Alejandro called up the stairs, anxious about the time.

Yesterday's hangover was taking a toll. Until the shower woke me up, I wasn't feeling lively.

"I'll be down in five," I hollered down the stairs, applying finishing touches to my makeup.

"Is that hours or minutes?" he shouted up.

His humour was quick, sarcastic, and a little dark sometimes, but he always made me laugh.

I was so nervous to meet Alejandro's father, his partner, Elizabeth, and his best friend, Jason, along with his partner, Cara. Alejandro had so few people in the world he was close to. I wanted to make a good first impression.

Alejandro pulled a stunning blue car out from one of the three garages at the front of the house.

"Why are you changing cars?" I asked.

"I might need to give Jason and Cara a lift later. Kinda need back seats for that. After yesterday, I don't feel like another heavy session, so I'll play taxi today."

"Ahh, I see. Very thoughtful."

We walked out to the car before I realized we'd forgotten the wine, cheese board, grapes, and flowers we were taking with us. I went back for them, locking up again.

"You're nervous, aren't you?"

"Yes."

"Why?"

"They're everything to you. I want to make a good impression, even more now you've won over my whole family in one day."

"Is that what you think happened yesterday?"

"I know it," I said, smiling.

"That's nice. Don't worry, just be yourself. You're beautiful, inside and out."

He always knew what to say, regardless of the type of mood I was in. He could stoke my flames with one look into my eyes or calm me on the stormiest of days. Maybe I'd never understand how he did it, but I couldn't deny the power he had over me, the way I knew I needed him in my life.

"You have a warmth about you, and everyone can feel it. I'm just the lucky bastard who gets to kiss you, feel it deeply."

"I love the way you see me."

Alejandro held my hand as he opened the door with one of the keys on his keyring and walked in.

"Hey!" he shouted to alert everyone. "We're here."

A very distinguished gentleman with predominantly short silver-white hair came around the corner. He had wrinkles and a scar on his forehead, which added to his character. He had a medium length broad nose, with a thin top lip, and thickset eyebrows. He approached with a smile, offering his hand to greet me, which I noted quickly. Not a hugger.

Alejandro must get his affectionate side from his mum.

"Dad, Leila." he introduced us.

"It's a great pleasure to meet you, Leila," he said, shaking my hand firmly, but not too firmly.

"Likewise, Mr. Steel," I said, a little formally, trying to offer him respect from the outset.

"Please, call me Jack. Come in, come in."

He ushered us to the lounge, an open room with a dining area.

"Are Jason and Cara still coming? I thought they'd be here by now," Jack asked Alejandro.

"They're running 10 minutes late, he just sent me a text," he said, putting his phone back in his pocket.

"Where's Liz?" Alejandro asked.

"She's finishing off the last bits of veg for the steamer."

"It smells wonderful here, a really homely aroma."

"We all love Liz's roast dinners," he boasted.

"I can't wait to eat. We deliberately kept it light this morning, so we had plenty of room," I said.

I was conscious of rambling. He was friendly. but he wasn't as warm as Alejandro, and my nerves had started playing up a little.

"I know, I'm starving," Jack said.

"Are you going out for New Year?" I asked him, trying to keep a good flow of conversation going to make a good impression.

"No, we're old and happy. Going out is for the youngsters," he said.

"You're not that old Jack," I said, being myself, as Alejandro told me to.

He laughed.

"I'm 63, old enough I don't want to be paying a fortune to get into some place that's going to be packed with people spilling beer over me. What are you and my boy doing?" he said.

My boy, how lovely.

"There's a club called Nocturnal that holds a New Year's Eve party every year. It hosts many parties and is, as the name suggests, open late. As it's secluded and off the beaten track of the main roads, they can get away with the volume levels being higher, without disturbing any neighbours. A lot of people drive in and then get taxis back. I'm going to my parents first. Alejandro's going to meet my housemate and her boyfriend a bit earlier for a drink, and then I'm going to meet them there later."

"So basically, they'll all be merry by the time you get there," he said.

"I would never do such a thing," Alejandro said mockingly.

Liz came in from the kitchen, looking lovely in a jumper of earthy colours – woodland green and oak brown, with gold leaves interwoven in a forest theme, with a pair of tan trousers. She was full figured and looked incredibly elegant with her copper-brown wavy hair and pretty necklace and earring set in colours matching her top.

"Sorry about that, I was right in the middle of peeling the carrots. I washed my hands. It's lovely to meet you, Leila," she said.

She walked straight over to me and to my surprise, held her arms open, hugging me tightly for a few seconds.

Such a stark contrast to Jack, and possibly the reason he was attracted to her.

"I've heard so much about you. I've been dying to meet the lady who has captured so much of Alejandro's affection. You're the first woman he's ever brought here," she offered.

I had no idea.

The doorbell rang.

"I'll get it," Jack said.

After hearing a couple of muffled greetings, he returned with both Jason and Cara.

"Good to see you, man," Jason said as soon as he saw Alejandro.

I could feel their bond immediately as they gripped hands.

Jason was huge, which made Cara look almost like a child next to him. She looked lovely, in a navy trouser suit and cream blouse. Jason was butch in physique, obviously a body builder. He had such a warm smile as he approached me.

"I'm so glad I'm getting to finally meet you," he said, as we had an awkward *do we hug* moment. He went to kiss my cheek, holding my upper arms briefly as he did.

"This is Cara."

She stepped forward, greeting me with a gentle hug.

"Leila, it's a pleasure to meet you. I've been looking forward to us getting together."

She had a beautifully soft Irish accent. Cara had elfin-like features, a small almond shaped face with pale skin, freckles, big green eyes, and ears pinned back a little, popping through light brown straight hair.

"Likewise, lovely."

I felt the gentleness of her personality. She had a soft aura. I felt us starting to vibe immediately.

"All I've heard is Leila this and Leila that for months now," Jason teased. "And because that's all I've heard, that's all Cara has heard from me."

"So sorry, I wouldn't inflict that on anyone."

"You must have spoken to him quite a bit while he was away then?" I asked, directing the question at Jason.

"Of course, we're best buds, we always look out for each other and check in regularly. He's more like a brother to me," Jason added.

"Plus, now that he's back, I've got my spotter back, too," he said smiling, punching Alejandro lightly in the arm.

"Can't wait for the new year and to get back to full size with you, bud," Alejandro replied.

I hadn't realised this was a smaller version of him.

"Am I not good enough as a gym partner?" Cara taunted Jason in her sweet Irish voice.

"I never said that darling. You know I love working out with you."

"Here we go with the comedy duo already," Liz said, laughing, and I realised this was going to be an interesting few hours.

"Sit down, get comfy," urged Jack.

"Would you prefer red or white wine?" he asked, generally addressing everyone.

"White, please," Alejandro said.

"Is that okay with you guys?" Jack asked.

"Yes, perfect," Cara replied.

"What made you choose to be a firefighter, Jason?" I asked, breaking the ice.

"I'm a naturally protective person. This role just felt right for me. There was a lot of heavy training," Jason said.

"I can see you lift very heavy weights. I assume you need to be fit, too, for stamina as well as strength?" I asked.

"Yes, I do cardio reluctantly, but I must do that, too. Alejandro and I sometimes do sprints, but Cara is the cardio bunny. She makes me run; we go on bike rides. Horrible things like that. She's so mean to me," he said, pulling a face at her.

"Oh, you love it really. What man doesn't want a beautiful woman bossing them around?" Liz chirped in.

"He wouldn't be half as disciplined if I didn't push him," Cara said, shaking her head, playfully tutting at him.

"You do know this is all wrong?" Jack said, motioning a circle at Jason and Cara.

"You mean because she's the little one and I'm the big one, I *should* be wearing the trousers. Yes, I know! Thing is, she says it's good for me or some mumbo jumbo," Jason shrugged sarcastically.

"Oh, you know it is, mister," she said.

Cara clearly wears the trousers in their relationship.

"So, you're a teaching assistant?" I asked Cara.

"Yes, I work with a special need's child, Isabella. She has Down's Syndrome. She's so adorable. She's a beautiful little girl and we regularly celebrate her progress in school as she learns. Some things are such small successes to others, but such incredible achievements to her. We all feel how open her heart is," Cara explained.

There was such a peaceful, calming vibe about her when she spoke. I can imagine her mere presence around Isabella would be a blessing. I already liked her and hoped we could become friends. Jack returned with a glass of wine for each of us.

"That must be so rewarding as a job. Mine is focused on a psychopath currently. I'd love to trade places with you," I said.

"Yes, you're a reporter, right? You're working on a serial killer? That must be so tough emotionally," Cara said.

"I feel a little overwhelmed some days, when I think about how twisted some people can be. A couple of weird things have been happening to Ellie and me recently. They're freaking us out. I pray it's nothing to do with the case I'm working on, but there are some striking similarities which are starting to make me nervous," I added.

"Has something else happened in the last week?" Alejandro jumped in; his ears sharpened like a wolf sensing danger.

"We got another package at the house last Friday. We've been so busy. I just haven't had a chance to tell you."

"That's no excuse. I need to know if anything happens, Leila," he said, in a surprisingly stern way, which made me flush.

"What did you get through the post?" Jack asked, showing signs of the same wolf-like instinct Alejandro had. I finally understood their connection.

They both had it. A sixth sense. A sense for danger.

"This time it was a book. *Tess of the D'Urbervilles,* by Thomas Hardy. The thing is, Ellie and I were talking about it two weeks ago. Privately. Just she and I in the house. Over dinner, we were discussing books we'd studied in high school. That's what's creeped me out the most. This feels personal. It's like he knew what we were discussing," I said.

"There's no such thing as a coincidence, Leila," Jack added.

"What makes you think it's related to the case you're working on?" he asked, interested and alert suddenly.

"The killer uses the same MO every time. He stalks the ladies he watches. Then he romances them, sending them gifts which can't be traced, normally cash purchases or hand deliveries. He is meticulous on every level. He's obsessed with making sure there's no evidence. This behaviour pattern increases over several months. Then eventually, the inevitable happens," I added.

"What does he do to them, Leila?" Liz asked, looking horrified.

"He rapes and strangles them," I said. "Over several hours. It gets longer each time, as well as what he makes them endure near the end," I added, feeling vulnerable thinking about it.

Jack shot Alejandro a look I don't think I was supposed to see, but it was enough to confirm they were both worried about what I was saying.

"There are many ways someone can find out what you're discussing, some more invasive than others. There are external listening devices that work within a range, internal bugs that could have been planted. I have a friend who can help me with things like this, someone I used to work with. For now, think. Have you had anyone in your house for any reason? Service men, engineers, anyone?" Jack asked.

"No, we've had nothing fixed, no meters being read, nothing like that at all."

"No strangers at all then?" he double checked.

"No," I said confidently.

"Then maybe someone has pirated a copy of your phone, downloaded spy software onto your computer, or has some other kind of spy hack tool. There is a myriad of ways they can listen to you these days," he added.

I looked at him blankly, not understanding or having any idea whatsoever what all these devices he was talking about were. Then I realised, nobody else normal did either.

Who are you really, Jack?

"Now this is important, Leila. Think carefully before you respond. Who referenced *Tess of the D'Urbervilles* – you or Ellie?" Jack asked.

I thought for a second.

"Ellie," I said with confidence.

"Then, assuming you're right, you need to warn Ellie she may be the target. It's Ellie who your villain is trying to romance and impress. The package was personal *to her*," Jack reinforced.

I felt sick.

"How do you know all of this?" Alejandro asked him.

"I need to be honest with you son. I'm 63 now, I don't want to die at some point knowing I didn't tell you the truth. You deserve to know. Now is as good a time as any, because my friend and I may be able to help you if you're in danger," Jack explained.

"Know what, Dad?" Alejandro looked confused.

"I used to work for MI6," he added.

The whole room froze. You could hear a pin drop.

"What? You said you were an international salesman. Why have you never told me this before, Dad?"

"Because I had to keep the cover that I was a normal man with a normal family, do nothing to raise suspicion. I was working undercover the whole time I was in Spain, investigating local drug lords, trying to stop international trade," Jack explained. "I had to get out in the end, after everything happened."

By the shocked look on her face, it was clear even Liz didn't know any of this.

I could tell Alejandro was overthinking. I can't imagine how he was feeling, finding out something so dramatic. His dad had basically lied to him the whole time. The whole time!

"I still don't understand why you left us, though. Was it something to do with your work, or were you grieving? You never gave me an answer I believed," Alejandro asked.

"That was because all of my answers were lies," he said, looking briefly at the floor.

"So, are you ready to tell me the truth now?" Alejandro confronted him.

"Would you like us to go into the study to leave you guys in peace?" Jason asked considerately.

"No, it's okay. There's nothing you don't know about me, Jace."

"What I'm about to tell you has to stay between these four walls and those in the room, do you all understand?" Jack asked.

"One hundred percent, Jack, you know you can trust us," Jason answered, while Cara, Liz, and I nodded in agreement.

"MI6 approached me and asked if I would go undercover for a drug operation responsible for many teenage deaths in Britain. They were incorporating a product known locally as N2 into their drugs. It increased the thrill of the pill, but then clogged up their arteries as a side effect, causing heart attacks within a few hours. In teenagers for goodness' sake. It was a great career move, fantastic pay into a private account, and I wanted to help save those kids. I was targeted for my expertise on drug trafficking, and because I spoke Spanish," Jack explained.

I hadn't realised his dad was fluent in Spanish, too.

"I infiltrated the gang successfully and was getting crucial information back to my team about targeted drop sites. There was a massive sting operation. We arrested several key drug lords, including the ringleader, Rodolfo Vasquez. Even though I was undercover, they found me, seeking revenge. People who worked for Vasquez abducted Dulce. I'm responsible for my own daughter's death, for your sister's death. I'm so sorry," he said, his eyes filling with tears, regret pouring from every word.

The whole room was heavy and thick, everyone sitting in absolute shock. No wonder his dad was emotionally repressed, he had been carrying guilt *most of his life*. To make it worse, he couldn't even tell anyone, the entire time. Alejandro's mother must never have known. She died not knowing who he really was, or what any of it was about. Maybe in some ways, that was a blessing.

"That's a lot to take in, Dad. All these years Mum and I had no clue. All those years."

"I'll let you guys' chat and serve up dinner in the kitchen if that's okay?" Liz said.

"I'll help you," Cara said tactfully to give them privacy.

Jason wanted to stay with his buddy. I couldn't leave Alejandro at a moment like this.

"How do you know that's who took Dulce?" Alejandro asked.

"They told me. They also threatened that no matter where in the world you were, they would hunt and kill both you and your mother, unless I quit the agency and Spain for good. They knew I had to live with the memory of Dulce for the rest of my life. They wanted me alive to feel it. They said both of you would remain untouched if I cooperated. I had no choice. They gave me their word, which is bizarrely the only honest thing about them. I couldn't live with myself knowing I had destroyed my entire family. I was deeply in love with your mother and my life and, with the four of us together. It was one of the happiest times of my life. I've mourned Dulce all these years, with a void in my heart eating me from the inside out. During the initial few months, I cried until the well ran empty. I haven't shed a single tear since, until now," he said, as one tumbled slowly down his cheek.

"They took my life, my family, my heart, my soul. No job was worth damage like that. I had to protect you both. Nothing in the world could replace what I lost. From that day forward, I tried to find a simple life," Jack explained.

"I'm so sorry," I said, directing it at them both.

I could feel their hurt. Jack's words were having a huge impact on Alejandro. He was tormented. His body language confirmed that.

"Sorry, man, that's tough to process," Jason said, in shock.

"So, it was all revenge? They took Dulce because your actions imprisoned Vasquez?" Alejandro questioned.

"Yes."

"Are Vasquez and the other drug lords still in prison?" Alejandro interrogated.

"Yes. For life. They were responsible for the death of 30 British teenagers. They won't get out now," Jack added.

"Did they say anything to give you a clue about what happened to Dulce?" Alejandro grimaced as he asked.

"They wouldn't say anything. Wouldn't confirm if, or how, they killed her. Nothing. Nobody ever found a body. They wanted me to suffer my whole life, never have closure. They created their own version of a mental prison for me, too. All potential leads eventually led nowhere. She's a cold case file now," he said, tears dripping off the end of his eyelashes.

"So, the reason you left Mum, and I, wasn't because you didn't love us anymore?" Alejandro asked.

"No, son. It was because I did," he replied, looking him directly in the eye. "I need you to know that" he implored.

He looked like a weight was being lifted from his shoulders. My fear was that it was now bearing down on Alejandro, though. His vibe and aura were heavy, and very dark.

"Thank you for telling me. You were right, I did need to know. All those years I thought you abandoned us. It never felt right. I could never understand why. That was one hell of a burden you carried, Dad. You couldn't have possibly known what would happen. They're the bad guys," Alejandro said, finally acknowledging the truth.

"I should have had a safer career so I could have a normal family life," Jack added. "But then I never would have met your mother. What started with a romance turned very quickly into love, becoming deep over time, especially with the birth of you and Dulce. Twins. You could have knocked me over with a feather when I found out. There was so much laughter and singing in your early years, Alejandro, much more than you'll remember. I remember it well, though," Jack said, smiling momentarily.

Liz came in the room.

"The food is ready. I've plated the meals. We can leave eating until later and reheat the food if you guys want to carry on talking?"

"I'm going to need a while to process everything that's been said anyway, a few days even. I think we should eat. We can talk about this another time, Dad. Let's try to enjoy Boxing Day together for now," Alejandro added.

I admired his strength. I was incredibly proud of him.

"Sounds good to me, bud," Jason chipped in, realising a distraction at this point would probably serve everyone best.

"Alejandro, would you come grab another bottle of wine and dish it out?" Liz asked.

"Sure," he said.

Liz was walking slightly ahead of him on their way to the kitchen, and she turned around before he went in, holding her arms open to embrace him.

"I thought you might need a hug."

"I really do," he said, giving her the type of hug, he could no longer give his mother.

Alejandro had always said Liz reminded him of his mum, her personality more than her looks. Maybe that was why his dad was drawn to her.

Alejandro came back with the bottle, topped everyone up and went to help bring in dinner for everyone. The conversation was lighter as we sat at the table.

Jason and Cara were brilliant at doing that. Her Irish humour was quick, having been raised with brothers.

We spoke about her family, as well as Jason's, in some depth, telling us about some of the hilarious antics they got up to growing up.

It was lovely to see Alejandro with the people he loved. Other than a black cloud hanging over his head, that is. I could sense it, feel him. I just wanted to hold him, to take him to bed, and make love to him.

That was how he dealt with emotions, letting them out through touch. I knew he would need to find a way to release the intense emotions beginning to clog him up. He put on a front, as always.

Alejandro and that mask of his, the one that was becoming increasingly transparent to me over time as I'd learned how to feel him. Looking him in the eye made it so much easier to read him than before, when we were separated.

What an incredibly tragic backstory to have carved out your softness.

We lightened up the rest of the evening, playing charades and chess, with interesting chat throughout. Everyone except for Alejandro had moved onto spirits from the drink's cabinet. We were quite merry by the end of the night.

Liz and Cara were yawning, and as I followed suit, I figured it was about time to go. I nodded secretly to Alejandro, so he could discreetly start making plans for us to move.

"Time to head home. We'll give you a lift, Jace."

"Cheers bud."

Alejandro went over to give Liz a big hug.

"Look after him these next few days," Alejandro whispered to her.

They both knew a can of worms had just been opened emotionally for him.

"I will."

Liz had been quieter after the announcement, possibly reflecting on what Jack's announcement meant to her. I wondered if it would make her question any part of their relationship, or things he'd done or said, knowing now he'd hid that from her for so long.

"Thank you for having us," I said to Liz, as I was next in line to embrace her. "The food was wonderful, and I've loved the company today."

"You're welcome, lovey, it was a pleasure to meet you."

Jack pulled Alejandro in for a long hug, which threw him.

"Promise me you'll chat to me anytime about this, okay? I know I threw a lot out there today. I want us to be able to talk about it whenever you need."

He sounded fatherly.

"I promise I will, Dad. It's going to take a little time to process it," he said, honest as always.

"I know, son. I'm here whenever you need."

"It was lovely meeting you, Jack," I said.

"You, too, Leila. Don't forget to speak to Ellie. If there is malicious intent toward her, her awareness could make all the difference. I will speak to my friend and see what I can do, too," he said.

"Thank you. She is safely away with her parents in Scotland for Christmas. She'll be back before New Year's Eve. She's in no danger while she's away, and I don't want to ruin her holiday with this."

"Good. As soon as she's back. Tell her to alter her routines immediately and think specifically about safety. You should too," Jack added.

"Understood," I replied.

We were so tired when we eventually got in, we got a glass of water, and headed straight to bed.

"Lay your head on my chest, Alejandro."

As he did, I stroked his head, running my nails through his hair until he drifted off. All I wanted was for him to feel how much I loved him.

What a horrific tragedy for all of you to bear.

49 MAKING LOVE

December. Thursday. Chester. Alejandro's.

After two busy and emotional days, we woke up late, feeling rested. Finally, we had nothing to get up for, nowhere to go. It was a nice restful period between Boxing Day and New Year Eve's where we could be together. No work, no rushing, just us, doing whatever we wanted.

Bliss.

I woke up slightly ahead of Alejandro and went down to prepare a light breakfast for him. Some toast, marmalade, pure orange, and a pot of tea. When I put the tray down in the room, clanging a little, he opened his eyes, flashing me a big smile.

"Morning, beautiful. What a lovely way to wake up," he said, as I poured the tea and milk into two mugs, passing him his breakfast.

"How are you feeling after yesterday's revelations? I know it hit you hard," I said.

I wanted him to open about how he felt and not allow it to clog him up emotionally. I was trying to get him to get into the habit of doing that, of expressing himself to me. I knew bottling emotions hadn't served him well in the past.

"Hurt. My whole life has been a lie. To discover Dad was the reason she was abducted ripped right through my heart," he said.

"I thought he'd abandoned us for all those years. In retrospect, to find out he was trying to protect us made those memories more bearable. The reality is, though, at the end of the day, he still wasn't there when I needed him, or when Mum needed him. It was painful growing up without a dad and we missed him so much. Knowing it was for a good reason changes nothing to the actual memories, it just softens them a little. I still felt deprived of his affection as a child. The times I saw him during the holidays, were never enough," he said, glancing down at the sheets, wiping away small crumbs.

"I'm so sorry, Alejandro, I know you loved him and your sister so very much," I replied.

"When I think about what Dulce might have gone through, all this pain wells up inside me, emotional pain. Was she tortured? Was she hurt for a long time? Was she made to pay for my father's mistakes? Did they kill her? Was it humane? I've had so many questions burning in my mind, and not one of them can be answered. I'm not sure if the not knowing hurts more, to be honest. It kills me, thinking she may have suffered," he said, his eyes filling up again.

"Oh baby, I'm so sorry."

I held him for a few minutes, while he shed a few soft tears.

"You don't have to be strong all the time. Please don't hold back with me, ever," I added.

I didn't want him to worry about being vulnerable with me.

"I can't help feeling confused by everything that's happened in my life. I had to shut off my heart to survive. I have spent so much time alone because I didn't want anything else to hurt me. My soul was exhausted. Every time I opened up to someone, they betrayed me, and it reaffirmed time and time again I could trust nobody," he paused.

"All male friends, other than Jason, have always let me down. Women only wanted me for my looks and didn't see me for the real me, so I felt empty without a connection. It all adds up. Eventually you shut down and close yourself off to people emotionally. You're the first person I've wanted to open up to for years," he added.

"It's called disassociation. It's a trauma response," I replied.

He was hurting. Raw. It was pouring out of him as he opened. I could feel years of pain. Dark. Heavy.

In a few impactful moments where he witnessed his father beaten and his sister abducted, his view of the world changed. It was harsh and frightening. Scared and mentally scarred, from the age of seven.

How do you mentally recover from something that wounds you so deeply it turns your whole life into an unanswered question?

"I will never abandon you. I will never hurt you. Do you understand?" I said emphatically.

"Fuck, I love you. You have no clue how deep this love runs for you," he said.

"It's soul deep. I know. I feel it, too," I said, placing his hand on my heart. "I need you, Alejandro."

The moment was incredibly raw. We were deeply connected emotionally, an invisible tether between us pulling with great strength.

One look into his eyes with his hand on my chest and I felt him, drawing me in, softly.

"Show me, baby. I need to feel it," he said, framing my face with his hand.

I undid the silk robe, letting it slide down over my shoulders, locking onto his eyes as I did.

I heard his breath catch, as he looked at the curve of my shoulders and breasts. He traced his fingers in a circle around my nipples, rubbing his thumbs over them, as he watched my expression change, arousal forming on my face.

"*Mine*," he said, as he pulled me on top of him, straddling him.

He continued thumbing my nipples until he saw my eyes mist and darken. My hips were rotating naturally, my breath changed, and I emitted a soft moan as I felt him harden underneath me.

"Mmm," he muttered.

I was sliding up and down the length of him, making him even harder. His beautiful chest and stomach were exposed. Desire filled my core. His cobalt eyes, framed with impossibly dark lashes, were drawing me in. I flicked my hair over to one side and lowered my face to him, my lips kissing him softly. We moaned at the same time, into each other's mouths as eroticism took over. It took so little for me to become lost with him.

Our kisses were full of passion, fed by the rawness of our emotions. I tasted his sadness, his need to be loved. It made me want to love him even more. He held my breasts as I kissed him, working them in his hands, squeezing them, teasing them. I allowed the feelings to spread as they swept through me.

I felt a tantric energy as it rippled through me now, one where arousal and love combined.

"You like that?"

His low muffled tone was erotic. He growled huskily in his sexy accent.

"Mmm, I love the way you make me feel."

He placed his left arm around me and spun me smoothly onto the other side of the bed, so he was on top of me.

"I want to play. We need to release some of our pent-up emotions," he said, leaning across the bed to the low side cabinet, opening the drawer, and taking out the set of leather handcuffs.

"May I?" he asked.

My breath was instantly erratic.

"I'll do whatever you need," I whimpered.

My heart was pounding as he instructed me.

"Put your hands up," he said, in his dominant voice.

I raised my arms for him, by the metal bed post.

"Good girl."

I immediately pulsed between my legs at the way he said it.

"Yes, *sir*," I replied.

He exhaled deeply.

It was never what he did, but the *way* he did it. It was never what he said, but the *way* he said it. I guess that was part of the whole RSD concept though. It was part of him.

He straddled me to secure the handcuffs. As they tightened, my thoughts drifted away, and I focused purely on the arousal. His erection was right in front of me and bobbed slightly as he secured me. As he looked down at me, he saw me looking longingly, and knew exactly what I needed.

He understood my insatiable appetite for oral sex. He had the exact same need, too. That was part of the sensuality of two givers together as lovers. As the relationship between us morphed into the sensual dominant/submissive roles when we roleplayed, my hunger for him was growing weekly, too. The further we fell into each other, the more we needed to let ourselves go.

"You want this, babygirl?" he added, holding the base of his erection.

As he did, I nodded, arousal gripping me tight now. Surges of it pulsed through me.

"Mmm, yes please, *sir*."

I watched the pupils in his eyes dilate and darken.

My dark wolf.

"You have to trust me completely in this position. Trust, I won't hurt you or push too far. Can you do that?" he asked.

"Yes, *sir*," I responded.

Sir came automatically from my mouth now, instead of an unnatural response when I first said it. It was a part of our roleplay, showing a consensual transfer of power from me to him. I now understood why it was so important to him. I willingly gave it to him on the grounds he would never abuse his power over me.

"How close do you want my thighs to be to your body and shoulders?" Alejandro asked.

"Really tight."

I felt such bliss in being restrained, to be trapped in such a way that I could focus on nothing but pleasing him. It was beautiful to me.

Alejandro brought his knees in closer on either side of me, pinning me with his legs. My arms were securely fastened above me. I felt wet. He shifted his angle to come at me slowly and softly, dipping his thighs down and bringing himself right in front of my face.

"I'll be gentle baby, open up," he instructed.

My mouth parted. His chest started to heave when the tip of his erection slid into my mouth.

"Mmm, that's so sexy."

He slid it in a little further. The warmth enclosed him now. I reacted as I took in more depth, my moan enclosing him completely, the echo of it reverberating around his hot flesh. The more pinned and out of control I felt, the more I needed to feel him deeper.

"Mmmmmm," I mumbled around him, so he knew to give me more.

He held my face briefly, stroking hair from my fringe away from my eye, then slid it all the way in. He was in so deep. I couldn't breathe for a second.

He slowly slipped it back out, before repeating the action. He was so gentle and in control. It never once felt like he would hurt me or just thrust into me. That trust was what defined us.

How fucking beautiful, to trust another human this deeply.

"Do you enjoy that? Do you like me fucking your mouth?" he asked, in his sexy bedroom voice.

I whimpered around him, lifting my head to fully take him in.

"That's fucking sexy," he said, moaning as I started moving my head, too.

I was twitching so badly.

"I'm going to move a little more. Make a noise if you want me to stop and I'll stop immediately," he said, ensuring I had a way to communicate, which enabled me to feel the trust between us still.

He was pulling out and pushing in with a little more pace, still nothing that hurt me. I felt full, so beautifully full of him. It was a sensation I found incredibly erotic.

Our sex drives matched perfectly, with the new added dimension of our roleplay erotically charging us in ways I never would have thought possible. He was so fucking sexy.

He started to lose his breath as I got carried away, licking, sucking, and moaning virtually every time he gently pushed into me, and then withdrew.

"You don't have to stop."

He knew he could take my mouth whenever he wanted because it was *his*. I was *his*.

"I know, but I wanted to use your other present," he said.

"Oh, fuck."

I remembered what he was reaching into the drawer for.

The wand.

"Oh fuck, is right," he teased, lifting it out.

He repositioned himself further down me, using his knees and thighs to separate my legs. He looked at me, unable to resist as he briefly licked me, his tongue flicking, making exquisite sensations rage through me as his tongue met my clit.

I instinctively went to move my arms, but couldn't, and I rattled against the railings. This thrilled him even more. He licked me even harder, stopping to suck me in between, enclosing his mouth over all of me as he French kissed me.

I was going crazy when I heard the buzz as he turned on the wand. The vibration was incredibly powerful and intense. He lowered it to me, watching my eyes for a response. I bucked as he pressed it against my clit, unable to take it at first.

"It's okay, look at me. Focus on me," he said, lowering it again.

The taste of him was still on my lips, a beautiful, stretched feeling and ache still in my mouth. He pressed it against my clit and swiftly sat lower on my thighs so I couldn't move at all. As it buzzed against me, I moaned out loud, the sensation sending what felt like a million vibrations through my body.

Alejandro kept it pressed against me, watching me thrash about, my hips bucking up and down, but with little movement, just enough to get relief from the stillness as I rocked against the intensity of the buzz. He was so good at immobilising me; it didn't take long before I was panting and losing myself.

My whole body spasmed as I came, shivering in fits at the intensity. The orgasm was almost violent. It seemed to go on for such a long time, sending ripples continually through me in huge waves, leaving me in an aftermath of tremors. He held it there until I bucked it away, too sensitive to have it against me post orgasm.

Much to my surprise, the vibration buzzed and continued after he took it away. I think he knew that, as he dipped down to lick me again, slower this time, to ease the sensation from me as I came down.

"You are so sexy, Alejandro."

My eyes were lost as I watched him pleasing me.

"Now I need to have you."

His voice changed with an increased urgency as he undid the handcuffs.

"On all fours baby and spread wide for me," he commanded.

I turned over. As he positioned himself behind me, he slapped my ass, three times, progressively harder each time. It was so sexy.

"Again," I said, breathless and lost, still trembling through the last flutters of the orgasm as he did it again, catching my sex mid twitch.

Fuck.

He held my hips, positioning himself, rubbing his erection up and down over my lips before he slid it inside and began pumping into me.

I was still pulsing, and it felt like he was completing me. The orgasm, the experience, the togetherness, the emotion. Everything. All our raw emotions were channelled into that one area.

I gave my body to him completely, relaxing all of it, so I could just feel. I could sense the release of the beast inside him by the way he gripped my hips.

All the little things added together in an experience. The adoration for him, the submission, surrendering my control, the way he loves making me come. All of it together made me delirious.

There was a slight bite to the pain from behind as he reached full depth. I whimpered, moaning as he drove into me, pumping in and out. His groans were sexy as fuck to me. They were a sign of him letting go and losing himself in the moment. I loved it. I could feel him getting closer and closer to the edge and was bracing myself for the beautiful flurry where he lost himself totally, when suddenly, he stopped, and pulled out.

"Turn over. I want to look into your eyes when I come," he said.

I turned over, positioning myself under him.

Damn, your eyes.

As he re-entered me, he lowered to kiss me at the same time, his face full of pure emotion. He loved me. It was written all over his face.

He slowed right down, sensually pure movements, emotional, full of expression. I placed my right hand slowly on the back of his head, while holding his upper face and cheek with my left, my shoulder curving and rounding inwards toward his face, as I pulled him in closer. Our mouths slid together, our tongues exploring each other. I felt every single ounce of his love poured into that kiss... those movements, our intimacy.

You feel so sensual, lover.

As he increased the pace, I was overwhelmed with emotion. His final few thrusts were deep and fulfilling as he released into me. I cried a little onto his shoulder at the purity of it all. He held me tight, moaning sexily into my ear as he came, his wet body sliding over mine.

I felt like something had been released between us, like our souls had just coalesced.

"I love you."

His body trembled and shook. The last few movements felt exquisite inside me. He began to still, kissing the tears that fell from my eyes, understanding it for what it was.

"I love you too, Alejandro."

I meant it with every part of me.

There was something powerful about the way we made love.

I wondered if he was the man, I would spend the rest of my life with.

50 NEW YEARS EVE

December. Monday. Liverpool. Home.

The days spent between Boxing Day and New Year's Eve all blurred together into a haze of eating, drinking, talking, and making out. I'd tried getting in touch with Ellie when she returned, but to no avail. Her phone had been off for days. She wasn't answering messages on any of her social media, either. Her bags from Scotland were in the house. She'd left a handwritten note by the kettle:

"See you tonight, same plan as we agreed before I went away, E x."

I really needed a face-to-face chat to warn you as soon as you got back, though, Ellie.

It's important.

Stop ignoring my calls.

I'm so worried.

Alejandro and I spent most of our time at his house after Christmas, on the build-up to New Year. It was beautiful, spending so much time together alone, connecting and chatting. There was something extremely beautiful about what happened after we made love, when our bodies and hearts were both sated, and we didn't want to go asleep afterwards.

We were left in a creative space, as we fired off ideas about poetry and songs, or things we were interested in. It was an enchanted bubble, where we were smitten, and we existed in and thrived off each other. To me, it felt as magical as the moments he was inside me.

I think I could love you forever.

New Year's Eve had finally arrived, and I was dressed for it in a stunning silver dress I'd bought with matching heels. I'd put on my rose and silver necklace with the silver/diamond earrings. I drove over to Mum and Dad's house to spend the afternoon, have a small bite to eat, and visit with them and my grandparents, to wish them a Happy New Year before everyone else.

I'd told Ellie I would be arriving late at the New Year's Eve party at Nocturnal, aiming to get there at 10 p.m. It started at 7:30 p.m., but I wanted to spend some time as the five of us.

Alejandro was meeting Ellie and Hayden there at 8 p.m. I was so excited I would be breaking in the new year with Alejandro. We were going to start a whole new year together and I couldn't be happier.

I'd missed him so much this year. I was ready to spend a lot of quality time with him. To explore him and our mutual desires together, chatting, being creative, making love. In our soul connection, lay the most beautiful peace I'd ever found.

I mentally reviewed the past few months as the year was ending. Alejandro had an ability to evoke emotion within me. I knew it was partially because we were separated, but looking back, I wonder now if it had been a blessing. We'd had an opportunity to explore each other's minds before we ever touched each other physically.

Who gets to do that? Who gets to fall in love before they become intimate?

Everything about him was romantic, sexy, and multi-faceted. He was thoughtful, kind, caring, focused, loyal, attentive, giving, loving, sensual, sexy, erotic, intelligent, charming, thorough, creative, challenging, exciting, unpredictable, persevering, and patient.

I was so lucky. Kissing him at midnight would finish off the year perfectly for me.

While my mum was busy chatting about some of the local news from the church and her circle of friends there, I hadn't heard my phone beep.

8:27 p.m.

It was a message from Ellie, fifteen minutes ago.

"help me," it read.

No capital letters, no punctuation, no context.

What's wrong, Ellie? What the hell does that mean?

I started to panic immediately. She'd never sent me anything like that before.

"Something's wrong with Ellie. I'm going to try and call her," I said, worried.

"Okay, love," Mum said, looking concerned, too.

I tried phoning Ellie, but it just kept ringing, only adding to my anxiety.

"I'm going to have to leave early Mum, something's clearly wrong," I said, starting to gather my things together to leave.

"Okay, darling, you do whatever you need to."

"I'll say goodbye to everyone quickly," I muttered, grabbing my coat, and rushing into the other room.

"Are you leaving already?" Dad asked.

"Yes, something is wrong with Ellie, she's asking for help, and I couldn't reach her on her mobile. She's supposed to be at the New Year's Eve party, so I'll head straight there."

He knew my worried look all too well.

"I'll come with you," Dad offered, immediately concerned.

"No, it's okay, Dad. Alejandro was going to meet Ellie and Hayden there at seven thirty, anyway, so I'll find the guys when I get there, and we will find her together if she's not there. Alejandro will look after me, I promise."

"Okay, sweetheart, but please phone us to let us know you girls are both safe as soon as you find her. If you need me, I'll be there in a shot, do you understand?"

"I'll phone you as soon as I can, I promise."

The drive over was only a few minutes, but it seemed such a long time. I was worried every second. I'd put my phone in the central holder and tried Alejandro's mobile on hands free several times, to no avail.

His phone was just ringing, too. Unfortunately, I didn't have Hayden's number, otherwise I would have tried his, too.

Why won't anyone pick up?

I arrived at the car park of the social club where the New Year's Eve party was held, realising how poorly lit the whole exterior was. There was a slight fog rolling in by the green outside the building, in front of the tree layering, surrounding the club.

The building itself was a former sports club. I'd attended various functions there with my parents before it was converted to a nightclub.

I couldn't remember the last time I'd been there at night. It was creepy as hell.

The lights in the car park flickered intermittently, like there were small electrical surges. It was as if the lighting would go off any second. Some of the fog rolled into the car park in drifts.

I parked easily. Several spaces were still available, as many locals came by taxi. There were still quite a few cars there. I grabbed my phone, wanting to get in there as soon as possible to locate Ellie, the cold air hitting me, taking my breath away, biting a little all over my face and hands, the skin areas exposed to the elements.

I bleeped the hand fob to lock the car, briefly acknowledging the eerie look of the glowing amber lights extending into the fog just in front.

I walked toward the building, my coat wrapped tightly around me, trying to retain warmth. There was a pathway of several metres to follow, which led between the car park and a disabled ramp and step entrance to the building. There was a temporary building erected within the car park, obscuring my view to the steps, a mobile I needed to circumnavigate.

As I walked toward it, just ahead, within the misty shadows, I saw a man bent over another man and, as my eyes slowly began to focus on the figure, to my absolute horror and shock, his elbow and arm were moving rapidly.

As I stepped a foot or two closer it became clear the other man was being savagely beaten. He was cowering in front of him on the floor, trying to protect his head with his hands over his face. The fists of the man standing over him were flying in rage, splatters of blood spread across the concrete floor.

The noise was a combination of a thud and a slap, along with the horrific realisation that it was the impact on this man's face making that noise. Worse still, he was kicking him in the stomach, too.

He was like a man possessed. Rage and emotion pouring out of him, like a demon that had been caged, right in front of my eyes. I could feel the anger, rage and hatred oozing out of this man, like he'd bottled it up for decades and the man on the floor was his arch enemy.

It wasn't a normal beating; not like I'd seen in the movies. It wasn't like a punch up or street fight. It was venomous. This man was highly dangerous.

I didn't know whether to run in the opposite direction, scream, or what to do. I needed to find Ellie, though. Her distress was playing on my mind. It had been the whole car journey. I was nervous about getting hurt in the process now, though.

How was I going to get past these men? The hairs on my arms and neck, even under my coat, stood on end through pure fear. I started to take a very wide berth, thinking I should call the police as soon as I got into the building. I wondered how I could slope around them safely.

As I got closer though, the shadow of the man who was raging, the frame, the hairline, the shape of his head, started to look all too familiar, as did his coat, his smart, long tan coat.

I was so busy watching him, I hadn't noticed an empty can on the floor. I cursed under my breath as I accidentally kicked it. It rattled against the corrugated steel building, echoing a noise into the night that sent a chill through me.

I'd disturbed them.

The man turned around instantly and, in the briefest of moments under the flicker of the car park lights, as they faded between amber and yellow, every single one of my worst fears were realised. I stalled as I recognised the face.

It was Alejandro.
What the fucking hell?
He had a look I'd never seen before. It was a look of pure and absolute rage, like an animal possessed, with his lips snarled, blood smeared across his cheeks and evident all over his hands.
No baby, no. Anyone but you.
In that exact moment I realised I'd made a huge mistake. An enormous mistake. Everything I thought I'd believed about Alejandro was a lie.
Every single thing.
The protective man I thought he was –was a lie. It was *all* a lie. Every word he'd ever said to me. Not only was he not protective, but he was worse than a lot of men I wrote about in the newspaper. He was aggressive and violent, one of the most violent men I'd ever seen in real life.
He's a con artist.
Seeing him there, with blood all over him. My heart cracked with the thunder of a full electrical storm, creating an instant break. It was the moment my heart shattered into a million tiny pieces of shrapnel, exploding in slow motion within my chest.
My beautiful Alejandro.
My songwriter.
My dancer.
My lover.
Who the hell are you?
What the hell are you?
I'd thought he was perfect.
How could I be so wrong?
I started to run away. My eyes filled up immediately, starting to drip large, heavy drops as they rolled down my face. My life, my illusions, my safety, the love of my life, my soulmate... everything disappeared within a matter of seconds. It felt like my life and all the dreams I'd built over the last few months were over.
Seconds. That's all it has taken to destroy my life.
As I reached the car and fumbled for my keys, my phone went off, signalling a text. I looked at my phone, the message was from Amelia.
"Ellie is safe with me. I found her in the toilets at the party crying her eyes out, and we took her out immediately and brought her back here. Come to ours as soon as you get this message."
I don't understand anything right now.
My flat mate was in tears and my love life was shredded and in ruins, all within a few minutes. What kind of hellish New Years' Eve is this?

I started the engine. Tears flooded my face as I drove away, my emotions spilling over until my soul cried out, from a deep well of despair inside me.

What the hell just happened?
What the hell is going on?
What if he's…?

BONUS CONTENT

If this story kept you up late, made your heart race or stimulated you, then you're exactly the kind of reader I love writing for.

Join my subscriber list and you'll get:
- FREE Exclusive Bonus Prequel Chapters to download immediately, written from Alejandro's POV, to thank you for joining. *Was it a coincidence they met?*
- Early access to new release information
- Chances to win exclusive giveaways, signed copies and reader only prizes
- Behind-the-scenes peeks into what I'm working on or writing next
- Upcoming events.

'Subscribe' via this link www.authoravamrose.com/contact

One last favour...

Writing this story was a journey, full of late nights and the kind of emotion that lingers. If any part of it moved, resonated with or invigorated you, or made you feel something real, I'd be truly grateful if you'd leave a review.

Your words matter more than you know, and they are vital to indie authors. Reviews help others discover these books and they also remind me why I write, to reach someone like you. It doesn't have to be long. Just honest. Even a short review makes a difference!

If you can leave a review on Amazon, Goodreads, or anywhere bookish, it would mean the world to me. The same goes for recommendations to other book lovers, book clubs, or groups.

Thank you for your support, and sharing some of your 'life time' with me...

Love always,
Ava xx

ABOUT THE AUTHOR

Ava M. Rose started writing poetry in 2016, releasing a poetry book "Sensual Words" in 2017. "Sensual Seduction" is her first novel from "The Sensual Series." This series allows her to expand her fantasy visions without restriction, exploring the sensuality of her characters. Her style is focused on feelings, evoking raw emotion in the reader.

Rose wants her readers to experience what the characters feel, journeying with her, while providing the fantasy of a safe space they may enjoy, too. Her words are vibrant, passionate, and exactly what you hunger for when you're looking for words to portray connection and intimacy.

Rose loves to write about sensory emotion, placing the reader at the heart of both the characters and the scene, with exquisite attention to detail. She wants her readers to experience what the characters feel, from the thrill of the centrally themed dark romance to the torment of the danger invoked by the villain. To feel the highs and the lows, the confusion, and the ecstasy; to understand the journey of each character. The sequel "Sensual Danger" is the exciting sequel in the trilogy and the final book in The Sensual Series, "Sensual Depth" is also available now, with a riveting conclusion to her dramatic trilogy.

"Ava is the epitome of beauty, passion, and dark desire. She is an enigma. Her way with words invigorates the mind and entices you to read more. Her words bring magic to the mind, heart, body, and soul of her readers. The highest compliment I can bestow upon her is to inform the world that she is quite simply an epic lady, poet, wordsmith, and author."

ACKNOWLEDGEMENTS

I wanted to say a huge thank you to Aria Blake for designing the covers of each of my books so far. I'm thrilled with the overall finish and think she's a creative wonder for conceptualising the contents of each with her amazing imagery. I also thank her for her patience with providing a uniform look and feel I can use for my current series and any future work. You can contact her on email: blakecoverdesign@gmail.com.

The Sensual Series

Book 1 – Sensual Seduction

Book 2 – Sensual Danger

Book 3 – Sensual Depth

Printed in Dunstable, United Kingdom

70439011R00170